ANN AGUIRRE

HORDE

ANN AGUIRRE

SQUARE
FISH

FEIWEL AND FRIENDS
NEW YORK

An Imprint of Macmillan
175 Fifth Avenue
New York, NY 10010
fiercereads.com

Library of Congress Cataloging-in-Publication Data Available
ISBN 978-1-250-05077-9 (paperback) / ISBN 978-1-4668-4855-9 (e-book)

Originally published in the United States by Feiwel and Friends
First Square Fish Edition: 2014
Book designed by Susan Walsh
Square Fish logo designed by Filomena Tuosto

10   9   8   7   6   5

AR: 5.9 / LEXILE: 790L

For Alek, who watched the puppy so I could write.
And Bree, who wins at fixing books.

one

impetus

"I smell a wild beast—that way, the way the wind is coming."
—George MacDonald, *The Day Boy and the Night Girl*

Quest

I left without looking back.

This wouldn't be easy, but it was necessary to leave our loved ones under siege to fetch help for Salvation. The decision hurt my heart too; my foster mother's face would haunt me, so wounded and brave, older than I'd known a woman could become yet remain strong and vital. She glimmered like a promise of hope that my flame needn't flicker and burn out before I had a chance to live. Once I'd thought *old* meant twenty-five, but my time in Salvation had changed my perceptions. Now it was strange to imagine I might not be entering the middle of my life.

Into the dark I quickened my steps, eyes sharp for Freaks prowling beyond normal perimeters. Behind us, I heard them shrieking challenges to the men guarding the walls. Rifles cracked out when they rushed, but I couldn't turn, no matter how much I wished otherwise. My course was fixed by the shadowy line traced on the priceless map secured in the leather folio in my pack. Before we'd left, I had studied it with complete focus, memorizing each twist and turn of the route, each handwritten note left by Longshot about good game-hunting or fresh water. It was two days to Soldier's Pond, two more back, once we mustered the necessary reinforcements. That dot on the parchment represented the best hope of saving the people who had taught me so much about life, that it could be more than just hunting and killing.

Momma Oaks. Edmund.

I couldn't let myself think of them or I'd falter. Instead I pressed on, silent and wary, listening to the Freaks behind us. With a glance over my shoulder, I reassured myself that Fade was still at my back. Tegan and Stalker walked on either flank, she with her lopsided gait and unshakable loyalty, he with his curved knives in his hands and his eyes fixed on the horizon, though he couldn't see what lay ahead as well as I could.

That came with being the night girl. Reflexively I adjusted my pack, reassured by the weight of the book that had traveled with us all the way from the ruins. Maybe I didn't need it, but it had become my talisman, every bit as much as the tattered playing card sewn into a hidden pocket inside my shirt. Edmund had explained that my token from down below was part of a fifty-two-piece set, and it was a low card. That seemed fitting, as it served to keep me humble.

"See anything?" Tegan asked.

"Just some night-prowling animals. The enemy's behind us."

"I know," she said softly.

The grass crisped under our feet, liberally sprinkled with early fallen fronds. It wasn't yet turning time, when all the leaves changed colors and dropped from the branches, but there were always a few to crackle as we went. We ran all through the night with periodic breaks for rest and water while I checked the maps by the moonlight shining overhead. By the time the sun crept over the horizon in delicate whorls of rose and amber, I was exhausted—and disgusted with my own weakness. Down below Fade and I had run a much more dangerous route in faster time, but we had to account for Tegan's slower strides too. Though the girl was all heart, her leg couldn't carry her indefinitely at the same pace that the rest of us set, and she was limping now, brackets of pain beside her mouth. I didn't make the mistake of noting it out loud, however.

"Time to make camp." I signaled for Stalker to scout the perimeter, and it was a measure of how much he'd changed that he didn't balk at the order, merely set off to do as I'd asked.

As I laid out my blankets, Fade asked, "No fire?"

I shook my head. "The sun will be up soon. We won't need it."

Tegan added, "We'll smell them coming if any of those behind us get close."

I nodded at that. This reminded me an awful lot of when we'd wandered the wilderness with only stories handed down by Fade's sire. *At least this time we have maps, a route to follow.* I wouldn't call it a road, exactly, but I spotted faint lines where Longshot's wagon—along with others, I was sure—had passed back and forth often enough to reassure me I was still navigating the proper course.

As I handed around the meat, bread, and cheese Momma Oaks had packed, Stalker returned. "The general area's clear, though I don't like the way it smells to the east."

"Are we being followed?" I asked.

I ate in economical bites, sufficient to keep me going, but not make it difficult to rest on an over-full stomach. The others did the same, experienced with balancing the need to stay strong against the wisdom of conserving our resources. After tonight, the meat would be gone, but the bread and cheese should stretch all the way to the end of our journey.

Soberly, Stalker nodded. "We should expect an attack while we're sleeping . . . and hope it's not more than we can handle."

I swore quietly, the worst word I'd learned during the summer patrols. "I'd hoped they didn't spot us coming out of the tunnel."

"I don't think they did," Fade put in. Out here, he was more his old self, quiet and alert, less of the bleak despair. "I suspect they can smell us just as easily we do them."

Of course. The minute he said it, I remembered—and recognized the truth. The Freaks didn't need to see us emerge; the minute we stepped into the wind, we entered their territory. Like any predator, they noticed such incursions and would take steps to eliminate the threat. If we were lucky, it was only a small hunting party, not a significant portion of the horde. Though maybe that would help Salvation if a large number gave chase—we could lead them away from the town toward Soldier's Pond. The settlers there wouldn't thank us for it, but they might believe the threat was real faster.

"How's that possible?" Tegan demanded, looking offended.

"They're animals," Stalker answered. "They have keen senses like a wolf too, and they notice anything that doesn't match the Freak stench."

"That's how I was able to—" I cut myself off before I said *rescue Fade*, knowing it would be hard for him to hear.

Too soon. Deep down, I wanted him to appreciate what I'd done, what I'd risked for him, because there weren't any limits on how far I'd go for my boy. But his black eyes flashed; he knew even if I didn't speak the words out loud. With a sinking heart, I watched him turn away to lay his bedroll with exaggerated care.

"Able to what?" Tegan asked.

Stalker replied for me with unexpected tact. "Sneak past some Freaks. Deuce rubbed herself with their parts—blood and worse stuff—until she reeked. They didn't notice her, though most of them were sleeping."

Some was a massive understatement. That was our first sight of the horde, sufficient to slay everyone in Salvation, and then sweep onward to pillage any surviving settlements. The memory swept over me, Freaks awful and staggering in their numbers, and armed with fire they'd stolen from our outpost. I battened down my alarm, knowing I wouldn't do the townsfolk any good if I panicked.

"That's ingenious," Tegan decided. "And disgusting." She cocked her head, thoughtful. "Does that mean they don't see particularly well?"

"I have no idea." To the best of my knowledge, nobody had ever studied the Freaks. Anyone who got near one chose to dispatch it instead, for obvious reasons.

"I'd like to find out," she murmured.

While I wished Tegan luck in her quest for knowledge, I preferred killing them. "It was dark . . . and like he said, most were asleep. I wouldn't count on them having impaired vision."

Stalker sat down opposite me, his icy gaze layered. The kiss he'd given me the night before felt like a weight, one I needed to displace before I could be worthy of Fade, who would hate it even more when I told him that I'd kissed Stalker freely in order to get him to promise to run back to Salvation to warn them if Fade and I didn't make it back.

At this point, however, we had more important things to worry about, so I set those matters aside, as Stalker said, "I'll take first watch."

"Second," I murmured.

The others claimed third and fourth respectively, which would grant us all a decent amount of sleep. Fade handed his timepiece to Stalker to make it easier to tell when the two hours were up; once Fade and Tegan would've argued at Stalker guarding the encampment alone, but both of them merely rolled up in their blankets as the sun rose higher. I was tired, so I dropped off immediately, and I dreamed of Salvation burning while Momma Oaks wept, and Silk, the lead Huntress down below, shouted at me that I was a Breeder, not a Huntress. Jolting awake, I rolled out of my blankets onto the sun-warmed grass and lay squinting up at the blue sky threaded with white wisps.

Clouds, they were called. Supposedly, this was where rain came from.

Not realizing anyone else was awake, I wondered aloud, "Of all the people in the enclave, why couldn't I keep Thimble in my head? Or Stone?"

My friends from the enclave might not have kept me from making the long walk, but I had fond memories of them. Thimble used to make us things even before she was officially a Builder, while Stone protected us both. I wished I could dream about them instead of Silk, who had put fear into everyone under her command.

"I don't know," Stalker answered. "But I think about this one cub all the time. He followed me everywhere. But he didn't have the heart to take power. He died young."

"What was his name?"

"Rule," he said. "Because he always followed them."

It sounded like the Wolves' naming traditions had been similar to ours, though they focused on a personal trait, not a naming gift. Quietly, I said as much, and Stalker nodded.

"The leader christened our cubs. At eight winters, we earned our names."

"How?" It was odd to think they had traditions other than capturing trespassers and stealing girls from other gangs, but by the way his face tightened, he didn't want to talk about it, so I added, "Never mind. You should get some rest."

"Thanks. It was all quiet." He handed me Fade's watch as he rolled into his blankets.

I pushed into a cross-legged position and served as sentry while the others slept. As I had done down below, I entertained myself with studying Fade, but the activity had more meaning now that I'd stroked his hair and kissed his mouth. The ache those memories roused in me were fierce as a rainstorm, thunder booming in my heart. With sheer discipline I looked away from the curled crescents of his lashes and the quiet curve of his lips. Those hours passed with only the quiet chatter of birds and the scramble of small creatures in the undergrowth. We had chosen a shaded spot, beneath a stand of trees, where the grass was soft and the light filtered through the foliage overhead to dappled green.

I was sleepy again by the time I woke Fade, but I was still alert enough not to do it by shaking him. Instead, I knelt beside him and whispered, "Your watch."

He roused instantly, one hand on his knife. "Anything?"

"No trouble so far."

"Good. Stalker's right, though. They're hunting us."

"I know."

I had been prey often enough that I recognized the prickling feel of enemies nearby. Unfortunately until the wind shifted just right, it was impossible to know how far away the Freaks were. We had to rest while we could and then press on. Fighting wasn't our top priority; our mission was to summon help, and I couldn't contemplate the cost of failure. If necessary, we'd take evasive action and head for Soldier's Pond even faster.

"I don't like our chances," Fade said.

"Of surviving the run or summoning help?"

He shrugged, unwilling to articulate his doubts. Deliberately I moved over beside him. I set my hand beside his in the grass. He knew—he had to know—that if things were different, I'd lace my fingers through his. But he didn't want that, couldn't stand that, and I read the awareness of my gesture in his altered posture. Fade straightened his fingers beside mine, and for a few seconds, I felt every blade of grass on my palm as if they were his fingertips.

"I hope I prove of some use," he said then.

"You're here. That's enough." I hesitated and decided there might not be a better moment—and I couldn't continue without telling him. So in a quiet rush, I explained what was bothering me about the good-bye kiss I'd given Stalker in the woods and the one he took by surprise the night before, and how those moments conflicted with the promise I'd made Fade regarding exclusive kissing rights. I felt like I'd broken faith with him, but I didn't regret bringing him back safe.

His expression went flat, his eyes dark as night-kissed water. "I don't understand why you're telling me this. You can do whatever you like. I already said, we aren't . . ." He trailed off and shrugged, as if I already knew what he meant.

Worse, I did. He was talking about the termination of everything we had been together, but if Fade thought we could just go back to being hunting partners, like we had been down below, before I understood anything about feelings or the way he held my heart in his hands without touching me, then he was purely mistaken. I clenched my teeth against an angry spate of words. Though Tegan had counseled patience, sometimes it was hard.

He went on in a quietly aching tone, "So it doesn't matter what you did to get me back. By then, it was already too late."

"It's not," I said. "I won't let it be. But you deserve absolute honesty. What happened with Stalker wasn't something I asked for, but I'd do anything for you, and that's a fact."

"Some things," he whispered, "you just shouldn't."

I didn't ask if he meant his rescue or the deal with Stalker that involved kissing. I couldn't resist pushing, just a little. "So it won't bother you if I find someone else?"

His jaw clenched, and I saw the muscle move before he got it under control. "I thought you said you'd fight for me."

"And *you* said it's too late." I offered him a faint smile along with his watch. "So it's a good thing I don't intend to listen to you."

The soft sigh puffed out of him in relief before he could stop it. That was all the confirmation I needed. At least in this regard,

I couldn't take Fade's word at face value. His mouth was saying things his heart didn't mean, out of pain and darker feelings that would probably cut me in two. At last I followed Tegan's advice about not pushing him too far, and I shifted back to my bedroll without further conversation. I didn't turn my back when I drifted off to sleep, either. *Let him look at me, if he wants to.* In fact, I hoped he did, and that he felt one fraction of what I did. It might bring him back to me sooner. Just as in this desperate quest, I was running blind and hoping that the journey ended with Fade beside me.

When next I woke, the world was a blur of snarls and yellow fangs.

Combat

By the angle of the sun as I rolled to my feet, it wasn't quite noon, but the Freaks had found us. There were nine monsters, strong and well fed, so this wouldn't be as easy as it had been before. Good thing my companions were all awake and preparing for a fight.

Stalker snapped at Tegan, "Get behind me."

My blades slipped into my palms and I lunged at the four encircling Fade. I caught the first off guard with a slash to the torso, opening a gash in its hide. I noticed these lacked the festering sores of other Freaks I'd encountered. Their skin was sleek but tough, if mottled, gray. The stained fangs were the same, however, as were the razor-taloned hands slicing toward me. I spun to the side, ending the maneuver with a dual downward strike. My left knife nicked the creature's arm, but neither wound was fatal. Bleeding and furious, the thing snarled at me, a challenge in its strangely human eyes. The irises were crystal clear, a stunning amber-yellow, with the sclera white by comparison. I had the unmistakable sense it saw me as a thinking person, not just meat, and yet it still meant to kill me. The realization stunned me, but not enough to keep me from dodging the next hit as another wheeled to face me.

Stalker dropped one of his with an efficient spike into the throat, leaving three. Fade had the next kill, gutting the Freak on the right from chest to groin. Entrails tumbled out in a meaty splatter, staining the grass at our feet. Another keened in grief—that awful, discordant cry that affirmed that the Freaks felt, that they suffered loss—and it went at Fade with a ferocity I found astonishing. It was furious, not just hungry. These behaved so differently from the mindless ones we'd fought down below.

I swiveled beneath the slashing claws and sank both my blades into the Freak's abdomen, then I pulled the knives sideways with all my strength. *That* was a killshot. The monster went down as the next one lunged at me. I blocked the strike, but took a rake of claws across my forearm in doing so; this Freak was *strong,* enough that I felt the impact down in my bones. I had to learn a new way to fight them since they didn't die as fast anymore. This was actual combat, not the havoc I once wreaked. Fade cried out as one of them sank claws into his shoulder and used the hold to reel him forward for a fatal bite. To my surprise, Tegan brought up my rifle from where she stood in the trees. I was none too sure of her aim, but the shot boomed out, opening the monster's chest and dropping the one who had Fade. I lifted my chin at her in thanks, then I whirled into motion, my strikes faster, faster.

Tegan shot another as I finished my second. Then I moved to help Stalker, who had two left on him. I stabbed one low in the spine, paralyzing it, then Stalker's lightning slashes finished the creature. I worked with him to bring down the last as Fade dropped another.

Finally, we had nine corpses and a bloody stink, while Tegan trembled, cradling the rifle to her chest. "I did it. I was afraid I'd shoot Fade but nobody else was close enough."

"Thank you," he murmured.

"They're different," Tegan said, staring down at the bodies. "Not just in physical appearance but in their habits, too. Did you notice they're not wearing rags anymore? These Muties actually made clothes."

She was right. They had poorly tanned skins fashioned into rough armor. But their oddities didn't change our mission.

"We have to move," I said. "Pack your gear. The rifle can be heard a long way off in open country, so I hope you all got enough rest. You'll need it. We'll tend wounds later."

In minutes, we had our blankets rolled and stowed in our packs. I handed around some bread for us to chew on the move, then I checked the maps and our route. Stalker helped me orient to the path and we set out at a run while I wondered how long it would take for more Freaks to track the rifle shots. I didn't doubt we could hold our own against most scouting parties, but each fight delayed and weakened us. Both Fade and I were injured; if we took more wounds, the trip to Soldier's Pond might take even longer.

Salvation doesn't have much time.

My feet pounded the earth, sending up a spray of dust behind me. "I think we should push to reach Soldier's Pond tonight."

"I can," Tegan said, "if that's what you're asking. My leg's fine."

It had been, and I was glad she wasn't defensive about it. We had to be realistic about our capabilities. "Good. You're surprisingly handy with my rifle. Keep it."

She flushed with pleasure, or it could be running in the heat of the day, which had warmed up with the sun. Light blazed forth, hurting my eyes, and I wondered whether I would ever get fully accustomed to it.

My forearm burned but it wasn't enough to slow me down. Fade wouldn't thank me for questioning his strength, so I didn't ask about the bloodstained patch on his shoulder. Still, he was moving well, keeping up, so he couldn't be in too much pain. I'd check on him later, provided he let me.

That was a long, grim day with only basic stops for sanitary functions and to gulp some water or swallow a handful of cheese. By nightfall, Tegan's face was white with exhaustion and pain she wouldn't acknowledge, but she didn't ask any quarter. According to Longshot's notes, this was a bruising trip, much longer than two days by wagon. But he had to care for the mules and let them rest, plus he was towing trade goods whereas we moved as fast as humans could.

The moon was high by the time I spied our destination across the plain. I didn't know what I had been expecting, but this wasn't it. From what I could see, this was nothing like Salvation, and a fearful sensation crawled up my back. I stopped, breathing hard, and when I did, exhaustion rushed in like a drowning wave, weakening my limbs to water.

"It looks like the ruins," Stalker said.

I nodded. "Only it's not completely destroyed."

This was an old-world town, but they had cordoned off the heart of it with metal fencing, embankments, and ditches. There were lights too, different from the ones that burned down below or even in Salvation. These were odd and fixed, not fire at all, but more like magic from the stories Edmund told of long ago.

"Have you ever seen anything like that?" I asked.

Both Stalker and Fade shook their heads, but Tegan was studying the glimmer with a fascinated frown. "Not since I was a little girl. We had some in the greenhouse at the university that filled up with light from lying in the sun. Those look a little like that, only bigger."

"I didn't know old things like that still worked," Stalker said. "We scavenged items sometimes but we couldn't figure out how to operate them, except the tins."

"That's because you're savages," she said.

"We were," he agreed quietly.

"How late is it?" I asked Fade.

He checked his watch. "Nearly midnight."

I sighed. "We don't have a choice. This isn't the right time to make our appeal, but waiting won't help, either. Let's go."

Though the perimeter looked deserted, I didn't trust my eyes. My senses told me we were being watched. So I picked an easily tracked path across the field, waiting for a warning or a voice asking me to state my business. Neither came, right up until I set foot on the metal ramp that led down into the pocked street, similar here to what it had been in Gotham. I could see where the citizens of Soldier's Pond had tried to keep the surface smooth, filling holes with packed mud and dirt, but it didn't seal well enough to hide the damage, even at night.

"Which are you," an unseen male called, "itinerant or tourist?"

I had no idea what either of those words meant. After glancing at Tegan, who shrugged—apparently she didn't either—I answered, "We're messengers, carrying word from Salvation."

"Why didn't they send Longshot?" the man asked.

I relaxed a fraction. If I wasn't mistaken, his tone contained a certain fondness, born of camaraderie and nights spent swapping stories. "I'm sorry. Longshot died in the last battle."

"I think you'd better come in." Something clanged, and a moving shadow showed me the security measure that would've crushed us had we taken another step down the ramp. "It's clear for you to cross. Hurry now."

Not wanting to inconvenience our host, I ran, and the others followed me. Behind us, the heavy weight went back up in cadence with grunting men who hauled it into place. Six of them stepped into the light afterward, led by the man I knew instinctively had invited us into Soldier's Pond. They all wore dusty green clothing, patched more than once, and they held themselves like warriors with shoulders back, spines straight, and their chins inviting trouble. All of them were pretty close to

Edmund's age with silver growing among the bristles on their jaws. They all wore weapons on their hips, similar to the rifle, only smaller, and long-handled knives on their thighs.

"You said you have word from Salvation and Longshot couldn't carry it. There's been trouble?"

"An incredible amount," I said honestly. "I mean no disrespect . . . but are you the elder?" That was what they'd called the leader in Salvation, and what we called Whitewall down below.

"That's an old word for it . . . and, no, as it happens, I'm not. I won't make you tell the story twice. Davies, you're head watchman while I'm gone. I'll take our guests to see the colonel."

One of the men nodded as our escort led us through the warren. This was old-world construction, patched and shored to retain functionality. We didn't have the means to build like this anymore, however. The size and shape of the structures was uncannily similar, one house after another stamped out with complete precision.

"It's eerie," Fade said beside me.

"More like a child's model than a real town," I agreed softly.

"This way. I'm Morgan. If we have to wake the colonel, I can't guarantee how well your news will be received." His tone held an odd, amused note that I couldn't interpret.

I didn't expect it would be glad tidings, so that hardly mattered, but the leader's reaction could determine whether we succeeded. Morgan led us to a large building with a long front porch; there were lights affixed all over the top of it, which made me think it was some kind of headquarters. Inside, it bore out that initial impression with tables and chairs littered with papers, some of which had yellowed with age, others appearing to be recently manufactured. I could tell the new sheets came from Salvation, as they carried its imprint in the form of a tree thrice encircled. So among other things, Soldier's Pond relied on Salvation for stationery, which was a fancy word for paper, according to Momma Oaks.

Candles burned, the wax crackling down into saucers, and there were a few lamps unfamiliar to me. They gave off an unpleasant smell as they burned, the flame flickering inside the glass like a trapped firefly. There were chairs too, where a few tired, worried-looking men were sprawled. I wondered which one was the colonel—and what a colonel was. It must be a title, similar to Elder Bigwater, since he wasn't actually the oldest man in Salvation, unlike down below. Maybe he played a role like the Wordkeeper's, consulting on important matters. But none of my speculations proved to be right when the colonel turned around; I could tell this was the person we sought by the way Morgan approached, and I smiled, both pleased and chagrined.

I let Salvation change the way I see the world. This never occurred to me.

It should have. Both Copper and Silk had played powerful roles down below. This woman was younger than Momma Oaks, but not quite as young as Ruth, Rex's wife. I didn't know how old that made her, but compared with the men around her, she seemed young. She wore her dark hair up in a complicated twist, and her clothes were crisp, despite the late hour. Likewise, her eyes were dark, ringed in faint shadows that said she hadn't slept much recently. Sharp features lent her an aspect of intelligence; we'd find out whether that was true once we spoke.

"Report, Morgan." Her tone was brisk but not impolite. In my time in Salvation I'd come to note the difference. Yet her eyes held warmth that belied her words. "What's the latest word in the territories?"

I figured she must mean all the lands described on Longshot's maps. Somehow I resisted the temptation to see if that word appeared anywhere on his papers. Instead I fixed my attention politely on Morgan, who was saying, "They come from Salvation, bearing news. I thought it best to bring them to you at once, Colonel Park."

"I imagine it's nothing good, but speak," the colonel said.

There was nothing for it but to lay out the problem. "Salvation is under siege . . . and Longshot died in the first onslaught. I'm sorry to carry such bad tidings if you were fond of him, as I was." I pushed past the lump in my throat, the fresh awareness that I'd never again hear his rasp of a voice or see his eyes crinkle as he smiled. "The town's surrounded and the Freaks—Muties, I mean—are armed with fire. We don't have the manpower to fight. So Elder Bigwater sent us to request reinforcements, and you're the nearest settlement."

Given my experience with people in positions of authority, I expected Colonel Park to say I was crazy and that I should eat some soup, then go to bed. Once again, I was wrong. Nothing in my experience prepared me for her reaction. She slammed a hand down on the nearest table, knocking over some pencils in a cup, scattering papers on the floor.

"I *told* you," she snapped at the men looking on with dawning horror.

Reinforcements

"You knew about Salvation?" Stalker asked, seeming incredulous.

The colonel shook her head. "I noticed a difference in Mutie attack patterns around here. Then they all moved off. I said it meant they must be planning something, but my advisors thought I was being an alarmist."

So not only did she believe us, she'd foreseen the progression. This would save us a lot of time begging and trying to convince somebody who didn't believe the world could change. Some of the tension left me, though none of the exhaustion. I was conscious that every moment I spent talking was one that Salvation lost, and I remembered the men on the walls, gray-faced with fatigue and firing gamely on, even as Smith fought to keep up with their ammo usage. Without Stalker's help, that might prove beyond his powers. We had to get back right away.

"Then you can probably imagine how things are," I said. "How soon can you send some men with us?"

A man with a mustache spoke for the first time. "We can't just send our standing forces off on a whim."

"It's *not* a whim," Tegan snapped.

Another advisor agreed: "Saving Salvation might mean losing Soldier's Pond."

"This could be what the Muties want. How do we know

their gambit in Salvation isn't a diversion? The minute we weaken our entrenched position, they'll attack," the last councilor predicted.

"They'll come for you eventually," Fade muttered.

"Enough." The colonel infused her tone with cold finality.

"Have you made a decision?" I asked.

She sighed, looking tired. "Unfortunately, it's not up to me. Something this significant must be put to a vote."

"Then call an emergency meeting," Tegan suggested.

I agreed with her. We couldn't afford to let people sleep. The colonel considered, then nodded at Morgan. "Go wake up the rest of the council. Get them here in the next half hour. These four need an answer, either way. I suspect you'll be returning home to fight, regardless of the result." She addressed the final statement to us.

"Yes, ma'am." Fade had internalized lessons about respectful modes of address faster than I did.

She put a hand on my shoulder. I was glad she didn't choose Fade for this gesture, as it wouldn't end well. "Are you hungry? The least I can do is feed you while you wait."

"That would be welcome," Stalker answered.

Colonel Park turned to one of her advisors. "Get something warm for them to eat. There should still be soup on the hearth in the mess."

Within minutes, we all had hearty stew and bread to clean the bowls with. I perched on a chair at the edge of the room, and the others followed suit. It was quiet while we ate, then shortly thereafter, five more people stumbled into the room, three men, two women, which gave equal power to both genders. I was pleased to see that parity, even as I finished my meal.

"What's the meaning of this?" a gray-haired man demanded.

Succinctly, the colonel summarized what I'd told her, then she added, "We need to vote at once as to whether we're sending aid."

A round, motherly-looking woman with fine blond hair put her fingers to her mouth in alarm. "If the Muties have organized, it won't be long before they march on us."

"My thoughts exactly," the colonel said.

They debated for a while. With a full stomach and an aching heart, I didn't attend to the proceedings. It only mattered what they decided, not how they came to consensus. Tegan slipped up beside me, looking determined. Wordless, she indicated my wound and I offered my arm for her to treat. I bit back a curse as the cleansing liquid trickled over the scratches, deep runnels across the top of my arm, adding a counterpoint to the healed scars on my inner forearms, courtesy of the enclave. I was proud of those six scars still, though maybe I shouldn't be.

When she was finished, she smeared salve on me and bandaged the injury with quiet efficiency. Then she whispered, "Fade won't let me treat him."

"Let me try." Once, he'd permitted me to do so. I didn't know whether he would, now.

Tegan handed me her supplies and I crept over to where Fade sat, propped against the wall. The ongoing debate washed over me, bits of argument about the viability of offering support to a settlement with whom they had no such defensive accord, only trade agreements. Then the counter-argument came, mostly about how if Salvation fell, Soldier's Pond would be next. I stopped listening again as I stilled. Fade opened his eyes, dark and wary in the candlelight. The flickering shadows painted his face hollow beneath his cheekbones.

"Your shoulder will fester if it's not cleaned and wrapped," I said softly.

His flinch was nearly imperceptible, then he pushed out a breath. "I'd prefer you to do it."

Happiness sang inside me. He still trusted me more than

anyone else, whatever his other problems might be. "Then brace. It will sting, but I'll make it fast."

And I did. Much as I would've liked to touch him more, I kept our contact quick and impersonal. He hissed when the antiseptic ran into the punctures, but he didn't move other than to curl his fists. He shut his eyes, his throat working, not against the pain, I didn't think. By the time I finished, he wore a sheen of cold sweat on his brow.

"Did it hurt that much?" I asked.

"No." His fists came to rest on his thighs and he wouldn't look at me. "When you touch me—when *anyone* touches me—I'm back there, in the pens. I feel it all over again."

"We'll work out a way to fix it," I promised.

"How? This is why I told you we can't be together. I wasn't strong enough to keep them from taking me and I'm not strong enough to shake this off. I can't—"

"You can," I cut in. "Maybe not today or tomorrow. But Tegan's doing better. She said you need time . . . and I have it to offer. I *promise* we'll figure it out."

As his head swung my way, his dark eyes burned into me. "Why?"

"Because I love you." It was easy to say it this time now that I understood what it meant. Then I quoted his own words back to him. "Not just when it's easy. All the time."

"No more deals with Stalker?" That told me he still cared; despite the pain, his feelings for me hadn't changed.

"He won't touch me again. Whatever's at stake, I'll find another way."

"If you had any idea how much I want to hold you—"

"I'm not going anywhere, Fade. You're my partner. I choose you. I always will."

After that, I simply sat beside him, listening to him breathe.

It wasn't enough, but it was more than he'd let me do before. Step by step, he would let me back in. My eyes closed and I tipped my head back against the wall. Stalker jostled me eventually—and by the angle of the light, a few hours had passed. They must've talked until nearly dawn.

The colonel finally said, "No more discussion. It's time to vote."

"Seconded," said the gray-haired man.

"All in favor of sending reinforcements, say aye and raise your hand."

The result came down in our favor, four to two. I exhaled slowly and closed my eyes in relief; until this moment, I hadn't realized how worried I was that we'd fail. Fortunately Colonel Park paid attention to the world she lived in and was willing to accept change even when it didn't mean good things for her town. I wished the elders in the enclave had been more like her.

But it still wasn't as fast as I would've liked because then they had to debate how many men they could afford to send without critically crippling Soldier's Pond. The endless talking was making me antsy, so I rolled into my blankets and went to sleep. I figured somebody would nudge me awake when it was time to move. This time there were no nightmares at least.

By the way my body felt, it couldn't have been more than an hour before Tegan touched my shoulder. "It's settled. We're taking fifty soldiers back to Salvation."

For the number of Freaks we faced, it wasn't nearly enough, but I couldn't complain when they were endangering their own citizens to help us. Shoving the hair out of my face, I rolled to my feet and collected my belongings. Everyone else was assembling outside. Fade and Stalker stood on opposite sides of the yard, and I didn't think I was imagining the narrow stare Fade offered the other boy. Though he'd claimed he didn't care what I did or with who, obviously that wasn't true.

Morgan stood at the head of the men given to our cause. In the dawn light, I saw that he had long dark hair, lightly sprinkled with silver, but his face didn't look as old as I'd first thought. He had lines at the corners of his eyes, but they came from humor, I thought, or sunshine, not the endless march of years. His mouth turned up at the edges as if he found it difficult not to smile, an expression echoed by the warm gray of his eyes; they were like smoke, warm and changeable.

Right now, he was giving orders to his men. "Infantry in good condition can cover thirty to forty miles a day on foot. We have to move at least that fast in order to prove of any help to Salvation. If any among you thinks he can't sustain that pace for whatever reason, speak now."

"I've got a bum foot," a man said. "Broke it a few years back and it didn't heal right. I'd only slow you down."

"Thanks for your honesty." Morgan turned to someone I took for his second in command.

The big, burly man responded by calling out another name, and a new soldier took the dismissed one's place in the formation. Unlike the guard in Salvation, these men were well trained. I could tell by their body language that they had drilled together extensively and fought real battles beyond the walls. Many of them had Freak scars, claw marks on faces or forearms, visible badges of their courage and skill. Touched by her valor and willingness to risk trouble for our sakes, I strode over to the colonel.

"I can't thank you enough, sir. You don't know what this means for us."

"God grant it's sufficient," she said, "but it's all we can do. Otherwise we'll be too weak to defend, should the Muties turn their ambitions west."

It'll happen, I thought.

But it wasn't the time for dire proclamations. Soon thereafter, we moved out, passing from Soldier's Pond in a concerted lockstep. I'd never traveled with such a large group before, top-side or down below. It seemed risky, but there was no avoiding it. We'd slaughter any scouting parties we encountered, unless the horde itself was rolling west. Letting my feet join their cadence was easy, but to my surprise, Morgan summoned me to the front of the column.

"I need to know how many we're up against."

"Honestly," I said, "I'm not even sure I can count that high."

Morgan laughed at first, probably thinking I was exaggerating but my sober expression assured him I wasn't kidding. Then he swore. "Give me your best estimate."

I thought about that. "I saw five hundred beans once. I'm pretty sure there are more." Then I described the nightmare of the horde encamped on the plain, along with the pockets of human prisoners and the multiple fires burning.

He made an odd gesture, touching his forehead, heart, left shoulder, then right. I had no idea what it meant but he seemed to take comfort in it. "I almost wish you hadn't told me that."

"Why?"

"Because now I'm the bastard keeping the truth from his men. If I tell them, they'll head back to Soldier's Pond. They'll know, just as I do, that this battle can't be won with our forces."

Sour sickness roiled in my stomach, born of fear, not because I feared dying, but because Morgan was right and I hated the idea of letting everyone down. For my new home, I wanted to do the impossible; I just didn't know how.

"Maybe we can create enough havoc to allow Salvation to evacuate." I was proud of that word. I'd seen it first in the ruins, then later Mrs. James, the teacher who had been the bane of my existence, had explained in a superior tone what it meant.

"Hit and run is our only option, but for the Muties, the woods are home ground. Guerilla tactics may prove difficult."

"I can help with that," Stalker said.

I hadn't noticed him joining us, which was a testament to how quiet he could be. Morgan turned to him with interest. "How so?"

"I know the terrain fairly well and I'm a good tracker. I can help by laying snares, planning ambushes. We can't fight them head-on, but I have experience with whittling down a superior enemy."

He must be referring to battles he'd fought in the ruins, destroying gangs with greater numbers until the Wolves were the most powerful force in the area. Overall, Stalker didn't seem proud of that experience, but I wasn't sorry he had it if it meant better odds for us at Salvation. He should realize that he could be proud of his skills without taking satisfaction in every bad thing he'd ever done. There were dark times from my enclave days that I would rather forget, now that I understood just how cruel our rules had been. Morgan listened to Stalker's comments attentively, nodding and occasionally offering a question or suggestion. After a few moments, I fell behind to join Tegan, who was bearing up better than I could've imagined.

"They have some good ideas," she said.

"Stalker does, anyway. Sounds as if he's fought against long odds before."

Her eyes distant, she nodded. "The Wolves went up against the Kings right after they took me. The Kings had more people, but Stalker cut them down. Half of his members were cubs, but he taught them to be merciless and cunning."

Thinking back, I recalled how my hesitation about fighting brats had led to Fade and me being captured. I just hadn't expected them to fight that hard or that well. Not at their age. If Stalker could focus that experience on defending Salvation, then maybe all wasn't lost. I exhaled as we marched on, glad to have this burden off my shoulders.

My skill didn't lie in planning battles, only in fighting them.

Destruction

By the time we reached Salvation, it was too late.

I'd feared that might be the case, but I'd forced the worst potential outcomes from my head and focused on my task. When we approached from the west, the darkening sky glowed orange from the flames devouring the settlement. I heard evidence of the horde nearby, but we didn't have men sufficient to face them. Pain lanced through me until I couldn't breathe. Unlike when Nassau sent the blind brat to our enclave for aid, we'd succeeded in fetching help but it didn't *change* anything.

"We should get back to Soldier's Pond." By Morgan's expression, he believed me regarding the number of Freaks massing, and he wanted to advise the colonel.

"You can go," I said. "But I have to get closer. If there's anything I can do to save my family—"

"There's not," Morgan snapped.

But I wasn't willing to take his word. I set off for the burning ruins of Salvation without asking anyone to accompany me. Tegan and Stalker didn't see me leave, but Fade raced after me. I didn't even have to ask.

"This is foolhardy," he said.

"I know."

It was nothing but open ground from the river's edge to the

carnage in Salvation. From this distance, I smelled burning wood, mingled with blood and charred flesh. The west wall crumbled before my eyes, fiery timbers collapsing in a shower of sparks; they soared in the night air like fireflies and the smoke curled upward, ghostly in the moonlight. Momma Oaks had told me that her people believed the soul lived on, after death—that it was a smoky sort of thing that filled your body and helped you remember to be kind. I wondered whether it looked something like this, slipping out of the nose and mouth as a person died.

A group of Freaks hit us—ten strong—and they snarled a challenge, fortunately drowned by the roaring fire they had started. Some distance beyond I heard townsfolk screaming, but I couldn't focus on them just yet. If Fade and I died here, I wouldn't be able to help anyone; I wasn't ready for my soul to drift out of my ears. In a smooth motion, I drew my blades and Fade backed up against me. This felt sure and natural. It was long odds, but I had been fighting this kind of battle since the day I was born, not against Freaks, but against hunger and disease—enemies that couldn't be faced down with a knife and a fierce look.

"We can take them," Fade said.

"We have to."

There was no other option. Either we killed them quick or the rest of the horde found us. Maybe we could drop ten, but not a hundred or a thousand. Or more. They encircled us so we couldn't flee, more signs they were employing tactics and strategy, but since we had no interest in turning tail, they only offered us better targets. I hoped the Soldier's Pond reinforcements didn't retreat, as we might need them to cover our return.

Too late to worry about it now.

The first one lashed out at me and I met the strike with a slice of my blade, opening its forearm from elbow to wrist. Oddly, the blood smelled less fetid to me, if not quite what normal humans had. I sniffed as I followed up with my left knife, carving a path across its chest. More salt and something else, but this Freak no longer reeked as if it were rotting from within. It just smelled . . . different, and that worried me, but I reacted with dead calm, blocking second and third strikes. The fourth one nailed me, and it hurt. With Fade at my back, I couldn't retreat. I had to hold my ground for him.

I felt his movements behind me, full of his old grace. Now and then he grunted a curse, muffled a sound of pain. I finished the first one with a downward arc of my knife. *Four to go.* Gunfire banged in sharp repetition some yards away.

So all the guards aren't dead. They're fighting in that inferno.

The Freak dropped at my feet, giving the others room to spread out. They didn't growl or keen in grief; no, these were warriors, bent on my death. With more room to maneuver, they could swing wider and at the same time. I battled two at once while the third and fourth snarled, looking for an opening, but they couldn't get to me without knocking their comrades aside. Freaks had progressed far enough that they didn't shove one another down to get at their prey.

They're fully organized. The thought chilled me, even as I severed two claws. Still twitching, they hit the grassy ground, smearing green with red, though in the dark it was impossible to tell. Blood spurted from the stumps, then the beast lunged at me with its other talons. Its partner came at me from the side and nearly took my head off. I was tired from the march, too slow to offer my best efforts. But Fade came across my shoulder and stabbed the Freak right through the eye.

When I glanced back, just for a second, I saw he'd already dropped three, and the other two were showing signs of fear. They hadn't broken and run but they'd backed off a few steps, snarling to show they meant business, but when that wasn't followed by an immediate attack, it meant he had successfully intimidated them. I loved seeing him back in fighting form, even as I was a little ashamed of my own performance. But maybe Fade needed me to be weak occasionally, giving him the opportunity to be strong. That was all right by me; it wasn't like I was doing this on purpose.

I'm just so tired.

"Don't make me do all the work." His tone was lighter than I'd heard in days.

"I'm trying."

But when I barely blocked a blow that would've impaled me, he snarled like a beast; and like he had done down below, I watched him come unhinged. I knew enough to scramble out of his way as Fade went berserk, his knives a silver blur in the starlight. Moments later, there were ten bodies at his feet and he was covered in blood, breathing hard through his nose.

I approached with care, keeping an eye on the periphery. "Thanks. I was flagging."

"Don't I scare you when I get like that?" he asked, low.

I said with conviction, "No. You'd never hurt me."

"I already have."

"Not with your knives. Come on." I cut the discussion and wheeled toward the burning town, determined to help if at all possible.

But the heat was too fierce near the walls and I couldn't cross. Maybe if I had a wagon or some buckets, I could work on the fire, but my knives were no help at all and I could hear Freaks nearby. This wasn't a rescue; it was just foolish. My heart dropped into my stomach. Then I saw someone moving near the walls.

Desperate, I yelled, "There's a secret exit under Elder Bigwater's house, a tunnel that leads out of town. Round up as many people as you can and get them out!"

"Thanks, Deuce! Will do," came the shouted reply. Through flickering orange flames, I caught a glimpse of the man moving off, and I was relieved to recognize Harry Carter. He'd saved my life, done me a good turn when Longshot died, and it was right to repay the favor.

Fade beckoned impatiently. "We need to get away, direct the others to the tunnel mouth if they're still here."

I nodded. "Lead on."

The run was harrowing since we were dodging prowling Freaks the whole time, and I was relieved to see Morgan and others right where we'd left them. "If you were one of my soldiers, you'd get a dishonorable discharge so fast it'd make your head spin."

"But I'm not," I pointed out.

The older man scowled. "Did you accomplish anything, at least?"

Tegan and Stalker were both talking over each other with incoherent recriminations. My fingers were bloody, and I was soot-stained, but I was no more injured than I had been in any other battle. I hushed them with a gesture, addressing Morgan.

"I think so."

Concisely, I explained about Harry Carter and the tunnel. Tegan and Stalker stood nearby, listening. Fear and pain crimped her brows together, flattened her mouth into a pale line. I knew she was worried about her family.

Me too.

"Why do you think they weren't evacuating already?" Tegan asked softly.

I shrugged. "Maybe Elder Bigwater died before he could tell anyone."

"Zach knew about it," Stalker said.

That much was true. But we wouldn't know why until we rescued some of the townsfolk, provided that was even possible. Hopefully Harry Carter could get people rounded up and make them listen, but terror made it hard to think straight. Between fire and Freaks, the citizens of Salvation weren't equipped to deal with danger on this scale.

"Can you find the outlet?" I asked him.

With a nod in lieu of a wordier reply, Stalker bounded off. Morgan was already signaling his men to follow.

"Stay sharp," he ordered.

Good advice, as it was likely we'd fight as a whole before too long. In the distance, I made out screaming from those who hadn't reached the tunnel. I couldn't remember ever being this scared. I wanted to rescue my family—Momma Oaks, Rex, and Edmund—and I didn't know whether it was possible. Truth be known, I'd rather save everyone.

"How big is the tunnel?" Morgan asked me.

"Not very. The townsfolk will be fleeing a few at a time."

"I hope they have the sense not to panic once they climb out," he muttered.

Though it sounded callous, I hoped so too. People running and screaming in the dark would draw the horde down on us, leaving no chance for escape. The rest of us ran after Stalker, who paused now and then to check a landmark. He kept the route in his head, no need for Longshot's maps. If he couldn't recall where the passage let out—

But he led us straight to it, and to my relief, we found a few citizens hiding nearby, mostly women and children. I didn't see Momma Oaks among them. My heart sank even as more people crawled out of the earth, filthy, terrified, some burned or wounded. Tegan got to work immediately, tending the injured.

Morgan drew me aside. "How long do you plan to wait? We need to move before dawn. We'll be easier to track escorting the refugees."

He was right, but that didn't make the truth easy to bear. "I know. Give us as long as you can."

The Soldier's Pond guard checked his personal timepiece,

similar to the one Fade had from his sire. "Three hours, then we march. No sleep tonight."

More screaming, cries of pain, echoed from the burning settlement. The report of rifles said that the guards were buying as much time as they could for the noncombatants to escape. I wished I could break from cover and go kill some Freaks, but that would only give away our position. It would happen soon enough on its own; there was no way to hide so many souls. The moment the wind shifted, it would carry our combined scents to the monsters. Then it would be up to us to cover the retreat.

Tegan wore a stony expression as she treated the wounded. I joined her and offered another set of hands, admiring her skill. Pain lurked deep in her eyes as she wrapped up a brat's burned arm. I didn't know the young one, but Tegan called him by name, then sent him to his mother, who was uninjured. It would be faster if we could go in and help, but the tunnel only permitted one at a time, which made the exodus interminable. A few minutes later, I recognized Momma Oaks crawling out of the hole. Tegan had to be watching for Doc, but she didn't pause her work.

I did. She clasped my hand and I pulled her up the rest of the way, then I looked for Edmund.

She shook her head. "He's fighting, along with the other men. I don't know if—"

Before she could voice her doubts, I hugged her. "Are you hurt?"

"No. Just tired. It's been awful." I suspected that was an understatement.

I could read Tegan's reaction. *Still no Doc. Still no foster mom.* I hadn't known her new parents well, but I suspected the doctor was still inside tending to the men and his wife would be helping him. The assurance of their courage didn't make Tegan feel any better, though; and I knew how she felt.

So I had to keep busy.

Morgan set guards on the perimeter and I sent Stalker to scout. He was the only one who could find out what was going on without alerting the enemy. We needed information, but not at the cost of bringing the horde down on us. At the moment our priority was extraction. I went back to helping Tegan by passing her salves and liquids, wrapping wounds and binding burns. Time ticked on; and as the final moments approached, I sagged a little in relief as my foster brother, Rex, hauled Edmund out of the hole. A few more men stumbled up into the fresh air, most of them badly injured.

"That's it," Rex said, his voice hoarse. "There's nobody else capable of following."

Tegan bit out a quiet cry, but she quickly bent her head and continued working. She was still at it when Stalker returned. I led him away from the others.

"What's it like out there?"

"A slaughter." In the moonlight, his scarred face looked pale. "And I swear there are even more than there were out on the plains."

"Where are they all coming from? And why?" I didn't expect an answer.

Just as well. He couldn't provide one. "We need to move. The bulk of the horde is prowling the burning wreckage right now, but there are scouting parties all over the area. There's a hundred strong just to the southeast."

A chill went through me as I imagined trying to fight off that many with so few warriors and fifty Breeders to protect. I nodded at Stalker. "Thanks."

Tegan was still bandaging the injured, her face a study in sorrow. She didn't look up at me until I put my hand on her shoulder. Then a sob escaped her as she tied off the fabric and sent the wounded man on his way. I put my arms around her and hugged tight; she buried her face in my shoulder.

"It's not fair," she whispered. "The townspeople need Doc more than ever and he's not—"

"They have you," I said.

"I'm not as good. There are so many things I haven't learned."

"I bet there's a doctor in Soldier's Pond. As soon as you get there, find him and tell him you mean to continue your studies."

That stalled her tears. "Will we be there that long?"

"I'm not sure," I said honestly. "But anything you learn will help down the line and bring you a little closer to feeling like you've earned the right to be called doctor."

Tegan hugged me back, then let go. "Thank you."

I didn't say any of the warm things bubbling at the back of my mind—about how she could cry later or that Doc and Mrs. Tuttle had been good people, well worth her tears. There was no time for softness. I strode over to Morgan.

"If your men are ready, we can move out now. I'm told we're within whistling distance of a battle we can't win."

To his credit, he didn't ask for particulars. The stench of burning buildings mingled with the unmistakable scent of seared flesh motivated him well enough. In low tones, he gave orders to his men, who began rounding up the injured. Some of them would require transport, which meant this journey would take more like three or four days instead of the two we had managed with a hard march. A knot formed in my stomach when I considered how many things could go wrong before I got the survivors to Soldier's Pond.

Ruse

ade came up to me as Morgan's men were lashing branches to make litters for the wounded. Despite the dire situation, his posture was loose and limber. Unlike most, he thrived under such conditions. Most likely, this trait permitted him to survive alone down below. When other people fell apart, he only got tougher and more determined, and the more he fought, the more he won, the higher his confidence rose. I didn't know if tonight's victory would improve his emotional state, but I hoped so. Tegan had made it clear there was no way for *me* to fix him. The shift had to come from inside Fade's own head.

My body ached. To cover my weakness, I asked, "How do you like our chances?"

"I don't," he admitted. "But I'd like it less if we didn't try."

That summed up my feelings, too. "We won't be sleeping for a while. Hope you're ready."

"How do you prepare for something like this? I wish it hadn't come to a desperate evac . . . but it's good to feel useful again." Fade gestured at the soot-stained faces and children terrified to silence at the upending of their orderly world.

Among their number, I saw Zachary Bigwater but neither of the elder Bigwaters, nor his sister, Justine. The kid looked older than he had a few days before when he'd begged to come with us because he was sweet on Tegan. In a heartbeat, everything could change. He wore despair like a necktie; it slumped his shoulders and kept his head low. For some reason, he couldn't meet anybody's gaze. Tegan tried to talk to him, but he turned away without speaking.

"He's carrying a pretty big burden," I said softly.

"Losing everything isn't easy."

Fade knew that better than anyone. Once, he had a sire and dam who loved him. First she got sick, then his sire did, ultimately leaving him alone. A lesser boy would've wound up in the gangs and let them take away everything his parents taught him. Instead he fled to the dangers and darkness down below, determined to hold fast to the person they'd taught him to be. Even down below, the elders hadn't touched the inner core that made him special. I admired him for that.

I loved him for everything.

Studying the refugees, I shook my head in perplexity. It was preposterous to imagine that we could herd such a large group to Soldier's Pond while escaping detection, but failure was unthinkable. Somehow we had to deliver them to safety; otherwise everything about Salvation would be lost. I understood that intuitively, seeing echoes of the ruins. All the people who lived and loved in Gotham had been decimated. I didn't want to see that happen to the people who had been kind enough to take us in.

"They have no chance without us," I whispered.

"It'll come down to avoiding enemy scouting parties," Stalker said, joining us.

"Do you have some ideas in that regard?" I asked.

He shrugged. "Maybe."

"Let's hear them."

"We could split into smaller groups, trying to lead them away from the refugees."

I shook my head. "That would leave them defenseless if the strategy failed."

"If it comes down to a straight-up fight, we've already lost," Stalker said flatly.

Fade prickled to life. "With that attitude, what're you doing here? Shouldn't you be saving your own skin? You excel at that, as I recall."

At the veiled reference to how he'd abandoned his cubs at the first sign of trouble in the ruins and threw his lot in with us because we knew how to fight the Freaks, Stalker narrowed his eyes and took a step forward. While I didn't want them arguing, I was glad to see Fade getting angry about anything, even strategy.

Still, I stepped between them and shook my head. "We should talk to Morgan. Presumably he's been fighting the Freaks longer than we have." He was older anyway, though that didn't always mean what I thought it should in terms of experience. "Come on."

The boys flanking me, I joined the guardsman. "Do you have any thoughts on how we can keep these people alive?"

"Pray to all your saints."

I had no idea what that meant or what a saint might be. This didn't seem like the time to ask. "Are you being serious?"

"Half," Morgan said. "But it's not the most practical approach. A group as large as ours will certainly attract attention. I propose we send scouts ahead to make sure the way is clear and keep sentries moving on the perimeters at all times. I'll also need a squad to guard our rear flank. That's the group most likely to see combat."

"I'll fight," I said.

"Me too." Fade spoke almost as quickly as I did.

Stalker didn't react to that quiet resurgence of our old dynamic; at least we weren't broken as a fighting team. "If I'm welcome, I'll volunteer as a forward scout."

Morgan glanced my way, probably for confirmation this was a good idea. So I said, "He's the best Salvation has."

"Then welcome aboard. Go see Calhoun for your assignment." Stalker didn't look at me again, merely went off to the fellow Morgan indicated. That told me he was annoyed that I hadn't let him hit Fade. To me, the guard added, "I'll leave my best fighting men with you."

"You're marching with the main group?" I asked.

Morgan nodded. "I'm not the best soldier, only the man the colonel trusts the most."

I could see why. He had a steady air and he gave the impression that he could handle himself in a crisis. That didn't always equate to raw battle prowess. "Tegan will be staying with you as well. She's the closest thing Salvation has to a doctor since Doc Tuttle didn't make it out."

"She'll be welcome. And I'll look out for her personally."

"Her leg bothers her sometimes," Fade added.

I frowned at him because she didn't like people treating her like she was crippled, but in a situation like this, Morgan needed to know. She'd already taxed her thigh getting from Salvation to Soldier's Pond and back again. Tegan must be hurting but she was more concerned with those who needed her than with her own physical limitations. There was only one thing left to do, so I wove through the milling crowd to check on my family.

Edmund was thin and hollow-eyed from the stress of the situation. As I approached, he put an arm around Momma Oaks, then reached for me with his other one. Up close he smelled of wood smoke and leather, though I couldn't forget the why of the former. Rex stood slightly apart, wearing the dull, shocked expression of someone who couldn't credit the sudden loss. I stepped into their embrace, quietly grateful that my family was intact when so many others weren't.

Momma Oaks kissed my cheek, her hand gentle on my hair. "There were just too many. You mustn't blame yourself. We didn't have the ammunition or the manpower to hold the walls."

She must've been so frightened, but there was little evidence of it at the moment.

"And then they figured out how to use the torches."

Edmund nodded, squeezing my shoulder with one arm. "But I told everyone you'd be back with help . . . and here you are."

"It's not enough," I said softly.

Rex started at that. When he spoke, his tone was incredulous. "It's more than anyone thought you'd manage. When Elder Bigwater said he'd sent the four of you on a rescue mission, most didn't think you'd come back. We didn't expect you to save the whole town, Deuce."

That was news to me. Maybe it was an impossible task, but I'd set out intending to achieve it. This lesser version of success hurt. Still, I'd take fifty-odd lives over none. I hugged my parents in turn.

"What happened inside?" I asked.

Edmund sighed. "Like she said, we didn't have the ammo to hold the walls. Smith fell behind on production, and once we started running out, the Muties got bolder. Then one of the monsters threw a brand. It got lucky and the wall caught."

"That gave others the idea," I guessed.

"Once a fire takes hold," Momma Oaks said tiredly, "there's not a whole lot you can do."

"Why didn't Elder Bigwater oversee the evacuation sooner?"

Rex's expression hardened. "Because he was too busy dealing with his mad wife."

"Oh, no. What did she do?"

Momma Oaks bent her head. "She kept ranting about how violating the covenant with heaven led to our downfall—that if we got right with our faith—the Muties would go away. Her supporters got in the way of defense *and* the water brigade, as if prayers ever put out a fire."

"I'm as devout as the next man," Edmund said, "but I don't

believe the Lord works that way, and I don't think these monsters are part of a divine plan."

Rex nodded. "Me either. I refute a god who would do such a thing to test people who have done their best to live according to his laws."

I had an opinion on that. "The Muties are like wild animals . . . or they were. Now, they seem more like us. I'd love to know where they came from . . . and why they're changing."

"Maybe someone out there has answers for you," Edmund said.

"Something you credit more than our stories," Momma Oaks added.

"I hope so." Changing the subject, I quickly explained the plan, then finished, "It's important that you follow instructions and stay close to Morgan. I'll meet up with you again in Soldier's Pond."

I glimpsed a thousand protests in my mother's eyes, but she voiced none of them. That made her brave in a way I couldn't match. Whenever Fade was in danger, I wanted to be right there beside him, fighting. It would be beyond me to watch someone I loved stride into jeopardy without me, even if it was best. Her strength surpassed mine by far.

Tears in his eyes, Edmund nodded. "We'll be safe, don't worry about us."

There was no way I could help it, but I took the reassurance as he meant it. He wanted me to go forth and fight without their safety preying on my mind. I appreciated the gesture. I repaid Edmund with an extra tight hug, then I went into Momma Oaks's arms. She wrapped them around me tight and I breathed her in, more smoke and blood, underlaid with the faintest scent of bread. It had been days since she'd baked, but the smell lingered to remind me of home.

When I came to Rex, I hesitated as I didn't know him well

and most of my interactions with him had come in the form of goading. He addressed my hesitation by hugging me gently. Close up, I could feel that he was shaking, barely putting a brave face on his wife's loss.

So I gave him a job to distract him. "Watch over them for me. I'm holding you personally responsible for their welfare."

"Noted," Rex said sharply.

But his shoulders straightened when we parted. I could see he was thinking about his parents now and not Ruth. There would be time enough to mourn her in whatever way he saw fit. Not now. Not with fires blazing in the distance and the muted snarls of Freaks prowling the woods in search of survivors. I couldn't remember when the stakes had been so high.

Soon enough, we split into three: scouting party, main group, and the rear guard. Fade, me, and five of Morgan's best men, who ranged wildly in age, composed the rear. Dennis wasn't much older than Fade or me, lean and nondescript, yet by the way he handled his rifle and knives, I could tell he was among the best. In contrast, all of Thornton's hair had silvered, though his beard still bore traces of black. His dark eyes revealed a canny knowledge; strong shoulders and a broad back made him a greater threat. To me he looked like a grappler, a man who preferred brute force to finesse. I also recognized him as the man who had been assisting Morgan in Soldier's Pond.

I guessed the third one, Spence, was five years or so older than me, short and wiry with shorn red hair. The first time I saw that shade, I was fascinated, as nobody down below had it. Now, I was only interested in how well Spence could fight, and his demeanor gave me no clue. He had a freckled, open-looking face, devoid of violence, yet Morgan had promised us the best. So I'd withhold judgment until I saw him in combat.

Morrow was the fourth. Thin and dark haired, he had a ready smile and a set of pipes slung across his back; you'd mistake him for a fool until you caught the glint in his eyes. Underestimating this man would be the last mistake you ever made, and I figured he couldn't be more than two years older than Fade. Yet he gave the impression of experience.

The last member was named Tulliver, Tully for short. Her green eyes were keen, set deep in a strong face. She was almost as tall as Fade and older than anyone but Thornton, but her hair was still fair. Most intriguing, she wore an interesting weapon strapped to her back. I'd never seen anything like it. I glanced at Fade to see what he made of it, but he wasn't paying attention to our recruits. Instead, he was staring at me like I was the last slice of cake on a plate, and somebody had told him he couldn't have it.

After a flurry of farewells, Stalker headed out with the scouting party. Tegan set out with the Salvation survivors, Morgan leading the way. My family cast a final look in my direction, then they followed as well. This was a terrifying gambit, and we wouldn't find out if it had succeeded until we reached Soldier's Pond.

Carnage

"Morgan put me in charge," Thornton said. "If anyone has a problem with that, you'd better speak up now so I can knock it out of you."

Nobody made a sound.

"Good. Let's move. Remember, we're not trying to practice good woodcraft. We're leaving a trail for them to follow. More than likely, we'll see some combat before we get home."

The word sent a pang through me. I'd just started feeling like I might belong in Salvation when Caroline Bigwater decided I was a plague sent from heaven, whatever that meant, and that the only way the town could be saved was by sacrificing me. For obvious reasons, I wasn't on board with that plan, so I'd gone for help in accordance with her husband's wishes. Now Salvation smoldered behind me, nothing but charred wood and piles of ash. I could trace this moment all the way back to the night the Freaks stole fire from the outpost; I'd known even then that the theft meant nothing good.

"I can't wait." Tully patted the giant knife strapped to her thigh, and from the shape of the sheath, it had a wicked curve, perfect for disemboweling Freaks. "Those Muties *better* bring an army because I'm pretty pissed off, after what they did here."

"They were good neighbors," Spence agreed.

I hesitated, then decided I wanted to get acquainted with the first female warrior I'd run into since coming Topside. "I've never seen that kind of weapon before."

As greetings went, it was rough, but the woman's face lit with enthusiasm. "It's a crossbow. I've been shooting since I was younger than you. I make the quarrels myself."

"She's amazing," Spence put in.

I'd come to that conclusion myself, but before I could ask about the quarrels, which I took to mean the projectiles in the container on her back, Thornton snapped, "Enough. Let's move."

As I fell into formation beside Fade, I refused to think about the hunting party—one hundred Freaks, Stalker had said—and though my math skills weren't the best, even I could figure that those were bad odds. The horde was way bigger, a number so huge I lacked the skill to calculate it. If you added up all the souls in Salvation, plus those who lived in Soldier's Pond, I didn't think you'd end up with that many humans total, let alone ones who could fight.

The first Freak hunting party found us some distance from the Salvation ruins. I counted more than twenty in the split second I had to assess our foe before the carnage began. As they charged us from behind, Tully whirled and drew the strange weapon on her back. She was fast with it, releasing four projectiles, one right after the other. Three Freaks died. She was a good shot, particularly in uncertain light on moving targets. Then they were on us, a mass of snarling monsters. I slashed with grim determination, my knives a blur in my hands. Like the old days, Fade fought at my back and he was death itself, dispatching the Freaks with complete efficiency.

The others battled around us; as I'd thought, Thornton was a brawler. He lashed out with weighted fists, smashed his way through three Freaks before I realized he was crushing their skulls with brute force. That roused my admiration even as Spence waded in at Tully's side. The redhead used shooting irons even close-up, a fighting style I'd never seen before. He was adept at knocking a Freak back with the butt, then he shot it in the chest at close range, and he used elbows and feet to boot. As for Morrow, he favored a slender blade, longer than any dagger I'd ever seen. He was elegant and willowy as he fought, his face a study in concentration. Dennis used shorter knives and he guarded Morrow's flank; I could tell they had fought together for a while, which spoke to how good Dennis was despite his age.

Two Freaks rushed me. Fade took the one on the left with a vicious jab through the neck, and his blow contained enough ferocity that he nearly took off its head. I dodged low and wheeled around to cut the creature across the back of the knees. It went down and I finished it with cold steel straight through the heart. The clearing reeked of blood, the grass damp with dew and worse, slick underfoot. I slid toward another, as Thornton was surrounded, and I didn't like his chances. No matter his strength, he still needed help.

Tully and Spence seemed to be all right. So were Morrow and Dennis. I stabbed a Freak in the spine, and was rewarded with an unearthly shriek of pain. The monster whirled, slashing with blood-tipped claws, but when I danced back, it couldn't follow. I had paralyzed it with that cut and Thornton finished the beast with a heavy stomp of his boot. Two Freaks tried to run, which unnerved me. What did they intend? Survival or something more, like carrying a message? Tully shot one in the back, the sleek shaft of the missile lodged in its hide. Spence took the other in a clean kill, but the noise made me wonder how soon we'd see more of these.

There were bodies everywhere, so much death. The corpses lay in pairs and triads, bones protruding, thickening blood pooled around fatal wounds. I couldn't forget that I'd seen these creatures going about their lives, much as human beings did—eating and chattering to each other. There had been no savagery in that Freak village, no monsters attacking one another. That lent another layer of menace to their enmity; they no longer killed indiscriminately out of endless hunger, which meant this was more than conflict over territory.

This was war.

"Everyone in one piece?" Thornton demanded.

I took stock in a glance. We were all lightly wounded, scrapes and bites here and there, but nothing serious or life-threatening. Dennis bound up a slash on his arm with calm competence. The rest of us could go without treatment until we hit Soldier's Pond.

"Good enough," Morrow said.

Thornton made a *get-going* gesture. "Then let's move out. We don't want to be here when another hunting party finds the corpses. They'll take it personal."

Which made me think Thornton knew about the change in Freak behavior. Maybe the colonel had shared some of her theories and observations with him. Our leader didn't look interested in entertaining questions, however, and that made me miss Longshot even more. This wasn't the time to try to figure things out, though. Too much rode on our diversion—too many innocent lives—for me to get distracted.

Unlike the progress to Salvation, we were noisy. Since it was our goal to attract hostiles and keep them from stumbling on the injured refugees, I stomped my feet like an angry child. With a puckish grin, Morrow got out his pipes. Thornton sighed over that, but he nodded his approval, then a merry melody echoed across the field. If the lilting tune didn't draw more Freaks down on us, then they simply weren't roving the area.

It was an odd procession through the woods. By the music that accompanied us, one could be forgiven for thinking it was a party and not the most dire of circumstances. I kept my weapons handy, listening at each crack of branches, each rustle of tall grass, but if the monsters were following us, they wouldn't be subtle about it, surely. They had the numerical advantage and didn't need to practice stealth or woodcraft.

Unless they're following you to Soldier's Pond.

Fade and I had thought that was why they didn't attack the outpost initially; they were waiting for us to lead them to more humans. The silence as we moved along the river unnerved me. Distant trees swayed in the light breeze, limbs shifting like skeletal fingers. Each step I took I expected the horde to descend on us, but it wasn't fear I felt so much as anticipation. Here, I was in my element, protecting those who needed me. Down below, I never expected to live long. As long as I went down fighting, I could be content.

We marched into the morning; as the sunlight brightened, Morrow played on. Soon enough his pipes drew down the next wave of monsters. They heard it from across the river, shallow enough to ford, and came loping across wet stones with fangs bared and claws extended. Tully drew her crossbow and loosed a quarrel to nail the closest one in the chest. I couldn't hear the impact over the rush of the water, but the creature went down and the current bore it away, the water frothing pink as it carried the body over the rocks.

When the rest drew closer, Spence unloaded, shooting first with one gun, then the other. He dropped two, then Tully killed her second and third. By my count, that left ten, a smaller band than we'd faced before. *There's a group of one hundred hunting us. Or maybe not.* It was possible they'd split up to cover more ground.

Please let the others have gotten away from Salvation.

Then there was no time for such thoughts. The monsters rushed up the riverbank and the battle was joined. I lashed out with my blades in crossing strikes that opened the Freak's torso. Blood spattered from Spence's next shot, and Morrow fought beside Dennis, his longer reach repelling the creatures from the younger man's back. They were all fierce and solid fighters, worthy to be Hunters. Fade was savage in his determination, his movements so graceful they looked like dancing. As he wheeled, I waded in, and we traded blocks and parries, slices and slashes with a natural elegance that moved me to my core.

All's not lost. We still have this.

With anyone else, I would have feared a misplaced blade, but Fade always knew precisely where I was. I never flinched, even when his dagger cut through the air, narrowly missing my arm and embedded in the Freak lunging toward me. He twisted the blade to widen the wound, and the strange stink hung heavy in the air, overwhelming the clean spray of the river and the crushed green scent of grass trampled underfoot. The birds were quiet in the reeds, and I heard no insects chirping, only the roar of my heart as I defended with all my skill.

A second wave hit us as we battled the first. Ten was easy; twenty became chaotic. Spence fired ferociously, keeping them off Tully, and Morrow's blade sliced through a beast charging straight at Dennis. Two more pushed through his guard, and I raised my knife to throw it. *Too slow.* Dennis went down beneath their combined weight, and by the time Morrow and I finished them, he was clutching his torn stomach, blood burbling out of his mouth.

The rest of us surrounded our injured cohort in a protective circle. I fought near Fade and Morrow, determinedly cutting down the monsters as they charged. Likely it was exhaustion, but the numbers seemed endless. My motions became clumsy as I blocked, letting a Freak push me back a step. Fortunately the others were enraged by their comrade's condition, and they fought like a hundred men.

Thornton broke the last one's neck and then kicked it for good measure. Breathing hard, I went down to the water to rinse my blades and then my hands. I wished Tegan was here. Maybe she could help Dennis.

"How bad is it?" I asked, kneeling beside Morrow.

"He won't make it." There was an awful finality in his voice.

Thornton dropped to his knees. "How do you want to play it, son?"

For a few seconds, I thought he was talking to Morrow, but the older man gazed down at Dennis, their eyes locked. "Make it quick, Pa."

"Aye," Thornton said.

In a dreadful, tender gesture, he scooped Dennis into his arms and carried him to the river. There, he held the boy's head in the water until he stopped struggling. When Thornton drew up the body, it was all limp limbs and bloody shirt. The older man's expression, as he cradled the young one, hurt me to witness, so I looked away.

"That was his last boy," Tully whispered.

Dennis was actually his son . . . like Rex and Edmund. It became clear to me just how grave a sacrifice I had asked of Soldier's Pond.

"What do you want to do about a funeral?" Morrow asked when Thornton returned.

"Gather as many stones as you can find. We don't have time to do a proper job."

We worked in grim silence, building a pile of rocks over Dennis's body. Any moment I expected more Freaks to set upon us, but it remained quiet. Thornton bowed his head and whispered some words I didn't catch. My heart squeezed.

The last thing the older man did was pull a hand ax out of his pack. In a fierce, furious motion, he beheaded the Freak that had killed his son. Since the monster was already dead, I didn't see the point, but I hoped it made him feel better. At last, Thornton ordered us onward. Over time I got tired of him belting orders, but since he was smart and I felt sorry for him, I put aside my irritation. We survived the first day, moving slow as we were, and we killed a lot of Freaks. By nightfall, I was exhausted and hungry, but I kept in mind that the longer we stayed alive, fighting and drawing the monsters, the better chance the other groups had of making it to Soldier's Pond. Since those people were all that was left from Salvation, including my family, I'd fight until the knives dropped out of my dead hands to make sure they were all right.

Yet we couldn't go without rest indefinitely. We paused beside the river at dusk with light falling like ripe plums, heavy with purple, so that it lent Fade a bruised aspect. All of us were tired; it seemed like months since I lay in a bed. There was bread, meat, and cheese from Soldier's Pond. Thornton divided it up brusquely, and we ate without the cheer of Morrow's pipes.

"Do you think they're all right?" I asked Fade softly.

I wasn't worried about Stalker; he had a way of surviving what the world threw at him. But Tegan, Momma Oaks, Edmund, and Rex? Yes, I couldn't help fearing for them.

"It's the best chance they have." I respected Fade for telling the truth, but his words offered no comfort.

I couldn't bring myself to say more so we finished our meal in silence. In the old days, he would've slung an arm around my shoulders, using his body to convey a sense of warmth. Until right then, I didn't realize how much I looked forward to those little moments, but they were gone like the last glimmer of sun below the horizon. The shadows lengthened, a chill setting in. Nibbling my bread, I wished I could touch his shoulder, his cheek, his hair. That didn't give Fade pleasure anymore, though, and such moments as when he put his head in my lap had to wait until his reaction changed.

Spence and Tully joined us, midway into the meal. His red hair was shorn so close I could see pink scalp. He wasn't big, but he was quick with his weapons, enough to keep up with Tully, which I took as a commendation. She stood four inches taller, ten years older too. But their body language made me think they came as a set.

"You both fight well," Tully said.

I nodded. "We were trained down below."

It wasn't until after I spoke that I realized they might have no idea what that meant. We were awfully far from Gotham, and maybe their stories didn't include survivors in the ruins.

Spence proved this guess to be true when he said, "Down where?"

With a glance at Fade, who nodded, I explained in as few words as possible. By the time I finished, both Spence and Tully were looking at us strangely.

"You *really* lived underground?" she asked dubiously. "That doesn't seem very healthy."

There was no point in explaining our culture: the fish pools and the mushrooms and the way Breeder women provided milk and cheese for the brats, or how we'd hunted creatures in the tunnels, kept them clear of Freaks. The life I'd known in the enclave seemed as if it belonged to someone else.

"It wasn't. We didn't live long," I said softly. "Not like people do up here."

"Tully." Spence evidently noted my discomfort with the topic. "Less talking, more eating. Thornton won't let us sit idle."

He was right about that. Just as soon as the last bite vanished, our leader barked, "On your feet, soldiers. There are more battles ahead."

Along with the others, I struggled upright. My stomach was full, but the rest of me ached. *And I'd thought Silk was tough.*

Sanctuary

An endless night of combat and bloodshed followed. At its end, my knives were crusted with dried blood, my fingers sore on the hilts. I had three new wounds in addition to my scars, and two of them needed attention from Tegan. The light of Soldier's Pond glimmered in the distance, a promise of sanctuary after the torment of the last few days.

My eyes burned as I picked up the pace without waiting for Thornton to give the word. For the first time in my life, I had no fight left in me. I had to know whether the refugees had arrived safely. The others caught my urgency, and soon we were all running, footfalls thudding over damp ground. I heard Freaks snarling in the distance behind us, but they were too far; they wouldn't find us before we reached the town perimeter.

As we approached, Thornton shouted the password and the guards went to work disarming the traps. In the moonlight I glimpsed spikes and weights, all manner of death waiting for unwary Freaks to charge. The fence wasn't solid like the one in Salvation. Instead, this one was made of metal, rusted, but still functional, and you could see right through the gate with a ramp leading to the town's heart. This had been a different kind of town once, clean and homey like Salvation, but the fortifications took away all the charm, making it clear the people who lived here were ready to fight for their lives. The people of Soldier's Pond understood the stakes and the penalty for failure.

"We made it," Fade breathed beside me.

He looked as tired as I felt. Breathing hard from that last burst, I followed the others into town and then the guards on duty secured the entry again. They all had rifles and other weapons, some of which I'd never seen before. Before I could ask about the others, our leader did.

"Status on the rest of the groups?"

"The scouts came in hours ago," the man on duty said.

"And the refugees?"

"Made it an hour past. Some of them are in bad shape. The colonel has set up a med center in the old granary at the edge of town."

"Where's that?" I cut in.

I didn't care if it was impolite; I needed to see Tegan and my family. Though Thornton offered me a sharp look, he did give me directions. I jogged off. I'd gone a good distance when I realized Fade was behind me, but I didn't stop to question him. It was enough that he didn't want me running off alone. *I have your back. Not when it's easy. All the time.* At least those words still held true. Everything else could be rebuilt with time and patience.

Here, houses were constructed of uniformly sawed timbers with faded, peeling whitewash, addendums to the odd uniform structures in the center of town. The granary was a long, raised building made of old stones. From the outside, I couldn't tell that it was being used for anything until I drew closer. Lights glimmered in the windows. I rapped twice, not wanting to alarm the occupants within. Momma Oaks flung the door open at once and I could tell by her expression that she had been waiting for me.

"You made it," she gasped, then she hugged me so tight I couldn't breathe.

"Edmund and Rex?" I asked.

"We're here," my father said.

His lined, dirty face was a welcome sight, so I hugged him too. I teetered on the verge of tears and couldn't restrain the apology. "I'm sorry I couldn't save everyone. I tried, but there weren't enough soldiers and the trip was too far—"

"Shh," he whispered into my hair, stroking my back.

Momma Oaks hugged me from the other side until I felt warm even in comparison to the hot trickle of tears on my cheeks. Rex stood back, looking beaten down by sorrow; the dead, uncomprehending look had faded, only to be replaced by pain.

"Have you any idea what's to become of us?" Momma Oaks asked.

I shook my head. "I'm not clear on how Soldier's Pond runs or who's in charge. I know Morgan's second only to the colonel when it comes to town defense. Beyond that . . ."

"We weren't here long enough to find out," Fade put in.

"You must be exhausted."

Momma Oaks had on her "I want to cook for you and fuss a bit" face but here she was dependent on others for food and shelter. By the twist of her mouth, that reality didn't sit well with her. I was relieved she was safe, but it couldn't be easy going from her own tidy home and plenty of food in the cupboards to this. In my experience down below, refugees had few rights, and some enclaves, like the one where I'd grown up, would refuse to accept them altogether, due to limited resources. Things might be different here in Soldier's Pond, but I had a feeling nobody from Salvation would relax until they heard whether they were welcome.

Knowing she wouldn't welcome my sympathy, I just nodded. "It was a tough trip."

"But necessary," Rex said. "We wouldn't be here without your efforts."

Praise made me uncomfortable, gratitude more so. I acknowl-edged his words with a jerky nod. "I'm going to help Tegan."

"You should rest," Edmund protested, but I ignored him.

"I can pitch in too," Fade said.

The room was a maze of prone forms, laid out with only a little space between them. These cramped quarters reminded me of the enclave, but instead of the makeshift walls built of scraps of metal and tattered curtains, there was no privacy at all. On the injured, I saw each shift of expression, every flicker of pain. It seemed wrong to efface their dignity, after all they'd suf-fered and lost. Tears trickled down one woman's face and she was too weak or sad to wipe them away. A stranger did that for her, just before tending the burn on the woman's right leg.

I drew strength from that kindness. As long as I had two hands, I could work beside my friend. Tegan had to be hurting, just as tired as I was, but she was still on her knees beside a pa-tient, doing what she could to give the man comfort. As I drew closer, I recognized Harry Carter, the man I'd fought beside on the wall. He had a terrible gash in his shoulder and another across his back, plus countless bites. It would be a miracle if he survived; I didn't know how he'd made the trip from Salvation.

Tegan read my look. "They put him on a litter. He was quite the hero before the town caught fire, I guess. Saved four families."

Harry's eyes opened, bloodshot and tormented in his dirty face. "But not my own."

"I'm sorry," I said softly.

He closed his eyes when Tegan went back to cleaning his wounds. When the astringent trickled into his rent flesh, it had to hurt but I saw no shift in his expression, maybe because the way he felt inside was worse. Wordless, I fell into our old rhythm, handing her things and wiping away the blood before she asked me to. There should be some words that would make things bet-ter, but I couldn't think of any. Maybe a Breeder would have the gentleness to comfort the ravaged sadness I glimpsed in Tegan's eyes. I worked on steadily.

It was the middle of the night when we emptied Tegan's bag; there wasn't enough salve or antiseptic to go around, so Tegan requested provisions from the women who had been helping us. Unlike the ones in Salvation, these females dressed in worn green trousers and they looked every bit as tough as Tully and the colonel. I suspected if not for the conditions surrounding our arrival, I might enjoy my time in Soldier's Pond. The women debated among themselves before sending a young runner off to ask the colonel if they could tap into their own supplies.

Tully popped her head in, her hair disheveled and her face lined with weariness. "Got everything squared away?"

I had no idea why she was asking me. "Not exactly. But we've done what we can for now."

"What's the problem?"

"We don't have enough supplies for the wounded. They sent someone to ask the colonel—"

"Ah." She got it, I could tell.

"Is she in charge?"

"From the outside, I suppose it looks that way. She's a bit of a benign dictator, but she's smart as hell, and she listens to her advisors. I only wish they paid as much attention to her warnings. If so, we'd currently be operating at a higher state of readiness."

Only a portion of her words made sense to me. "Readiness?"

"She's been telling us for a while now that the Muties are gearing up for a major offensive—they aren't the same mindless creatures we've been fighting for years. The last time I went out with her, I noticed the same thing. They set perimeters. They have patrols now. And they use scouts." She paused, her features yielding to a worry that troubled me. "Then at Salvation we saw evidence they've mastered fire. What's next, tools? Weapons?"

"We won't survive that," I said grimly.

"I'm aware, believe me. I just don't know what to do about it. Alone, every settlement will end up just like Salvation. And I'm taking that loss personal . . . because last winter, when sickness set in here, Longshot came out in the middle of the cold snap to bring us medicine. A woman in your town made tinctures out of herbs, and without her, I suspect we'd have all died."

"I wonder if she survived the fire."

"If she didn't, then the next time the bleeding fever rolls in, we're done for. Did she have an apprentice, somebody who knew her recipes?"

"I wasn't in Salvation very long," I said in an apologetic tone.

"That's right. You come from the underground tribes." Her tone still sounded a little skeptical, as if I sprang from some mythical land beyond her reckoning.

And maybe it was exactly like that, as she couldn't fathom the way I'd been reared, like the night girl, outside the reach of the sun. Even now, it hurt me more than it did normal people, and my eyes burned to the point that I put on my glasses when other people were staring right up at that glowing orange ball like it was the best thing they'd seen all day. At my core, I feared it as I did fire. Maybe it could warm you up and cook your food but it could be deadly as well.

At that point, I caught sight of Fade, who was reeling on his feet. From what I could tell, they had set him to hauling water and dumping out the bloody, dirty pails, rinsing rags, and generally doing scut work. After a hard march like we'd experienced, he must be feeling like the devil. *If only he'd let me hold him or stroke his head, rub his shoulders.* I knew I couldn't make all bad things go away with a kiss, but it hurt not to be able to show how much I cared. I'd only recently learned the power of a gentle touch and now that freedom between us was gone.

Tully followed my gaze to Fade, a brow arched in curiosity. "He's yours?"

Once I might've argued or hesitated to claim him. Not anymore. I nodded.

"You seem a trifle young to be married."

That wasn't what Fade and I were to each other. Momma Oaks and Edmund had spoken promises in front of the whole town. Fade had sworn his intentions were honorable, which I took to mean he intended to speak those vows someday, but we hadn't gotten to that point. Still, it was nice to imagine things ending well, more than I'd permitted myself to envision before. Usually, I saw my life finishing on a bloody note, surrounded by Freaks. Until now, I'd always accepted the obligation to make that sacrifice for the good of the whole.

Those rules didn't apply anymore. I was allowed to want things. More, to strive for them.

Belatedly, I realized she was waiting for an answer. "We're promised."

"Ah," she said. "Well, you should go tend him before somebody else does. I see young Maureen looking him up and down like he's a sweet she wants to try."

"We'll see about that." I clenched my jaw and picked a careful path through all the pallets strewn on the floor.

Fade was saying in a taut voice, "I'm fine. I don't need medical attention."

"But your arm—" she started, reaching for him.

When he jerked out of range before she touched him, I knew a little shock of relief. It was small and wrong, no doubt, but his reaction proved that he wasn't being difficult. His problem wasn't something he could make up his mind to get over. What the Freaks had done to him left damage it would take time to heal. I wasn't glad Fade had been hurt, only that he wasn't lying to me.

I shouldn't have doubted even for a second. He never lied, even when it would be easier.

"I'll take care of him," I said to the girl.

She was my age, or thereabouts, with red hair caught up in a tall tail. Her eyes were dark brown, though, an interesting contrast. Boys would probably call her pretty, though her thwarted expression marred the overall picture. As I recalled, Tully had called her Maureen. After glancing between us and seeming not to like what she read, she stalked away with shoulders set.

"Thanks," Fade said.

"You have to let me." This time, I was prepared for his reflexive recoil.

"I know."

I was about to suggest privacy when the runner returned, laden down with boxes. *So the colonel is generous in times of need.* That was a good sign for the refugees, I thought. Fade followed me when I collected the necessary supplies from the stockpile the girl had brought, just enough to tend his wound. Others required attention, and as I strode toward the back wall, Tegan went back to work.

Kneeling, I set down the salve and bandages, then beckoned Fade. He sat beside me, his expression grim. "What can I do to make this easier for you?"

"Just . . . be quick," he said.

Hope

"I can do better than that," I answered, as an idea struck me. From what I understood of his problem, being touched made him remember everything the Freaks had done to him and the pain came back, along with the shame and revulsion.

"What do you mean?"

"Think about the best thing you ever felt, the moment you were happiest. Fix that in your mind and don't let it go."

Fade studied me, a frown gathering. "It's not that easy."

"Try. It can't make things worse while I bandage you up."

"True enough." With a deep breath, he closed his eyes. "Do it."

For the first time, he didn't flinch when I touched him, but I still did the job quickly, cleaning, smoothing on the ointment, then wrapping up the wound. He pushed out a breath as my hands dropped away. His gaze met mine, something new present in his dark eyes—hope.

"Was that any better?" I asked, sitting back.

"Incredibly, yes. I mean, it wasn't good, but I could stand it. The memories flickered at the edges, and I kept shoving them back with that one bright moment, like you said."

"What did you—" I cut the question, fearing the answer.

But Fade knew what I was going to ask. "The night after the cherry blossom festival. Holding you, kissing you. When you said you loved me . . . that was the happiest I've ever been."

My heart compressed. "Love. Not loved. Nothing's changed."

"I have."

"Not in any way that matters to me. I'm sorry you're hurting, but even if I can never touch you again, it won't change how I feel."

"It won't come to that," he said with sudden determination. "I'm not letting the Freaks get the best of me."

Deep down I was delighted to hear him say that. The Fade I knew didn't accept defeat; he'd always fought—and won—against unbeatable odds. But I didn't feel like I could put a limit on him or say the way he was acting was wrong when I hadn't suffered the same pain. I could only stand by him and offer a shoulder, whether he took me up on it or not.

"I'm glad."

"It will take time," he warned. "I can't wish this away. Believe me, if I could, I *would*."

"I know. And we got by before, just thinking about touching." Or I had, anyway. I hadn't been bold enough to stroke his hair down in the enclave, but I'd spent a lot of time watching him and wondering what it would be like.

"The thinking might do me in," he muttered.

It took me a few seconds to process what he meant, then heat washed my cheeks. So he missed it, too. "Well, maybe that's a good thing."

"I was dreaming about you. When they took me." Since he was talking about it—when he'd said he would only tell the story once—that had to be good. "It was warm and lovely, and I half roused, thinking you were coming to me in the night. Since Frank was there, I was afraid to make any noise, afraid we'd both get in trouble. I was wrong, and then it all turned to pain."

"I should have heard something," I said, clenching a fist.

"Don't blame yourself. You weren't on watch."

"But I knew there was a problem with the sentries. I could've stopped it. But I think you were right . . . neither of us can change what happened. We can only move on."

"You know what bothers me most? I didn't smell the one that took me. I've gone over every moment, and I should've scented the Freak. Why didn't I?"

"We all should have," I said, frowning. "But there was no stench the night one of them crept in and stole our fire, either."

"So what does that mean?" Fade asked.

"Nothing good." I was too tired to speculate this evening.

I didn't bother asking where we could sleep. Answers might require waiting longer than I could stay awake. My body demanded I get prone at once. If I didn't listen, I'd collapse, and though I might not be a Huntress, I didn't want to be seen as weak, either. So I found a quiet corner near the back wall, away from the wounded clustered in the center. Fade and I would be fine on the floor with a roof over our heads; we'd slept in worse places.

"Rest well," I said softly, and Fade replied with the first real smile I'd seen in days.

He bedded down a small distance away, just out of arm's reach, and I rolled up in my blankets, facing him. His familiar features comforted me. Over my time at the outpost, I had developed a soldier's ability to turn off my brain and snatch sleep when I could, but it was a light doze. I roused at a touch, and half pushed myself upright, expecting to see someone who needed my help. Instead, I found Fade pressed up against me, still wrapped in his covers. I squeezed my eyes shut for a few seconds, startled by the urge to cry, just from the welcome pressure of his arm across my waist. It meant everything that he was drawn to me like this. There were problems in his waking mind, but when he dreamed, like he'd said, it was of me. I couldn't resist. Gently, I touched his hair, stroking my fingers through the tousled strands, and he puffed out a contented sigh. It wasn't enough to wake him.

I drifted off happier than I had been since before they took him. Drowsily I decided the last time I'd felt this good was the night of the festival; it was *my* golden moment too. In the morning, I woke to light slanting into my eyes. Fade was still wrapped around me, sleeping, and I didn't stir, even though I needed to for various reasons. I feared waking him and seeing the conflict in his eyes.

I braced for it; and when he shifted, bumping against me, I was surprised by what he must be dreaming. Or maybe there was no mental aspect needed. For all I knew, males might wake up in the morning, ready to breed. I had little information on such matters, but as he moved, my breath caught. I had no idea what to do, whether to encourage him or wake him before he really craved what was currently impossible for all manner of reasons.

"Deuce," he whispered drowsily.

That made my confusion better, more worthwhile. "I'm here."

His hand drifted to my hip to pull me closer, and I didn't struggle. From the angle of the light, I didn't think anyone else was awake. That didn't mean I should encourage this, but it felt so good to be close to him. Love surged through me in a drowning rush; it took all my self-control not to wrap my arms around him as tight as I could and beg him not to go away again.

Stay. Stay with me. Just like this.

But wishes were empty thoughts, cast down a dark hole. They didn't come true unless you worked for them. I'd learned that about the world, if nothing more.

Fade nuzzled his face into my neck, his lips warm on my skin. My heart pounded like mad, and it was an effort to remain still and soak up whatever affection he offered in his sleep. I touched a fingertip to my tingling mouth, wanting a proper kiss. *Maybe if I'm slow and careful . . .* I warred with myself about the right way to manage the moment, whether I should wake him.

In the end, selfishness won. I threaded my fingers in his hair and shifted back until his lips were near mine, our breaths mingling. His eyelids fluttered, then he pressed in. It was a delicate butterfly of a kiss, as if he'd never touched me before. Then possibly his dream changed and the flavor of the kiss did too. It gained layers and heat, hunger and ferocity. Dazed, I responded in kind, thinking this was what he wanted in his secret heart and had been afraid to show me. I was swept away by his need, then it became mine, until the moment he woke—and remembered.

Fade shuddered. I started to draw back, but he set a hand on my arm. "Don't move."

"I didn't—"

"I know. I came across the space toward you, not the other way around."

"Is it awful?" I asked in an anxious whisper.

"No. I want you too much to feel anything else right now."

I took that to mean he was extremely interested in breeding, a fact I could confirm through our double sets of blankets. "What's the solution?"

"I just . . . need a minute. Then I'll go find some cold water to dunk myself in repeatedly." The wry amusement in his tone made me smile.

As promised, he rolled away, but without any of the prior repugnance he'd shown before. He was too preoccupied with minimizing embarrassment, I thought. In the brightening dawn, his cheeks were touched by high color, and Fade ducked his head as he crept out of the granary, presumably to find the icy bath he'd mentioned. I lay in my blankets for a few seconds, torn between discomfiture and quiet pride. It wasn't something a Huntress would be pleased with, but the girl inside me was glad he wanted me enough to seek me in his sleep—and it was more than a physical need, I suspected.

Smothering a smile, I crawled out of my pallet and rolled my blankets tightly, then stowed them in my pack. I checked to be sure I still had the splendid legacy of Longshot's folio, containing the map of the territories with all his notes learned over long years on the trade runs. Thus reassured, I tiptoed over to Tegan, who was stirring on the other side of the room. As I knelt, she sat up, shoving the dark hair out of her face.

"Let's find some breakfast," she said.

I nodded. With quick fingers, I subdued my hair in the braid Momma Oaks had taught me to create, ladylike, but also good for fighting. I tied the tail with a scrap of leather, then trailed Tegan out of the building. She followed her nose to what looked like the barracks from Salvation, only bigger.

Inside, the room was swarming with soldiers, all in grungy green. Some looked more alert than others. All were in various stages of breakfast. There was a food line, and with a puzzled look at Tegan, I joined it at the end. There was a place for us to get plates and cutlery, so we went through, telling men with spoons what we wanted. Most of it looked disgusting, cooked in such huge quantities, and a few items I'd never seen before, especially a dish that was lumpy, white, and brown. It looked filling, though, so I indicated it along with a thick hunk of bread. I also found some apples, so I took one of those as well.

A glance across the room told me no tables were vacant. As Tegan came up beside me, I picked one at random with a few empty seats. The men shoveling their food down didn't look up as we sat, merely kept eating with a single-minded focus that seemed unnatural to me now. I had gotten used to small courtesies in Salvation, I supposed, as down below, we devoured our meals as fast as we got them, fearing somebody might decide we didn't merit that much food after all.

Tegan cocked a brow at me. "It must be good."

"It's terrible," one said. "But edible, and we know better than to dally in the mess."

I repeated the last three words with a question in my voice.

"Short for mess hall," another man clarified.

That didn't help me, but Tegan made the connection. "Is this a military facility?"

The question earned her a strange look, but the soldier proved willing to answer. "A long, long time ago, it was just a small town. After the first outbreaks, the army stationed men here, provisioned a base to receive and support survivors."

"Outbreaks of what?" I asked.

Before the man could answer, a bell went off. I tensed—had my knives in my hands and was on my feet before anyone else at the table responded. Tegan just looked worried, but she still had her spoon halfway to her mouth.

Then someone laughed. "You're skittish, girl. That's just the signal that breakfast is over and those of us on duty need to get on with training, the work roster, or patrols, depending on what we've been assigned."

"Good to know," Tegan murmured, going back to her breakfast.

Once the room cleared out, I said, "It sounds like they know more about what happened than the townsfolk did in Salvation, something more real than religious stories."

"No history is ever unbiased."

I considered that, eating a bite of the brown-and-white lumpy food. It wasn't horrible, but it seemed like it needed something else, so I spooned some onto my wedge of bread, then took an experimental bite. *Better.*

"What do you mean?"

"It's been a long time, but my mom used to teach me, before people got sick. There were books all over the university, and she read to me, explained things as best she could."

"And she said history is biased?" I wasn't positive what a bias was. From school, I knew history was the study of things that happened in the past, but I couldn't understand what Tegan was getting at. Surely something was either true, or it wasn't.

"Not on purpose. But people see things differently. So I might see a blue flower growing below an apple tree and write all about the blue flower whereas you might see only the apples. Your account would contain information about the fruit, never mentioning the flower."

"Because the food would matter to me more," I said in sudden comprehension. "So it's not that the people in Salvation are trying to lie. They just include the part of the stories that they care about."

"Exactly. Since they're devout people, they interpreted the terrible things that happened in the world as punishment from God for their sins. I don't think we'll find that bias here."

Now I understood. Thoughtful, I ate my breakfast in silence, considering all we might learn in Soldier's Pond.

First, though, we had wounded to tend.

Verdict

The rest of the day, I helped Tegan.

Not only did the bandages need to be changed, cuts and burns had to be tended. There were broken bones too and once we'd dealt with the long process of treating them, they also needed food and broth. I'd never seen myself as a caregiver, but since Tegan needed my hands, I was willing. I didn't know as much as she did but I followed directions well enough.

"No, hold that with your left hand," she said briskly. "Don't move."

She was so good with the injured, offering endless patience and kindness. I had less of her natural aptitude, but since I was only her assistant, not the doctor, my skill didn't matter as much.

By nightfall, I was as exhausted as I had been after the battle outside the Salvation gates.

"How many of them do you think will live?" I asked Tegan.

The room was starting to reek of putrid wounds, masked lightly by antiseptic and healing salve. In some cases, her proficiency and desire to help wouldn't be enough. I felt sorry for those poor souls because a slow death was the worst kind.

She puffed out a weary sigh. "Half, I hope."

That was even fewer than I expected. "It must be hard."

"I wish Papa Doc was here," she whispered. "He could probably save more."

"You're doing your best."

"It's not enough," she said, stalking off.

I didn't take it personally. Tegan wanted to save everyone but life didn't work that way, no matter how much I wished otherwise.

As I came out of the granary, I ran into Stalker; he had fallen in with the scouts and went out regularly with them. He didn't look as if he'd rested much, his bones sharp beneath his skin and dark circles cradling his eyes. He jerked a nod, then moved to push past me. I stayed him with an abortive movement, not quite touching him. I suspected by his taut expression that there would be no more quiet moments between us, and that was for the best. False encouragement would be wrong when my heart belonged so completely to Fade.

"What?" he demanded.

"I just wondered what you saw out there and what the trip from Salvation was like."

"Awful. I had no idea if you were safe, if I'd ever see you again. And this time, I didn't even get a kiss good-bye."

"That's not what I meant." He had to know I was looking for concrete information about the terrain and the number of Freaks.

"Forget it," he said. "The colonel is waiting on my report."

It wasn't hard to read his mood. "That's not the only reason you're hurrying off."

Stalker eyed me, his mouth flat. "I get it. You'd rather have him, broken, than me whole. If that didn't clarify my chances with you, nothing would. But you can't have what you want either, Deuce. I can't be your friend, feeling like this. Give me some time, and then . . ." He shrugged. "Maybe. No promises. Just . . . leave me be."

"Take care of yourself," I said softly.

He strode off without looking back, shoulders straight. *At least his leg's healed.* Part of me was glad it was over—that he'd finally given up. The rest felt bad that I'd hurt him and given him the wrong signals out of ignorance. Sighing, I went to the mess hall, where they were wrapping up dinner; I was among the last to be served, then I spotted Momma Oaks and the rest of my family across the sparsely populated room. I wove through the tables and sat down with them. They all looked a little better than they had the night before.

"Have you heard anything?" I asked, regarding their official status.

Edmund shook his head. "There's a council meeting this evening to decide our fates."

"They wouldn't just turn us away," Rex said, but he didn't sound as sure as he wished.

I didn't reply since the enclave made a practice of exactly that. In all the years I lived there, they'd made one exception—for Fade—and only because his will to survive fascinated them, the way he'd lived feral and alone, bereft of protection or support. That implacable core made me admire him more, even as I promised myself I'd always be there to fight for him. It was time *someone* did.

"It sure is strange here," Momma Oaks whispered then. "They don't pray before meals, did you notice? And the women go around dressed like men." She aimed a look at me, as if she'd just realized something. "Is that how you felt when you first arrived in Salvation?"

I smiled at that. "Yes. But if I adapted, you can, too. I don't think people here mind that you have your own customs." But that brought a question to mind. "How come you don't know more about the other settlements? I can tell none of you have ever been here before."

My mother looked shocked at the idea. "Of course not. Long-shot handled all contact with outsiders. It's been our policy for hundreds of years to limit our exposure to worldly ways."

"It was supposed to keep us safe," Rex whispered.

Edmund's shoulders slumped a little. "Yes, we believed that by conforming to the covenant the original settlers made with heaven and by living plain, simple lives, God would spare us from the trials that plagued others."

"So . . . Longshot kept Salvation from being . . . sullied?" I wasn't sure that was the right word, but my parents nodded, so I must be in the vicinity.

"He acted as a buffer, handled all of our trade runs and when trappers and traders came to town, he did business with them outside the walls," Rex added.

That much, I remembered; I just hadn't known why. "But if you were so worried about bad things getting in, why did you let the four of us stay?" Before, I just thought they were kind folks in Salvation. I hadn't realized they were so insular. Now I was genuinely curious.

Momma Oaks answered with a quote from the book Caroline Bigwater used to haul around. "'Train a child in the way he should go, and when he is old he will not turn from it.'"

"You took us in because we're young," I guessed. "You thought we'd learn your ways."

Edmund smiled at me. "That's not why *we* welcomed you, Deuce, only the official town policy on strangers." Then his face fell. "Or it was."

"Don't think about it," my mother whispered.

Drawing in a breath, Edmund rubbed Momma Oaks on the shoulder. "We can build a life here, if we're welcome. Surely even soldiers need good shoes."

I glanced down at the worn, poorly made boots that most of the men were wearing. "I'd say they're crying out for you here."

"I'd like to apprentice and learn the family trade," Rex said hesitantly. "I understand if you won't take me back, though. I'm pretty old to start from the beginning and I've likely forgotten what little you managed to cram into my head, before—"

Edmund smiled. "Of course, I'm happy to have you. That only applies if I can find a workshop here, of course."

Momma Oaks was scrutinizing the green shirts and trousers that everyone wore. "Their clothes are in rags. I wonder if they know how to weave or sew, here. I could set up a shop, too."

It was good to see them making tentative plans, imagining how they could build. Their hope renewed my own, fortified my determination to find the place I belonged. So far, I liked Soldier's Pond better than I'd enjoyed Salvation—not that I had wanted the town destroyed. They took us in and kept us safe to the best of their abilities, and I'd always be grateful.

Shortly after I finished my food, the rest of the men filed out. Rex rose to follow them, and Momma Oaks and Edmund did likewise. I came last, watching as the soldiers jogged toward a large building on the opposite end of town. I figured that was where the meeting would be held, more organized than the impromptu sessions Elder Bigwater called on the green. Curious and apprehensive, I slipped into the hall along with the last trickle of soldiers.

Inside, there were rows of benches, similar to the mess hall, but none of them were stained, and there were no tables. The wood gleamed, attesting to the fact that they discussed serious matters here. I slid onto a bench beside soldiers I didn't recognize. Spread throughout the crowd, I spotted a few familiar faces: Spence, Tully, and Morrow, though not Thornton—and I imagined he was mourning his fallen son.

The colonel stood up front, talking to the same group who had agreed to let her send men to Salvation. Along with everyone else, I waited to see what the verdict was. I couldn't make out the conversation from this distance, though I could tell they were still talking. The fact that they were meant I had reason to hope for a positive outcome.

Once the room filled up, two men swung the doors closed, then locked it. They took punctuality serious in Soldier's Pond. Then the colonel called the meeting to order by whacking the table with a small wooden hammer. The crowd quieted at once, turned expectantly toward the front as the council took their seats. Once everyone was settled, the colonel leaned forward.

"A motion has been brought to permit these folks to stay as permanent residents." In Salvation, people would already be shouting objections or support, but the room remained calm and orderly. Colonel Park went on, "I now formerly call this meeting to order to present our decision. Mr. Walls, will you do the honors?"

The gray-haired man I remembered from their first emergency meeting stood. "Yes, Colonel." He addressed the audience then. "After a lengthy debate, we've decided to offer provisional citizenship status to any families willing to comply with the terms, which are as follows: one member of the household, male or female, must volunteer for service and pass basic training, then take his or her place on the active duty list. The rest are then free to assume support roles in town."

Though I wasn't sure, that sounded like joining the guard in Salvation. From what I'd seen of the training program here, it would be more rigorous; they took defense and discipline seriously. A support role must be someone who helped the soldiers do their jobs, likely by making shoes, boots, and uniforms. So that meant if Rex or I volunteered, then the Oakses could stay here and be safe. Well. Relatively speaking. Someone as smart as the colonel must understand the severity of the threat. Her scouts were good or Stalker wouldn't be roving with them. He had little patience for incompetence.

"Are there any questions?" the colonel asked. Silence. "Objections?"

I expected a spate of complaints but the men and women in the hall merely nodded agreement with the decision. On some level, it made sense to permit new blood, but a favorable decision would never have been reached in the enclave. Resources weren't quite as strained Topside, however, so Soldier's Pond could afford to be more generous in their terms—and they still benefited from the influx of new faces. This ruling increased the size of their defense force.

Tully and Spence whispered together, though I wasn't sure how they felt about the verdict. Morrow was watching me, and when I caught his eye, he touched two fingers to his brow in greeting. The gesture made me lonely for Longshot. Once the meeting broke up officially, I strode to the front of the room, my decision made.

"I'll join up for the Oaks family."

The colonel frowned at me. "How old are you?"

"Sixteen."

She sighed and shook her head. "While I admire your enthusiasm, you're not old enough, Deuce. We require minors to be eighteen before they can volunteer."

Horror washed through me. "I've been training since I could hold a knife, ma'am, and where I'm from, you're considered an adult at fifteen. Can't you make an exception this once?"

"I'm sorry. I respect your courage, but an adult from your family must fulfill the requirement. Come see me in two years."

That would be too late. Momma Oaks might be strong and resilient, but if Rex died in service to the town, she would have no children left at all. I didn't think she could bear it—and even if she could—she shouldn't have to. Edmund probably couldn't pass basic training; I'd noticed the slow way he moved in the mornings, as if his joints pained him, and his back wasn't the best from long years hunched over his workbench.

"What about the wounded?" I asked. "Some of them have no surviving family."

"If they can't recover enough to serve, then they have to go," the colonel said. "We can't afford to support those who give nothing back."

So they weren't wholly unlike the enclave, here. They just had the resources to permit a façade of kindness, but ultimately, the result wasn't too much different. "How long will you give them to heal before sending them away?"

The colonel seemed surprised by my question. "We discussed this issue, and a month seems fair. So we'll assess everyone in thirty days."

I had to admit, that was reasonable. If a patient wasn't on his feet and in fighting form after all that time, it was unlikely he or she ever would be. Sending the injured out into the wilderness was the same as a death sentence, but that wasn't the colonel's problem. She had to look out for the welfare of her citizens foremost. I understood that well enough.

"What about able-bodied souls? If they don't have anyone who can fight, how long before you ask them to move along?"

"There's never been a time limit set on trading parties or visitors," the colonel said. "But they wouldn't have citizenship rights."

"What does that mean?"

"It means they need a way to earn their food and shelter, and we give priority to businesses run by those who have someone in service."

So the Oakses could stay, but there was no guarantee anyone would buy from Edmund's shop. With a faint sigh, I turned and walked toward the exit. The others had mostly filed out of the hall; they milled around discussing the decision in low tones.

For the most part, their reaction sounded approving. I stopped short when I realized my family was waiting just outside the doors.

"You already volunteered for us," Momma Oaks said with a touch of anger.

The failure stung. "I tried. They won't take me. Said I'm not old enough."

It never even occurred to me that there would be some arbitrary age that qualified me as old enough to fight since I'd been doing it for years. The schooling requirement in Salvation might've given me some clue, but there, the magic number was sixteen, and I'd reached it. I wished I'd known about the rule before; to help my family, I would've lied. Frustration surged through me.

Too late now.

"You aren't," Edmund agreed.

Before I could protest, Rex said, "I'll do it."

I wondered if his parents noticed the despair in his eyes. He wasn't stepping forward so they'd have a place to stay. Ruth's loss ate at him, making him just not care about the consequences. This couldn't happen.

Momma Oaks shook her head. "Absolutely not. I've already lost one son."

"So we rest up a bit and gather supplies." Edmund produced a cheerful, determined look. "Then we move on. There must be a settlement that doesn't require military service. It's just a matter of finding one that suits us."

Given the distance between towns and the danger of the territory, I wasn't sure it would be that simple. But the way Momma Oaks brightened, I could see that Edmund's words had the desired effect. And I couldn't bring myself to kick dirt on the fire of their hope.

So I offered, "I can check the maps. Longshot has notes about all the towns and settlements on the trade routes."

Edmund sighed. "I wish I'd paid more attention to his

stories, but the rest of us weren't permitted to travel, even if we wanted to. So it seemed better not to indulge in curiosity."

But I had noticed that he had a secret yen to know more about the world he hadn't been allowed to explore because he'd asked me all kinds of questions when I went out on patrol. I wondered if Edmund had ever felt stifled by his life in Salvation. Not enough to want it to end this way, I imagined.

"Don't worry," Rex said. "We'll find somewhere to settle. This is a good enough place, but maybe it's not where we belong."

I agreed. "If they can't see that I'm capable of fighting, they don't deserve my blades."

"They don't know you," Momma Oaks said. "Like us, they only understand what life has shown them. And I'm willing to bet there's nobody here like you."

Given the smile she was wearing, that felt like a compliment.

Accommodation

Spence broke away from his conversation with Tully when he saw we were done discussing our options. "If you'll come with me, I've got your temp quarters assignment."

"You have houses standing empty?" Edmund asked.

That was interesting since Salvation had gotten to the point that land within the walls was at a premium. There had been talk that families would need to start doubling up in the next generation. That would never happen now, of course. Sorrow settled in my stomach like a lump of stone; so many people had died. I saw far too few familiar faces in Soldier's Pond.

"There was an epidemic last winter. We lost more men to it than we have the Muties."

"How is that possible?" Momma Oaks wondered.

If she hadn't asked, I would have.

"We have stockpiles of weapons and ammo. After the army conscripted this location, Soldier's Pond became a military base. They didn't expect to be here long, so they went light on certain provisions."

"Like medicine," I guessed.

Spence nodded. "It makes things tough. There are always plenty of people who can teach you how to fight. In other respects . . ."

"Then it seems like you'd be happy to find craftsmen in your midst, whether any of us are willing to fight or not," Edmund said in the sharpest tone I'd ever heard from him.

"Are you a smith?" Spence asked.

He shook his head. "Cobbler. I made the finest shoes and boots in Salvation."

The man studied his feet, clad in obviously substandard gear. "I'll talk to Thornton—he's in charge of goods and supplies—see if I can get a special dispensation for you. Policies always have exceptions."

That was intriguing, too. By rights, he should be applying to the colonel, if things ran as they should. The idea that Thornton quietly did as he wished without regard to his leader's wishes both interested and alarmed me. But I didn't speak of these misgivings.

Momma Oaks brightened. "That's kind of you, sir. I'm a seamstress. Would that help?"

"Not as much, ma'am. This way, please?"

"You go on," I said then. "If I know Tegan, she plans to tend the wounded through the night. I'll help her, and when we're finished, I'll camp out in the granary like before."

"Get some rest," Edmund cautioned, and Momma Oaks bussed me on the forehead.

I watched the path they took in case I needed to find them later and waited in front of the hall until I saw them go into a dark house. Then I turned my steps back toward the granary. In the dark, the paths between buildings were rocky and rutted. Some of them looked like the ones in the ruins, evidence of a facility for building that we no longer possessed. The rest of the trails were only worn in the dirt, pressed flat from repeated use.

"What're you doing here?" Tegan asked when I stepped in.

"Lending a hand."

"Why?"

"Because you're my friend, and I care about these people, too."

She nodded, her dark eyes full of sorrow. Because a number of our volunteers from the first evening didn't return, it took us most of the night to complete treatment. The young warrior, Morrow, came in somewhere past midnight, to help out. She put him to work at once, turning the men who were too heavy or too hurt for us to manage. By morning, four of our patients had died. Tegan wept after the first; when the third one stopped breathing, she was pale and dry-eyed, which worried me.

"I don't know where their families are," she said flatly. "Or what kind of funeral rites they preferred in Salvation."

"They were religious," Morrow said. "They didn't permit visitors, or I'd know more. Not sure if their minister made it. I can ask around . . . and if not, our chaplain could say a few words." He hesitated, then went on, "They can't stay with the living. It'll increase the risk of infection."

Tegan snapped, "I know that. Go ahead."

For the first time, I understood why people were always saying I was too young to fight. Because looking at my friend, I had that same thought. Someone older should've removed this burden from her shoulders; she shouldn't be suffering like this. But with Doc Tuttle gone, she was the closest thing to a doctor these people had, and Tegan wouldn't abandon them. I wouldn't leave her dealing with this alone, either. Morrow removed the bodies with care, I'd grant him that. He didn't treat them like dead strangers. Tegan's sharpness softened a little, then.

"Thank you," she murmured to him when he came back for the last time.

He only nodded.

"We need to sleep," I said then. "The bandages have all been changed, and you'll be no use to them if you fall asleep in the middle of treatment."

With a reluctant nod, she agreed.

That set the tone for the next week. I had rarely been so tired in my life as I left the granary only to wash up and eat, then I came right back. It gave me the greatest satisfaction when our patients got well enough to move around, tend their own needs, and head to the mess instead of opening their mouths for broth like baby birds. I saw Stalker and Fade little. At the end of ten days, over half the casualties had healed, and fourteen died. By then, eight remained, among them Harry Carter. I had my doubts that he would make it. His wounds were severe and with his family gone, he didn't seem to care that much about getting better.

I was exhausted and I ached all over when I stumbled out of the granary to eat. It had been weeks since I slept anywhere but on the floor, longer since I felt rested. Tegan had to feel just as bad, but she had more resolve for this kind of suffering. My own pain, I could deal with. I'd learned to tolerate it, shake it off, and keep fighting. I'd never learned how to handle anguish from people I was helping. Maybe I'd get better at it. With eight patients left, it wouldn't be much longer. Then the burning of Salvation would only be a terrible night that lived in the memories of the survivors.

I collided with Fade as I turned toward the mess. His hands came to my shoulders in reflex to keep me from falling. Blearily I expected the same recoil, but I was too tired to mind. To my surprise, his hands lingered past the point where I was steady.

"You look exhausted," he said.

"It's been rough," I admitted.

Fade fell into step with me. I hoped they would still be serving, as there were no other options for refugees. Inside the building, there was still a short line and the impatient server was ladling out soup; farther on, I took some stale bread. The food wasn't good, but I'd had much worse on the road and down below. Fade took his meal and followed me to a table.

"What've you been doing?" I asked.

"Helping Edmund."

I guessed I'd know that if I had visited the shop. News had funneled to me; as patients went for a walk, then limped back to the granary, they brought word from around town. So I knew Spence had made good on his promise to get an exception made for my family, and Edmund was hard at work, tanning and making boots. There had been some leather on hand, and Edmund had the skill to make more from skins the patrols brought in. Unlike theirs, his was high quality and butter soft. Somebody here knew the rudiments of a cobbler's trade, but his work was shoddy and poor. Once the soldiers were all outfitted in better gear, though, I feared my family might be asked to move along.

"How long do you see us staying?"

Fade shrugged. "It doesn't seem like home, but Salvation didn't, either. I'm used to making the best of things."

"What *does* make a place feel like home?"

"You," he said quietly.

"So you weren't at home in the enclave until you got to know me?"

"I never was, there. But you made things better." He changed the subject then. "Have you seen much of Soldier's Pond?"

"Mostly just the field hospital." That was what the soldiers called it. "And the mess, of course. I'm awfully familiar with the ground in between the two buildings."

"If you think Tegan could manage for a while, I could show you around."

"I'd like that . . . and I think she can. We only have eight people left."

"Is that good or bad?"

"Mostly, it's good. But we lost a number of patients, and Tegan's taking it hard."

He nodded. "She feels like Doc Tuttle would do a better job

if he were here because she didn't complete her training with him."

"He might know about treatments but there's no way he could care more." I finished my meal, then said, "Let me tell her, so she doesn't worry."

"She's already eaten?"

"I always send her first. She won't leave unless I make her."

"Then let's go," he said.

Since I had Fade with me, despite my weariness, I ran the distance to the granary and darted inside. Today, it smelled less of putrid wounds and more of antiseptic. The scent of blood had dissipated days past. Two of the pallets were empty, so I hoped that meant they were moving around, not dead. I didn't ask since Tegan wasn't crying; I decided to assume the best.

She actually smiled when she saw me enter, Fade behind me. "Let me guess, you want some time off."

"Just a little while. Will you be all right?"

"Of course. You've been more help than I could've asked. Go." She made a shooing motion with both hands.

This time I took her at her word. As we stepped outside, Fade stilled me with a look. Once he was sure he had my attention, he reached out and laced our fingers together. Heat curled up my hand all the way to my forearm, but I was afraid to move, afraid I was dreaming. I could feel the difference in his fingertips, new calluses from working with Edmund. He rubbed his thumb across the back of my hand and I shivered in pleasure.

"You're better?" I breathed.

"Not wholly. But I've been doing what you suggested, picturing the happy moments when it gets bad. I don't like being grabbed unexpectedly—" From his expression, that was awful. "But I . . . can manage when I'm the one reaching out, and it's even easier with you."

"The memories will fade." I sounded more sure than I felt, but it seemed like a reasonable guess. After all, I couldn't remember much about going hungry as a brat, but during lean times, we all ate less than we wanted. Time had a way of smoothing out the rough edges.

"I suspect you're right," he said, surprising me.

He led me toward the town gate; apparently we would start the explorations at the beginning. In daylight things looked even more forbidding. I would've been able to tell that a military force was responsible for this settlement, even if nobody had told me. From the fortifications to the hidden defenses, Soldier's Pond appeared more ready for war than Salvation, despite the lack of wooden walls. To my mind, now that the Freaks had fire, that might prove an advantage. Deep into the grass beyond the gate, I glimpsed defensive countermeasures: unnatural bulges in the ground and hidden pits, stands of wire, wrapped around devices I couldn't identify.

In the distance I heard chanting, but I couldn't make out the source until a group of recruits, all dressed uniformly in green, came loping past. I was awed by the matching cadences of their strides, the way their echoed words came perfectly in unison. At once I grasped the value of such training; not only were they strengthening their bodies, but the chant got them used to one another's rhythms, which would translate to better combat timing.

Fade followed my glance. "You want to run with them?"

"Will they let us?"

"Officially? No. But they won't break stride to drive us off, either."

"Then let's go."

As the soldiers approached, we fell in behind them. I got my tour while moving at a smart clip, and I took everything in—the houses were functional at best, and some of them had a strange look, as if humans hadn't built them. The cuts were too neat, and I had no idea how a person could construct something out of sheets of metal. Here and there sat the rusted remnants of old machinery, a few of which had once been automated wagons, but they didn't move anymore. The whole town was ringed in open steel fencing, so you could see right through it, and then it had spiked wires across the top. I suspected it would be hard to climb, difficult to maneuver over the top, and it didn't burn, either. There were eight watchtowers posted around the perimeter, and from what I could tell, the men on duty were fully alert, scanning the horizon for any sign that the trouble from Salvation had followed us.

I didn't learn the words to the running chant until our third circuit of town. By then, I was singing them out along with everyone else. It made me happy to keep up with grown fighting men, even with the long hours I had been working in the field hospital. When we finished, I was sweaty, but glowing with pride. Fade looked more or less the same as we ran through what the leader called cool-down exercises; it was mostly stretching, flexing, bending, and walking around, but he was right. I felt better when I stopped gradually.

"You sure you don't want to join up?" the leader asked Fade. "You're a natural recruit."

He shook his head. "No thanks. Deuce isn't old enough yet."

The man's expression hardened. "Think about your answer, son. Your thirty days will be up in a couple of weeks. What do you plan to do then?"

Belatedly I realized what that meant. Fade must be eighteen, or thereabouts. He wasn't sure of his naming day, I suspected, as the elders had guessed down in the enclave. But based on his appearance and prowess, these soldiers were willing to take him on faith.

I swallowed hard. "If you want to sign up and take their training, I understand."

"You're crazy if you think I'm ever leaving you."

That's not what you said before. I must've said it with my eyes, as I would never do so out loud, because he registered my pain with a remorseful look.

"I wasn't in my right mind," he said softly. "You have no idea how much I regret hurting you, how much I wish I could take back what I said. I'm grateful you didn't listen."

It was frightening how happy he made me with a mere handful of words, but my heart, stupid bird that it was, sang on.

Torn

Before returning to the field hospital, I took a quick bath; there were private facilities for men and women. I'd asked how they managed it and received an explanation about rainwater, cisterns, and gravity. To me, it meant only that I could pull a lever and a trickle of water fell on my head while I stood in a narrow room. This was similar to how it had been down below, but the water was warm in Soldier's Pond. They used the sun to heat it somehow.

The shower felt great but I didn't linger. Afterward I dressed and ran back. I found Tegan with six patients, one of whom was Harry Carter. The other two pallets had been rolled up and stacked for laundering. Since she was smiling, I took that for good news.

"They recovered?"

"Enough to decide to leave," she said.

Her gaze roved over my wet hair, clothes still sticking to my damp skin because I hadn't taken time to dry off properly. "Do you mind if I go to the bathhouse too?"

It had been long enough that she desperately needed to clean up, but I hadn't wanted to say something like, *Get out of here already, Tegan, you stink.*

"I can manage," I said.

Since I'd watched over three times this number, not long

ago, and we didn't have any treatments due for a while, it should be easy. For the moment, I was content—full belly, muscles pleasantly lax from the run with Fade, and I was quietly glowing, too, over those moments afterward. Though things might be terrible again soon enough, right now everything felt all right. Or as much as it could be, considering what happened in Salvation.

Once Tegan had gone, I settled in the middle of the room, so I would hear if anyone called me. Sometimes the patients needed water or had an itch they couldn't reach. At first it was quiet, then the pervasive whisper reached me. It was a thread of sound, my name rustling through dry lips. I brought the water pitcher with its ladle with me, expecting Harry Carter wanted a drink. But when I settled beside him, he opened his eyes. His face was terrible and sallow, which Tegan said was bad.

"Why am I still alive?" he asked.

It was an awful question, and I made up an answer. "Because you have work to do yet."

"Do you truly imagine I'll recover enough to be useful to anyone?"

I ignored the bitter, angry words. We had been keeping his wounds clean, so I checked them. He should be healing better than he was. I found that the bites had begun to fester—*again*—which meant they needed to be opened and cleaned. I hated this part of the job. Sucking in a breath to brace myself, I got one of Tegan's knives and treated it with antiseptic as I'd seen her do. When I came back, he shifted away from me, horror in his gaze.

"Don't do this. Not again. I'm never going to be whole. Just . . . let me go. Better yet, kill me. It would be a mercy. Please, Deuce."

It was impossible to hear a strong man like him beg, and for a few seconds, I was tempted. The Huntress in me wanted to give him the end he craved since he had been denied a warrior's death. But the girl in me shook her head vehemently. *Tegan will never trust you again, if you hurt him.* My fingers trembled on the knife as dual instincts warred within me.

Gently, I said, "I'm not doing that, Harry Carter. You might've lost your family, but you saved a good portion of the town. I hear you fought like the devil himself, keeping the Freaks away from the Bigwater house, so that others could escape."

"That's done. I'll never hold a rifle again."

"That's a lie," I told him. "You took most of the damage else-where. If you'd just make up your mind to heal, you could get out of this place and take some revenge on those monsters."

His retort was sharp with bitterness. "'Revenge not your-selves, my dearly beloved; but give place unto wrath, for it is writ-ten: Revenge is mine, I will repay, saith the Lord.'"

I recognized that as a quote from the old book Caroline Big-water had been prone to toting. "I don't mean to urge you to sin, Mr. Carter, but if it was me, I'd want blood in payment from those Muties, not the word of a man who lives in the clouds."

"So you won't have mercy?" he asked, low.

The Huntress in me protested, *This isn't how I'd want to end my days.* But I ignored her.

"No," I said. "And what I'm about to do may seem cruel."

My hands were clean; so was my knife. With careful finger-tips, I traced the puffy edges of the first bite. Yes, it was hot and swollen, already filling up with pus again. He screamed when I opened the wound, and he yelled more as I expressed and cleaned it. The other patients called out words of encouragement as I worked, likely hoping to ease his pain. Harry Carter was a strong man, but he passed out when I got to the fourth one, which was a blessing. I finished my task quickly, then bandaged the affected areas. By the time Tegan got back, I was shaking.

Being a healer is harder than being a Huntress.

"What happened?" she demanded.

I didn't share with her what Harry had asked of me. Instead I gestured to his fresh wraps. "I had to open him up again."

Her dark gaze softened. "Poor man."

"I hope this is the last time. I'm starting to feel cruel inflicting this on him."

She nodded. "I've never treated so many Freak bites before, at least not on the same person. It's almost like their mouths are poisonous."

I stared at her, wondering if that was possible. *"Are they?"*

"I need more information. I've been treating this like an infection, but so few people survive an attack, fewer live through the kinds of injuries Mr. Carter's suffered. I wish Doc was here."

"He wouldn't know what to do, either," I said, but from her expression, that was no comfort, so I shut up.

"Stay with him," she ordered.

I sat down cross-legged on the floor, keeping an eye on Mr. Carter. For me, this man's recovery had become a personal battle. He *had* to get better; it was a sign of things to come. As I watched, she went to her bag and drew out some stoppered vials. Each contained dried, crushed herbs, and Tegan muttered to herself as she set a kettle on the hearth, added water, then pinches of this and that. The resulting mixture smelled really vile.

"Is he supposed to drink that?"

She shook her head. "I'm going to pour it into his bites."

"What is it?"

"I have no idea. I'm combining ingredients that Doc told me were good for various things: fever, bee stings, snakebite, pain, swelling. I might make things worse, but I have to try."

Studying Carter, I didn't think it was possible to make him sicker. He was already begging for death. "We should do it before his wounds close and we have to hurt him again."

"My thoughts exactly. It has to cool a little first, or we'll burn him."

That took a while. But it was a kindness that Carter didn't rouse while we doused his injuries and wrapped them up again. It was too soon to say whether it helped, but I liked that we were trying something new, not just repeating past efforts and hoping for the best. I spooned some water into him and figured that was all I could do tonight.

Tegan sat back with a weary sigh. "Now we wait and see."

By morning, however, we saw a vast improvement. His skin tone was better—bright and warm—instead of the ashy gray that marked a man for death. Tegan hugged me, and I squeezed her back, though I hadn't done anything except stick around. We sped through our morning rituals, the cleaning and tending. At least we didn't have to feed patients anymore; they were all well enough to hold a cup or a spoon.

Carter's eyes were sharp and alert as I handed him a mug of broth. With my help, he struggled to a sitting position for the first time since we arrived in Soldier's Pond. I took it as a personal victory. His hands shook but he downed it all.

"More?" he asked.

I refilled him. "Decided to live, have you?"

"It's obvious you won't let me die, so I better quit malingering and get back to the fight." In his quiet expression, I saw gratitude.

"Thank Tegan," I said. "She's the doctor, not me."

I felt so incredibly proud of her. With nobody's help, she had come up with a successful treatment for Freak bites. I hoped she recalled the exact proportions of the remedy because I had a feeling we would need that tincture again in the near future. The Freaks hadn't quit the field; they just hadn't reached Soldier's Pond yet. So that meant this was, at best, a lull before the worst of the storm.

Part of me felt anxious and unsettled. We should be laying battle plans, but I had no part in any such arrangements. Here I wasn't even old enough to join the military. Once again, I had been relegated to the rank of child, regardless of what I could offer. I didn't regret the time I had spent on nursing, but my skills were better suited to fighting the enemy.

Carter seemed to read my mood and his own expression grew somber. "Don't worry. I'll be on the front lines when the time comes."

"That means a lot to me."

I wasn't joking. If I couldn't have Longshot, then Harry Carter was the next best thing. He was Salvation's hero, and I had no doubt that once he recovered his strength, he would be a powerful force in the war against the Freaks. He wore a determined look, as focused on recuperation as he had been on despair. If they weren't terrifying monsters, I'd pity the beasts.

"I don't mean to be rude," Tegan said then. "But isn't it time you rejoined your family? I appreciate your help and all, but I can manage these patients on my own."

"Are you dismissing me?"

"I believe I am."

"I'll swing by to check on you tomorrow," I said to Carter.

He bobbed his head. "I'll look forward to it. I might even be strong enough to eat my next meal in the mess I've been hearing so much about. Still say food cooked in a place with a name like that can't be too delicious, though."

I smiled. "You're not wrong."

Though Fade hadn't showed me the way to Edmund's shop, I followed my nose. Tanning leather created an unmistakable smell, so it was fairly easy to locate. The workshop was located near the house they had been assigned, closer than it had been in Salvation. I stepped into the shop, inhaling the familiar scents. The process of creating leather from skins was noisome, but the finished product smelled better. Edmund was behind a make-shift counter, checking measurements before he cut the sole. Noises in back said Fade and maybe Rex were here too.

"Are you settling in all right?" I asked.

Genuine pleasure dawned on my father's face. He came around to hug me. I'd never been touched so much or so easily, and I was adjusting to the idea that it didn't have to mean weakness. Still, I hugged him back, reveling in my ability to be a girl, not just a Huntress. I was a little backward in some regards, and I wanted to fix that.

"Are you finished in the infirmary?" he asked.

I nodded. "Tegan sent me away. She had some idea you might be missing me."

"You've no idea," Edmund said. "Your mother is worrying herself sick, so I'd count it a personal favor if you would reassure her."

"What did she think would happen to me, working with the wounded?" I asked, puzzled.

"You could catch something or get an infection or be hurt by a delirious man—"

"So she's making up reasons to fret so she doesn't have to focus on the real problem."

Soberly, Edmund nodded. "Go see her, please."

"Is it all right if I have a word with Rex and Fade, first?" I gestured at the back room.

"Go ahead. Just don't dally too long." I could tell by his narrow-eyed look that he meant sparking, and I sighed.

With Rex in the room, it was unlikely I would crawl all over Fade, even if he could stand for me to do so. Despite my wishing, we weren't back to our old standing yet. I just nodded as I moved past Edmund, navigated the counter, and stepped into the dim room where all the materials were gathered. Fade was smearing something that smelled awful on a stretched skin while Rex handled another portion of the process. They both glanced up on my arrival, and Fade actually smiled.

"Come to admire my work?" he teased.

I pretended to study the rack, then offered a patently false criticism, as I had no idea what they were about or if it was well done. Rex laughed, which was the point. It was good to see my foster brother getting along with Fade. We chatted a while, but I couldn't linger, as they had work to do, and I had to reassure my mother that I numbered among the living, despite her fears.

With a wave for Edmund, I hurried out of the shop. Though it had been dark when I watched them go into their little house, I found it fine. It was smaller than their place in Salvation had been, just a room full of beds, really, and they were odd, too, stacked on top of each other, so there was no privacy at all. I found Momma Oaks sweeping a floor that didn't need it. Here, she had no place to cook, she'd left her beloved dog behind, and the soldiers didn't seem to value her work. When you got right down to it, our circumstances were similar.

But she brightened when she spotted me. "I'm so glad you're here."

Few people had said that to me and meant it. Other than Fade, I couldn't think of anyone who treated me like the sun. Momma Oaks genuinely loved me, however, even when I was difficult for her to understand.

"This is an odd place," I said.

At best, it was shelter. Surely there were normal homes, where families cooked their meals and gathered in the parlor to share stories. I'd seen them dotted here and there, but my family had been allotted this instead. Refugees had no rights, though, no reason to expect better.

But my mother didn't show a hint of dissatisfaction.

"I'm told it used to house soldiers who had no family, but many people died of fever last winter and the Muties have gotten others. So it was standing empty, waiting for us." She put on a smile. "Isn't that lucky?"

I loved this woman so much that my heart hurt with it. I wanted to keep my whole family safe and happy, and it cut me to the bone that it might be beyond my power.

Summons

T rue to his word, Harry Carter had supper the next night with Fade and me in the mess hall. He took short walks around town, building his strength, and I admired his determination. The following day, a runner came to the workshop, where I was pitching in. Since they wouldn't let me train with the men, I had to keep strong somehow—and cleaning served the purpose. This soldier was young, barely older than I was, but apparently of age to volunteer. He stared at the industry as he'd likely never seen people practice a trade before.

"Do you need something?" Edmund asked.

"I've been asked to fetch the girl and her friend to the colonel."

I couldn't imagine why, but I dusted my hands on my thighs, then called to Fade, "Can you pause for a bit?"

He said something to Rex, then stepped out into the main room. "What's going on?"

"The colonel needs you," the messenger said.

Fade shrugged. "Let's go see what she wants."

Soldiers were running as usual. Others practiced with melee weapons. From the perimeter, the sentries kept calling the all clear. It wasn't too far, distance-wise, so the silence from the enemy troubled me. If Stalker wasn't so mad at me, I'd ask for an update on the horde's position; and it wasn't his anger that prevented me from inquiring, only the surety he'd snarl and refuse to reply.

I figured the town leader had a job for us. There was no other reason for such a summons. Fade was quiet until we reached headquarters, then he said, "How bad do you suppose it'll be?"

"If she had anybody who could do whatever it is, she wouldn't need us," I answered.

He nodded as we passed into the staging room. If anything it was messier than before with documents and papers spread all over. There was a huge map laid on a battered table and it had markers on it, spread in no pattern I could detect, some red, some black. Morgan cleared his throat to draw the colonel's attention, and she managed a weary smile. That told me things were dire. People in power only smiled when they wanted something.

"Good, you got my message. How much do you know about our preparations?"

"Nothing," I muttered. "They wouldn't let me join up."

"We're trying to avoid involving a generation of children . . . but we might not have a choice down the line. If we lower the enlistment age, you'll be the first to know." She paused, looking us over in way that made Fade bristle. "But I can make an exception for covert and special operations."

That sounded like a fancy way of breaking the rules, just like they had done for Edmund, because they needed new boots. The government of Soldier's Pond would do whatever it wanted and then come up with an explanation to justify the decision later. I folded my arms and waited, giving her nothing. My silence set her to pacing, which told me she was worried. I had no interest in going to fetch help, if that was on her mind. It hadn't saved Salvation, and that tactic wouldn't work here, either. The Freaks outnumbered us, plain and simple; we needed a new strategy to defeat them.

The devil if I know what, though.

"What's that?" Fade asked, when it became clear I was keeping quiet.

"Special ops are initiatives undertaken for the good of the town, but not common knowledge to the other soldiers."

"A dirty secret then," I said.

"Not exactly, but I could see how it would sound that way. First, how familiar are you with what we've laid out here?" She indicated the map and all its markers.

I shrugged. "I can see what it is, but I don't know what those wood pieces mean."

"The black ones stand for settlements," she explained. "And the red represents all the Mutie movements scouts have spotted in the vicinity."

"Has the horde broken into smaller groups?" I asked.

"No. This is it." The colonel touched the biggest red piece on the map.

It covered what looked like impressive ground in the middle of the territory, plus there were all the smaller forces to contend with as well. I had *no idea* it was this dire. *Stalker probably did. And he didn't tell you.* And there was nothing I could do about it. I curled my hands into fists. My knives were paltry against such a threat.

"What do you want?" Fade asked. "It's fine to show us how bad things are, but that's not why you summoned us."

"No. After talking to some of my men and hearing stories, some of which I don't entirely believe, I've come to the conclusion that the two of you might be the best suited to undertake a mission for me."

"Let me guess—" I started.

The colonel held up a hand. "Don't waste my time with sarcasm. Hear me out. It's a simple yes or no. We need info from a settlement to the northwest . . . and it'll help us combat the Muties. But getting through enemy lines won't be easy, and I need someone who's used to traveling quick and quiet. Your mission is simple—avoid detection whenever possible, find Dr. Wilson, retrieve the scientific data, and get back here fast."

Fade arched a brow. "Is he a medical doctor?"

Good question. If so, Tegan would want to meet him for sure. Now that her patients were better, she was currently working with the doctor in Soldier's Pond, but she didn't think highly of his skills. So maybe we could persuade Wilson to come to Soldier's Pond. If he wasn't used to travel, that might make the return journey difficult, but it'd be worth it to see her smile again.

But the colonel shook her head. "Not exactly. He's a scientist, and he's been studying the Muties for twenty years. Last contact we had, he was close to finding a weakness, something we can exploit to counter their greater numbers."

"That won't be enough," I said. "You need an army, not facts and figures."

Her expression went flat. "We have one, but I won't send them out ill-prepared when Wilson could potentially save lives."

"Your army is too small." I had been thinking about this for a while, and the truth crystallized for me like candy Momma Oaks used to make. "The only way we win is for all the settlements to band together, pool their people and resources."

She laughed at me, then shook her head ruefully. "It's a nice idea, Deuce, but folks have gotten too used to their independence. We can barely come to consensus *here*, let alone get another town to agree on the action we should take. The territories have turned into a bunch of separate city-states . . . we haven't cooperated in over a hundred years."

I didn't know what a city-state was, but it sounded counterproductive. *It's unlikely we can win this war with all the towns acting alone.* But the colonel wasn't interested in my advice, only in using me.

"Then we've already lost," Fade said. "And this trip is

pointless. We may as well go about our business until the horde swoops in. You'll last longer since your fortifications are metal and you have an ammo stockpile, but sooner or later, they'll overrun you."

His assessment matched mine completely, and I gave a short nod. The colonel planted her hands on her hips, trying to stare us down, but it didn't work. Silk had a much worse glare and her punishments had been truly cruel. I doubted the colonel had anything like that kind of ruthless streak—until she proved me wrong.

"Do you know what conscription is?" she asked me.

Immediately, I tensed, more at her tone than the word. "No."

Her smile genuinely frightened me. "What about a draft?"

"Like when a cool wind gets in through cracks in the house?" I guessed that wasn't it.

She shook her head, proving me right. "Historically speaking, armies and navies could demand that a person sign up for service and enforce that requirement by any means necessary in times of war. I'd say this qualifies, wouldn't you?"

Since I'd long thought the Freaks weren't just killing us for food—that they saw us as their enemies—I could hardly dispute her statement. So I stared at her hard, hoping she felt my active dislike. In her smooth tone, I sensed a trap; I just couldn't make out its shape just yet.

"No need to answer. Your eyes speak plainly enough. So that being the case, I might have no choice but to call someone else up for active duty, if you refuse this mission." She paused delicately, pacing a step or two, as if contemplating who it might be. "Your brother, Rex, perhaps. He seems strong, hearty enough."

"You'd send Rex out into the wilderness? That's the same as executing him. He doesn't have the skills to survive." The words burst out before I could stop them, showing the colonel that she had me exactly where she wanted me.

It didn't matter what I thought of this task, or the relative worth of the information she wanted me to retrieve. Momma Oaks would be heartbroken if anything happened to her sole surviving son, especially after the sack and pillage of Salvation. She was clinging to the tatters of faith that a rough life had left her, and I'd do anything to keep her cheerful spirit as bright as it could be. I bit down on my lower lip against the curses that sprang to mind, some I'd learned from Gary Miles and his cohorts, but somehow I doubted I would succeed in shocking the colonel, now watching me with a faint smile.

"That's up to you," she said softly. "I won't risk my own people, and I need that data."

Fade growled, taking a step toward her. I threw out a hand, not touching him but keeping him from going after her. He wasn't altogether rational when people threatened me, and this qualified. But it was more emotional duress than physical danger, and he knew it, which was probably why he stood down at my gesture. By his look, he was furious, however—and so was I.

"Don't expect me ever to join your military," I said in a low, lethal tone. "You'll get this one job out of me, and nothing more, ever. Plus, I have some terms."

Her mouth twitched. "I can't wait to hear this."

"Clear the room."

"My advisors are privy to anything you—"

I drew a knife and spun it in my palm, a habit that had unnerved the men in Salvation. "I said, clear the room. I won't ask twice."

She appeared to come to a rapid decision. "Everyone out. Give us five minutes."

"But, Colonel," one of the men protested, and she waved away his concern.

"If I can't keep one girl from killing me, then you need

someone else leading your armed forces. Post a guard at the door and see that we're not disturbed."

"I'll do your dirty work willingly," I said, once we were alone, "under one condition."

"What's that?" she asked with a faint smile.

"You let me make my pitch to your men. I intend to raise an army that owes its allegiance to no town. It'll be full of humanity's best and brightest, and we'll eventually take the battle to the horde. Your part is simple"—I mimicked her brisk tone from earlier, using almost the same words—"you let me speak and you don't deny anyone who wants to march with me. They go, free and clear, when I leave Soldier's Pond. And finally, you leave my family alone. No more threats against them, or so help me, I'll find a way to cut your throat as you sleep."

Colonel Park actually looked shaken by my ferocity. Then, to my surprise, she inclined her head in a terse nod. "That's fair, especially since my men will laugh their arses off at the idea of joining an army raised by a little girl. So you're welcome to anyone crazy enough to follow you, so long as you complete the mission first."

Her mockery burned, but I'd known worse. And maybe, just maybe, I'd surprise her. It wouldn't be the first time someone had underestimated me.

"Deal," I said, offering my hand.

We shook, then she tried to execute a restraint maneuver, probably to humble me, but Stalker had drilled me on that move in Salvation. I blocked and twisted her arm, so that she had to drop to her knees, or I would've broken it. My gray eyes must've looked cold as dirty ice as I stared down at her.

"I made that gesture in good faith. Now swear on something you hold sacred that you'll keep your word."

"I promise," she gasped.

I relented just before I did permanent damage and she sprang to her feet, stumbling backward. There was a new wariness in her gaze; and I saw she'd take me seriously from now on. That might not be a good thing, but it meant I wasn't a tool to be used anymore, either.

In an easy movement, I slid my blade into its sheath. Fade stood at my shoulder, ready in case she decided to pursue the conflict. Eventually, her shoulders relaxed. She needed us for the mission; therefore, we couldn't be executed or even punished. Soon enough I'd find out whether her pledge meant anything.

"Show me on the map where we're going," I said, smiling. "There are plans to make."

Misdirection

F ade and I slipped out of town early the next morning. The colonel was running a drill with mandatory attendance for all, creating enough commotion that nobody would notice our absence until it was too late. Fade was worried about letting Edmund down in the shop, and I felt guilty not telling my family about the assignment, but they would only fret longer if they knew, plus I'd have to deal with another emotional goodbye. Sometimes it was more expedient to get on with your work and apologize later.

Not since we first came Topside had Fade and I taken a journey alone. Though I didn't say so out loud, it was nice having him to myself. There was no one to note how often I admired his sure strides or the strength of his broad shoulders. At once I chastened myself for such thoughts. They had no place outside the safety of town limits; in the wilderness, an instant's distraction could have disastrous consequences.

"According to the maps, it's a three-day run," I said.

"You think we can do it faster?"

"I hope so. If we're gone for a week, Momma Oaks will have a conniption." That was a new word, one I loved. When I'd asked what it meant, Edmund described it in such an exaggerated way that I didn't want to see such a fit for myself, in case he was telling the truth.

"Times like this, I miss my folks most," Fade said softly.

"Because you want to be in trouble too?"

"No. I wish I had somebody to worry about me."

"You do," I told him. "I fret over you all the time. I just don't say anything because it doesn't seem like something you'd want to hear from me."

He flashed me a smile as we put Soldier's Pond behind us. "Feel free to fuss a little. I wouldn't mind."

It occurred to me then that his life had been bereft of small kindnesses, like when he put his head in my lap, and I stroked his hair. For me, it wasn't such a large matter; I hadn't even known I was supposed to want such things, until I met Fade. But with his desire to be touched struggling against the weight of bad memories, however, I wasn't sure he could bear it, and I wouldn't do anything to hurt or trouble him, even with the best intentions. But maybe this trip could reassure him that he was strong and competent—that the Freaks hadn't changed anything.

The sun was just creeping above the horizon as I broke into a run. It felt good to be away from the settlement, even if it also carried risk. I was used to that, less prepared for the pain and exhaustion that nursing left behind. Fade jogged alongside me and I remembered our desperate journey to Nassau down below. Topside, the light was better, and the air was clean. I smelled the dying leaves and broken blades of grass beneath my feet, faint musk of animal droppings and the honeyed purr of clover in the air. In a few more months, the snow would come; my family needed to be settled before that time.

Toward the end of that first day, we dodged Freak patrols like it was our reason for living. They were only hours away from Soldier's Pond, but I guessed the military settlement had given them reason to fear a direct attack. I'd rather fight and clear the area, but I had been instructed to get there undetected, and I had to admit, it would only complicate our mission if we had monsters chasing us. With only two of us on the move, our scent shouldn't be strong enough to attract a big hunting party. Chills crawled over my body when I caught the rare scent of the Freaks on the wind—not the old, rotten reek, but the new, meaty animal smell. It told me that these creatures had changed for good, and if we couldn't work out how and why, then we might not survive the coming conflict.

Fear might have paralyzed me if not for Fade. He beckoned with a determined look, then guided me around the danger zone. I kept my footfalls light and soft while we passed through; and in the distance, I heard it—the rustling foliage and cracking branches that said we had company. The Freaks called to one another in a whuffing, growling tongue—what dogs might sound like if they could speak. I could hardly hold the question until we were out of range.

"Do you think they have their own language?" I whispered.

"I think so." His voice was low and grave. "I'm pretty sure they spoke to one another while they held me. But I don't care to stick around to ask."

I shivered. "Me, either."

There was no way to tell how many were lurking nearby without a scout. For the first time, I wished Stalker had come with us. If anyone could give us the lay of the land and warn us of dangers ahead without being spotted, it was him. But Fade and I would manage. We had before, though the stakes had never been this high.

"This way. The air smells clean."

That was no longer a foolproof system, but we didn't have a better option. My heart thudding like mad, I followed Fade. As he moved, he kept to the shadow of the trees, as the forest grew thick and uncut to the northwest of Soldier's Pond with the river glimmering in the distance like a silver snake. The day warmed as it wore on, one of those perfect fall mornings with the sky so blue that it looked like a painting, yet the sun wasn't so bright that it hurt my eyes. For that reason, I preferred this season to all others, even spring planting.

When the sun hit its zenith, Fade found a shaded spot beneath the red-tinged canopy. I broke out the bread, dried meat, and water, then we ate with efficient speed. There were so many things I wanted to say to him, but we had at least four more hours of running ahead of us. Town life had softened me; I noticed the burn as I wouldn't have before. I'd put on weight, too, softening in ways that were occasionally inconvenient, though I hadn't minded when Fade examined those curves.

By nightfall, we had dodged four Freak patrols and outrun the trees, leaving us only open ground upon which to make camp. We could do without a fire, but it would get colder as the night wore on. I ate only a little of our packed food, thinking we might need it before the trip ended; things seldom went according to plan. The water, I downed generously, as I heard the river burbling nearby. We weren't encamped on its banks—that would be asking for trouble since Freaks had to stop to drink—but it was close enough to be reassuring. Clean water was always a concern in the wilderness.

"Can I see the map?"

I handed it to him. "How did we do?"

"We shaved some time off the estimate. If we maintain this pace, though, we'll be burnt to nubs when we arrive in Winterville."

"The alternative is stretching this out. Sooner we get there, find this Dr. Wilson, and get back with his data, the faster we can put Soldier's Pond behind us."

"Did you mean what you said?"

"About what?" I asked.

"Raising an army."

I tilted my head. "One town won't be enough to defeat the

horde. With the Freaks organizing and banding together, we have to do the same. It can't matter where somebody's from or why they want to fight. It only matters if they're committed."

"The colonel laughed. You really think we can do this?" While it warmed my heart to hear that instinctive "we," the question also showed me how much the Freaks had damaged his confidence. He'd had my back in the meeting, but now the doubts emerged.

"I think we've lost if we don't try," I said.

"Then I'm with you." He pitched his voice low so it wouldn't carry—and in that moment of everlasting sweetness, it felt like a secret pact, Fade and me against the world.

Too soon, dark fell and cradled us in night. We had come far enough from Soldier's Pond that there were no lights apart from moon and stars. How odd that I could've so quickly forgotten that darkness like this existed, beyond banishing by candles or the crafty glow of old-world lights. I held my hand up to my face, marveling at the smudgy lines. To my annoyance, I was too keyed up to sleep.

"I'll take the first watch," I said.

Fade shook his head. "We both need to rest. I'll put dry branches around the perimeter. If anything crosses, the noise will wake us."

"Good idea." I helped him gather them, then we created a box far enough from our bedrolls that it should give us time to draw our weapons.

My time at the outpost had left me sleeping even lighter. Though I had never mentioned my bad dreams to anyone, between memories of the enclave and Fade's abduction, I didn't sleep well most nights anyway. Between my nighttime troubles and Fade's precautions, I doubted the Freaks could sneak up on us. Of course, before it happened, I would've said they couldn't steal fire or take two men from an armed encampment, too. Those facts left me faintly unnerved.

"It'll be cold tonight." I nodded as I curled into my blankets, too preoccupied to wonder at the statement. The reason for it became clear when Fade added, "You could sleep next to me."

"Would that be all right?"

"It was before. I rolled toward you . . . and I might as well save us that step."

"I'd like that if it wouldn't bother you."

He exhaled slowly and with obvious trepidation. "I'll let you know."

Feeling like I was taming a wild creature, I eased my back up to his front by increments, and I stopped when I could just barely feel him. He came a little closer on his own, so the heat was immediately palpable. Delight cascaded through me when he dropped his arm over my waist. I braced for rejection, but instead he seemed to be settling in, and I felt the warm gust of his breath against the back of my head.

"You have no idea how happy this makes me," I whispered.

His voice was somber. "It makes me feel less broken. It helps when I can plan it and consider all the reasons it's a good thing, first. I still quake like a child over loud noises, sudden touches, people popping out at me unexpectedly—"

"That's normal," I said, though I had no idea whether it was. Then it occurred to me how I could best help him—by reassuring him he wasn't alone. "I never told you this, but I have nightmares. The blind boy from down below, usually. Since we came Topside, there are more . . . being taken by the Wolves, and later, when I feared I'd lost you forever . . . that's the worst. I'm in the woods again, it's dark and I'm alone, and I'm surrounded by the horde, only this time, I'm covered in my own blood, not their entrails, so they're all staring right at me. I know I'm going to die—that I failed you and it'll be *my fault* that—" The tears sur-prised me, choking my words.

That you die. I don't save you.

Before this moment, it hadn't occurred to me that my weak-ness would matter to him. Fade levered up on his elbow and tugged on my shoulder. I could tell he wanted me to face him. Another gentle pull, and I succumbed. His eyes were wide and soft, surprised even, in the moonlight, like he hadn't known I could suffer the same way he did. Well, maybe not the same, but if *he* was damaged, I surely was too. I strangled the weeping with a few sharp breaths.

"You're not as strong as I thought."

"I know," I said miserably. "Silk always said that. She told me over and over that I have a Breeder's heart, and I'll never be a true Huntress."

"You're stronger. Much as I love you, I always thought you don't feel things like I do. But the truth is, you just hide it better. You carry it around without ever asking anybody to help shoul-der it. I'm so sorry. I just . . . left you, hurting, and I was so wor-ried about being worthy that I never once suspected you need me too."

My voice came out small in the dark. "I do."

For once, the Huntress was in complete agreement with the girl.

Fade trembled when he touched my hair. "I promise I won't go away again, even inside my head. And you tell me about the bad dreams from now on. Please don't hide. Not from me."

"Then in the interest of full honesty, I really wish you'd kiss me right now."

Apart from the blind nuzzling in his sleep, he hadn't touched me like that since his return. Considering it hadn't been very long since we started sparking, I missed it a whole lot. His breath misted my forehead, and Fade pressed a kiss there, delicate as a moth's wing. That wasn't what I had in mind, but I feared spooking him. He dusted kisses along my temple down to my cheekbone, then I couldn't help it. I turned my head so my mouth met his. He made a soft sound, and I was in accord.

I didn't grab on to him, though I wanted to. He had conveyed to me that touching went easier when he was in charge of it—braced for it—and so I kept my hands still. Somehow that only made me more conscious of the hot glide of his lips, and the way his body lit mine up like a summer night, all heat and starlight. His tongue grazed mine; it was all I could do not to leap on him. Proud of my self-control, I lay in the circle of his arm after he broke the kiss, dreaming of the day when I could again touch him freely.

With a soft sigh, Fade rested his forehead against mine. "We should get to sleep. It will be another long day tomorrow."

He was more right about that than he knew.

Winterville

reaks harried us all the next day.

Past dawn, they caught our scent, and Fade and I ran like the devil was at our heels. At one point, we crossed the river, hoping they'd lose us in the water, but no such luck. Since it was shallow enough for us to pass, they could too. I found it interesting that two people in the wilderness could draw so much attention. Was it possible they suspected the importance of our mission? If so, we were in more trouble than I'd reckoned.

With them prowling in our wake, there was no chance to stop for more than minimal food, water, and hygiene breaks. Sleep was out of the question, so we ran on into the night, until the pitch darkness made it likely we'd break an ankle on the uneven terrain. I slowed, scanning the horizon as the noises grew louder behind us. If I didn't spot shelter, the Freaks would find us, and we'd end up fighting in the dark. My night vision could compensate but Fade might not fare as well. Therefore, I was determined to find us a place to hide.

I spun in all directions, then pointed. "This way."

To his credit, Fade didn't ask. He just followed me as I ran. The dot resolved as I drew closer. From this range, I made out an abandoned house, bigger than the one we'd camped in that first winter after we left the ruins. There were outbuildings on the property too; and from my history lessons, I suspected we had stumbled on a farm. Ancient machinery sat in rusted hulks, creating eerie shapes in the darkness. I ignored them as I darted past.

The door was still standing, though hanging drunkenly on its hinges. I had hoped for a secure location if not a secret one, but this would have to do. Inside the house, I found pests and scavengers, droppings and old nests. A rickety flight of stairs led up, and at the top, there was a door with a wooden crossbar. I shut it quietly and lowered it in place. If they tracked us here, we could defend the room better than an open field, plus they would expend strength and energy in breaking down the door.

"This is as good as it gets," I said, surveying the dusty space.

My muscles trembled with weariness. In hindsight, I had no idea how Fade and I had functioned down below on so little food. No wonder my people died young.

"At least we have a roof and four walls. More than we had last night."

But last night we had kissing.

That didn't seem like a worthwhile protest, however. I sank down to the dirty floor, one hand on my knives. If the Freaks proved as relentless as they had been all day, they would be here soon. I didn't suggest sleep for obvious reasons. Fade sat down near me and we listened.

He heard it first and crept to the window with me close at his heels. Through the smudged and filthy glass, I glimpsed a cluster of Freaks doggedly tracking us toward the house. I counted at least ten, a large party for the two of us. But if they had taken to traveling in small war bands, then we were lucky there weren't more of them.

"I don't know if I can take five of them," I admitted in a whisper. "Is this how aging goes? First you feel incredibly tired, you weaken, and then your reactions slow—"

Fade was laughing softly. "You're ridiculous. You're not getting old, Deuce. It's just been a rough run, and you got precious little rest, helping Tegan. You're also recovering from multiple injuries, and we had an exhausting trip to Soldier's Pond."

Put that way, it *had* been a tough month. "If a straight fight is out, what should we do?"

"I have an idea," he said.

The Freaks were at the door downstairs now. I heard them snarling in the yard, then the front door banged open. Their claws rasped on the wood floor as they prowled below us. Despite my faith in Fade's cleverness, a chill raced through me.

"Make some noise," he said, as he piled things up in the center of the room: broken bits of furniture and rags that might've been curtains, ages ago.

That seemed like a bad plan, but I trusted him enough not to argue. I stomped my feet, walking in circles, then I heard the monsters scramble up the stairs. The first body hit the door and the bar bowed with the pressure; it wasn't strong enough to keep them out indefinitely. A snarling discussion followed, as if they were debating their options.

I understood when Fade touched his father's lighter to the rags and dry wood. The flames curled up immediately, spreading to the floor that was riddled with dry rot. He ran over to the window and slid the sash up. With an impatient gesture, he beckoned.

"We need to get out of here and set a couple more fires downstairs. With any luck, these Freaks aren't part of the group that burned Salvation, so they won't understand the danger until it's too late."

He intends to burn them alive.

Without further hesitation, I scrambled over the sill and dangled by my fingertips. There was no tree branch to swing onto as there had been at the Oakses' place so I dropped and hoped for the best. I landed hard, but I didn't break anything. Fade came down more gracefully and tugged me to my feet. Time was critical. We gathered more rubbish to serve as kindling and lit the house up at both doors, front and back. The fire spread quickly, fanned by the breeze blowing through. Soon the whole building was engulfed in orange flames, creating a huge glow against the night sky. This might cause more problems for us down the line if the blaze attracted more enemies, but we wouldn't be here to see it. I lingered only long enough to hear the monsters screaming as they burned, then I ran after Fade, who was already on the move.

"They won't bother us again," he said with certainty.

Still, to be safe, we traveled through the night and didn't stop until we had a full eight hours of distance between that hunting party and us. At last I collapsed, winded, and I couldn't go on. Fade was right there with me, his face flagged with windburn. He leaned against me, seeming not to realize how easy the gesture was, and I didn't remind him.

"We won't make Winterville without a break," I panted.

"You sleep. I'll keep watch."

Before, he'd said we could afford to rest at the same time. His caution had to mean he thought there were more Freaks in the area. I didn't hear or smell them, but Fade had better instincts for such things, no doubt honed by his years alone down below, where his survival depended on knowing where the monsters were before they found him.

"Just an hour or two, then you. And we'll press on."

He neither agreed nor argued, and I lay down. Fade rested his hand on my hair. I expected to be so conscious of him close by that I couldn't sleep, but I underrated my exhaustion. When he jostled me a few hours later, I couldn't believe how soundly I'd gone out.

"Any problems?"

"A few squirrels threw nuts at you."

"That's not the kind of problem I meant."

He smiled. "I know, but things were quiet. Your watch?"

"I'm on it."

Luck held long enough for Fade to catch a nap, and I had food ready—such as it was—when I woke him. We drank and ate in silence. I hoped we reached Winterville soon; and to that end, I checked the map, comparing Longshot's notes with where we were. Sometimes it was hard to judge since he kept mostly to wagon routes whereas Fade and I ran cross-country, taking the most direct route. But near as I could tell, the Freaks had only driven us a little off course. Longshot and I hadn't spoken much about the other settlements, so I was glad he'd written memos along the edges of his maps. It was like receiving his advice when I needed it most.

Another day of breakneck travel and dodging the monsters found us outside the city limits. I said city because it reminded me of the ruins, only it wasn't damaged in the same way. It wasn't nearly as big as Gotham, either. Around the edges, Winterville had buildings made of brick and stone, towering compared with the homey structures I had admired in Salvation. Well-kept stands of grass lined the avenues, which were paved with stones and neatly swept. There was no gate, either—no wooden wall or barbed metal fencing—but I mistrusted my eyes. Surely no settlement could be wholly unprotected. Fade and I exchanged a glance as we approached. I expected to encounter some security measure, some hidden threat, like a man with a rifle aimed at us, but we passed into Winterville without a single warning.

"This makes me uneasy," I said.

But I didn't smell anything, or at least, the scent was too faint for me to place it. If the Freaks had destroyed the place, they would still be there, and the buildings wouldn't be so intact. The monsters tended to break windows and doors in their desperation to kill all humans hiding inside. Here, it was like nothing bad ever happened, as if Winterville was a special, blessed place. Momma Oaks would say her god smiled on it.

Just when I was starting to think nobody was here, a woman stepped out her front door. She looked startled to see us, but she lifted a hand in careful greeting. "What brings you around, strangers?"

There's nothing stranger than this.

Fade answered for us. "The colonel sent us from Soldier's Pond. She said Dr. Wilson has been working on a project and should have some information."

"Ah." The conflict in her expression cleared. "Then you want to follow this main road through town. When you come to the research annex, hang a left. Then go down two blocks, turn right, and knock on the back door of the lab."

"What's a block?" I asked.

She eyed me like I was simpleminded. "Two streets. The lab is where Dr. Wilson works. It's a white building, no windows at all."

That should be easy enough to find, though Winterville was bigger than I'd expected, based on what I'd seen of the world so far. "Are all these houses occupied?"

"No," she said sadly. "Less than half, now."

"Did the Muties get them?" Fade remembered to use the topside word.

"No. Since Dr. Wilson spread the pheromones, we've had less trouble with attacks, but . . . there have been other problems."

She didn't volunteer what those might be, and I didn't ask. Our job wasn't to fix Winterville, only to get the necessary information and survive the return trip. But I did wonder: "Do you have a standing military?"

Once again, she shook her head. "It's possible to coexist

peacefully with the mutants if you know how to avoid enraging them."

With a polite smile, I decided she was insane. I followed her directions, hoping they weren't as crazy. No matter her personal delusions, she did tell us how to find Dr. Wilson. As we stood outside his lab building, I felt properly grateful.

"It looks like a giant box," I said.

The lack of windows made the place distinctive, but it also looked rather like a cage, a place where you hid things you didn't want the light to reveal. Mustering my nerve, I circled around and rapped sharply on the back door, as instructed. I waited what seemed like a long time before I repeated the knock. Fade tapped his foot, no more pleased by the delay than I was.

Eventually I heard shuffling movement within and a white-haired man opened the door, squinting at me with obvious annoyance. He looked as if he hadn't bathed in days and a noisome stench wafted from the darkness behind him.

"What do you want?" he demanded. "I'm a busy man."

"I'm sure," Fade said politely.

"May we come in? We bring word from the colonel in Soldier's Pond."

"Ah, Emilia, yes, has it been that long already? I suppose it has or you wouldn't be here. Just let me fetch my notes, come along." He babbled the words with scarcely a pause for breath, shuffling back the way he'd come with the apparent expectation we'd follow him with no questions asked.

We did.

Fade shut the door behind us. The slam made me flinch, but it also meant this was a good solid door, and it wouldn't give way, no matter how the Freaks battered at it. But the crazy woman had said they didn't have trouble with raiding—and the state of their town supported her claim, however outlandish it sounded. Dr. Wilson moved ahead of us, turning left and right, seemingly at random. The hall was dim, so I was left blinking when we stepped into a large, well-lit room.

These lights were similar to the magical-looking ones in Soldier's Pond that they claimed were powered by the sun. But if possible, these were brighter still. I had never seen anything like them and, as Wilson peered at a mess of papers, I crept closer to the lamp. It hurt my eyes a little.

"Don't touch it," the doctor snapped.

I drew my hand away, guiltily. "I'm sorry."

"It'll burn you. I suppose you're a savage who's never seen electricity before?" Wilson sighed the question.

I shook my head, though I wasn't sure what he was asking. The scientist launched into a complicated explanation about windmills, grids, power sources, and currents, and I understood none of it.

But Fade was looking at him in amazement. "My dad told me stories about the old wonders. And you got them working?"

"It's not so great a thing, the least of my discoveries," Wilson said modestly.

It was clear Fade had a burgeoning case of hero worship. *Tegan would love to meet Wilson,* I thought, *and ask all kinds of questions about doctoring.* But the colonel had said he wasn't a medical man, so maybe his knowledge about windmills meant he couldn't tell her anything about fixing the human body.

"I can report limited success in the trials," he said, "but I wasn't able to weaponize the pheromones as Emilia hoped, and there were . . . complications."

That was only so much gibberish to me, but before I could say so, a snarl echoed through the warren of hallways. I froze; I *knew* that sound down to my blood and bone.

Somehow, there were Freaks in here.

Shock

I expected the old man to panic, but he didn't look worried. He waved a hand dismissively, still rummaging in his papers. "That's just Timothy, nothing to be alarmed about."

Fade said, "Where we come from, sir, Muties inside a dwelling means big trouble."

The scientist sighed. "You won't be satisfied until I prove there's no threat, will you? Come then. Let's get this over with."

He led us out of the main room, which was full of equipment for which I had no name, but I recognized the articles as belonging to the old world, which I had believed to be lost. I was a little awed that any of the things still worked and that Dr. Wilson employed them as a matter of course. Soldier's Pond had more such artifacts than Salvation, where they eschewed old technology by choice, but this was a veritable treasure trove of functioning equipment. The Wordkeeper—the man who guarded our relics down below—would've been astonished.

The same bright bulbs—long strips of light that flickered—lit the halls, lending the pale walls a milky tremor. Fade stayed close and I noticed he kept a hand on the knife strapped to his thigh. Wilson opened a door on the right, and the reek was unmistakable; this reminded me of the tunnels, where the Freaks had lived and bred for years undisturbed apart from the occasional run-in with our Hunters.

I expected to find a breach in his security. Instead, I saw a row of man-size cages. They were all empty, save one. To my abject shock, a Freak occupied it. The monster rattled the bars, prompting a sigh from Dr. Wilson.

"Yes, all right. It's past feeding time. Just be patient." He went to a white rectangular unit and withdrew a bucket, then hauled out a substantial portion of bloody meat, which he then tossed into the cage as if the Freak were his pet.

The beast fell on the food with its claws and it ate voraciously, hunched over because the cage wasn't quite tall enough for it to stand upright. I watched with a growing sense of horror. What was the purpose of this? Tegan had said once that she would like to study the Freaks to understand how their bodies worked and possibly to work out what drove them. Maybe that was what Dr. Wilson was trying to do here?

"This seems cruel," I said.

"Don't fret. Timothy is old, only a year or so left. In the wild, he would've already been slain for his weakness. And he's contributing to my ability to understand their culture."

"My friend Tegan is curious about them too. What have you learned about their eyesight?" I recalled how she'd wondered when she heard the story about the way I slipped past the horde to rescue Fade.

"It's on par with ours, meaning not good. They rely on their olfactory senses more."

"What do you mean, 'not good'?" Fade asked.

"Compared with some animals, humans have terrible vision. A hawk, for instance. The mutants have an advanced sense of smell, however, akin to a hound or wolf."

At that, the Freak glanced up from its gruesome feast, strings of meat threaded through yellow fangs. Now that Wilson had pointed it out, I could see that it was missing four teeth, crucial ones for ripping and tearing. From context, I figured he meant their society—and once, I'd have found the idea absurd—that they could have customs and rituals similar to ours, but that was before I'd glimpsed the Freak village hidden in the trees. I realized that Dr. Wilson could probably give us a better picture of what happened to the world . . . and what we could do about it.

So I put aside my shock and asked, "We came to retrieve information for the colonel, but I wonder if you could answer some questions first."

"As long as it's not about Timothy."

The Freak looked between us as if it recognized that Wilson was talking about it. I shivered. "It's about what happened before, actually."

"You want a history lesson? Well, I have time to indulge you. Let's have a drink then and I'll answer your questions."

Fade was still staring at the Freak, but he followed when we left the room. The thing whimpered as Wilson pulled the door shut, like it was lonely. That bothered me too. I didn't want to sympathize with the monsters, not even a little; that would make it harder to kill them.

This time Wilson took us to the kitchen, though it was unlike any I had ever been in before. There was no hearth for cooking, only more rectangular units like the one where he'd gotten the meat. It was bright and clean, though, and he gestured for us to take a seat at the table. I did, feeling like the world had once again stopped functioning according to the rules I knew. Fade perched beside me; he looked every bit as flummoxed as I felt.

Wilson turned a lever and water gushed into the pot he was holding. The scientist moved a dial and concentric rings kindled to a glowing orange. It was astonishing. Then he set the pot to boil; at least that much hadn't changed. He joined us at the table with an expectant look.

"Go on, then. I'll grant you the time it takes the water to heat and our drinks to steep."

I nodded. "At this point, sir, I'm not even sure what to ask. So whatever you can tell me about what left Gotham in ruins and Muties everywhere, well, I guess I'd find that helpful."

"You really don't know anything?" he asked, visibly surprised.

"Only what we were able to glean from old papers, but they weren't clear," Fade put in.

"Then let me be concise. A long time ago, in labs similar to this one, scientists developed all kinds of terrible things. You probably don't know what biological or chemical weapons are, do you?" He sounded like he pitied our ignorance.

I squared my shoulders. We were trying to amend that lack, weren't we? "I don't."

Fade shook his head silently. His father's stories only went so far, and he was young when his mother died. There was a limit to what you could learn when the people who raised you didn't know the truth, either.

"They came in many forms—gas, powder, liquid—but they served only one purpose, death and destruction. Whenever such things are created, bad men want to test them. That led to war among the great nations of the earth. Are you with me so far?"

I could tell he was simplifying matters for us, and while somebody else might be insulted, I appreciated it. What good were answers if I didn't understand them? So I nodded and said, "I've heard part of this story, but with a religious slant. My foster father told me men were full of hubris and meddled with matters best left to God."

"Some might agree with him," Wilson said.

"Edmund also said there were horseless carriages and flying wagons," Fade offered doubtfully.

"He's correct, but they were called cars and planes. You can find wreckage of them to this day."

"Do you still use them?" I asked.

The scientist shook his head. "Fossil fuels are no longer in production. The only reason we're able to continue using technology that runs on electricity is because we're positioned favorably for our windmills to generate enough power to keep the town going."

"What's a windmill?" Fade wanted to know.

"If you came in from Soldier's Pond, you won't have seen them." Wilson got a scrap of paper and sketched, then he launched into a complicated explanation of how the thing turned in the wind and that generated the power.

I had no interest in that. As the pot whistled, I grasped that the man's limited patience with our curiosity would soon be coming to an end. He had important work to do. "What about the Muties? How did the world end up like this?"

"I mentioned the war," he said, spooning some herbs into three cups. "It was . . . long. But it wasn't fought with guns and bombs. We tested new horrors on one another, time and again, usually in the cities, where the populations were highest. The last of these synchronized strikes was more virulent than anticipated."

"Virulent?" Fade asked.

"Powerful. It took effect quickly and the results were horrific. A vast number of the population died and the bioweapon created lesser plagues that troubled us for years to come. Governments created quarantine centers and tried to control the contagion, but all such measures failed. In fact, one vaccine even made the problem worse." Here, his account faltered. "My forefathers were responsible for part of that . . . and I've continued their terrible work."

"You must've had a good reason," I said.

He lifted a shoulder, continuing the account. "But not everyone died. The pathogen affected others differently. Some DNA chains mutated, a systemic devolution. They became primal and savage, concerned only with the urge to feed."

"The Freaks," I breathed, forgetting to use their Topside name. Though I didn't grasp everything, I had the gist.

The scientist looked interested. "Is that what you call them? Fitting, I suppose. And, yes." He paused as if trying to figure out how to phrase a complicated idea so that we'd understand. "Others simply changed. DNA is the building block of our bodies, containing all the code that makes us who we are. It's the reason you have brown hair and blue-gray eyes. It also carries incredible amounts of data regarding your ancestors and lineage."

I stared at the back of my hand, awed. "Can you read this code?"

Fade's eyes were wide because this sounded like more of Edmund's stories. "Can the code be broken?"

"It's not cipher in that sense, but, yes, if I had the proper equipment, I could show you what I mean." He took his pencil and sketched out what looked like a long figure eight on its side. "This is what I'm talking about."

"And it's hidden in our bodies?" I asked.

"Somehow I don't think this is pertinent to what you really want to know. You're curious about the changed folk, yes?"

I nodded, remembering Jengu and the small people who had saved my life down below. They'd been changed, definitely, but not monstrous like the Freaks, so I understood what Wilson was talking about.

"This is an unproven hypothesis, of course, but I suspect that an alternate evolutionary track was activated in their DNA. Some other animal in their genetic history took precedence, creating a divergent physiology, and since the pathogen was so powerful, it forced these changes much quicker than should've been possible in nature, occasionally with horrific results. Such a shift would naturally take millions of years."

"So the world was poisoned," Fade said, "and it made monsters out of some people and changed others, and a lot more died?"

"In a nutshell, yes."

"But why is everything so broken?" I asked.

Wilson strained the leaves out of our drinks and brought them to the table. I made up my mind to sip slowly, so I could keep accruing information. I wasn't altogether sure whether I believed him, but his account dovetailed with Edmund's just without the religious shadings. Fade cupped his hands around his mug, and I wondered if he felt as overwhelmed as I did.

"After the quarantine centers failed, governments tried to protect their dignitaries. Evacuations of the wealthy, influential, and powerful took place in cities around the world."

"Leaving Gotham empty apart from the people who were expendable," Fade said grimly.

"Yes. They were left to fend for themselves without support or infrastructure."

"Are those governments still out there?" I asked.

"To the best of my knowledge, no. The information I have comes from historical records. Those new enclaves fell in the chaos that followed, and new towns and settlements sprang up, populated by pockets of survivors."

"Like Salvation and Soldier's Pond?"

The scientist nodded. "Granted, since I have no way of communicating long distance, I cannot tell you what it's like in other parts of the world. But if things were different elsewhere— and if they had the means—surely they would've made contact by now."

That made sense to me. "How do you know all of this?"

"Journals. My people have always been scientists and they

kept meticulous notes on everything that occurred, insofar as they were able. Would you like to see them?" When I shook my head, Wilson looked troubled. "I wish I had a child to whom to pass on this legacy. My wife passed and I never found anyone—oh, never mind. That isn't why you came."

In that moment, I saw him as he was, an old man surrounded by relics of a lost age, irrevocably lonely with only a caged Freak for company. He might be the smartest person I'd ever met, but he was also the saddest. I restrained the urge to pat his hand, thinking he wouldn't appreciate it.

Fortunately Fade distracted the man from thinking about his dead wife. "I have a couple more questions, if you don't mind. Unrelated."

"Go ahead."

"My parents both died of sickness in the ruins. It swept through and carried a lot of people with it. Was that one of the lesser plagues you were talking about?"

"The initial deployment was such a long time ago," Wilson said gently. "So I rather doubt it. But there are a number of diseases that could account for it. What were the symptoms?" Fade told him, then the scientist asked a number of questions about their living conditions and the water they drank. "It sounds like dysentery, but I can't be sure."

Fade didn't look as if it helped to have a name for what took his parents away. But it was good to know that our stories down below were so much rubbish—that the poison that started the problems had long since vanished, leaving the world to heal as best it might.

"Why didn't I die too?" he demanded. "I drank the same water, lived as they did."

Wilson shrugged. "Perhaps your immune system was better. Or possibly you were just lucky. Do you recall whether you were sick at all?"

Fade shook his head, obviously frustrated. "Maybe a little, but never as bad as my mother, first, and then years later, my dad."

"You said you had multiple questions. What's the other?" Though we were obviously nursing our drinks, I could tell the man was eager to get back to work by the jogging of his knee.

"The Muties . . . why are they getting smarter?" The moment Fade asked that, I wished I'd thought to do so.

Wilson appeared delighted with this question. "Again, this is an unproven theory, but I suspect the mutants have what I'd call genetic memory."

Fade and I swapped looks, then I said it for both of us. "I don't understand."

"Genetic memory is when a species recalls everything its ancestors know, so with each successive generation, the offspring is a little smarter than those that came before."

"So that would be like if I remembered everything my dam and sire knew, and their dam and sire . . ." I trailed off, overwhelmed by the idea.

"We shouldn't have seen such a shift so quick, though," Fade protested.

"Ordinarily, no. But the mutant life cycle is much shorter than a normal human's. I suspect that's the price they pay for their exceptional speed, strength, and olfactory sense."

"How short?" I asked.

"Two years of childhood. Four to maturity, and they rarely live to be older than ten."

"But . . . the ones down below didn't change that fast," I said.

"I imagine there were fewer resources, so they were probably starving. From extensive dissection, I've deduced that they've evolved into optimal predators, but in times of privation, their bodies cannot cope. They cannibalize their own systems to survive, but once they begin digesting their cerebral proteins, cognitive ability cannot help but suffer."

Fade said quietly, "They look, smell, and act different now. The ones we're fighting seem organized and they're not covered in sores anymore."

"I can only guess, young sir, but I'd say their evolutionary shift has stabilized and they're turning into beings capable of competing with humans on all levels."

Discharge

Those questions exhausted Wilson's patience. He downed his drink in one gulp, then escorted us back to the main room, where he returned to gathering up documents for the colonel. Eventually he presented us with a leather folio, similar to the one that housed my precious maps. The scientist wore a hard expression as he handed the papers over to us.

"Make sure you tell Emilia that the pheromones aren't a solution. The complications I spoke of earlier have a significant impact on the general populace."

"What does that mean?" I asked.

He sighed. "For some, exposure to mutant pheromones imbues certain irresistible urges. They become violent and in some cases . . . feral."

"So they attack and try to eat you?" I was horrified. "How is that better?"

I'd much rather fight Freaks; at least I understood why they hated and wanted to kill us. If they truly remembered everything their people had suffered over the years, then I was right, and they *did* blame humanity for their pain. That didn't mean I'd let them annihilate us.

"It's not," Wilson said. "I thought if I distilled a compound, based on excretions from the mutant endocrine system, it might make them think this territory was already occupied by their brethren and leave it without need for conflict. That part of the spray works as intended. But I didn't anticipate how certain human physiologies would react."

Of that, I only understood that he was coating the area in Freak-stink and it was driving his townsfolk crazy. "That's the colonel's plan? Her soldiers will massacre each other."

"If they're susceptible. So make sure you tell her, this is not the miracle cure she's looking for."

Fade laughed. "She's not thrilled with us right now. I can't guarantee she'll listen."

"Since I'm not sending any of the treatment with you, she'll have to send another envoy if she wants to discuss the matter further. I hope not," Wilson added, looking worried. "I don't have the personnel to defend the lab if she decides to take the compound by force."

"Destroy it," I said flatly.

I could see he was conflicted because it was an idea that he'd had that actually worked, if not as intended, but in the end, he came to the same conclusion. The colonel couldn't be permitted to unleash this plague on Soldier's Pond. People using questionable mixtures on one another was what started this trouble in the first place, a long time ago. We didn't need another mess before we cleaned this one up.

"Now I need you to go. I have work to do and a round of experiments ready to check."

I put the packet of papers in my pack. "Thanks for your time, Dr. Wilson. We appreciate it more than you can know."

The old man actually colored. "It was a pleasure to shed some light on the world for you. I don't often get to play the role of instructor. It will be safer if you travel during the day, but I suppose you already know that. Mutants aren't any more nocturnal than we are, though there are occasional exceptions. There's a woman who will rent you a room for the night, if you have anything of value to trade." He gave us directions, then added, "Stay out of the south side."

There was no need to tell us that it was full of feral humans, who might try to eat our faces. "Why didn't you just kill them?" I asked.

"Because I'm working on a cure. It was more humane to pen them up until I can figure out how to heal them." But he didn't look hopeful anymore, so maybe it was more that he couldn't bear to admit failure and order those poor people to be killed.

I read the caution and regret in his eyes as Wilson lifted his hand to us in farewell. Fade led the way out of the lab, following the turns perfectly. He had an excellent sense of direction Topside, better than mine. Soon enough we were standing outside the house where we could rent a room; I was less sure what we would use to do that. Before knocking, I rummaged in my pack and then looked at Fade.

"What do you think she'll want?"

Fade shrugged. "Let's go ask. We need a good night's sleep before starting the trip back."

I noticed he didn't say home, and I felt the same way. At best we were biding time in Soldier's Pond. Idly I wondered how they'd controlled the savages in the southern section of Winterville, but I didn't intend to go see how bad it was. It did explain why the place was so quiet, however; I imagined there had been casualties.

Fade rapped on the door and within moments, a young woman answered, no more than five or six years older than I was. She wasn't what I'd expected; I supposed I had been looking for someone like Momma Oaks, as she was the one who sheltered us when we first arrived in Salvation. I cleared my throat.

"Dr. Wilson said you'd be willing to put us up for the night."

"Did he now? Then I'd better not make a liar out of the old goat. Come on in. I'm Laurel, by the way. Nice to meet you."

Inside, her home was cheerful, decorated with cushions in colorful fabrics. The furniture was old and battered, however, which told me they didn't have many skilled woodworkers in Winterville. She waited for us to take a seat, then said, "What are you offering for a night's lodging?"

"News," I said.

By her expression, I'd surprised her. "If you don't find what I know useful or interesting, we'll camp outside. No harm done."

The woman nodded. "That sounds fair."

Quietly I summarized the sacking of Salvation, the gathering horde, and the unrest in Soldier's Pond. Then I finished with "I realize you have the treatment that's supposed to keep the Muties away, and so far it's working, but that's not exactly a permanent solution."

"No," she said shakily. "It's not. There are those in town who will prize this information highly, so I can use it as leverage."

I didn't ask what she meant by that. "Is it enough for you to put us up for the night?"

"I'll throw in soup for each of you," she said. "Let me show you to your room."

Fade and I were tired enough that we went straight to sleep and only roused when she knocked much later to tell us it was time for the evening meal. We ate quickly, then retired once more. I felt like a miser, hoarding sleep, because it would certainly be scarce on the return trip.

In the morning, Laurel packed us some bread for the road. I hesitated, as I hadn't discussed this idea with Fade, but it seemed right to me. So in parting I said, "Will you let the men in town know we're raising an army in Soldier's Pond? Anyone who wants to enlist should make his way there and can march with us. There's no way around it—we have to fight."

If the men thought I meant the colonel, well, that wasn't my fault. A flickering look from Fade told me he'd caught the slight deception, but he didn't say anything.

Laurel nodded. "A few might make the journey. We're not warriors by and large."

"That's all we could ask."

Since we'd slept almost a full day and eaten well, the return trip went smoother. Freaks still prowled in our wake, but we outran them and in some circumstances outsmarted them. It took us two and a half days of constant running with only short breaks for food and rest. I didn't sleep more than three hours at a stretch until I saw the barbed metal fencing glimmer in the morning sunshine.

"We made it," I said to Fade, pushing out an exhausted breath.

I slowed to a walk then as the shout went up from the sentries not to shoot us. *Reassuring.* Freak corpses lay at irregular intervals outside the perimeter. So a hunting party had tested the defenses here at Soldier's Pond while we were gone; they'd fared poorly too, but it wouldn't be long before others came in search of their lost brethren. I foresaw a repeat of what happened in Salvation, though these warriors could withstand a longer siege.

As we approached, they neutralized the defenses long enough for us to enter. Fade quickened his step, no doubt eager to have this errand done. I agreed with him. But we didn't get to the colonel before Tegan found us. And I had *never* seen her so angry.

"You left me!" she shouted, then she hauled off and hit me.

I was so stunned that I didn't even try to block the blow, so she punched me square in the nose. The resultant crunch hurt like the devil, blood trailed down over my upper lip and into my mouth. Gaping at her, I scrambled in my bag for a scrap of cloth to blot it up.

"You've been training," I said.

"Not really." By her shocked expression, she hadn't expected her strike to land, and now she was looking faintly horrified by her own violence. But Tegan didn't let it sidetrack her from her grievance. "I can't believe after everything we've been through, you just took off and didn't tell me. Do you have any clue how worried we were?"

"I was coming back," I said guiltily.

"We didn't know that! Your mother has been crying off and on for two days. Two days! What's the matter with you? Don't you understand how much the Oakses love you? If the Tuttles had survived, there's no way I would . . . would ever—" And then Tegan broke down, tears trickling down her cheeks.

I hugged her because I didn't know what else to do and whispered, "I'm sorry. I am."

"Don't tell me. Tell Momma Oaks and Edmund and Rex." Tegan speared Fade with a hard stare next. "And you. I'd think you would know better. Deuce has all the natural instincts of a wild partridge but *you* had a family once. Why did you let her do this?"

He shuffled, and it kind of delighted me to see him so nonplused. Finally he mumbled, "You try stopping her from doing something once her mind is made up."

By rights he could've blamed the colonel, who was behind all of this. It was to his credit that he just accepted her anger without excuses. We *had* hurt the people who cared about us, and it didn't matter why. Time to make amends. The colonel could wait.

It took two hours of eating, explanation, and constant apology before we were forgiven. In the end, I think my family was just so glad to see me back and alive that they couldn't hold on to the anger. Plus, when Momma Oaks saw my swollen nose and two black eyes, her maternal sympathy got the best of her. She fussed at Tegan for picking on me, which I found hilarious.

But my mother wasn't happy when I said, "I have to go see

the colonel before she sends somebody to haul me in. Tarrying could be grounds for her deciding not to honor our deal."

Edmund was saying, "What deal?" with a worried look as I hurried out, Fade close behind me.

We found Colonel Park in her usual spot, poring over the maps that tracked Freak movements nearby. "I take it you've seen some action in our absence," I said.

She shrugged. "Nothing we can't handle yet. Do you have my data?"

I handed her the packet, then repeated Dr. Wilson's warning.

From her narrowed eyes, she thought I was making up the obstacle, until she broke open the seals and started reading. Then her frown became a scowl but I saw the worry lurking underneath. When a warrior came up against a foe that couldn't be defeated under existing conditions, it was genuine cause for alarm. If her men found out how poorly equipped they were to face the horde, discipline would break down. Yet I sympathized with her position. She couldn't strip the town of all defenders and go on the march, leaving the place unprotected. The colonel was between a rock and a hard place, right enough.

"What was it like in Winterville?" she asked, surprising me.

I guessed the reason behind the question right away. "Unnaturally quiet. I'm guessing they had twice the population before he spread the potion. Fade and I only saw three souls while we were there . . . most were hiding, I gather, due to the problems in the south."

With a weary sigh, she set the information aside, bowing her head. I saw the moment she decided to abandon the idea, choosing not to sacrifice her own people. I liked her better for it too. "Then this was a waste of time. I suppose you want to address the men now."

I inclined my head. "I held up my end of the bargain."

"Let me gather them for you. But don't blame me when they laugh you off the platform."

Nerves fluttered in my stomach. This was the real beginning of our resistance. I felt it in my blood and bones, but it could also end before it began. Talking had never been my specialty; I was good with weapons, not words.

"You can do this," Fade said softly.

At his faith in me, I squared my shoulders and followed the colonel out. She led us to the training yard, where she stopped somebody and said, "Gather all the men except the sentries."

It took a while to muster soldiers from the far corners of town. By their mien, they were annoyed at being dragged from their duties. Soon enough those looks would be turned on me.

The colonel climbed up on the platform that she used for addressing her troops. "The messenger from Salvation has a few words. Please give her the same attention and courtesy you'd offer me."

My stomach lurched as I climbed up. I was alone up here, and they'd think I was just a stupid brat, being absurd and presumptuous. Dryness prickled in my throat. Then I spotted my family in the back of the crowd, eyes focused on me. Oddly Momma Oaks seemed proud and Edmund was nodding. They had no idea what I was up to, and they still thought I could succeed.

I pushed out a breath and raised my voice to carry. "Some of you don't know me. I'll keep my story short. I come from the underground tribes, a place so dark that you can't even imagine. I had never seen sunlight until I was fifteen. But I came to the surface and I survived when everybody told me it was impossible."

A rumble greeted those words; plainly they doubted me. I ignored it and carried on. "I found people who wanted to kill me in the ruins of Gotham. Girls didn't fight in the gangs . . . but I did. And I survived. I made a friend out of one of those savages and brought him with me."

Stalker met my eyes and jerked a nod, his scars in sharp relief compared with the smooth faces around him. I took courage from his anger. This time I wasn't sure if it was for me.

"We only had stories of safety to the north. It should've been impossible for us to find help in such a vast wilderness. There were Muties everywhere, and we had no maps. Yet we did. Longshot guided us to Salvation, and they took us in. I fought for them with my last breath, but it wasn't enough. They sent me to fetch aid, and I was too late, too slow. That haunts me."

I had no fancy words to persuade them, only the truth of my life. So I dug into my pocket and produced my bloodstained playing card. "I'm called Deuce, and I take my name from the two of spades. I'm telling you now, from the things I've survived and the places I've been, that there is no such thing as impossible. According to everyone else, I shouldn't be here. But I am."

The yard was deathly quiet, and the soldiers had lost their irritation. In some faces I read incredulity and amusement. Others were merely listening. One man tapped his foot.

I gathered the last of my nerve and concluded, "It's only a sure defeat when you stop trying. We need an army who fights for the whole world, not one town, and I mean to raise it. Your colonel has given me her blessing to recruit from your number. If you join up, from this point, your loyalty will be to this cause only. Step forward, brave souls. It's time to do the impossible once again."

two

onus

He saw that the creature was a tremendous wolf, rushing
straight at him.

—George MacDonald, *The Day Boy and the Night Girl*

Absurd

When my speech ended, I hoped for a massive outpouring of support. I gave them everything I knew to be true, and in return, most didn't even take the time to laugh at me. They went back to their duties and their old routines. Feeling like a fool, I hopped down from the platform, my stomach a knot of embarrassment and shame.

One soldier said, "This is absurd. I can't believe the colonel thought this was worth our time. That girl can't even defend herself from a punch in the nose."

Humiliation cascaded through me. My story meant nothing to them. They probably didn't believe me, and that was a fresh pain. Nobody had mistaken me for a liar before.

Once the training yard cleared, a few people lingered. I eyed them with caution, wondering if they meant to pick a fight. But as I stepped closer, I recognized them: Morrow, Spence, Tully, and Thornton. *Every army has a beginning, no matter how humble.* Wary, I picked a path across to them.

"What can I do for you?" I asked.

"We're in," Tully said, speaking, I presumed, for all of them.

"Why?"

Thornton wore a grim look. "I'm an old man, and I have no family left. I'd rather go out fighting Muties than from some ailment nobody can figure out how to cure."

"We like to live dangerously." Spence exchanged a look with Tully that I didn't know how to interpret. But it didn't really matter why they were joining up, only that they could fight, and I'd seen them in action.

"And you?" I asked Morrow.

"At heart I'm a teller of tales," he said. "And this looks like it might be a good one."

That could be entertaining in the field, and I already knew he was good in tough situations. So I inclined my head. "I'm waiting on word from Winterville. We'll give them time to make the journey, then head out. So you'll want to rest up."

"Yes, sir," Tully said, and she didn't seem to be sarcastic about it, either.

"I'll send word the night before we march. That's all."

It seemed odd to be giving orders to people who were all older than I was, but I figured I'd get used to it. With Fade at my side, I went across the yard to talk to Edmund and Momma Oaks. I could see in her eyes that she was scared for me, but her mouth was smiling. That looked like love to me, when you put a brave face on your heart breaking because it was what the other person needed.

"There are other towns," Edmund said bracingly.

Momma Oaks nodded. "These men just don't have enough imagination to grasp what you're trying to do. They've been following orders too long. It will be different elsewhere."

In my heart I wasn't too sure of that but I appreciated their support. "There might be some men coming from Winterville."

"What was that like?" Edmund asked, fascinated.

He seemed almost as interested in my stories as I had been in his, early on. As we walked, Fade and I took turns explaining what we'd seen and learned. Both Edmund and Momma Oaks marveled over the electric lights and windmills and Freaks being kept in cages. Tegan and Stalker accompanied us, listening to the account.

Stalker stopped me outside the Oakses' house. I hoped this was about repairing our friendship, but judging from his expression, it probably wasn't. This square structure without a hearth for cooking made me sad. Momma Oaks would never be happy in Soldier's Pond; they'd taken away her life's work, much as Salvation had done to me, but at least she was safe.

"Go on inside," I said to Fade and my folks.

They did, after Fade gave me a meaningful look.

"I hear recruitment didn't go as well as you hoped. My opinion, you went too soft. You appealed to their better natures. You should've called them cowards lacking the spine to take the fight to the Freaks. That would've motivated more of them."

I folded my arms. "If you just came to mock me, I'm not interested."

He shook his head. "That's not why I'm here. It's only advice for next time."

"Then what do you want?"

"There will be no gentle words between us. No more of me begging for a scrap of your affection."

"I never asked you to," I protested.

"Fair enough. This is what I propose—and you should be aware I have another offer on the table. You give me command of the scouts and accept that I'm not answerable to you. I lead my own men. I'll fight with your group, but we're free to come and go, pick our own battles."

"If I don't agree?"

"Then I'm staying in Soldier's Pond. I don't expect you care. But they appreciate my skills. I won't be in charge of the scouts, but I can work my way up. And it'll get me away from you." He said it like distance was a necessary cure for a disease against which he'd been fighting a losing battle.

"Maybe it will be better if you do stay here. I don't want to hurt you, Stalker. I never wanted that. Except when you first took us. Then I intended to kill you."

A reluctant laugh escaped him. "And I intended for you to lead the Wolves alongside me. I figured you'd see the advantages soon enough."

"No," I said gently. "I'd have died fighting you. I don't have it in me to bend. For me, it's always been Fade. It always will be."

He nodded, his eyes cold. "I understand that. And I can live with it. Do we have a deal?"

Part of me didn't think it was a good idea to take him along, but he was an excellent scout. Only the fact that he wanted to lead his own men had driven him to offer this agreement. He had been in power in the Wolves, and he didn't much like following orders, which he'd have to do if he stayed in Soldier's Pond and formally joined their ranks. While the scouts might have more freedom, there was still a chain of command, and Stalker wanted to be at the top.

"Right now, there's nobody for you to lead, but I accept."

He nodded. "That's enough. I've seen what you can accomplish."

That sounded an awful lot like a vote of confidence. Before I could thank him for it, he turned and strode away. In time, I hoped he would get over his hurt feelings. I missed training with him. Fade stepped out of the house when I approached the door.

"What was that about?" But his tone wasn't sharp or fearful; and that, too, was a relief. I didn't need to deal with jealousy on top of everything else.

Quickly I summarized the offer Stalker had made.

"He'll do well with that, provided we can find him some scouts."

I sighed. "That's far from sure, at this point."

"At least you're taking action. Every big thing starts small."

Maybe I was just tired, but that seemed profound. Fade took

a breath, then framed my face in his hands, contact initiated wholly by him. I gazed up at him, enjoying the warmth of his palms against my cheeks. Then he brushed a kiss against my brow, amusement in his dark eyes.

"Tegan got you good."

"She did." I ducked my head. "But I had it coming."

He kissed my temple next, and I closed my eyes with a shiver of pleasure. "Thanks, Deuce."

"What for?"

"Being patient. I don't know why, but it's better and easier when I'm in control. When you just let me—I don't know." Fade's hand curled into a fist because he was obviously frustrated at not being able to explain. "It's just better."

"That's all I care about. If it means I have to wait for you to hold my hand or to kiss me, that's fine. I fully believe there will come a time when you don't even think about it anymore."

"It might be a while," he warned me.

I smiled. "Then I'll just have to depend on your urge to touch me."

"You *can* count on that." His dark eyes held a hungry light, like he wanted to eat me up. I rather wanted to let him.

That night, we all slept in the same room, the small barrack house my folks had been assigned. Edmund snored a little; so did Rex. At some point, Fade climbed down from his bunk and into mine. Since he was warm, I didn't protest . . . and since he *wanted* to be close to me, I took it as a personal victory. His arms went around me, so natural that I drifted back to sleep at once. When I woke, he was gone, probably down at the workshop with the other two men.

Momma Oaks was listlessly sweeping the floor, which didn't need it, when I rolled out of my bed and bundled up some clean clothes, intending to head to the washhouse. Impulsively, I went over and hugged her. She squeezed me back, patting my shoulders as if I were the one who needed comfort. And maybe I did. Yesterday sure hadn't gone as I'd hoped.

"I'll find us a better place," I promised her. "Just hold on, and when the war's over, I'll look for a town that will suit us all better."

She smiled. "It'd be impossible to have a better daughter or for me to love you more."

Stepping back, I took her hands in mine, feeling so many things that I just didn't even have the words for them. "I'm sorry about Salvation. I wish I could've done more, if I had stopped that Freak who stole the fire—"

"Oh, honey, no. Put that burden down. It's not yours to carry. The Lord sends trials as he sees fit. In my heart, I thought you could try harder to fit in Salvation. I love you but I didn't always understand. Perhaps this is His way of making me see."

"You think he took away your home in order to teach you something?" That sounded like a mean, petty thing to do for someone who supposedly had all the power.

"Could be. But speculating is pointless. His ways are beyond our understanding."

Nodding, I stepped back and collected my things. I would have to rush to get cleaned up and make the breakfast service in the mess hall. I ran to the bathhouse, past the center of town, where a number of houses had been demolished, and that was where they planted their crops. In addition, there were gardens just inside the metal fencing. Soldier's Pond made excellent use of the space they defended. It was efficient, certainly. There was also a pen full of livestock, but they used the meat sparingly from what I'd seen. I hurried through my shower and arrived as the last latecomers joined the line. I didn't like this part of our new life; I preferred Salvation's way of eating meals at home. Cooked in such quantities, the food was bland and savorless.

You won't be eating it much longer.

Skimming the crowd, I saw no one I knew until Morrow beckoned me over. He was sitting alone with a sheaf of papers, his fingers ink-stained. As I approached, he nudged them aside, making room for my plate. I sat down on the bench opposite him.

"You weren't kidding," I said, surprised.

"When people stop writing down their stories, the soul of the world is lost."

"So what was it like, growing up here? Did you have a choice about becoming a soldier?" I wasn't clear how that worked.

"I'm not from here, and I'm not one, really. I come and go like the wind." Though his tone was light, he definitely meant it.

"But the colonel sent you with us to Salvation, among her best men."

"You saw my work with the foil. Would you not agree that I have skill?" I couldn't argue that. He went on, "And she didn't send me. I *chose* to go. Big difference."

I raised a brow. "Because you thought it would make a good story?"

Morrow indicated the scattered papers. "What do you think I'm writing?"

I didn't know how I felt about that. On some level it seemed disrespectful to make an entertainment out of what the folks of Salvation had suffered. But another part of me said it was good and fitting that they would be remembered. Mulling the two conflicting thoughts, I downed the rest of my food without much enjoyment.

"Thanks for the company," I said, rising. "I'll be in touch in a few days, once I see how many men are coming from Winterville."

"Not many, I expect. It's why Dr. Wilson was working on a peaceful solution to the Mutie problem."

I wondered how he knew about the pheromones or if he

knew anything at all. Morrow might be testing me to see what he could learn for his blasted stories. While I needed his blade, I didn't fully trust him or his motives; he had his own reasons for joining me. Still, it was better to have men who could think for themselves instead of those who followed blindly.

Three days later, four men arrived from Winterville. They were exhausted and two of them were wounded from a skirmish with the Freaks. Tegan treated their wounds, which weren't serious. They were all angry when they realized the message hadn't come from the colonel, but they'd all lost their families to the madness Dr. Wilson created when he sprayed the town. So they had nothing to go home for and a strong reason to fight.

The next day, as we assembled in the training yard, I did a head count. Four from Soldier's Pond. Four men from Winterville. When Tegan presented herself without a word, angry eyes daring me to protest, that gave us four from the ruins of Gotham. That made twelve—such a small number to set out toward such a big goal. My family came out to watch us go. There was no fanfare; the soldiers never paused in their work or their drills. They probably figured we were going to die.

It was up to us to prove them wrong.

Otterburn

I had never been in charge of anything before.

So when Stalker stepped in and interrogated all the new men from Winterville, then claimed two of them for the scouts, I let it happen, partly because we needed skilled sentries, and partly because I felt guilty that I didn't care about him the way he wanted. That was an illogical reaction and I had to banish it. But it would help the rest of the squad, small as it was, to have good intel. The scouts would still fight when it came down to it. Before we left, I had checked the maps and memorized the route to Otterburn. It wasn't far from Soldier's Pond, only a day up the river via hard march. Wagons would take much longer. I didn't anticipate trouble, but it was best to be prepared.

"Stalker, would you mind—"

"We'll scout," he said.

His team hurried off to check the path ahead. I understood why he didn't let me finish. He was making it clear this mission resulted from his choice, not because I asked.

I turned to the rest. "Let's go. We'll make Otterburn by nightfall if we push."

Tegan fell into step, looking sheepish. "I'm sorry I hit you."

"You were mad. I understand why."

"I figured you'd *stop* me."

"I scared you and hurt your feelings. That deserved a smack

in the face." I smiled at her, wincing a little at the way it pulled my sore nose. "I'm just glad you came with us anyway. We'll need a medic something fierce before this is through."

"I don't just want to patch you up," she said. "I want to be able to defend myself. I don't want always to be the weakest one in the group."

I nodded. "We'll figure out what weapon works best for you and go from there."

Tegan didn't hug me around the shoulders because we were soldiers now, but I could tell she wanted to. "Thanks, Deuce."

The scouts found us a clear path to Otterburn, but there were Freaks sniffing all along the river. It bothered me that I could no longer smell them as strongly, only a whisper of corruption carried on the wind. Things were changing faster than I could keep up. Part of me doubted my ability to complete this task I'd set for myself.

A smaller voice was saying, *Just find a safe place to hide. You can't save these towns, and you're crazy for considering it.*

Then the Huntress squeezed out the cowardice, reminded me I'd rather die fighting, like Thornton said. If that was the case, well, at least like Longshot, I'd make my death mean something. Living down below, I wouldn't have had that many years left anyway. So I'd make them count Topside; the Huntress who would always be a part of me, as much as my scars, wouldn't let me do less.

The sun was sinking below the horizon when we arrived at the edge of town, long orange and pink streaks staining the sky. Otterburn was more like Salvation than other settlements I'd seen. The buildings were rough-hewn, but there were no walls here, no whitewash either. The wood was weathered, but it wasn't like Winterville. There were people in the mud lanes, going about their business. Yet this was a small settlement without visible means of protection. The proximity to Soldier's Pond meant they might receive aid in times of trouble, but I wouldn't care to rely on a neighbor's goodwill. I counted thirty buildings, total, twenty-five of which looked like people lived in them. The others were probably for tradecraft. Given the apparent lack of precautions, I had no idea how they hadn't been wiped off the map.

I turned to the recruits from Soldier's Pond, including Morrow in the look. "What do you all know about this place? Have you been here before?"

Tully and Spence shook their heads, and he said, "Our patrols didn't rove this far."

"I did trade runs for a while," Thornton said, "so I've been here, but it was a long time ago. I retired from the road after my boys were born." A flicker of sorrow shifted his set expression, a reminder that he had come along because he had nobody left in Soldier's Pond.

The storyteller added, "I've been here, but I didn't see anything worth staying for."

He was likely the most traveled member of our group, making me glad he'd volunteered. "Do any of you remember the layout?"

"Nope," Thornton said.

Morrow admitted, "I didn't make any mental notes. This place is a bit of an eyesore."

"No matter. We'll figure it out," I murmured.

Tegan was still beside me, though she was limping after a day on the move. But her leg wasn't as weak as it had been, so she was improving. Asking more of herself would only increase her stamina too. I wasn't worried about her keeping up. Everything else? Absolutely.

I called a halt in the center of town, then said to Stalker, "Take the measure of the place. See if you can find a local gathering spot. A shop or a market?"

Fade had told me about those long ago, how people got together to trade things. A place like that would be exactly what we needed.

Unlike other settlements, there were no guards. No sentries. People walking with bags and baskets glanced at us more than once, but nobody asked our business. Given what I knew about the world, I didn't see how this place could continue, long term, without everybody dying in a massacre. Glancing at the rest of my men, I could tell they didn't understand it, either.

The people seemed well fed. They wore simple clothing, similar to what folks had used in Salvation, except the women here were in trousers, too. I smelled bread baking along with the rich, savory scent of soup. After the swill we'd eaten in Soldier's Pond, my stomach growled.

"I hear you," Thornton said.

Before I could reply, Stalker returned. "I found what they call a public house. Half the men in town seem to be inside."

"Then that's where we need to go."

The place Stalker mentioned had a porch across the front, and it was noisier than other buildings. I stepped inside, wrinkling my nose at the strong scent. It smelled like rotten fruit only with more yeast, combined lightly with unwashed bodies. Conversation stalled at our entrance, resumed a few seconds later as the men inside decided we weren't that interesting.

"It's a drinking house," Morrow said.

"What's that?" I asked, low.

"They serve alcohol." He forestalled my next question by explaining, "It makes you stupid, loud, and removes a good half of your coordination."

"That sounds like a bad way to pass the time if you want to live," Tegan said.

Yet another reason that Otterburn didn't seem to be like the other towns. I just had no idea why.

There was a man behind a counter, a big, bald lout with a scarred face, and an even bigger cudgel behind him. For obvious reasons, he looked like he was in charge, so I picked a path through the tables and said, "Do you mind if I address the men?"

"That depends. I don't want you stirring up trouble in here and causing a fight."

I didn't think my words would have that effect, but it seemed better not to make him mad. "I'm looking for soldiers to fight the Muties."

An enormous belly laugh erupted from him. "Why the devil would we do that?"

Fade stepped up from behind me, his body language declaring that he'd happily pound this big idiot into paste. He didn't like when people mocked me, regardless of the reason. I held up a hand, not wanting to provoke the fellow when I didn't understand what was going on.

"You don't have problems with them here?" Thornton asked, visibly skeptical.

"I don't meddle in *your* business," the man said.

Tegan tried a conciliatory tone. "If you told us how you manage to stay safe, it could help a lot of other towns."

I already knew it couldn't be some technical solution like they'd tried in Winterville. Nothing in Otterburn made me think they were using old-world salvage. Like in Salvation, there were lamps and candles in here, adding to the room's stink. The counterman rubbed his chin, looking thoughtful.

"A story for a story," Morrow suggested.

"Make yours more entertaining than mine and I'll throw in soup and beer for the lot of you." The man gestured to the crowd. "A happy crowd stays . . . and drinks longer."

Our teller of tales nodded. "Explain how this works and I'll keep them laughing."

"Before, we had trouble with the Muties, same as anybody.

They were mostly dumb beasts and we hid in our root cellars. They were too stupid to find us. So they'd break doors and furniture, sniff around until they got bored. Occasionally, they'd eat a straggler who didn't get hidden in time. About a year ago, all of that changed."

"How?" Stalker asked.

We were all riveted, even the bitter, silent men from Winterville. I bet they wished they'd had this secret before Dr. Wilson infected the town and made their families go crazy, so they had to be penned up away from everyone else. But what else would you expect from a fellow who kept a Freak as a pet? Smart as he was, the man wasn't right.

"About six months ago, the Muties called a meeting. Instead of attacking, they sent one of theirs that could talk."

A rumble of disbelief echoed through our small group, followed by some creative cursing. I took note of a few. Even Morrow looked skeptical—and he specialized in stories. But I wasn't so quick to dismiss the claim. I remembered the Freak addressing me in a raspy voice. When the fighting was fiercest outside Salvation's gates, I'd stabbed a Freak's slashing hand, and it had pulled back, screaming its pain. Its murky, almost-human eyes had glared at me in shock, I'd thought.

Did you think I'd just let you eat me? I had demanded.

Eat me, it growled back.

I'd dismissed its words as a beast's trick, an act of mimicry. Now, given what the Otterburn fellow claimed, I wondered if I had been wrong. Maybe that was the start of the monsters' evolutionary stabilization, as Dr. Wilson put it. I wasn't altogether sure what that meant, but nothing good for us; that was sure.

"The Mutie spoke to you?" Thornton clarified in a tone usually reserved for fools.

"That's right. And it offered us a bargain."

"What kind?" Fade asked.

"We stay inside our town limits. We don't hunt Muties in the wilderness. And we provide a regular tithe to show our good faith."

Oh, I had a bad feeling about this. "What do you mean?"

Fade's hand slipped into mine, whether as a caution or a comfort I didn't know, but it was both. The counterman narrowed his eyes as if he could feel the weight of my judgment. "It was for the best. And things have been so much easier since the deal was struck."

"Just finish your story," Morrow said. "So I can tell mine."

"The tithe is simple. We offer food to the Muties and leave it in a certain spot, once a month."

Maybe it wasn't as bad as I feared. In the enclave, we gave them our dead to appease them, so they took less interest in trying to breach our barricades. A similar practice in Otterburn would be smart and practical, though I imagined most Topsiders would find the idea repugnant. As I glanced around, the rest of my men looked quietly horrified, so I didn't volunteer that information.

"Exactly what're we talking about, here?" Tully spoke for the first time.

The man cleared his throat. "Anybody who dies naturally, they receive the bodies."

"And if there are no deaths?" I asked.

Things were better on the surface, so I imagined that in good times, people probably didn't pass on that often. And the Freaks wouldn't understand failure to honor the agreed-upon terms. I was shocked to hear they had proposed any kind of deal at all, instead of mindlessly attacking. That development was . . . beyond worrisome.

The lout hunched his shoulders. "It wasn't my idea," he said, low. "But to pay the tithe, we draw lots. And the loser goes out to the meeting place."

"That sounds an awful lot like human sacrifice," Spence snapped.

The man flattened big hands on the counter, both angry and defensive. "We don't kill anybody."

Thornton leaned in. "The Muties do that for you. How long do you reckon you can maintain your population, paying in that coin?"

"It's not a permanent solution, and you don't understand how frightened everybody was after the attacks accelerated, how tired we were of hiding. You never knew when the Muties would strike or who would get to shelter. At least this way the deaths are predictable and you get a chance to say good-bye."

It was horrible, but true. That didn't mean I could see myself accepting such a deal.

The counterman went on, "And that's why I won't let you speak your piece in here. Nobody wants to anger the Muties by encouraging folk who mean to kill them."

"Then I'll honor my part of the bargain," Morrow said. "If you'll keep yours."

"Certainly," the man replied.

He was obviously relieved as we put a couple of tables together, then Morrow leapt up on one. At first the Otterburn men yelled at him to get down, stop making a clown of himself, but he played a few bars on his pipe, and they took an interest. The tale that followed was wild and improbable—about a boy wizard who lived in a cupboard, then a giant came to fetch him to a magical school, thus commencing a bunch of adventures. We were all hanging on Morrow's words when he wrapped up:

"And that's the end . . . for now."

To my astonishment, I had cold soup and a lukewarm drink before me. If I had anything of value, I'd pay him to keep talking. Sadly I didn't and Morrow must be parched. I ate my meal quickly, sad for the folks of Otterburn and sorry for myself.

There were no warriors here, so I'd failed on our first leg of the journey. I couldn't defeat the horde without more men.

Then I put such self-pity aside because I did have a small troop and I had to provide for them. So I signaled the counterman and asked him, "Sir, if I promise to be gone in the morning, would you consent to let us bunk on the floor by the fire? It would be nice to pass the night under a warm roof before we go back into the wild."

He looked undecided, then Morrow pointed out, "I marked how many pitchers of beer you sold while I was sharing that tale."

But the man wore a shrewd look. "That was part of our old arrangement, but I've a mind to offer you another if you're interested."

"Not the same sort you gave the Muties, I hope," Thornton muttered.

I shot him a quelling glance. "I'm amenable to bargaining."

"Then you lot clean the common room after I close up, then you can move the tables and bed down. Sound fair? I sleep upstairs, mind, and I'll count all the jugs and bottles before I retire. If there's even a drop missing in the morn, there *will* be trouble."

"Fine." I had no interest in more of his warm beer, which smelled like piss to me.

A few hours later, we were mopping as a unit. That wasn't the kind of action I had in mind when I set out, but maybe the next town would bring better luck.

Of a certainty, it couldn't get worse.

Failure

It was always a mistake to tempt fate with thoughts like that. Tegan had explained the idea of fate, a concept passed on by her parents. She knew lots of odd things. And I shouldn't have thought what I did, because the situation could always deteriorate. In the next month, we visited Appleton and Lorraine. The former was a village similar to Salvation, though they had more modern amenities; I could see why Longshot had enjoyed the trade runs. In both towns, I used his name to open doors, and folks were sad to hear he'd passed on, more so to learn of Salvation's fate. Those facts were enough to get them to let me say my piece.

But I'd come to recognize the light in a man's eyes before he laughed in derision. When it was forty or more, the sound could be demoralizing. They took one look at my ragged group, listened to my idea, then fell to uproarious chuckles. And those were the nice ones. A few men threw food.

Today, we stood on the outskirts of Gaspard. We had made a complete circuit, and now we stood on the coast. It had been so long since I saw the great water that rather than continue on toward the town I saw in the distance, I paused on the rocky beach to marvel. The men came up beside me, weary and travel stained. I had pushed them hard for little gain, but so far, nobody had complained. I had no illusion that they'd continue to follow me, however, if we kept wandering without progress.

"I've never seen the ocean," Thornton said.

I gazed out over those blue-gray waters, the waves rocking toward shore. "It's worth seeing." I turned to Morrow. "Is this going in your story?"

"It might," he answered.

Gaspard was built on a jut of land that reached out over the water. It seemed foolhardy. What if a great wave drowned them all? But with Freaks roaming, maybe the sea was the least of their worries. To the front, they had the ocean as a bastion and at the back, they had chipped a towering wall out of the rock and mortared it. It stood higher than any defense I'd ever seen, impressive enough to deter fire and claws, any attack the Freaks could devise. There was only a narrow pass covered by a metal gate. The town had a forbidding air, but it was a stronghold.

The world is bigger than I would've believed, down below.

If anyone had told me there were so many people living Topside, I would have laughed. Everyone knew the world above was ruined, uninhabitable. It was hard seeing a constant reminder of how misinformed my people had been. These towns weren't huge like Gotham, but each held hundreds of people, all living according to different rules. Now I understood how foolish my proclamation to Colonel Park must have seemed. I'd simply go unite everyone because it needed to be done? No wonder she laughed—and people kept doing so.

"One thing I don't understand," Stalker said.

I turned to him. "What's that?"

"What's the purpose of the tithe? It's not like one person is enough to feed a large number of Muties, so it can't be about food."

Ah. So he was still thinking about Otterburn. I had to admit, I was puzzled too.

"It's symbolic," Morrow said.

"Explain." Fade looked curious.

The storyteller's face gained a grim aspect. "It means the Muties are letting those people live on sufferance. They're the victors, the overlords, and the battle hasn't even been joined."

"Do you think it could be like an experiment?" Tully asked. "On a small scale. They're wondering how humans will react to such proposed bargains and whether we can be relied on to keep the terms."

"If any of that's true," Thornton said, spitting onto the sand, "then things look bleak for us. We don't want our enemy learning more about our ways, how to cow settlements into bending at the knee."

There may not be anything we can do. But I didn't speak of how disheartened I was.

On the map, this settlement had a slash mark by it. I could interpret most of Longshot's symbols but this one defeated me. But if Gaspard was dangerous, surely he would've noted it in a more obvious way. There was nothing for it but to push on. Turning from the ocean, I led the way up the shore and over the uncertain ground until we came to the metal lattice that sealed the town. A man in a helmet stepped into sight; his armor was crafted of reinforced leather, so it lent him a martial air. The sight gave me hope. Maybe there were warriors here, and some might be interested in taking the fight to the Freaks.

His hard glance swept our group, then the guard snapped, "We don't open the gate for beggars and thieves. Go plead for charity elsewhere."

Indignant, I replied, "We have skins to trade."

After two impressive failures, I knew better than to share our true purpose with a man who worked the gate. While he might pretend to be important, if he were truly a policy maker, he wouldn't be stationed here. Behind me, Fade held up the string of pelts he carried. We had hunted as we traveled and Stalker prepared the furs, so they would survive long enough to lend plausible credence to our reason for visiting Gaspard.

"You're an awful big group of fur traders," the man said doubtfully. "The ones I've known traveled in ones and twos, better to avoid the Muties."

Morrow cocked his head, his manner quizzical. "There won't be any new armor for you with that attitude, my man."

The gate guard swore. "Fine. You can come in and trade, but if I hear of any problems from the lot of you, I'll have you in the stocks before nightfall."

From Salvation, I was familiar with that punishment. And it was definitely to be avoided. The only positive thing about all the traveling was that we'd gotten good at eluding detection by the Freaks, as they roved in great bands. It was as if they were taking some kind of measure of our defenses, and I wondered if they meant to offer similar deals to other settlements, like the quiet conquering of Otterburn.

Maybe it wouldn't be so bad, I thought, *if they just let us live.*

But my stomach turned at the idea of offering our dead, now that I knew it was wrong, and I couldn't sit idly by while someone I loved sacrificed for the greater good. Even the old Deuce, the one who desperately wanted to be pure Huntress, would've caviled at that tithe. Freaks couldn't be permitted to win the war that way.

The gate clanged as they hauled it up. I strode forward before the guard changed his mind. Inside, I saw that it had taken six men to get the thing open, which meant it was incredibly heavy. That offered safety, but I also had the sense of stepping into a trap when it banged shut behind us. All the guards were dirty and unshaven with a hard look in their eyes. When she noticed it, Tegan stepped closer to me while Tully instinctively reached for her weapon, checking the motion when she realized it would be unwise to seem hostile.

Unlike other towns we had visited farther inland, all the houses were made of stone. This added to the cold, forbidding air when I was used to homey timber structures. Of course, sometimes, like Winterville, the town had been expanded using salvage from the old world, but even that looked more welcoming than endless rows of squat stone buildings. Most of the windows were shuttered at this hour of the day, which struck me as unusual. If I lived in a house like that, I'd want all the warmth I could muster.

"Where's the market?" Morrow asked.

Wordless, the guard pointed. Apparently he wasn't wasting more time with a bunch of eccentric trappers. We had met such traders—and the surly man was right—they tended to travel in groups no larger than two. It was common to see a man alone, covered in furs and skins, with a beard all the way down his chest. Dressing in that fashion—so many parts of other animals—probably made tracking difficult for the Freaks.

Once we moved deeper into town, I didn't send Stalker to scout. I couldn't explain the instinct, only that I felt it best for us to stick together. Fade stayed close at my back, too, and I could tell by Tegan's expression that she felt the sensation of countless watchers, like the entire town had their eyes pressed up against their shutters. A chill went through me that had nothing to do with the weather.

At first I feared the guard had directed us wrong out of spite, but eventually the narrow lane between buildings widened into a public square. Vendors sold their wares out of baskets and wooden carts; there was food, clothing, piles of kitchen items, and used goods. Beckoning to Fade, I beelined for the man who was running a knife across some damp skins, preparing to turn them into leather.

"I'd like to trade," I said.

The tanner pawed through our bundle, examining each fur

with a critical stare. Then he nodded. "I can use these." He counted out fifty bits of metal, then handed them to me.

They jingled in my palm. "What's this?"

His look turned scornful. "Haven't you spent any time in a real town? That's money, you idiot. You buy things with it. Food and lodging, goods and services."

I already didn't like Gaspard. "Other towns use different items, like wood tokens."

The tanner became less critical. "I didn't know that. Interesting."

Most likely, I was better traveled than he was, especially after the past month, but I didn't comment further. This seemed a likely place to speak my piece, but I had misgivings. I told my-self I was just hungry; and it made sense to buy some supplies since we had local chits. Once we finished our business, then I'd make my speech.

I hate this. So much.

I gave four to each person in the group with two left over and we split into pairs to shop. Fade came with me. He slipped his hand into mine without thinking about it; and the casual nature of the gesture made my heart sing. We stopped first to look at a basket full of brightly painted wooden squares.

"What are these?" I asked the vendor.

Delighted, he broke the thing into pieces. "It's a puzzle box. It goes together like this."

I watched him do it, and it seemed easy, but when I tried it, I found it impossible to assemble into a neat cube. Instead I had a jumble of components going every which way. Smiling, Fade took it from me and put it back together.

"But what does it *do*?"

The seller seemed puzzled. "It's a toy. Children play with it."

There hadn't been any fun down below. Even the brats trained in basic knowledge necessary for survival and when they weren't training, they performed minor maintenance and sanitary tasks that the older enclave citizens didn't have time to handle. I remembered running all the time with few moments to myself. As a Huntress, I'd had more leisure because my job was more dangerous.

"Thanks for your time," Fade said, replacing the box in the basket.

He knew my thoughts too well. Since we had eight bits of metal between us, we had to buy things the group needed, not a funny little box. In the end, I bought dried meat and herbs and a lightweight pot so that we could have stew as we traveled. Later, we met the others in the middle of the market, their packs bulging with whatever they'd spent their money on.

I could delay no longer.

Taking a deep breath, I hopped up onto an overturned crate. But the reaction wasn't usual. No laughter. No derision. The silence was worse somehow, but I pushed on, until I'd finished. It was the same speech I had used in Soldier's Pond; I wasn't one for talking. And maybe that was why I kept failing.

Then a vendor shouted, "Call the watch! They're disturbing the peace!"

"Did you hear what she said? Coming out of the earth from where she lived down below . . . she's either a madwoman or a witch!"

I had no idea what a witch was, but I recognized fear and anger when I heard it. This wouldn't end well for any of us. I bit out a curse. If we ended up in the stocks, the few men I had would probably leave me once they cut us free. I ran toward the gate, hoping to outpace the commotion in the market. No such luck. Armed men surrounded us, their blades similar to Morrow's, only not as light and graceful. These were weapons made for brutality and strength; they could hack off a head or a limb with equal facility.

"What did I tell you about causing trouble?" the guard demanded.

"You were against it, as I recall," Tegan said.

It was awful, but I wanted to laugh; she looked so small and innocent, the least likely of our group to give anyone lip, but appearances could be deceiving. In an instant, however, circumstances changed. My men drew their weapons and stepped in to protect me. They put their bodies between the guards and me. I didn't move, didn't protest.

I had no idea how to resolve this standoff.

Change

"Did you hear what she said, Sarge?" a guard asked.

The commander snapped back, "No, I was on duty, like you were supposed to be."

His cheeks colored. "I only popped down to the market for a drink, and there she was, bold as brass, declaiming like a loon. She wants to steal our soldiers!"

"Steal" was a strong word. I drew my knives, calculating the odds. We could kill these men, but it would do our cause no good to be hunted by the Gaspard townsfolk. With the Freaks massing, that was a complication we didn't need, so a peaceful resolution would be best.

"We didn't realize there were ordinances regarding public speech," Morrow said soothingly. "Why don't we call it a misunderstanding? And we'll leave at once."

It was lowering to have him speak on my behalf, but he *was* better at it. Maybe he should make the recruitment speeches from now on. People thought *I* was crazy. But the guard shook his head, and his men stepped closer.

"We're big on abiding the law here. You broke it. So you'll pay the penalty."

"For speaking in the marketplace?" I demanded, incredulous.

"Inciting a public disturbance," the guard corrected.

That was patently absurd. It didn't seem like a huge problem that a few people got agitated and yelled a bit. For that, I deserved to go into the stocks?

But the guard went on, "And now you're resisting arrest. Tell your men to stand down immediately. If they don't, that's a hanging offense."

Fade snarled. I knew what that sound meant. The half-feral boy slept lightly under his skin, and that ferocity kept him alive down below. I wished I could soothe him, but given his precarious emotional state, that might make things worse. Touch was a trigger, and I didn't want Fade to go off like a flint to dry kindling.

"Bend the rules for a change," Stalker suggested in a low tone. "Let us go. Or not. It's your life."

I couldn't be sure whether it was the way the rest of the men lofted their weapons or the shine in his icy eyes. From his set jaw to his livid scars, in that moment, he looked every bit a savage, like he could slay them all himself. The Gaspard guards took a collective half step back, giving us some room.

One of them offered in a small voice, "Perhaps this once—"

"Get out," Sarge snapped. "If you come back, I'll see you dead if it's the last thing I do."

He barked an order at the men to raise the gates for us. Behind us, the citizens from the market were gathering, yelling questions and protests. We got out as fast as we could, and the gate slammed shut behind us. Instead of offering up some recruits, they'd threatened us with a hanging and booted us out of town.

Excellent.

My spirits hit an all-time low as I found us a suitable campsite. Thanks to the rocky beach and the low hillside, I did manage to find a windbreak. The others set up their bedrolls while Tully and Spence built a fire. I put a pot on it and used our fresh supplies to set soup boiling. We each had shallow wooden bowls and spoons, but so far, we'd eaten mostly foraged fruits and nuts, along with meat roasted on the spit. This reminded me unpleasantly of our journey north out of the ruins, and I missed Salvation with a sharp pang. I hadn't loved all their rules, but it offered safety with good food and warm beds.

"This isn't what I signed up for," Dines said quietly.

He wasn't much of a talker, too much sorrow and bitterness in him. Along with Hammond, Sands, and Voorhees, he'd traveled from Winterville in response to what he believed to be the colonel's call. They had come looking for battle, and I'd wasted their time. At the moment, I felt weak, powerless, and small. The world was too big; and *I* was incompetent. It had been hubris, just like Mrs. James said, for me to imagine I could change anything. The gray sky overhead echoed my shame and the ocean dwarfed me. I was a dot on the sand, a whole lot of nothing. With a soft sigh, I sank down by the fire, grateful for the rock face at my back.

But the men were looking at me, expecting a bolstering word. I had made such promises before, after Appleton and Lorraine, after I wiped the rotten fruit off my face. This most recent failure bit deep, and I had no more promises. But if I didn't do something—say the right words—I'd lose them.

"Me, either," Hammond said, staring at me.

The Winterville men didn't know me. They had no idea if my stories were true.

"I have a new plan," I murmured, though currently it was to eat soup for dinner instead of meat on a stick.

They didn't need to know that. Surely I'd figure it out.

Stalker set a hand on my arm, the first time he'd touched me since the night we left Salvation. He looked angry too, though. "I need to talk to you in private."

"Let's take a walk," I said. "Thornton, you have the camp."

That might be a stupid thing to say, given how little anybody thought of me just then. I wasn't in charge of anything but a big mess. Yet I was trying so hard, and the girl part of me just wanted to curl up and cry. The Huntress wouldn't let her, a fact for which I was grateful.

In silence we strolled all the way down to the water, too far for the others to hear us. The wind blew cold and salty against my skin. I shivered but I didn't react otherwise, fixing my gaze on Stalker's angry countenance.

"What the devil is wrong with you?" he demanded.

Of all things, I hadn't expected him to yell at me. "I—"

"Girl, you're not a talker. That's why you're failing. You can't go around asking people to fight a war with you. Tegan and me, we'll follow you anywhere but it's because we've seen you fight. That's how you win people to this cause."

I started to protest the logistics—because how was I supposed to impress strangers in far-flung towns with my battle prowess—but he held up a hand to forestall my response. "Let me finish. That quarrel at the gate in Gaspard will do us more good than anything we've done so far. We made those guards *back down*. You don't think people will talk about that? There was a fur trader in the crowd, watching. He'll carry word."

"I don't see how that adds men to the group," I muttered.

"You wouldn't. You've never built anything."

"And you have." I wasn't being sarcastic. He'd fought his way to the top of the pack within the Wolves, and then molded them into a gang to be feared, wiping out all opposition. So I was seriously listening to his advice.

"Enough roaming around. We pick our home ground, probably near Soldier's Pond to make it easier to get supplies. We claim and . . . protect it. It doesn't sound like much, but it's how you start something like this. It's not so different from the gangs. I was defending buildings and streets. Out here it's plains, beaches, and forests. So pick one."

I thought about that and decided he was right. "Forest. There will be plenty of wood for us to build, varied terrain offering cover. Easier to defend than an open field."

Stalker jerked his head in an approving nod, his pale eyes glimmering in excitement. "That sounds better. Once we settle, the Freaks will find us. It'll just be a matter of whether we can defeat them. But that's a fight the men can get behind. Most of them came out expecting to die anyway or looking for the thrill of battle. You haven't been offering that."

It was true. I'd thought it best not to engage or rile the Freaks more than necessary while we built our numbers. But that wasn't happening. Time to change strategies.

"Thank you. Without you, this would be doomed to fail."

"Probably," he said with a trace of his old cockiness.

But the look wasn't leavened with wistful yearning. Stalker had closed the door on that desire at last. I followed him back to camp, where Spence was stirring the soup. Everyone else talked quietly, tended to their weapons, or both.

I cleared my throat to draw their attention. "I'm sorry our efforts haven't been as fruitful as I'd hoped. But that part is done. From here on out, we're taking the fight to the enemy, hard. Maybe we can't fight the horde, but we can keep our part of the world safe."

From there I outlined the strategy Stalker and I had agreed on. The men seemed enthusiastic, eager even, to defend the forest near Soldier's Pond. Satisfaction replaced a fraction of the shame. We might not be marching an army to face the horde, but this, we could do. I recalled how the Freaks had created a village in the forest near Salvation; we would do the same to them at Soldier's Pond, and we'd learn every root, branch, and tree, every shadow, until there was nowhere they could find us. If we couldn't face them en masse, we'd kill them one by one.

We would be ghosts of the forest.

That night, everyone seemed in much brighter spirits. The return trip took us over a week, as we had been traveling steadily east since we left Soldier's Pond—all the way to the ocean—and that was a hard march. There were settlements to the west too, but we hadn't gotten that far before failure squashed me like a bug. But I felt better, now that we had an attainable goal.

Nine days of tough travel later, I glimpsed the prickly green trees rising in the distance. Soldier's Pond lay on the other side, flush with the river, but we weren't going that far. In addition to occasional hunting, our supplies from Gaspard were holding out fine, and we had to support ourselves in the wilderness. The Freaks were smart enough to study our habits, so if we made regular runs to town, they'd strike when we stepped into the open.

I didn't intend to make it easy. "There may not be many of us, but we'll teach the Freaks to fear us. Too long we've cowered in ruins and in settlements. It's time to take back our land."

Yes, it was just one patch of forest, but I felt like we were drawing a line. Maybe that was just optimism, but I preferred it to despair. The men knew better than to cheer, but they raised their hands in silent anticipation of the killing to come. A few drew their weapons and flourished them. That put a smile on my face. I might not have an army yet, but I'd choose these valiant warriors over a horde any day.

"Will you scout the area?" I asked Stalker.

He nodded. "I'll take Hammond and Sands."

"Find us a likely spot, something defensible," I suggested.

He acknowledged that remark with a vague gesture and the three moved off. The rest of us waited in the green shadow of the trees. Dried needles carpeted the ground here and there, relics of a drought. Tegan came up beside me; she was thin and tan from our time on the road, and she hardly limped at all anymore. I didn't err by asking how her leg was, either. She was more than an old injury.

"This isn't how I pictured it when we left," she said.

"Me either."

I had imagined myself at the head of a glorious army, unlike any seen since the old world imploded. Instead, at the end of six weeks, I still had twelve volunteers and we were preparing to take a stand in a wood near the town where we started. Momma Oaks would say this was a lesson in humility, teaching me not to put the cart before the horse—and probably, she was right.

Spence said, "It's better to be out here, preparing to fight. It makes me feel like I'm doing something, at least."

Tully aimed a fond smile at him. "He hated the endless drills. Said it made him feel like they were training him for a day that would never come."

"They want us ready to fight, but they don't really *want* to battle the Muties," Spence snapped. "We don't spend nearly enough time on patrol or hold enough ground. If I wanted to work in the animal sheds, I wouldn't have enlisted."

I'd noticed that about Soldier's Pond. For a town full of warriors, they saw relatively little battle. They sent men out on patrols only enough to keep the immediate area clear, and that was a curious way to live, like the Freak Dr. Wilson kept caged in Winterville. I'd call it mere existence because a barbed metal fence defined their lives. To some extent, I'd felt that way in Salvation too. In my heart, I wanted the world to be safe for humans to travel.

At length, the scouts returned with word that they'd found a suitable location. And when I saw it, I approved the spot at once, a clearing with bits of blue sky showing through the canopy, and the tree limbs overhead were tangled enough that they could support small structures. When my eyes turned up, Fade glanced that way too. He was pale beneath his copper glow; and I feared this reminded him too much of his abduction.

Then he said, echoing my thought, "We could start by

building platforms, walkways amid the trees. Cut some timber to use the branches to form a makeshift roof."

Tully pointed to a straight, sturdy limb. "I could perch up there, shooting Freaks."

She was walking death with her crossbow, and the monsters had no comparable weapons. The others spread out, assessing the terrain and deciding how they could best turn it against our enemies. With a smile, I turned to Stalker and his men.

"Perfect. Great work." Then I called to Thornton, "Do you have that hand ax?"

"Of course. Never go anywhere without it."

I pitched my voice to carry. "Then get to work. There's no telling how long we have until the Freaks find us. I intend to be ready."

Embattled

We worked undisturbed in the forest for a week.

That was good, as it gave us time to implement some of our plans. The roof would take longer, of course, but we cut and split enough young trees to establish the walkways Fade had mentioned. With judicious use of our limited supplies, we employed twine, vines, and resin to fix the logs in place. Tully got her shooting perch as well. By the time we finished, the camouflage was complete, and you wouldn't notice our camp in the boughs unless you were looking for it. Cooking still took place on the ground, of course, but it looked more like an isolated fire than a settlement, which was exactly what we wanted.

In time, the smoke drew enemies to us. That, too, was part of the plan.

A Freak hunting party stalked into the clearing just before dawn, probably expecting to catch a trapper unaware. They stopped, all twenty of them, to stare at the unattended fire. This was a risk, but they already *had* fire, thanks to our outpost, and they'd demonstrated no problems protecting the flame for long periods, which showed cognition of the consequences should it go out. The way they were developing—and with what Dr. Wilson had said about their collective memory—it wouldn't surprise me if they figured out how to start one on their own ere long.

One of them snarled at the rest, then gestured. *He's giving or-ders.* Then the Freaks fanned out, sniffing around the clearing. But before they could figure out we were up above, I signaled Tully, and the attack commenced. She loosed a bolt from her perch, spearing the leader through the throat. The hit was clean until the beast clawed the metal out of its neck, then blood sprayed everywhere. His soldiers reacted with less panic than I'd expected, but without his leadership, they needed to be more focused in order to take out opponents with a battle plan and superior placement.

From beside her, Spence shot two more. Using shooting irons was a risk. If there were more in the vicinity, they'd hear the noise and come to aid their brethren, but the alternative was putting the rest of us on the ground before we softened them up. From what Stalker said, the horde was east of Salvation, not west. Once they found Gaspard, they'd probably harry that area for a while, not that it would do them any good. The way that town was situated, unless the beasts could approach by sea or find a way over that massive wall, then the only way they could hurt the people within would be to starve them out.

That left us with seventeen Freaks to kill. I nodded my ap-proval to Tegan, who still had my rifle. She inched forward on the platform, braced, and fired. Though her aim wasn't all that good, the higher vantage helped. I suspected she hadn't intended to shoot one through the back, but it worked. The monster cried out in rage and spun, snarling a challenge. Not a fatal shot. She unloaded again, this time catching the Freak in the chest, and that ended it. From her exultant expression, it felt good to assert her strength. I didn't undervalue her healing skills, but defensive ability made a person feel powerful, and she needed that.

Tully reloaded and killed another one, Spence accounted for two more. That was what I had been waiting for—slightly better odds. The men needed a decisive victory to restore the morale we'd lost wandering around and begging for help. I gave the signal to leap down and began the next stage of the battle. As one, we attacked from above. To me, the others were a blur of fists and blades. I had my knives out before the first Freak reached me. It lunged and I replied with a lightning slice of my wrist.

It felt good to cut its throat.

Another took its place. The clearing was a mass of snarls and lashing claws, snapping fangs. Fade fought his way to my side and took his position at my back. We fought as we always had, like one person, and the beauty of our coordinated movements felt like sparking. Stalker was a whirlwind of graceful savagery; everywhere he moved, the beasts went down. Tegan's gun went quiet, and I suspected she didn't trust herself to fire while we were fighting. I respected her for knowing her limitations, even as one of Tully's bolts slammed into the monster I was battling.

As I took on another, I glanced over at Thornton, who stunned a beast with his weighted fist and Morrow ran it through. They were efficient together, brute force coupled with finesse. Morrow saw me looking and winked, then he whirled back into the fight. Behind me, Fade fought with his whole body—elbows, shoulders, knees—while deftly avoiding their snapping jaws. I blocked a feint in my direction, then tried a new maneuver; I launched a kick, and when the Freak leapt back to avoid it, I disemboweled it on a low, forward rush.

Our plan turned into a chaotic melee with Freaks moving wildly. Some lashed out at whomever was nearby; others fled. Tully and Spence dropped the last two as they bounded toward the edge of the clearing. I was breathing hard but euphoric. This definitely counted as a victory. All around me, the men were celebrating.

"It's only one fight," I said, "but this is where it begins."

They responded by stomping their feet and hooting. Tegan moved through, checking us out. Apart from Tully and Spence, we all had minor scrapes, bruises, and claw marks, but nothing serious, no wounds that required much medical attention. We'd needed to prove our ability like this; it would bolster our resolve through the tough times, and I had no doubt those were looming on the horizon.

I went on, "Let's get these bodies out of here. They'll soon be stinking up the place."

"What should we do with them?" Spence asked.

After considering how they had tormented us and ultimately destroyed Salvation, the answer came to me. My heart felt cold as ice as I replied, "Drag them past the edge of the forest. Take their heads. Then burn the rest."

"What're we doing with the heads?" Thornton demanded.

Stalker answered for me, an approving light in his eyes. "I suspect we're planting them on stakes in a perimeter around our territory."

"That's exactly right."

Morrow frowned. "That seems barbaric."

"It is. It's also a warning they'll understand because it's one they issued to us."

By their expressions, a few didn't like this, especially Morrow and Tegan, but I was done playing. The Freaks knew precisely what this meant—and that was the point. If they respected our boundary posting, then we'd get bored and have to change our strategy. If they did not—and I both hoped for and expected an enraged challenge—then things would get interesting.

Alongside the others, I helped with the hauling. Stalker kept a sharp eye on the terrain around us, as this was a dangerous point. We were off guard, dealing with the aftermath of the battle. Plus, we stood in an open field while stacking the headless Freak corpses in preparation for burning. Tegan gathered dry grass and other kindling in order to speed the bonfire along and Thornton donated a splash of liquor he'd picked up in one of our many stops. Once lit, the monsters made a fearful stink with a column of smoke pluming up like a signal fire.

And that was when the second wave appeared.

They swarmed from the south, and Fade's warning shout gave us enough time for Spence to fire off a few rounds and Tully to unload two bolts before they hit us. I drew my blades, dancing back enough that I had room to move. It would be the worst luck and the ultimate irony if I fell over a Freak corpse and got clawed to death for my clumsiness.

They came too quick for me to get a count, and that fast I was fighting for my life. Four of them. *Where's Fade?* I blocked with my right forearm, slicing two talons with my left so they hung from a spider spool of muscle and skin, dangling, dangling. Another slash cut through entirely and left stumps of bloody bone jutting from the maimed hand. The other three reacted as one; and I couldn't block all of their blows. I flipped backward, arms extended for balance, but didn't land clean since the grass was damp with blood. My feet slipped, thus yielding the advantage to my enemies.

Fortunately, I recovered fast enough to avoid everything but two swipes of their collective claws. Blood bubbled in the runnels they left in my flesh, but I spiked my daggers into the first one's chest, then tore it wide open. Freaks tended to be predictable in their attacks. Over the years, I'd learned how they fought: swipe, swipe, snap with teeth. If they sank them into you, however, they locked their jaws. I rolled away from a snarling attack, using the damp ground to carry me out of range.

Before they could reach me, I rolled to my feet, ignoring the pain in my arms. What were a few more scars? Around me, I caught a glimpse of Fade, fighting to reach me, and Stalker, who was killing like it was his favorite thing in the world. I heard grunts from Thornton and nothing at all from Morrow. Spence was conserving his ammo, favoring knife and boot, while Tully shot from behind him. The chaos of killing was beautiful in a way, and I contributed to it by opening another's veins as it ran at me. Blood spurted from its wounds, not fetid, just salt, copper, and that strong, meaty tang.

When the last monster fell, there were thirty of them on the ground, and we were all standing. More cheers sounded, as we'd just put down fifty Freaks. *Not a bad day's work.* I was exhausted and drenched in blood, most of it not my own, but as I wiped my eyes, I knew the precious glow of satisfaction. The others looked as if they felt the same with the possible exception of Morrow. I couldn't read him at all. The man was talented with a blade, but he didn't show a warrior's pride.

"Take these heads too," I said. "Then add them to the pile."

It took us the rest of the day to complete the burning and further into the night to post all the warning pickets around our base. A grisly job—Morrow and Tegan opted to remain at camp. By the time we returned, I was starving, filthy, and exhausted, but also hopeful. This was why the men had followed me from their homes. They didn't care about the scale; they only wanted to kill Freaks. In some cases they wanted retribution. Others needed to feel like they were making the world a little safer. As for Morrow, I had no idea what he was doing here, but by firelight, he scribbled some notes in a book that he kept in his pocket.

There was a brook not far away, so Fade and I took some jugs to haul water for drinking and bathing. I didn't think there would be more trouble—I suspected we'd cleared all the Freaks in the immediate area—but I was still on my guard as we pulled the full containers back toward camp. In the moonlight Fade looked as tired as I felt.

"How long are we staying?" he asked.

"Until they stop coming or we're dead."

"You think they're capable of learning to fear us?"

"I hope so. I don't know what else to do. When the horde marches this way, there will be no resisting them, unless you live in a place like Gaspard."

"And most settlements aren't so well positioned," Fade said softly.

That bothered me. I saw Otterburn's future for all unprotected towns, and I didn't believe the Freaks would honor that bargain forever. That was a ploy to make the humans feel safe in the custody of monsters. To my mind, it was a way to get those residents used to the idea of bending at the knee—of being subjugated. I recalled the pens where the Freaks had kept humans—and how they'd treated Fade—which told me all I needed to know about their true intentions.

In this part of the forest, it was so dark, only slivers of moonlight trickling through the canopy, but for me, that was enough to make out the shapes of trees and the fans of the leaves, others with limbs full of prickling needles. I heard the distant bubble of the brook and the quiet chirrup of insects. The air smelled of sap and sweetness, crushed herbs and the slight musk of animal waste. Sour notes bled through from the distant fire, a smoky char full of burning bones.

I wished the flames could drive away the monsters forever, but it didn't work like that, and according to Edmund, wishing was only a thing you did when you looked up at the stars. From here, I couldn't see them—and for a few seconds I yearned for the relative innocence of when I'd imagined the lights came from a city set high above us. Things had been much simpler then, my quest smaller. We'd found safety in Salvation, but it didn't last. There could be peace only if we forced it down their throats and choked them with it.

I stopped, bowing my head. "It's insidious."

Fade put down his jug; he was carrying instead of hauling it, as he was stronger than I was. Though he was better, I didn't expect him to reach for me. I had grown accustomed to standing alone, no strong arms or warm body to lean on, so for a few seconds, I froze, like I was the one with a problem being touched. Then I melted against him, eyes closing.

"It is," he agreed.

"Right now, I feel so small."

His lips grazed the top of my head. "I believe you can do this. I've lived through all of your impossible stories and I know them to be true. So if anyone can change the world, it's you."

Questions

I n the days that followed, I clung to those words.

The battles came fast and fierce, so that our bonfire on the edge of the forest burned all the time. Eventually we piled stones to keep it from spreading to the grass and then the trees. While we meant to warn our enemies, there was no value in burning down the woods.

In between the fighting, we built more. A roof went up across the branches, as we'd planned, and we widened the platforms so we could sleep up there too. At first it felt precarious and I hardly got any rest at all. But I'd had problems when we first came Topside, too. In time, I adapted. Everyone did.

Tully and Spence worked with Thornton in digging pits, then lining them with sharpened stakes. For obvious reasons, we all memorized the danger zones and avoided them. Farther out, Stalker and his scouts added snares and trip lines. Most often, we caught our dinner in the snares, but occasionally they trapped a lone Freak. The snarls gave away the location, so each time, one of us ran to kill the thing before it chewed through the line.

We had been in the forest for about a month, as far as I could tell, when Tegan approached. Her steps were light if uneven on the wooden perch. She had gotten nimble at climbing, and it was improving her confidence. She no longer skittered away from any of the men or failed to meet their eyes. Sometimes she even joined in the roughhousing with Spence and Morrow. I noticed Stalker studying her, but it wasn't the look he used to give me, more like he was considering the terrible things he'd done and wishing he could change them.

She sat down beside me and let her legs dangle. Others were on watch. Morrow and Stalker were facing off in the clearing below. The Winterville scouts had taken off a few minutes before to check the perimeter traps and see if any of our severed heads had been removed. Sometimes the Freaks crept up and took them away, but they were cautious about attacking the camp now. We'd taught them wariness, at least. In time, it might become more.

I lived with the daily fear that some Freak would carry word to the horde, which had to be on the eastern coast by now. There was no way for me to confirm, however, without parting with one of my scouts, and I was unwilling to do so. It seemed like too big a risk for too little gain. So we fought on, poised on the razor's edge. One day these trees might fill up with far more Freaks than even our skilled band could hope to defeat.

We'd fight until that time.

By this point, my black eyes had gone and my broken nose had healed, though it was a bit crooked. Fade said it gave my face character. I didn't know about that, but other minor injuries distracted me from such concerns.

"Remember what we talked about, just after we left Soldier's Pond?" Tegan asked.

"Your self-defense training?"

"Yes. When do you plan to teach me?" Her approach was direct and brusque, her expression daring me to object.

Her bravado made me smile. "I was waiting for you to ask."

"Are you kidding? I already did!"

Just to annoy her, I modulated my voice to Silk's lecturing

tone. "If you want something bad enough, you chase after it. You don't wait for people to bring it to you."

Sure enough, Tegan's dark brows spiked, but she swallowed her protest, probably thinking I wouldn't teach her anything if she sassed me. First, however, I had to figure out what style would suit her. She had a small handicap in her weak leg; firearms might be best . . . yet that came with the worry about ammunition, and Spence was already running low.

So I decided to ask some questions. "Whose style do you admire most? Forget what you can do for a minute, just consider our fights."

"Morrow," she said eventually.

There was a lot to like with his limber grace and his elegant form; he also employed agility in his spins and feints, leaps and flourishes I wasn't sure she had the reach to match—and her balance was probably off—but it was possible we could adapt the style to fit her. So I swung to my feet and clambered down, beckoning for her to follow.

Stalker had just leveled both his blades at Morrow's throat when the other man brought his arm up in a lightning maneuver. It was so fast that Stalker lost one of his curved daggers, something I'd never seen before. But instead of reacting with anger or outrage, his pale eyes narrowed.

"Show me," he demanded. "Again."

Obligingly, Morrow duplicated the move until Stalker could counter it. They were both breathing hard when they noticed Tegan and me.

Morrow doffed an imaginary hat, a gesture he was fond of. I couldn't imagine where he'd learned it, but faint color touched Tegan's throat and climbed toward her cheeks. Stalker waited to hear what we wanted. The others went about their business, but I sensed their interest.

"Tegan can handle a rifle already . . . and we can't waste

ammo on target practice out here. But she wants to learn to fight better."

"That's a good idea," Stalker said.

Morrow looked thoughtful. "What's your weapon of choice?"

She shrugged. "I've used guns. A club, once, but I wasn't very good with it."

"It was too heavy." I missed that club, though, because my brat-mate Stone had made it for me. Not for the first time, I wondered what became of him and Thimble and why they had been so quick to believe the charges the elders levied against me.

Down below, hoarding was a crime, and I'd been accused of stashing old-world treasures for my own personal gain. Since I loved shiny things, it would've made no sense for me to squirrel away stacks of reading material. Sometimes I enjoyed the pictures but even after going to school in Salvation, reading was hard work, so that was the last thing I'd steal. I shook my head over the foolishness of that accusation and focused on Tegan.

"Walk for me," Morrow said gently.

Tegan's eyes shone with misery but she obliged, showing him her stride. There was high color in her face as she came back toward us, but she didn't drop her gaze. *Yes, I have a limp,* she said with a silent, defiant lift of her chin. *But I can still fight.* Morrow didn't seem to be focusing on that, however—at least not in any judgmental way.

"What do you think?" I asked.

He addressed Tegan, not me. "You need a weapon that helps you compensate and plays to your strengths. You're small enough to be a deceptive target and strong enough to surprise your enemies when they get close to you."

"What do you suggest?" Tegan sounded happier, confident he could help.

In answer, Morrow ran off into the woods. Stalker gazed after him, one brow raised. "Well, that was odd."

But I had a feeling I knew where he'd gone . . . and why. Sure enough, he returned in a few moments with a relatively straight tree limb. With some judicious carving, it would make a fine staff. A little banded metal on top and bottom—which could be done once we returned to Soldier's Pond for supplies—and the weapon would serve.

"This is yours," he said, offering it to Tegan.

"You want me to kill Freaks with a stick?"

"Make some room," Morrow said.

The rest of us complied, then he demonstrated some of the moves. In his hands, the branch became beautiful and danger-ous, whirling in defense, striking hard, blocking phantom blows. When he finished his demonstration, even Stalker looked impressed.

"Could I really learn to fight like that?" Tegan asked.

"Not exactly," Morrow told her frankly. "But I can adapt the style for you and the staff is long enough that you can plant it if you stumble and then adjust your footing. It's the best weapon for you."

Stalker added, "Plus you can keep it with you. It may not even occur to your enemies that you can smash their skulls with it . . . until it's too late."

That sounded like exactly what Tegan needed. I didn't want the Freaks making right for her because she was dropping them too fast with a rifle. This was a quiet competence, exactly suited to her personality, a subtle threat right out in the open. For her part, she seemed pleased when she took the branch from Morrow.

He turned to me. "Unless you have something else for us to do, I'd like to start now."

"Go on," I said.

Afterward, I decided it seemed strange—him asking *me* for permission. But there was no question I'd started this endeavor, so that made me in charge by default, no matter whether I was doing a good job. I wondered if Silk felt this way when she first took command of the Hunters, as if it were wrong for all of them to look to her for orders. At that moment, I realized it had been a long time since I heard her voice in my head; I wasn't sure what that meant, precisely, but I suspected I had changed until my mind no longer worked in the same way. And that meant my memory of Silk had no insight to offer, no oft-repeated homilies.

In other words, I was on my own.

I moved off to give them space to train. Stalker followed me, likely with the same goal. But he looked troubled, and I was determined to be a friend, even if he didn't want me to be.

So I asked, "What's wrong? It can't be the lack of action."

He smiled wryly at that, the movement pulling at his scars. We'd just burned twenty-nine more Freaks. For a band of twelve souls poorly armed and living in trees, our body count was impressive. As long as the hunting was good, the snows held off, and the horde stayed out of our territory, we could continue like this indefinitely.

"No. I was just wondering . . . do you think I could ever make things up to Tegan? I know I apologized and she said she forgave me because I didn't know any better but . . . I feel like I need to do something more. It's eating at me."

"That sounds like a guilty conscience." Momma Oaks had explained the idea to me a while back, and once she did, I understood the bad feelings I had regarding the blind brat and certain things I'd done to earn my rank as a Huntress down below.

"Maybe," he said, sounding unsure.

So I ran through the explanation I'd received from my mother, and he nodded. "It wasn't just her, either. We stole a few other girls, but none of them were treated so bad . . . because they came from other gangs, and they understood our way of life."

"So they didn't fight."

I hurt for my friend, thinking about how she must feel. Maybe she hadn't wanted the two brats they'd forced on her, but she couldn't feel good about losing them, either. While I'd pondered, Morrow had gotten his own staff and was demonstrating the forms. Patient and skilled, he'd teach her without making her feel like she wasn't good enough. Part of me wished I'd known an instructor like him instead of the Hunters who screamed at us down below, telling us we'd never be fast enough or strong enough—that our best would always be pathetic. *It made you strong*, I told myself, but all the same, I wasn't sad that Silk's voice had gone quiet.

"No," he said, still standing expectant.

Belatedly, I went back to Stalker's original question. "No. There's nothing you can do. She has to live with it and so do you. Some things can't be made right . . . but it's good that you want to."

"I might be a better person now," he said with a sigh, "but I'm not happier."

If his feelings hadn't lain between us like a spike-filled trap, I would've hugged him. But things could never be so simple between us. Now that I understood what he wanted of me and I knew I'd never offer it, I couldn't cuddle him like he was a brat in need of solace. He'd take it as encouragement and the cycle would start all over again. Maybe someday, like he'd said, we could be friends without all the complications. I'd hated the savage I met in the ruins but Stalker wasn't that boy anymore, just as I wasn't a pure Huntress. The world was a big place, full of wonders, and it had taught us both so many things. For his sake, I wished so many lessons hadn't been hard, sad ones.

"I am. Mostly." I was also panicked and exhilarated by turns.

"One thing I've wondered . . ."

"What's that?" I asked.

"Why does it have to be you?"

I wasn't sure what he meant . . . and I said so.

"You're out here when you could be safe in Soldier's Pond or Gaspard, even, if you hadn't nearly started a riot. At any point, you could lay your weapons down. Nobody's ordering you to fight anymore. So why? You seem so committed to making things better. And I don't understand it."

The answer seemed obvious. "People go about their lives, trying to be small, hoping the Freaks will kill someone else, attack another town. How long does avoidance work until the whole world is drowning in blood? Somebody has to draw the line. And if not me, who?"

It was a compulsion, I supposed. The idea of sitting idle while everything burned? I just couldn't do it. It would end me to do nothing when I could fight. Maybe I wasn't meant for a peaceful life, and I could accept that. My only regret would be if I didn't manage to improve the world a little before I went.

Stalker studied me with a mixture of emotions I couldn't interpret. "We would've owned the ruins, you and me."

I didn't dispute his assessment. In another life, I might've been queen of the gangs, as he'd envisioned, but never in one where I knew Fade. That, too, was an immutable truth.

It was my turn to ask, "Why do you think there were no Freaks in your part of Gotham?"

"I wondered that. You said they were down below with you, as long as you can remember. Maybe they started there. People died of sickness Topside in our territory, but we never ran across any Muties, not like we saw in other ruins on the way north."

"So you think the mutations happened belowground, and they were too dumb and weak to find their way out, at first?"

He nodded. "Maybe. As they got smarter, they located the exits."

A sudden, chilling thought occurred to me. "Then that means

the Freaks now swarming Gotham came from the enclaves, however long ago."

Stalker looked thoughtful. "You told us Wilson said the monsters were born of weapons they created in the old world. It was a disease first, and the . . . vaccine made it worse?"

I nodded.

"Well, we don't know how sickness spreads. So maybe people went underground to hide, not knowing they already had it."

"It makes sense," I admitted.

That was scary and awful. I hated the idea that diseases could hide in your body and you'd seem perfectly healthy while giving the illness to friends and family. I preferred enemies you could fight. At least the old world, with its hidden perils, was long lost.

And these days, the monsters came with claws and fangs, not in tins and bottles.

Triumph

ventually the Freaks grew more cunning about their attacks. They came while we slept and in great numbers, but our traps maimed a good third of them, and we decimated the rest, first with death from the trees, and then in a hard-fought ground battles. Between skirmishes, we worked on improving the camp. And after the last fight, we went days without seeing a single monster. I took that as a good sign.

"It's working," Fade said. "Word's getting out and they're starting to avoid these woods."

I hoped he was right.

As time wore on, the air took on a familiar chill, and the sky overhead went pale on those odd moments when I glimpsed it through a tangle of tree limbs. Morrow trained Tegan daily, and she grew proficient with the staff. As I watched her drill, I thought she'd do well. Life had taught her to be brave and strong—that as long as she didn't give up, there was no such thing as defeat. Which made her a fighter as well as a healer, and I envied her that. Sometimes I wondered what—and who—I would be without my blades.

On days without combat, the rest of us sparred and scouted, tended the fire, enhanced the aerial defenses, set more traps, hunted, and cooked. The work wasn't exciting, but it helped to have a routine, occasionally punctuated with violence. It had been two days since they'd attacked last, and I was starting to get restless when Stalker burst into the clearing.

He was out of breath, which usually meant inbound monsters. But this time he wore another expression. "There's someone on the way to camp. I've been watching for a while, and he's negotiated all of our defenses. What should we do?"

"He's human?" Fade asked.

"Definitely."

I made the decision swiftly. "Let him come. It'll be a nice change to have company."

The scouts dogged the stranger's steps until he found the clearing. The older man wore an amazed expression as he took in what we'd built: the platforms and pulleys, the nets and makeshift roof built across the top. We'd created a tiny town in the treetops, and I was proud of it. Tully didn't smile when she spotted him; she occupied her usual perch and, if he made trouble, she would shoot him without a qualm.

I recognized the fellow but couldn't place where I'd seen him. He wore the raw skins and furs of one who made a living traveling the wilderness. All towns were glad to receive hides suitable for tanning. Along with other traders, trappers also played the role of messengers, carrying news from town to town.

"You didn't find us by chance," I said.

Fade stepped up beside me, then Stalker and Morrow flanked my other side. Part of me approved of this show of solidarity, but the other half was annoyed by the implication that I needed help dispatching one weathered old man, who killed animals for a living. I made mine battling something much more dangerous.

"I did not," the trapper admitted. "I've survived the wilderness for years and I didn't manage by being careless. When I noticed the Muties veering away from here, I was curious . . . and concerned. Then there was that giant plume of smoke . . ."

"You wondered what could be enough to frighten them away?" Morrow guessed.

"Exactly so, young sir." He assessed the camp in a glance. "And I also wonder what you hope to gain by claiming this stretch of wood."

That was a complicated question. He didn't know about my big dreams or my larger failures. So I just leveled a hard look on him. "I reckon that's our business. You're welcome to our hospitality, provided you mean no harm, but our food and protection isn't free."

The trapper looked interested then. "What do you propose? I can't imagine you're interested in these skins. With all the traps I spotted on the way in, you must know how to hunt."

"You must've learned some tricks over the years. So spend some time with my scouts. Teach them what you know, along with how you spotted our defenses and any tips you have for making them less visible." I glanced at Stalker, asking with a silent brow whether he had anything to add to my offer.

He responded with a slight shake of his head.

"That's fair," the trapper answered, seeming pleased. "I'm John Kelley, by the way."

"Deuce. Nice to meet you."

We shook hands then, and out here, that was as good as a promise we wouldn't try to kill each other. "Are you hungry?"

"I could eat."

I fixed him a bowl of stew. For the moment, it was quiet; the scouts currently in the field would warn us if they detected an imminent attack and surely Kelley would've mentioned it if he'd spotted any Freaks in the vicinity. In past weeks, we'd gotten good at quick response to incoming enemies.

"Where did you come from?" Morrow asked.

"Most recently, Gaspard. I had enough credit to board for a

while. But then the chits ran out and I have to stock up on skins to afford a warm place to spend the winter."

That was where I'd seen him before. He had been part of the crowd watching the altercation with the guards. I felt better after I figured that out; it relieved the niggling suspicion that he'd come for some reason other than curiosity.

"You're in a dangerous line of work," I observed.

"Says the girl camped out in a Mutie-filled forest." He had a point. "But I saw how you handled yourselves in town. You trying to keep the area clear?"

I nodded. "It'll be better for Soldier's Pond if the Muties think this territory's more trouble than it's worth."

"That where you're from?"

"Some of us." I didn't bother to tell my real story.

But the minute I went off to tend other business, Morrow did. I heard him sharing the story as I had in my various speeches, only with considerably more eloquence. Heat flooded my cheeks, and I pretended they weren't talking about me. Now and then, Kelley threw me an incredulous look as if he was thinking, *Really? That girl?* Morrow was a teller of tales, though, so there was no imagining what embellishments he might be adding. Good thing he was so skilled with his blade or I might stab him.

"Your face is on fire," Fade said, smiling. "Just think, John Kelley will be able to say he met you just as it was all beginning."

"What was?" I raised a brow.

"Your plan to save the world."

I'd never put it in those precise terms, but I did want to improve things. Some people—like Tegan—were smart and could learn anything; they could make life better in all sorts of ways, but I had only one talent, just the one. It would be wrong not to use it as best I could.

I hunched my shoulders, feeling silly. "I don't know if it can be saved. Things are pretty well broken. But maybe I can dig in and defend a corner of it."

"That's more than anyone else has tried to do." Carefully, Fade wrapped an arm around my shoulder and I leaned into him.

His quiet support meant so much. Most of the others just wanted to kill Freaks. They didn't have any faith that this served a greater purpose. Truth be told, I didn't, either. I had learned a hard lesson. Just because I wanted something, it didn't mean I could instantly achieve it, and this goal might be beyond my reach. I'd also realized what I should've known already—that anything worth doing took hard work. There was no wand like in Morrow's stories, where problems went up in purple smoke.

So I'd keep on, even if it seemed fruitless, on the faint hope the world would be a safer place someday. I didn't ever want to go through that fear again, as I stood beside the tunnel mouth, peering into darkness, and wondering if I'd ever see Momma Oaks and Edmund again.

"We can't winter here," I said softly. "Even if we haven't made definite progress before the first snowfall, we still have to return to Soldier's Pond."

The idea horrified me, but I wouldn't let the men starve or freeze over my pride. I'd bear all the jokes and the smug looks from Colonel Park, who thought I was a stupid girl with overly ambitious dreams. Maybe I should just take John Kelley's arrival as proof that our efforts out here mattered. It was a big world with few travelers, yet he'd noticed us; we had changed the way the Freaks in the area behaved.

That was something.

"We have a few more weeks of autumn left. Something might happen," Fade answered.

As it turned out, he was right. John Kelley had been eating our food and training our scouts for four days when the impossible occurred. Only, since it *did*, that meant it wasn't impossible, just unlikely. I was standing beside the smoldering fire in the field past the forest, tending the bodies of the last beasts we'd slain, when a lone Freak loped toward me. I wasn't frightened. I had my weapons and a few men nearby, including the trapper, John Kelley. Earlier, he had been much impressed by our efficiency in dispatching our enemies, and he'd expressed curiosity about how we handled the bodies.

There were five of us: Morrow, Fade, John Kelley, Tegan, and me. Tully and Spence were guarding the camp while the scouts kept an eye on our perimeter. Briefly, I wondered if this was a trap, but if so, it was an odd one. As it drew closer, the Freak slowed, something I had never witnessed before. The beast came toward us at a walk, head lowered as if in respect. The claws stayed at its sides.

"Well, what in the world do you make of this?" Kelley asked softly.

I shook my head. The counterman in Otterburn had said the Freaks had sent an envoy to make them the offer to submit, but they couldn't be dumb enough to ask us to surrender when we were *winning* the War of the Trees. It was a small campaign, to be sure, but we had killed an impressive number of monsters in the last two months.

"Not fight," the Freak called through a mouthful of fangs. "Talk."

It had an odd voice, as if someone had mutilated its tongue, then strangled it; but it was unquestionably speaking, not echoing us, as none of us had yet said a word to the thing. Fade had his knives in hand already, and I admit, my fingers were twitching. I didn't know how I felt about this development, but it couldn't be easy, facing us beside the smoky corpse-fire of its own kin. That required a special kind of bravery . . . or stupidity. Possibly both.

I motioned the others to back up. "All right."

"Not happening," Fade answered.

His knuckles whitened on his blades; it seemed to require all of his self-control not to slay the monster straightaway. So I let it go and he remained at my side. The others backed off, but shock and amazement dominated their expressions.

Morrow whispered, "It seems the chap in Otterburn was speaking the truth after all."

Tegan drew in a sharp breath, her eyes wide. "I never dreamed . . ."

The Freak stopped eight paces away. At this distance, I could see its eyes—and they were different, even more than the ones I'd killed outside Salvation. Savage intellect glimmered as it studied me in turn. I wondered whether it had learned our language from its captives. My heart was pounding like mad. Though I'd killed hundreds of these monsters, I'd never conversed with one. I didn't know anyone who had. Beside me, Fade made a sound deep in his throat, full of rage and pain. Quietly I offered my hand to ground him and he took it.

"What do you want?" I demanded.

"Forest yours. Not to pass. If not pass, not kill." It seemed to require a great deal of thought for the creature to produce this scant number of words.

I clarified, "You acknowledge that we own the forest? And you want us to stop killing you, if you stay out of it?"

I suspected it was asking us to let the Freaks alone, as long as they didn't trespass inside the woods. Since they had to go through those trees to get to Soldier's Pond, that sounded like a step forward, a success I could take pride in when we returned to town. The Freak's prominent brow furrowed as it apparently tried to sift the meaning from all my talking.

Then it said, "Yes."

Yet I didn't know whether I could trust it. "Give me one good reason not to add your body to the pile here."

"If no return, others join big group."

It means the horde. A shiver worked through me. "So you're not with them?"

The Freak appeared to recognize my dread. "No. Could make alliance. Bad for you."

This was a stunning revelation: There were different factions among the Freaks. Did that mean they all had different agendas? With each generation, their ideas and priorities changed more. Since humans didn't all have the same goals, I could credit that the Freaks might disagree about the best course, so maybe most of them—the horde—wanted to kill us, a few reckoned they should rule us, like in Otterburn, and a small number feared us. The situation would only worsen too, if they kept getting smarter. Soon they'd know all our tricks; and if the horde won over the rest to the idea of extinguishing the human race, well. At this rate, it wouldn't take long.

So if the Freaks who roved near Soldier's Pond agreed to a truce, it would grant the settlement time to improve their defenses as well as some much-needed peace of mind. Yet I couldn't assent too quickly. It would make us seem weak—and terrified of the horde, which we were, but it was better if the messenger didn't see that.

Tegan asked, "Who does this truce apply to? I mean, which of you will honor it?"

"Mine," the Freak answered. "All of mine."

That didn't give me enough information, as there were different subgroups—tribes—within the whole. I'd love to know how many, where their territory ended. We'd speculated about that when we found the Freak village near Salvation. Some monsters hunted and killed, and there were small ones, so that meant they bred like any natural creature. A portion must stay home to care for the young, but I had no other insights regarding their customs or culture.

Fade pulled me aside before I could ask anything else. "Are you sure about this? I don't trust it."

Morrow stepped up with one hand on his blade, making sure the monster didn't try anything while we were distracted. I appreciated his vigilance even as John Kelley loosened his rifle from its comfortable perch on his back. Fade and I didn't have long to talk before this encounter turned ugly—and I had no reason to doubt the Freak when it said the survivors in the area would join the horde, if it failed to return. Not the most desirable outcome. Fade had terrible memories of his time in captivity, and it hurt me to think of adding to his suffering.

"You don't think we should accept?"

He curled one hand into a fist. "I'd rather kill it. But then, I want all of them dead. So I'm not impartial."

I turned back to the Freak. "Has your tribe ever taken human hostages?" It was the only question I could think to ask that might give Fade some peace with this arrangement. If the answer was affirmative, then I'd turn them down, however grave the consequences might be.

"What is 'hostage'?" it asked.

Tegan offered, "Stolen humans, kept for food?"

"Old ones do. For us, too much trouble. Humans noisy."

"Are the old ones part of the big group you mentioned?" Morrow inquired.

"Yes." The monster snarled, seeming agitated. "No more talk. Deal or no deal?"

I glanced at Fade. "Can you live with this?" Drawing a deep breath, he nodded. We had only this monster's word that his tribe hadn't kidnapped and hurt Fade, but it had to suffice. "Deal. But it will go hard for you if any of your folk break this bargain."

We were already slaughtering them in droves and burning their bodies as a warning and posting their heads on pickets. The men had even started taking fangs to wear on leather thongs around their necks, trophies from our kills. I wasn't sure I had it in me to do worse, but the Freak didn't know that. It seemed to take my threat seriously as it lowered its face almost to the ground. A glance at John Kelley said he was taking it all in, eyes huge in his weathered face.

"Why *aren't* you with the horde?" Tegan asked, frowning in puzzlement. "You'd have a better chance of surviving."

" 'Horde' is big group?" At my friend's nod, the monster replied, "Horde wrong. Better to die than follow. Good-bye, Huntress."

Morrow exhaled in a long rush. "That sounded like a moral judgment."

They know of me? I was stunned into silence.

When the Freak ran off, Kelley rubbed his bristly jaw. "That was . . . something. Did you notice how it showed submission there at the end?"

Fade nodded. "It made my flesh crawl, hearing it speak. I'm not used to thinking of them as anything but mindless monsters."

He wasn't alone in that.

Morrow tipped his head toward the woods. "That's our cue. We should tell the others, then pack things up. We've won a concession from the Freaks, and the colonel needs to know that it's possible."

I didn't know whether it was the best course to abandon the ground we'd only recently gained but with the first snow due any day now, I couldn't rationalize keeping us in the field much longer. Historically speaking, the winter months slowed Freak activity. They might be faster and stronger and might be able to go longer without food and water, but they froze just like humans. The horde might diminish through starvation by the time spring rolled around again.

I could hope anyway.

"Let's give it two days, make sure we don't see any movement. They might've put a sentry near the camp to see how we respond."

"If there are any Freaks in the wood," Fade said, "then the scouts will find them."

Homeward

Though we waited the full two days, the scouts spotted no Freaks within the posted boundary. At that point, I gave orders for us to move out. It was just as well, for as we gathered the last of our supplies, the first white flakes drifted down through the bare branches. I was a little sorry to be leaving, but we couldn't survive the winter here. Game would be scarce, and exposure would end us.

John Kelley traveled with us to Soldier's Pond. "I was on my way there anyway. The trip to see about your smoke signal was a detour."

That reminded me. "Is that common? Once, somebody saved us because he saw our fire. Does it usually mean the party needs help?"

"Depends," Kelley answered. "But often, yes. A smart traveler doesn't light a fire, unless he needs it for some vital reason, and he never lets it get big enough to be seen for miles. Anybody who does is essentially inviting all travelers in the area. It could be benign, a request to trade, could be somebody's sick or hurt, could be a trap. So it's best to be prepared if you ever answer one like I did."

Like Longshot had.

"I understand."

"I feel like I have to ask. Is everything that rascal Morrow told me true?"

"About me?" I shrugged. "Some of it. Not the part where I was raised by wolves, suckled by bears, and that I can fly."

Kelley laughed. Before he could respond, though, we were approaching Soldier's Pond, close enough that the guard called out in surprise, "I thought the lot of you were dead. You've been gone a long time."

Morrow shouted back, "Tell the colonel she owes me a drink."

That made no sense at all to me, but I didn't have the chance to ask what he meant as the guards were lowering the defenses to permit us inside. The town looked more or less the same, squads running even in this weather, all dressed in drab green. Soldiers at the gate peppered us with questions about where we'd been—what towns, what was it like out there—and it occurred to me this wasn't so different from Salvation. People were being strangled in Soldier's Pond in the name of security. Colonel Park kept them safe, at the cost of their spirits. More than ever, I wanted to change the prevailing conditions so that people could visit nearby Winterville or Otterburn without losing their lives.

"This way," Morrow said, sidestepping the questions. Over his shoulder he called, "If you wanted to share our adventures, you should've signed on. Now you'll have to wonder."

That was unlike him, but the rest of us followed. People watched and whispered as we passed through. A few of them called out to John Kelley, who apparently wasn't a stranger. He'd probably visited the same towns we had, only with less resistance and difficulty. A woman stopped him and asked for news in Appleton. He waved to let me know he'd be along.

The lot of us went directly to HQ in all our forest dirt. It wasn't as bad as it might've been since there was a brook nearby, but scrubbing with pine branches was scratchy, incomplete, and left you smelling of sap. I hadn't washed my hair properly in weeks. But I wasn't worried about any of that as Morrow interrupted the colonel's meeting with the grand pleasure of someone about to prove a point.

I opened my mouth, but he shushed me. Glancing at the others, I decided they had no idea of his agenda, but I obeyed and quieted. At that point, he spun an impressive tale of a long journey and an impossible goal full of obstacles and monsters. That was when I figured out he was crafting a *proper* story about what we'd accomplished since we left. When he finished, every soul in the building was quiet, even Colonel Park.

She stared at him. "Swear to me on your mother's name, everything you've said is true."

"The meat and bone of it," he promised. "I always paint a pretty face, but I never lie, Emilia." Then, to my surprise—and I think everyone in the room—he kissed both her cheeks. Clearly I didn't understand their relationship. "This changes everything."

"I didn't think it was possible for those monsters to learn," she said, almost to herself.

I spoke for the first time. "They're definitely changing."

It wasn't clear to me what our role was in Soldier's Pond. We didn't report to her, but it seemed polite to offer what knowledge we'd gathered in exchange for supplies and shelter. So I picked up where Morrow's tale left off, and I filled in details, mostly related to altered Freak behavior, but also about towns we'd visited and the deal the Freaks had offered Otterburn.

Her normally detached expression faltered, revealing a trace of pure horror. She mastered it swiftly, but not before I saw the truth. The colonel averted her eyes, directing them to her maps. With a pencil she outlined the territory we had secured.

"So this is promised to be Mutie-free?"

I nodded. "We weren't fighting the horde, just hunting parties, but it should help. If the larger group decides to attack, however, the truce means nothing."

"It's more than I thought you'd achieve when you set out," she admitted.

"Just think what we could do if your men weren't all such cowards," Stalker said flatly.

Things went downhill from there. Shortly afterward, I left HQ, longing for a bath and to see my family, definitely in that order. I shrugged deeper into the coat Edmund had made for me—it was soft leather lined in fleece shorn from the sheep they kept in the animal pens. That part of town was noisy and smelly, unavoidable when space was limited. In Soldier's Pond they addressed that by making people sleep in narrow cots stacked one atop another; there was little focus on private space like there had been in Salvation. In some ways, this town was more like down below with its focus on duty to the collective, the dearth of amenities, and savorless food. On the plus side, they didn't seem to mind who did the killing or wore pants. From what I could see, everybody here worked as a Hunter. They just had to turn their hands to other jobs too. That probably explained why the clothes were poorly sewn and the food was terrible. Anyone with a grain of sense knew you needed Builders like Edmund too.

"I'll meet you in the mess for dinner," I said to Fade, who kissed the top of my head.

I lifted a hand in farewell and hurried to the bathhouse, empty at this time of day. The scarcity of the sun meant the water was only a little better than ice cold; I bore it, though the soft soap didn't lather much and it took me twice as long to scrape the wilderness out of my hair. After, I dug out the clean traveling clothes I kept aside for special occasions. As I tugged on the dun brown trousers with a tie at the waist, I knew a moment's regret for the loss of the dresses I hadn't even wanted at first. But by the time I had my shirt on, my lovely, polished boots, and the lined jacket, I didn't care so much. It was better to be warm than pretty.

My hair went into neat plaits, and I hoped they didn't freeze as I stepped out into the biting air. The snow had followed us from the forest, white stars now slanting downward from a gray sky. I ran all the way to the house where I'd find my parents waiting; it was late enough that Edmund might even be done at the workshop. To my delight, I found all of them there, just gathering for dinner.

"Deuce!" Momma Oaks had her arms around me before I was halfway in the door.

"I don't think I ever said it, but I love you all . . . very much."

Edmund and Rex both grabbed me close until I was squashed on all sides. It was pretty close to the best I ever felt. I tried to hug my whole family at the same time but my arms weren't long enough. My mother kissed me all over my cold cheeks. Her eyes were sparkling when she stepped back to look at me.

"Well, you're not bleeding, so I take it your mission was a success?"

"In a manner of speaking. I'll tell you all about it over dinner."

"Are you home for a while?" Edmund asked.

They got their own coats and stepped out. My father stared up anxiously at the sky, and I could tell without him saying it that he was worried about us traveling in this weather. "I think so. There isn't a whole lot we can do during the snowy months."

Momma Oaks nodded in satisfaction. "It's odd here, but we're pulling our weight, and the men seem to like Edmund's work awfully well."

"I imagine." I'd seen what they wore before; Edmund's shoes were magical by comparison.

"They've got us making leather grips for weapons," Rex put in.

"I suspect they'll make a permanent exception for you," I said. "If you want to stay."

"Where would we go?" Momma Oaks asked.

It was an excellent question. So far, in my travels, I hadn't found a place I thought would suit them better. Considering all the soldiers, the metal defenses, and cache of weapons, plus the extra breathing room I'd won from the Freaks, I couldn't fathom a safer place. Whether they were happy and comfortable, if they actually felt at home, those were questions I didn't dare ask.

To my astonishment, when I strode into the mess hall, applause broke out. Some of the men rose to their feet and saluted me, just like they did the colonel or some other important person who ran around barking orders. I glanced over my shoulder in reflex, thinking they must mean somebody else, and Edmund nudged me.

"You have to acknowledge them somehow, so they can go back to their meals."

This was all completely new to me, so I racked my brain for what would serve, then I touched my brow with two fingers as Longshot had when he was being respectful of some good idea. The soldiers loved it; some stomped their feet, and others banged cutlery on the table until the cook yelled at them to pipe down.

"My goodness," Momma Oaks said. "What in the world did you do out there?"

"Let's get our food, then I'll tell you."

The story was half over, though not as exciting as Morrow made it sound, when Fade arrived. Since the rest of us had barely touched our meals, he had plenty of time to catch up. Rex and Edmund offered their hands to shake and Momma Oaks contented herself with a warm smile, though she wanted to squeeze him. But she was an observant woman, and she'd doubtless noticed the way he pulled his body in when surrounded by people.

"You missed the hero's welcome," I teased.

Fade shrugged. "That was for you anyway."

"We all earned it."

"I'm just so proud of you," Momma Oaks said.

Once, that kind of remark would've puzzled me. She'd had nothing to do with my training, so why would she feel anything about my accomplishments? But now I knew that love made her care about all things related to me—and I felt the same way. I would never tell them, because it would worry them more, but I might be more interested in waiting out the time until I was old enough to enlist, and then just quietly joining the soldiers here, if it wasn't for them. But I wanted them to be happy; I wanted to give them a home as snug and safe as the one they'd freely offered me. Accomplishing that required more than mere patience.

My family asked us questions others didn't think to pose, like what kind of shoes and clothes they wore in other towns. Did I think they could master the patterns? Dinner passed in an agreeable fashion, and as we left, Fade whispered, "I could really use some time alone with you."

There was no privacy in the bunks where we all slept, and I didn't know of any conveniently empty houses here. I must've looked conflicted because he added, low, "Just meet me out back after everyone's asleep."

Then Edmund dragged him off to see some improvements he'd made to the workshop and Rex went along. That left me to walk back to the house with Momma Oaks. She put an arm around my shoulders, which took some doing as I was a little taller than she was. I hunched a little to make it easier, and she gave me that glowing look, the one that said all kinds of happy things, like, *I love you* and *I'm proud* and *I'm thrilled you're here.*

Before I met the Oakses, nobody much cared about my comings-and-goings, so long as I followed orders.

"I've been wondering about something," I said, as we stepped into the house.

This time, I got a better look at the place, and I saw she'd made it homier. The beds had been moved to a less rigid arrangement, and she'd found some chairs—or maybe Rex or Edmund had built them. There were other small touches as well: wall hangings that I was sure she'd made from scraps of cloth, most of which were green. It seemed to be the only color this settlement knew how to produce.

"What's that?"

"Some people have two names, like you and John Kelley, the trapper we met. Why?"

"The first is the name my parents gave me, the last a family one." She fixed a stern look on me. "And you do have a second name, missy. You're Deuce Oaks. We claimed you as ours, and I'll tell Edmund if I hear any nonsense about you rejecting our surname."

I was astonished. "Nobody told me that joining a family meant taking their name."

"I suppose not." Her gaze softened.

"But what about Fade? Is he a Jensen now?" I curled one hand into a fist, ready to fight at the idea that he had to carry a permanent reminder of the man who'd hurt him.

She shook her head. "He's one of ours too."

"So we're *both* Oakses?" I asked.

"To my mind, you are. I love that boy like a son."

"But if I'm your daughter and he's your son—"

She cut me off with a harried wave of one hand. "Don't make things complicated, Deuce. There's no blood relation."

That wasn't even what I was about to say. I knew I wasn't

related to Fade on the bloodline tree, so that we could breed, should I want that down the line. "No, you told me once that when people join up and make their promises, they take the same name. Does that mean Fade and I already did that?" I was a little confused by this point.

She sighed. "No. But you're all set for when you do."

I liked how she had no doubt that we belonged together—like the day boy and the night girl, we'd end up together forever. That was good enough for me . . . but much as I was enjoying this reunion, I couldn't wait until my family fell asleep.

Interlude

The moon was a silver crescent brightening the gauzy veil of the midnight sky. With the snow still coming down in lazy flutters, I saw the cold in the smoky whorls of my breath. I gazed up as I followed Fade silently. My feet crunched on the layer of snow, untouched apart from the watchmen who patrolled the town at night. There wasn't a curfew, but if they caught us wandering at this hour, there would be questions. I didn't imagine they would look kindly on "we missed sparking" as an answer.

Fade's hand was warm when he wrapped it around mine. He tugged. "Come on."

"Where are we going?" I asked.

He shushed me with such obvious delight that I didn't have the heart to ask again. He wanted to surprise me, so I let him. Our destination was a medium-size building with smoke wafting up. That meant there was a fire lit inside, and considering how cold it had become and how much snow had accumulated during the day, I was glad to see it. After jiggling the door just so, he popped it open. Within lay some kind of meeting place, but more comfortable than HQ. Instead of tables there were padded chairs and sofas scattered throughout. Shelving contained a few old books, most in worse condition than *The Day Boy and the Night Girl.*

"What is this?" I asked, stepping in.

"The officers' club. It's where they go in their off hours to drink and avoid their families."

That sounded odd. "Are you sure nobody will catch us?"

He shook his head. "They're asleep by now. I've come here to think more than once, and nobody bothered me. The enlisted men are afraid of punishment, so they don't trespass. As long as we don't turn on any lights or make a ton of noise, none of the watchmen will come in."

The fire had burned down low, so Fade moved to stir it, churning the glowing orange sparks through the ashes, then he added a length of wood from the pile. With careful management, the blaze caught, then he beckoned me to the sofa nearest the hearth. It was old and worn, like most things in Soldier's Pond; I could see where the leather had been poorly patched.

It was toasty in here compared with the outdoors. I imagined being in the woods and shivered. Fade pulled me down beside him, probably believing I was cold. I didn't enlighten him as I settled against his side. Warmth prickled over my skin, both from the cheerful fire and his proximity.

"This is a nice surprise." I hadn't known there was anyplace we could escape to, here.

"It's not the same," he said.

I knew what he meant. The first night we stayed together, there had been candles and kissing, whispered words and inexpressible sweetness.

"There's only one way to find out."

Holding his gaze with mine, I waited until he offered permission in the form of a quick nod. Then I touched his cheek with gentle fingertips, tracing over to his temple. I feathered my hand into his hair. His breath caught, but I didn't think it was because I was hurting or scaring him. Still, I paused to make sure he was still with me. His eyes were dark and hot, half lidded.

"More," he whispered.

I obliged. Shaping his head with my fingertips, I petted him as I had done the night he slept with his head in my lap. And by his expression, he remembered. Maybe I could help by reminding him of all the good feelings that came along with being touched. I was slow and gentle, no sudden movements, and when I grazed the nape of his neck with my nails, he actually shivered. Fade leaned closer, then wrapped his arms around me. He didn't seem to be thinking at all anymore, his face soft and dreamy.

When he kissed the side of my throat, I bit my lip. It felt surprisingly good. He followed with more kisses just beneath my jaw. His skin rasped slightly against mine, reminding me that he was a man, not a boy, and he'd shaved off the scruffy beard grown over weeks in the wild. My heartbeat quickened as his mouth grew more heated, and he hadn't even touched my lips. He was breathing fast when he put a hand on my shoulder. He urged me back on the sofa, and I let him because I had the odd desire for him to cover me like a blanket. Fade made a satisfied sound as he lay down, and then he kissed me.

My eyes closed. The feeling exploded like embers of the fire, kindling into a full burn. It was a summer sky of a kiss, breathless and endlessly blue, full of berry sweetness and sunshine. That long, luxuriant tasting turned into smaller kisses, our lips touching again and again, until we were both shivering, despite the warmth of the room. Fade drew back and framed my face in his palms; I could see powerful emotion working in his eyes.

"I was afraid," he whispered. "But I was wrong to be. This . . . this is still perfect, even if I'm not."

"I'm not, either," I whispered.

I moved beneath him and his expression grew pained. He pushed back before he could help himself, teasing us both. In that moment, I'd have given him anything.

"This is . . ." He trailed off as I settled beneath him, finding the right fit.

"We could." I knew exactly what I was suggesting.

"Not here, with no guarantee of privacy. It should be special."

Fade shifted then, drawing me into his arms. We twined like tree and vine, his legs tangled with mine, and I lay so I could feel the warmth of the fire on my back. I kissed his neck.

"I love you." His voice came low and rough.

"I love you too." My response was smooth and easy, as if I had been waiting my whole life to offer him those words. No doubts, no hesitations. This feeling was woven through me until it seemed like it would kill me to root it out.

"Thanks for not giving up on me."

"Have you ever known me to walk away from a fight?" I cocked a brow in challenge.

Fade laughed softly. "Never."

"We should get back before someone catches us . . . or Momma Oaks notices we're gone."

With a groan, he let go of me. I took that for agreement. As we slipped out of the officers' club, the night was still quiet with the moon reflecting off the new fallen snow. Our tracks had been covered so we made new ones back to the barracks.

But Fade left me there with a rueful shake of his head. "I can't come to bed yet. I'm going for a run."

I blushed because I understood why. So I slid into bed, but not before Momma Oaks raised up on an elbow and fixed me with a sleepy, pointed look. It said, *You haven't gotten away with anything.* For some reason, I wanted to laugh, but that would wake Edmund and Rex, so I just rolled into my blankets. I barely stirred when Fade got into the bunk above mine.

And in the morning, everything was different.

I didn't understand the shift at first, but soldiers I didn't know greeted me by name. A few stopped me to ask about the Freak fang necklaces my men wore, and a sentry called down from the tower, "Let's hear it for Company D!"

In the mess, I found my men all sitting together, including Stalker's scouts. They waved me over to join them. I brought my food, surprised by their camaraderie. Both success and failure created bonds, I supposed, and we'd seen our share of each while we traveled.

"Does anyone know why we're getting VIP treatment?" Tully wanted to know.

"What's a VIP?" I was glad Stalker asked, because I didn't know, either.

"Very important person." Morrow grinned. "I might've had something to do with that. Between my account of the treaty and the talking Freak, they think we can move mountains."

"Deuce especially," Spence noted.

I mumbled a curse. "What did you *tell* them?"

"So what's the plan for the spring campaign?" Thornton interrupted, changing the subject.

They took it for granted we'd be going out again—that we wouldn't rest on our laurels once the cold weather passed. In all honesty, I had no grand scheme, but I didn't care to disappoint them. So I considered while I ate my breakfast, listening to them swap jests. Fade sat beside me, quiet, but not in a sad or brooding way, more quietly watchful, the way he'd been before the Freaks took him.

"Scouting first," I said in the first lull. "After the thaw. To plan, I need intel on how much of the horde survived the winter. Fortunately, the Muties aren't as good at strategy yet."

"Yet," Tully muttered.

I nodded at her. "Who knows how fast they'll catch on? Once we know how many are left and where they're headed, we can decide what to do."

Nobody laughed or said that twelve soldiers couldn't make a difference. We already had.

"You know my favorite part of this?" Spence grinned as he asked the question.

I shook my head. "What?"

"We're all off the regular duty rosters. That means no midnight watches, no patrols outside the fence, no cooking, cleaning the bathhouse, or working in the animal sheds."

Thornton smirked. "That *is* a boon. I can't remember the last time I had an easy winter."

"If anyone complains," Morrow put in, "tell them you're part of Company D."

I glanced at Tegan, who shook her head. "I heard it, but I don't know what it means."

"It's our squad name," Morrow said.

"Who came up with it?" Stalker asked.

The storyteller's expression grew crafty. "The men who want to join up. I've been spreading the word about our success, and they decided the squad should be named after Deuce."

I suspected there might be more to say, but he didn't, and I was too delighted at learning we had more potential recruits to pursue the matter. That day, ten men approached me quietly and asked whether I'd consider letting them volunteer when we marched out for the second time, Harry Carter among them. He'd wanted to come before, but he wasn't strong enough. Whether it was the first taste of success or the idea of getting off the duty roster, I wasn't sure, but I told all of them that they were welcome. The following night, I spoke to five more.

A week later, Zach Bigwater approached me. He was the only member of his family to survive the fire, and for a while, I didn't know whether he'd make it. For weeks, he didn't speak and it was a chore for Tegan to get him to eat. But he came to me that afternoon.

"I want to join Company D," he said without preamble.

"Why?"

"Because I'm tired of feeling helpless."

"I think you need to tell me what happened in Salvation."

He squeezed his eyes shut. "So many people died because of me."

"The town was under siege. It wasn't your fault."

"It was," he said heavily. "I ran and hid. I was paralyzed when the walls came down. I should've told somebody sooner about the tunnel, but I couldn't make myself move, even as people died all around me. I'm a coward."

His actions didn't recommend him as a volunteer, but I thought I understood why he wanted to fight. "And you're looking to redeem yourself now, prove something?"

"If it's possible," he whispered.

"Then welcome aboard." I'd keep an eye on him, but I couldn't turn anyone away.

The number of fresh volunteers trickled off as the weeks wore on, and the snow piled higher. During the cold months, I kept my men sharp. I asked for—and received—an indoor training yard. The colonel responded with her typical ambivalence . . . and put us in the cowshed. With the animals in their stalls, there was room for us to spar . . . and I pushed the others, myself as well. We drilled hard, practiced fighting as a group, worked out silent command signals and battle strategies for all kinds of scenarios. Word got out about our sessions, and the men who had asked to join up, but were not yet officially part of Company D, worked in their off hours, concerned about keeping up with us.

By the time the snow started to melt, we were all stronger, and Tegan was a wonder with her staff, banded properly with metal for optimal impact. All over Soldier's Pond, they called us an elite unit, which meant we were really good at fighting.

To my astonishment, I trotted out Silk's old lectures. *I think she'd be pleased.* "Don't waste your energy. Kill quickly. We'll be battling superior numbers, so save your strength. No showing off, just take your opponent down, then move on to the next."

I watched them spar for a few seconds, shaking my head. "Thornton, you're working too hard. Yes, you're a brute, but crushing skulls is exhausting. I need you to kill faster."

"I'm an old man." But it wasn't a protest; it was a statement— unbelievable to have this grizzled veteran taking criticism from me so readily. "Show me an easier way."

Over the past month, it had become apparent that he had little hand-to-hand training, so I put him with Stalker. Eventually I got him to use two small hand axes instead of weights in his fists. The blades were heavy enough that he felt comfortable with them, well suited to efficient hacking motions that should drop Freaks quicker.

In early March, Stalker and five scouts went out to locate the horde. It was a risky mission, and I worried the whole time they were gone. The rest of us continued training; I had to feel confident we'd function as a unit when we moved out. A week later, the scouting party returned, half frozen and starved, but full of interesting information. Stalker dismissed the others while he and I went to the mess. It wasn't open for meals, but there were always drinks available.

I poured two mugs of herbal tea from the warm pot and settled at our usual table. Stalker's skin was ruddy and chapped, his lips split. Despite melting snow and occasional bursts of sunshine, the weather was still raw. I hoped that meant bad things for the enemy. With so many animals in hibernation, game was scarce this time of year. With any luck, the horde had to turn most of its attention to finding food rather than attacking human settlements.

"It's bad," he said quietly. "Appleton is gone."

That hit me hard. They'd laughed at us there, less extreme than the hanging they threatened in Gaspard, but still bad enough that I had unpleasant memories of the place. Appleton was bigger than Salvation, but less defensible; I suspected it hadn't been a problem when the Freaks were scattered nuisances. People who hadn't seen the horde before it swept down on them couldn't imagine the sheer numbers . . . or the horror, so I didn't blame them for the reaction, but it was horrible they'd paid such a high price for their skepticism.

"Survivors?"

"No. They butchered the townsfolk, and the horde seems to be digging in. Looked like fewer bodies than last time, but there's still a couple thousand of them."

"I hoped the cold would cull more of them."

Stalker shook his head, sipping his hot drink. "I bet that's why they took Appleton. They're roasting the townsfolk, plus they have shelter and supplies. They'll be fine until spring."

This was just the kind of news I dreaded. I was sure Appleton's relative lack of defenses had contributed to the horde's decision to sack that town first. Soldier's Pond would've required a lot more time and effort. And in the cold with a weakening force, it made sense to take out a soft target. Come spring, however, every town in the territories would be at risk.

"Will you tell the colonel?" I asked.

He nodded, offering a half-smile. "I appreciate you asking me instead of ordering."

"You run the scouts, not me. I just thought she might benefit from the information."

If the loss of a town within two weeks of travel didn't alarm her, the colonel wasn't as smart as I thought. This gave the horde a terrifying foothold in the area. When the weather improved, they'd consider what target to eliminate next. If they came to

Soldier's Pond, it'd mean a long, ugly siege. Eventually, the Freaks would figure out how to get around—or tear down—the fences, or the ammo stockpile would run out.

I couldn't let that happen to my family. Not again.

Entreaty

I t was just after the noon meal when the messenger arrived
from Winterville. I had been braced for bad news since I
heard Stalker's report, so I wasn't surprised by the urgency.
The runner was ragged and thin; and by his various wounds, he
wasn't accustomed to traveling. The odd thing about his injuries, though . . . they didn't look as if a Freak had inflicted them.
I strode up to the guards listening to his breathless stammers—
and my status in town had changed to the point that none of
them questioned my presence. They were used to seeing me
roam in and out of HQ, consulting with Colonel Park on concerns she didn't share with anyone but her advisors.

"We need help," the man was gasping.

"Muties?" Morgan asked. I had learned that he was married to
the colonel, not that they were effusive in their public affections.

Since Winterville was closer than Salvation, it was possible
we could mount a successful defense, depending on the nature
of the attack. The weather wasn't ideal for mobilizing, but if we
packed well and moved fast, we might be able to hit them from
behind. As I recalled, the research annex was mostly built from
a peculiar, wrinkled metal, so at least it wouldn't burn before we
got there. The rest of the houses might well be gone, however.

The messenger shook his head, startling us all. "Dr. Wilson

said to find Deuce. He said to tell her there's trouble on the south side—that she'll know what it means."

I bit out a curse. Whatever they had done with their feral humans, containment must've failed. And from what I recalled of Winterville, they had no dedicated warriors. It was an odd little town, no mistake, but that didn't mean they all deserved to be killed because Wilson was a madman who invented crazy potions and tested them on his own people.

"Get this man some medical attention," I said to the guards. "Then find him some hot food. I'll take it from here."

It wasn't until I was walking away, and I heard Morgan say, "Come on, we'll take you to see Doc Tegan first," that it fully sank in just how much things had changed.

Those men took my orders *without question,* and they weren't even part of Company D. My shoulders squared, and I walked a little taller on the way to HQ. Inside, the colonel was waiting for my word on the situation.

Quickly I summarized the problem, then reminded her of what Wilson had told me. She listened with her usual acuity. Since our go-round earlier in the year when I'd threatened to cut her throat, the colonel treated me with caution and respect. I'd come to the conclusion she wasn't a bad person, but like Silk, she had the ability to make awful choices for the good of the whole. It wasn't a trait I coveted.

"Do you have any idea how many infected souls we're talking about?"

I shook my head. "They won't be as smart as the Muties we've been fighting, though. Wilson said their higher brain function was compromised." Though I wasn't fully clear on what that meant, I guessed they'd be like the Freaks I fought first, down below.

"So you don't know how many men you need."

"I have forty-four at last count." Such a small crew, compared

224

with the horde, but we'd likely be equal to the problems in Winterville.

"Then handle it. By the way, I've decided to commission Company D formally for rescue operations. Given what we know of mutant intentions and numerical advantage, it seems likely more of these requests will arrive. You'll retain command and will assess all threats and determine the best response, according to our resources."

"I thought I wasn't old enough to enlist," I said.

"And you haven't. Elite squads aren't subject to the same regulations." By her smug smile, she was pleased at getting around the rules while still finding a use for my team.

"With respect, sir, I decline your offer. I intend to take anyone who will join up, not just men from Soldier's Pond." I struggled with how to word my explanation. "Our cause still isn't about defending towns . . . Company D is meant to end the Mutie threat. So while we'll handle appeals for help if they come while we're in town, I can't guarantee we will be. The fight's out there, and I intend to be too, as long as the weather holds. Right now, we don't have the numbers to face the horde, but someday . . ." I trailed off, my meaning plain.

This time, she didn't laugh.

"I understand." Her eyes were sad, but her tone was brisk when she added, "You'll need to brief your men and get moving. No telling how bad it is in Winterville."

"Yes, sir." I didn't salute her when I left, as the others did.

Colonel Park wasn't my leader. I shared information with her out of respect, not obligation. I'd meant it when I said she'd get nothing else out of me. I wasn't a little black piece on her maps, willing to move against the red markers at her will.

When I met the men, already assembled in the shed for afternoon training, I gave them the quick rundown. I finished with "Get your gear. We're moving in an hour."

It didn't take long to raid my footlocker and pack my things. I was lacing up my boots when Momma Oaks found me. She was carrying a bundle; I first thought she'd made some more clothes. Then she unfolded the fabric, and the shape marked it as wrong for a shirt or a gown.

The material was plain, the first I'd seen since my arrival that hadn't been dyed olive drab. She had cut it into a triangle and banded the edges in green. Square in the middle sat a stitched version of my personal token, a black spade with a two on top of it. The dark symbol looked powerful against the pale background, more so because she'd embroidered a red border. She had precious few supplies left from her seamstress work in Salvation, and I couldn't believe she'd used them up to make such a thing for me.

I also didn't know what it was.

"It's a pennant," she explained. "I read in a book where warriors used to fly their colors when they went to war, so all their enemies would see them and despair."

This . . . this was the truest love. She hated it every time I went out, but because she loved me, she supported me, even though it scared her. A fist tightened around my heart.

"Thank you," I said. "It's wonderful. How am I supposed to display it?"

"On a short pole, I think. I have Edmund working on it."

"We're leaving soon," I said, hating to disappoint her.

"I know. He'll be along shortly." Momma Oaks paused. "Do you trust me, Deuce?"

"Of course."

"Then let me have your token."

My hand went to the hidden pocket in my shirt reflexively. Over the course of my travels, the card had become more bloodstained, but I had never lost it. I fought the urge to ask why; instead I proved my faith by producing it and offering it to her without a word. My mother smiled as she got out her needle, then she sewed the card into the center of the banner.

"Now it's finished. This represents your fighting spirit and I truly believe as long as you keep it safe, you cannot fail."

Tears sprang to my eyes at how she had combined her greatest skill with my custom, one she probably didn't even believe in. Shakily I hugged her and whispered, "Thank you."

She pushed out a long breath, then said, "Rex wants to go with you."

I froze. "How do you feel about that?"

"When we first arrived, he was grieving over Ruth, and I was afraid he'd do something foolish. But now it's been long enough . . ." I heard what she didn't say. She wanted him to follow his heart, even if it was worrisome.

"He hasn't said anything to me or attended any of our drills. Tell him if he still wants to join up, it needs to be after he's worked with us some."

"He'll ask why you've accepted strangers over him, no questions asked."

"Because they're trained soldiers and he's not. It would be irresponsible to take him into action without first teaching him how to fight."

"That sounds fair." She was visibly relieved that we weren't both marching off today.

I ended the discussion with a hug, but I couldn't linger. It wouldn't look good if I ordered the men to be ready in an hour and I showed up late. *Lead by example,* Silk always said—and though I didn't agree with everything she'd shouted at me, that tenet stuck. Momma Oaks accompanied me to the gate, and as she'd promised, Edmund arrived soon after with a light metal rod. It wasn't so long it would be unwieldy or so heavy it would be a problem to carry. In efficient motions, she stitched the pennant to the pole while I counted heads. Fade was here, Thornton and Tegan too . . . Zach Bigwater, Harry Carter, all the scouts, along with Morrow, Tully, and Spence. I'd memorized all the men's names because they weren't numbers to me. I ran down the roster mentally.

"Everyone's present," I said. "Company D, move out."

It was a miserable march, though our official flag cheered the men up considerably. They took turns carrying it and eventually took to wagering over who got the privilege. I had nothing to do with that; they awarded it to one another for whimsical reasons: a good song, stealthy movements, a cheerful tale. Though I expected some of the new men to complain, as they weren't used to life in the field, none of them whined. That was a good start.

The ground was marshy from melting snow and frozen by turns, so I watched my step. Stalker and his scouts ran vanguard, finding us a good, safe route to Winterville. Since I didn't know what we'd face once we arrived, it seemed best not to expend our energies more than necessary. There would definitely be fighting in town, and I hated the thought of killing humans. The handful of times I'd done so, I only enjoyed it once. Gary Miles, the Salvation soldier who thought girls were good for only one purpose, was no loss to the world.

Despite the weather, we made good time.

On the outskirts of Winterville, I waited while Stalker and his scouts surveyed the opposition. The rest of us were tense, listening for any sign that the afflicted were venturing past the Winterville boundaries. Now and again, I heard inhuman shrieks, wordless growls, awful but distinct from any sound I ever heard the Freaks utter.

"This is horrible," Tegan whispered.

I nodded. The scouting party didn't return a moment too soon.

Though the former Wolf was tough, even he was shaken when they returned. "I've never seen anything like it," Stalker said, still panting. "Every house is barricaded from the inside, windows and doors. And the town itself . . ."

"Go on," I prompted.

"There are people everywhere, attacking anything that moves . . . *eating* each other."

Horror ran through me. Regardless whether the scientist, Wilson, had good intentions, he'd experimented without considering the consequences, and it now seemed that his work would end as badly as those that started all the trouble in the first place. *If these people turn into Freaks . . .* With some effort, I curtailed my urge to speculate and focused on the facts.

"How many?" I asked Stalker.

"Seventy-five to a hundred. That's just an estimate."

"Are they working together?"

Stalker shook his head. "No. If anything, they're competing to get into the houses. It's . . . grim, maybe the worst thing I've ever seen. You'll understand when we move in."

Considering what he and I had been through, that was quite a statement. But I didn't doubt him. Armed with this disturbing information, I went back to the others and gave the orders. "We're splitting into four teams of eleven. I'll assign squad leaders to each, and you'll follow their instructions as if I had given them. Understood?"

"Yes, sir," they chorused.

I went on, "We have a devil of a mess to tidy up. While it's true we didn't make it, the people trapped in those houses are counting on us. I have no idea whether what Wilson did to these poor madmen is contagious, so protect yourselves from their teeth."

Tegan bounced, which I took to mean she had something to

add. "Blood can carry diseases, too, so be careful. Try not to get it in your eyes or mouths, and if you have any open wounds, make sure they're covered before the battle begins."

"Anything else, Doc?" She flushed with pleasure when I called her that, but she shook her head. That was the extent of her warnings, apparently.

"Excellent. Some of you may hesitate when it sinks in—that we're fighting people. But remember, there's no help for them. That's the reason Wilson kept them penned up; he was trying to find a cure, but they're broken beyond fixing, and it's a kindness to put them down." The words sounded hard and cold to my own ears, but the men were nodding. "Now then, team leaders: Stalker, Fade, me, Morrow."

The storyteller looked surprised to be called out, but he was smart, and he'd lead his men with the same care and wisdom he'd offered Tegan during their training sessions. To avoid any question of favoritism and for the sake of speed, men counted off by fours and then divided up accordingly. I ended up with Thornton and Spence, but not Tully, along with Tegan, three scouts, Zach Bigwater, and three fresh recruits. It was a good mix of skills with enough veterans that we should be able to compensate if Zach panicked under pressure.

"Everyone knows who's in their squads?" I asked.

They agreed in unison that they did.

"Good. Then, Stalker, you take the eastern section. I'll go west. Fade, you have the north, and, Morrow, you've got the south, where the problem started. But from what Stalker said, there's trouble all over Winterville now."

"I'm clear on the objective," Stalker said.

Morrow inclined his head. "Me too."

But Fade stepped close, gesturing to his men to wait a second. They were checking their weapons, talking in low voices about the fight to come.

He leaned in with a furrowed brow. "Are you positive you want me in charge?"

I understood that he thought he wasn't the Hunter he had been, and he had doubts about his leadership. But Fade needed to stop treading in my shadow; he was every bit as fierce and strong as he had been, maybe more so. Blasted few people could survive an experience like his. Even less would be able to wade into battle afterward. He was one of the strongest, bravest people I'd ever known, and it was past time for him to acknowledge that.

One step at a time.

When I met his gaze, I didn't do so as the girl who loved him or the Huntress partnered with him down below. My tone was firm and cool. "Are you questioning my judgment?"

I read the shock in his gaze, quickly veiled by a thick sweep of lashes. Then he stepped back. "No, sir. I have my assignment."

I pitched my voice to carry. "When you clear your quadrant, head for the lab at the center of town. You can't miss it." I described the building, just in case. "Now let's get this done."

Slaughterhouse

If anything, Stalker understated the chaos and carnage.

Winterville reeked of infection and death. The wind carried the stench from all corners, which told me nothing about where we'd find the afflicted ones. I stepped over a puddle of blood and scanned the area before I led my group west. Bloody palm prints stood out in sharp relief on the pale metal of the buildings. Zach Bigwater was an unknown quantity, but fortunately, I had veterans to compensate for his inexperience, and the rest of my team should be competent. My nerves drew taut as I listened. With a glance at Tegan, I confirmed that she heard it too.

Forty paces on, we ran into the source of the noise. Ten feral humans surrounded a house, scrabbling at the barricaded windows, and their utter wrongness pierced me like a blade. As we approached, they turned—an uncontrollable impulse more than a decision—and ran at us with lips curled away from their teeth. I caught a glimpse of rabid eyes with starbursts of blood in the corners, normal human hands with nails untended until they were curled and yellow.

Though I'd cautioned my people not to hesitate, I hated it when I drew my knives. These people didn't deserve this; Wilson had done it to them—with the best of intentions—but still, their suffering could be laid at his door. When the first lunged at me, I saw that he was Edmund's age. He might've been a farmer before, a normal man who loved his family and hated parsnips. *Please, give me the strength to do what's needed.*

With a rush of sorrow, I took him down, and that kill set the tone for everyone else. I glanced around for Tegan, but she was executing the staff maneuvers Morrow had taught her with complete precision. We all accounted for one except for Zach; he froze while the rest of us defended. Afterward, he hunched and lost his breakfast.

"How *can* you?" he asked in a low whisper. "They were *people.*"

Tears filled Tegan's eyes. "I know. But it was a mercy. They couldn't ever be who they were again. If they were in their right minds, it wouldn't be necessary."

I checked all the bodies to make sure they were dead, taking care with their blood as Tegan had suggested. Thornton watched, then he etched what I'd learned was the sign of the cross. I'd seen Morgan do that as well; and he had explained it had spiritual significance when I asked. My family had religion, but they didn't favor that gesture.

"What's wrong?" I asked him.

"Lying there, they look so normal, almost like us," the older man answered.

"I know."

It *was* eerie. This was what it must've been like long ago, before everyone changed; I glimpsed the Freak genesis in these poor lunatics, and it chilled me to the bone. With care, I closed all the eyes, so they weren't staring at the sky with eternal hunger. At last, satisfied they were all dead, I straightened, though part of me couldn't help a primitive fear that these corpses would rise and shamble after us. Apparently the others felt the same because they backed off, and didn't turn until we moved more than fifty paces away.

I fell into step with Zach, keeping my tone low so the others couldn't hear, though they might well guess what I was saying. "The next fight might be more challenging, and we can't carry your weight. Don't let me down."

He nodded, looking ashamed. "It won't happen again, I promise."

I felt for him, this boy who had lost his whole family, and now had to learn to fight when that hadn't been his role from the beginning, as it had mine. But in this world, people had to adapt, or they died. Cowardice would haunt him all his life, if he didn't find the courage to raise a weapon and hold his ground. It wasn't that I thought people who couldn't fight were worthless; that judgment came from deep inside the kid. He needed to earn his own self-respect.

The next group ran at us from around a corner. There were no telltale sounds, but in a blink, there were twenty on top of us. I should've smelled them, but the miasma hung over the whole town; the stink was horrendous, and they were near starvation. Some had gnawed their own flesh—or maybe they'd done it to each other—but the bites were infected and livid, sour milk flesh imprinted with savage red teeth marks.

Our drills held up, though. The men fell into a circle as we had practiced, forcing the enemy to push through if they wanted to surround us. I expected Zach to falter again, but this time he brought his knives up and held the line. We were outnumbered, but these were creatures of madness and hunger, the way the old Freaks had been. They knew nothing of tactics or strategy, only of the need burning like fire in their blood. The fight became an intricate dance of death. When Tegan swung her staff to sweep the legs and knocked one down, Thornton finished it with an efficient blow from his hatchet.

I worked with Zach, keeping them off him while he discovered his confidence. He might not be a natural warrior but he was determined, offering a block and feint to draw the snapping teeth. That opened the throat, and I cut it, then followed with a kick to avoid the spraying blood. Some spattered on my pants, but it couldn't be helped. Spence worked as he usually did with knife, gun, and boot. I didn't count how many I killed; I just fought until they all lay dead.

"Injuries?" I asked. "Any bites?"

There was a heavy, fraught silence while everyone scrutinized their fellows.

"Me." Danbury was one of the new men, recently recruited. He cradled his forearm, and as I stepped closer, I saw the purple bruise with a scarlet heart where teeth had broken the skin. The wound would heal, but I glimpsed raw fear in his eyes.

"You can't become a Freak through bites," I said, though it was a hollow reassurance. "Maybe this isn't catching the same way."

Tegan offered, "I told you to avoid the blood as a precaution. These people went mad after exposure to that potion Dr. Wilson created, not from biting each other."

"You should shoot me," Danbury said. "Just in case."

I shook my head. "We'll finish clearing the town, then I need to have words with Dr. Wilson. I'll ask him if there's any risk."

Danbury curled his hand into a fist. "If I go wrong, promise me you won't let me turn into that."

I gazed down at the bodies. "I'll take care of you. Don't worry." The statement sounded tender when it was, in fact, a pledge to end his life.

"Let me clean and wrap it." Tegan took the soldier's arm. She put on thin leather gloves, then poured antiseptic into the bite to flush it. Afterward, she smeared some healing salve and bound it with a length of cloth. The soldiers watched her as if mesmerized; I didn't know if it was the grace of her movements or the silent threat of what might lie beneath the bandage.

Spence holstered his gun. "This is no challenge at all. I'm surprised the townsfolk couldn't handle them."

Thornton added, "It helps that they're stupid and weak."

"The people here aren't trained to fight," Zach put in.

He was right; it made a difference. Most folks, when confronted by a nightmare, tended to run and hide. It was a rare soul that took up whatever weapon came to hand with no prior experience. But somebody else might be able to explain why most people fled and one in a hundred decided to do battle.

After that, we met only stragglers, one so weak he was on his knees when we encountered him. Spence murmured, "Poor sod," and put a bullet in his head. The madman tipped over backward, and I swear at the moment of death, he was relieved to have it done—or maybe that was just what I wanted to see in his tormented features because otherwise this day would create a weight too heavy to carry.

"I'd like to speak with this Dr. Wilson, too." Thornton smacked the haft of his hand ax against his palm, which I took to mean he wanted to lop off the scientist's head.

I held up a hand, signaling quiet. After few seconds, I was certain. There were more nearby. How many, I couldn't be sure. I wished Stalker had been able to provide a more accurate count. The men moved behind me, their fang-and-bone necklaces rattling. Down the street I found the source of the noise. This house had proven unable to withstand the onslaught, and the front door stood open like a gaping wound. A blood trail led inside.

I swallowed back my dread, whispering, "There won't be room for all of us. I need four with me, six outside on guard."

"I'm with you," Thornton said.

Spence didn't answer, but he stepped closer. Then Zach moved in . . . and Danbury. Those two wouldn't have been my first choices, but it was better for squad morale if I didn't play favorites. The house was dark with the windows shuttered, shadows heavy as the souls of the dead. I inhaled, tasting the air; it was sick and stale, tainted with decay. Then I heard movement deeper within, and all the hair on my nape stood up.

A few seconds later, the creature that shuffled into sight, dragging a severed arm, barely registered as human. Her skin was too tight, bloated from the feast we'd interrupted. Her eyes were bright but sunken in her swollen face and so smeared with blood that they were the only bright points in a ruddy mess. She lumbered toward us, and we scattered, giving Spence a clear shot. There was no point in letting her get close enough to bite. He leveled the gun and took the safe shot right in her chest, but it wasn't enough. Despite that wound, she kept coming.

"Again," Thornton snapped.

Spence fired another round, nailing her right between the eyes. She dropped like a stone.

I pushed out a breath I hadn't realized I was holding. "I doubt she left anyone alive, but we should make sure. Thornton, with me. The rest of you, watch the door."

"Yes, sir."

It was a moderate-size home. From what I could tell, it had originally been all one space, almost like a storage facility, but it had been repurposed as a house and someone had built rickety partitions. A lot about Winterville reminded me of down below. Unlike many settlements, this one looked like it didn't belong; it was more than half made up of old salvage, used by people who didn't fully understand what to do with it, and those foreign materials struck a strange note in the new world.

The whole house was awash in blood and feces, as if the madwoman who had broken inside had been a wild animal. She ate and excreted, and from what Thornton and I saw, that was *all*. In the sleeping area, I stumbled into the worst scene I'd ever encountered.

Is Appleton worse than this?

Thornton caught my shoulders as I rammed into him in an instinctive recoil. Chunks of meat and bone were everywhere, and the former residents were so chewed up that I couldn't tell what parts belonged to which person. It was a slaughterhouse of a room, a scene that would haunt me forever. The sheds where they slaughtered the meat in Soldier's Pond had more kindness. Then the woman, who was half devoured from the waist down, opened her eyes and whispered, "Kill me."

"Let me," he said.

I couldn't have gone into that room—my feet were frozen—so he strode across the blood-smeared floor, and with a clean stroke of his hatchet, ended her misery. I moved back until I couldn't see the massacre anymore, squeezed my eyes shut, but the images didn't go away. Hard tremors shook through me, and I was ashamed of my weakness, until I felt Thornton's big hand on my arm.

"Girl, I'd be worried if you could handle that. Only reason I could is because I've worked in the animal sheds, butchering beasts."

I didn't ask what mental tactic he'd employed, but I suspected he must've pretended she was one of those animals and he had a duty to make it quick. Thornton kept a hold of me as we stepped out and cleared the rest of the building. My heart was in my throat, fearing there would be brats, but I found none. I hurried back to the front door, and I guessed my expression gave away how bad it was because nobody asked me a single question.

"Let's go," I said. "We have more ground to cover before dark. I can't speak for the rest of you, but I'm not making camp until I'm sure we've killed all of them."

"You're dead right about that," Spence said with a hard look.

That day, I killed six more feral humans; after what I'd seen in the house, I was only just functional. My squad accounted for more, but the situation was tense. I had Danbury fretting about his bite while the rest eyed him like they wanted to cut his throat as a precaution. Finally, I called it, after we searched every structure in our part of town. It had been exhausting, and the sun was already gone, darkness driving out the streaks of vibrant color.

"This whole town is cursed," Zach said, his skin washed red by the sunset. "There are old-world relics all over the place, no wonder they came to grief. God has forsaken them."

"None of that crazy talk," Spence snapped.

Before sharp words could burgeon into a full-fledged argument, I beckoned. "Let's go find the others. I hope they didn't run into more trouble than they could handle."

That sparked a frank discussion of the other squads' capabilities, which lasted until we reached Dr. Wilson's lab building. Stalker's crew was already waiting; they were bloody but relatively fit. Right away, Tegan went into action with her medicine bag and about half the soldiers looked like they would walk on hot coals for her. *There's just something about a girl who can heal you . . . or crack your head open with a staff.*

As soon as he saw me, Stalker strode over to me to make his report. "We killed thirty-odd feral humans. Found some dead citizens. I'm not sure as yet how many survived the attack."

I shrugged. "Hard to say. They're unlikely to come out until they're sure it's safe."

"True."

When I did a head count, I belatedly realized he was down a man. "What happened?"

"There was . . . resistance inside one of the houses. By the time I got to him, it was too late." From Stalker's expression, he was taking the loss hard, so I just nodded.

Soon Fade's crew joined us. He bore several new wounds,

but after I scanned him head to toe, I was relieved to find no bites. There was no way I could grant Fade a merciful end, should it come down to it. I might as well ask Spence to shoot me. Morrow arrived last, also one man down. That put our current number at forty-two. I greeted Fade with a smile, though I wanted to kiss him. His dark eyes lingered on my mouth, and with effort, I recalled myself to business. We couldn't carry on like Breeders in the field.

"Time for Dr. Wilson to account for this mess," I muttered.

Lull

The door was bolted or barred from the inside, so I banged on the lab door with both fists until Wilson called out, "Who's there?"

"Company D!" the men shouted, before I could reply.

That was enough to reassure him, apparently, because I heard the sound of latches being unfastened, then the door swung open. I felt safer once we all stepped inside, but not happier. If possible, the man looked older since the last time we'd been here, by years instead of months, and he was thinner too. They used windmills to generate power—that much I knew—but I wasn't sure how well town commerce had stood up to the crisis. If the people who went mad normally worked at some trade, farmed, or crafted trade goods, then their supplies must be running low. Salvage could only take people so far.

"Lock up, please," Wilson said.

The soldier closest to the door complied, then we followed Wilson to the large room where he'd hosted us first. My men didn't relax; none of them looked at ease in this place. It was strange to them, just as it had been to me, and I hoped the scientist wouldn't give his windmill lecture again. That might be the last straw.

"Somebody string this bastard up." The demand came from one of the scouts, but I couldn't see who'd spoken.

I whirled, fixing a hard stare on them. "We're here to help, not impose punishment. His own people will decide if he's guilty of anything."

Wilson slammed a hand on the counter, rattling his glass odds and ends. "Who do you think begged me to find a solution? I told them it would take *years* and that the mutants might have changed by then. They insisted on a live trial over all of my objections, and I had pressure from Emilia in Soldier's Pond too."

That shut everyone up for a few seconds.

For the first time, I noticed how quiet the lab was, no ambient snarls or growls, and there was no accompanying Freak stench, either.

"What happened to your pet?" I asked.

Wilson lifted one shoulder, the posture of abject weariness. "Old age. Once it sets in, they go downhill fast. I did what I could to make him comfortable."

The rest of us were horrified; he had been nursing a monster while his people ran amok and ate one another? Wilson really *was* crazy.

But Tegan showed signs of fascination. "Did you learn anything about the creature's physiology while you had it in captivity? I've never heard of anyone studying a mutant."

"We study all kinds of things," Wilson said. "Or we did. The last year has been hard on the scientific community."

"What the devil are you talking about?" Tully demanded.

Wilson sighed. "Winterville has always been split along two lines, the scientists who gathered to study the Metanoia virus and eventually developed the vaccine to treat it, and the lay people who supported them."

"You mean those who did all the real work," Thornton muttered.

From the rumble of agreement, other men felt the same. I sensed the mood getting ugly, after everything we'd seen today.

To prevent a hanging, I needed to divert their attention, but Tegan did it for me. She was plainly curious, moving about the room with apparent absorption.

"So this was a research facility more than a town?" she asked.

The scientist indicated the lab, stocked with all manner of gadgets. "That's the only reason I have this equipment. Most of it has long since stopped functioning, of course, as the people who knew how to repair it are long dead. A few things, my father taught me how to maintain, and it's the reason I was able to extract enough genetic material to create that serum." His face fell. "As it turned out, that was an appalling idea."

"Seems to me you didn't pay nearly enough," Spence said. "You made this mess, then you nearly got some poor fellow killed calling us to clean it up."

"Did Marcus get there safely?" Wilson asked then.

That would've been my first question, and his belated concern didn't endear him to the rest of the men. I was familiar with how humans thought; they wanted somebody to blame for the evil they'd witnessed here. A time or two, I'd been accused of things I didn't do, according to that mob justice. So as much as I'd wanted to hang him myself, I couldn't let my men make Wilson a scapegoat.

"He did," I said. "He was resting in fair health when we left."

"What's the Metanoia virus?" Tegan asked.

"It's what started the end of everything."

"Ah." Doubtless she remembered my summary of our conversation with Dr. Wilson and what he'd told us about what led to the collapse.

Red-eyed and fearful, Danbury cleared his throat, reminding me that we had a problem. I said, "I need to know how dangerous it is if we were bitten by one of the afflicted."

"No more than any human bite," Wilson answered. "The human mouth is filthy. But the mental deterioration you noticed sprang from adverse bioreaction to the mutant pheromones I released, not from viral or bacterial infection." The scientist shook his head. "Regardless of the external pressures, I'm not reckless enough to experiment with viruses. They're the most dangerous and insidious form of contagion."

What he'd done with the potion seemed plenty irresponsible to me, but I didn't know what a virus was, so maybe it *was* worse. From that moment, Tegan looked at Dr. Wilson like he wore a silver crown, and she pelted him with questions regarding things I might've wondered about too if my men weren't tired and hungry and Winterville still such a mess.

"In the morning," I said, "we'll advise the townsfolk that it's safe and help with cleanup. For now, find a place to bed down and eat whatever you have left in your pack. I'll make sure we get a hot meal tomorrow."

Danbury was frowning. He peeled back the bandage to stare at the bite on his arm. The afflicted must've died before he or she could really dig in. "What did all of that mean?"

"Just watch for infection. You won't go crazy."

That seemed to relieve him. All around the lab and in the hall, men laid out their bedrolls. I had no idea how late it was, but between the day's horrors and the hard travel behind us, I was too tired to be hungry. On impulse, I left the lab and followed the turns of the corridor until I found the cages where Dr. Wilson had kept Timothy. They all stood empty, and they had been cleaned, so the room smelled sharply of vinegar, no hint of Freak at all.

Without turning, I recognized Fade's footfalls as he came up behind me. "It's so odd to think of them dying of old age."

"Like people."

That was part of what bothered me about all of this. The more the Freaks changed, the more they became like us. How many more generations before they spoke and thought as well as we could? At that point, their faster development meant they would outpace us in the breeding department. Another question ate at me—maybe the monsters were *supposed* to survive. Not us. And how could I fight nature on such a scale?

Weary, I leaned my head against the door frame. I should go back and lead by example, but I needed a quiet moment. *Just one.* Fade put his arms around me, looping them so that he could rest his chin on my shoulder. His warmth felt good, and the men were safe for the moment. That was a heavy burden, thinking about so many other people all the time. I didn't ever want to be an elder if it meant this much pressure. Maybe it was why so many lost their minds and made decisions for all the wrong reasons.

"You were right," he said quietly.

"About what?"

"I needed to lead today, though I was mad at you for making me do it."

Oh. I guessed our current position meant he'd gotten over it. "You brought back your whole team, so I knew it went well. But I had no doubts."

"I did," he admitted. "I was afraid I'd lock up or panic."

"You've fought since you were taken."

"It's harder when your choices affect other people," he pointed out.

So true.

"But you coped. No matter what life offers, you just fight harder. I love that about you."

I could tell he was smiling when he nuzzled the curve of his lips into my neck. "Let's see if we can find a place to clean up."

Since I didn't care for the idea of sleeping in travel dust and the blood of the day's battles, I followed him. The lab complex was bigger than it looked from the outside, as corridors criss-crossed the length and breadth of it. There were also stairs down, but I'd had enough of darkness, so I steered us away from there. At length we found a cleaning room with a spigot that provided a gush of water.

Fade and I took turns rinsing off, and I was conscious of my heart beating in my throat as I scrambled into clean clothes. I'd like to see what he looked like with nothing on, but this wasn't the time or place. I cursed those girlish impulses as Fade strode out with damp hair flopping into his eyes. In the winter months, he tended to let it get shaggy, providing more warmth, and then as the sun shone brighter, he often hacked it off. It didn't matter to me what he did with it; I enjoyed gazing at him regardless. By his expression, the feeling was mutual.

Fade appraised me with warm, dark eyes, and it was as powerful as a kiss. "I could look at you forever and never get tired of your face."

His words flooded me with pleasure so sharp it pierced like pain. That was better than saying I was beautiful, though he'd done so before. This moment felt like a forever-thing, because he saw me when he looked in my eyes, and I'd always be that person, no matter how the years changed me. With that tender weight between us, we returned to the main hall. When the men saw we'd found hygiene facilities, they demanded directions. In twos and threes, they went off to tidy up as well before breaking bread—and I decided I hadn't done such a bad job of leading by example. A girl could do worse than inspiring soldiers to bathe. Fade and I ate dry meat and stale bread, typical of road food. As I washed it down with tepid water, I imagined a roast goose like Momma Oakes used to make in Salvation with all the trimmings: creamy sweet potatoes swimming in butter and honey, brown bread, green beans, and berries in cream.

"You look like you're in pain," Stalker said.

His face was drawn, eyes shadowed in the flickering light.

The death of his teammate weighed on him, I suspected. We'd lost a lot of good men in the summer patrols as well, but it was different when you had the charge of them. Instead of a bad turn in battle, it felt like a personal failure.

"A little." I told them both what I'd been envisioning, and Fade groaned.

"You delight in cruelty." There was a sweetness in his teasing that I hadn't seen in so long, like he was before, when it was just him and me against the world.

Stalker turned to Fade with a polite expression. It sat oddly on his scarred features, like a hat tailored to another head. "I'd like to speak with Deuce in private, if you wouldn't mind."

"It's not up to me," Fade answered.

Stalker nodded. "It's not personal, if you're worried about that. I have no intention of causing any trouble between the two of you. I just need a word."

Part of me felt aggravated that he'd asked Fade, like he was in charge of who got to talk to me. But the rest appreciated the gesture, thereby acknowledging that Stalker understood how things stood between Fade and me. I ignored those conflicting reactions and accompanied him all the way to the door. That seemed like an excessive precaution, if he feared somebody eavesdropping. The men were all seeing to their own needs.

He took a deep breath. "There are a few things I need to say, if you'll hear me out."

"Go ahead."

He folded his arms, but not in a defensive way, more like he needed a hug, and there was nobody to give him one. I didn't move. Touch was a precious gift, and I didn't offer it freely. The distance between us came for good reason, as he didn't seem to be able to separate the quiet warmth of a friend as opposed to the way I reacted to Fade, who had exclusive kissing rights.

"In the gang, if I made up my mind to do something, it happened. And I started believing there was no obstacle I couldn't overcome, nobody I couldn't turn to my will."

"If nobody ever gainsaid you, I understand how that could happen." I was less sure what that had to do with me, but I trusted that he'd get to it.

"So when I met you . . . and I wanted you, I figured it was only a matter of time until I changed your mind. I didn't factor your thoughts or desires into it. At first, you were more a prize to me than a person." He took a deep breath. "I apologize for that. And when I realized you were never going to return my feelings, I didn't take it well. I'm not a good loser."

"Few people enjoy it," I said dryly.

"My point being, I'd like to accept your offer of friendship, if it's still open. I'll talk to Fade; make it plain I don't intend to get in his way. I get why he doesn't like me. He has reason."

"I'd like that." *All of it.* I'd never wanted any competition between them.

"The next thing is, I need you to lock up after I leave."

I tensed. That sounded like good-bye. "Why?"

"Don't worry, I'll be back. I just need to rove for a while. I can't sleep tonight."

I nodded, guessing the loss of a man under his command was bothering him. He probably thought if he had been faster or smarter, he could've saved the scout. But Longshot's death had taught me that sometimes you couldn't, no matter how much you wanted to, because other people made their own choices, however little you liked them. Sometimes they were brave and heroic; other times, it was just stupidity, and those losses were the hardest to bear.

"Be careful," I said.

"I will." Stalker unfastened the bolts and chains and strode into the dark.

Recovery

I slept poorly that night.

The conversation with Stalker plagued me. I expected to hear a tap on the door at any moment during the night, so I lay awake listening for it, but it never came. I snatched my rest in fitful bursts, but I roused with everyone else, took my turn washing up, and then I went out to see what Winterville looked like. The men followed me, something that struck me as odd, though it was what I'd wanted. In the daylight, the damage was apparent, but it seemed as if it could be readily repaired. Dr. Wilson joined us, shading his eyes as if he rarely saw sunlight. Since most of his work took place in the lab, that might be true.

"There's a bell four blocks that way," he said, "at the church. It's the building with the point on top. If you ring it, the townsfolk will know it's safe."

I was ready to put this grim and broken town behind us, but I'd told the men we'd help with the cleanup, and despite my desire to move on, I'd keep that promise. One day spent in repair and recovery wouldn't cost us the war.

"This way," I said, following Wilson's directions.

As we moved off, he went back inside. Tegan fell into step with me. "Where's Stalker?"

"He's taking Hammond's death hard."

From the ground, I could see the bell, but it required me to go inside the church. I left the bulk of my men outside, taking only Fade with me. The damage seemed especially wrong in here; the wood was scarred with countless scratches, more blood and excrement from the feral humans who had squatted here. It smelled rank, like death and rot; I covered my mouth as we moved through the shadowy interior to the stairs on the right. They were steep and skeletal, leading up to a narrow tower where the bell hung. Fade pulled the rope and the peal rang out, echoing to all corners of town.

"It's worse," he said. "Knowing that people caused all this destruction."

The cause and effect haunted me. Long ago, people feared one another, so they invented terrible things, capable of creating monsters. Then the monsters killed so many of the people that we were in danger of dying out. So once again, we devised something awful, trying to drive off the beasts. It was like an unbreakable cycle, and it exhausted me, made me wonder if I was mad for thinking I could make a difference. I preferred to imagine I'd survived the long walk to serve some purpose, but the world might not operate like that. Maybe there were no reasons why, just an endless chain of bad and worse, leavened by occasional brightness.

"Yes. It is."

Fade laced our fingers together as we left the church. Sometimes it felt as if he could sense when my heart hit its lowest ebb, then the smallest sign from him, and it sailed away again, soaring on the wind like a bird. The lightness couldn't last, of course, with the dire nature of the task ahead of us, but it was enough to keep me from seeing only the dark.

The citizens of Winterville emerged from their homes slowly, careful as squirrels. An elderly woman asked, "Who do we have to thank for our salvation?"

"Company D!" the men replied as one.

A ragged cheer rose up. In their wan and tired faces, I glimpsed true adulation. I'd seen it a few times down below in the faces of brats who dearly wanted my approval. Several men and women clasped my hands, kissed them, even, and I glanced at Fade in confusion. He lifted a shoulder, fending off the worshipful attention, but not in a way that made me fear he was about to panic and attack them. He only looked puzzled.

"Enough," I said. "There's a lot of work to do. Who's in charge here?"

A couple pushed to the front of the crowd; they looked to be of an age with the Oakses, lined but not incapable. "I'm the mayor, Agnes Meriwether, and this is my husband, Lem."

"Do you intend to punish Dr. Wilson?" I asked.

She looked as if I'd suggested murdering a child. "Why? He only did as we implored. For years, we had no need to defend ourselves. The Muties were different then. They didn't band together like they do now . . . and we could handle the odd scavenger. It was no different from running off a rabid wolf. But in the last year or so, things have gotten much worse. We didn't have any trained men or many weapons. So we thought science might offer a solution."

"From what I've seen," Tegan said soberly, "you can't have both fast and safe. It just isn't possible."

"We know that now. I should've listened when Dr. Wilson warned me that it wouldn't end well. But it worked at first. The Mutie bands just veered away, but then people started going mad. Fourteen people died while we were rounding them up—"

"There's a prison camp in the south," Morrow said to me, low. "Barbaric. It would've been kinder just to kill them."

"That's what I said," Lem put in.

Agnes seemed genuinely tormented. "I couldn't bear for so many people to die, if there was any way to prevent it. I asked Dr. Wilson to devise a treatment."

I nodded. "But he couldn't. And the temporary prison didn't hold."

"I don't want this responsibility," she said softly. "I've made too many mistakes."

A woman called from the crowd, "If you think we're cleaning up your mess, you're out of your mind, Mrs. Meriwether. You put this town to rights."

I cut off the argument with an impatient gesture. Once we left, I didn't care who held office. My objective was to restore Winterville to some semblance of order. So I divided us into teams as I had the day before, only this time we were hauling bodies. It seemed disrespectful to burn them as we had done the Freak corpses, so I set five men to digging a mass grave. That wasn't a whole lot better, but it would take too long to dig so many separate ones. Down below, we'd have fed them to the Freaks, but I'd come to understand that was wrong, and Topside, it would attract scavengers.

I labored alongside everyone else, dragging bloody burdens out of buildings to where they could receive a decent burial. By noon, my back and arms were aching; it was the grimmest work I'd ever done. Only Tegan tackled other tasks; she checked the townsfolk over and helped those she could. I saw her frustration when she encountered illness or injuries she didn't know how to treat. Guilt blazed like a signal fire in her eyes; she thought if Doc Tuttle had lived instead, he'd be of more use.

Once we finished moving the bodies, they fetched us shovels, and everyone pitched in to plant the dead. When I first heard of this custom, it gave me nightmares because it seemed so similar to putting seeds in the ground; and my sleeping mind conjured all kinds of horrific plants that might sprout from a corpse. It was silent work, raking dark soil over the faces of the dead. I heard only the rasp of the shovels and rakes and the breath of those who labored beside me. Black and still, the freshly dug mound rose up from the grass surrounding it. There should be some marker to commemorate the tragedy, but maybe the memory of the people who had loved and lost would do the job instead. Then the men of Winterville came with wood and stone, nails and hammers, and they built a monument. I rested in the shade nearby, weary in body and soul. Once the noise quieted, Mrs. Meriwether fetched the minister, who had a holy book similar, but not identical, to the one Caroline Bigwater read from when she disapproved of someone.

I gathered along with everyone else. These words were soft, and they slid like silk from the holy man's mouth. "'For everything there is a season, and a time for every matter under heaven: a time to be born, and a time to die; a time to plant, and a time to pluck up what is planted. Weep no more, my children. He will wipe away every tear from their eyes, and death shall be no more, neither shall there be mourning, nor crying, nor pain anymore, for the former things have passed away.'"

After the service ended, the people of Winterville swallowed their tears, pretending their loved ones had gone to a better place. I didn't know the truth, so maybe they were right. Company D stood silent and respectful through the completion of their rites, then the men gathered around me. It was late in the day by then, and while I didn't especially want to spend another night here, I didn't think it was wise to leave the protective perimeter with dark coming on. The pheromones—though they drove part of the town crazy—still seemed to be functioning as a deterrent to the Freaks. So we could rest safely here, I imagined. Before I could announce the decision, however, Mrs. Meriwether stepped toward me.

I met her halfway, brow arched in inquiry. "Something else, ma'am?"

"We'd like to thank you. At the moment, we don't have much, but it's customary to share a meal in honor of the deceased. We cook their favorite foods, talk about good times, and remember them kindly." She lifted a plump shoulder. "It might be a silly tradition, but it comforts people, and supposedly it allows the spirit to move on, like a rite of passage."

After so much death, it seemed wise to pacify the spirits. I wasn't convinced such things existed, but *if* they did, it would be bad for feral souls to stick around. They'd soon drive the survivors mad.

So I nodded. "We'd be honored to share a meal with you tonight."

The houses were too small to host so many people; there was no mess hall like they had in Soldier's Pond, so they made do in the town square. People carried out what they had left in their cupboards, and men and women shared the cooking; a good idea, I thought. Soon, there was meat roasting in multiple fires, vegetables bubbling, and sweets being stirred in pots. Other townsfolk went about the business of removing all signs of the bloodbath from the day before. Stern-faced, weary men worked with rags and buckets. For a time, those labors made people forget the high cost of survival.

What will they do with the makeshift prison they built to house the afflicted? And why didn't they just confine them in their houses? It was possible they tried that and that measure failed. I closed my eyes for a few seconds, breathing in the savory smells. Belatedly, I realized I was starving. Dry meat and bread had been the norm on the way, and I'd pushed the men hard. I'd feared we would arrive too late, but now I could relax a little. The crisis was past.

Someone sat down beside me, then I recognized Tegan's voice. "Do you think things will ever be the same here?"

"I don't know," I said honestly.

"Where are we headed in the morning?"

I had been thinking about that a lot. "We'll try our luck

nearby, see if our success in the fall was enough to change people's minds."

"Good idea."

As the cooks finished up the evening meal, a trading party arrived from Lorraine—and that seemed like a sign. They were grizzled men with permanently sun-browned skin and silver beards. Their easy manners reminded me of Longshot, and a hole opened up inside me. I'd lost people before, but never like that. Nobody ever thought so much of me that he'd die so I could live, and I was finding it hard to carry that gift, as there was no way of repaying him.

"What happened here?" the lead driver asked, for it was obvious the town was recovering from an attack.

"Private dispute," Mrs. Meriwether told him.

"Not Muties?" the man demanded. "There's a huge mess of them over in Appleton. The whole town's overrun."

The woman blanched but she shook her head. "So far, we've seen nothing of them."

"I wouldn't fret. I hear there's an army on the march. I had word on the trail from John Kelley. These soldiers killed about a thousand mutants out past Soldier's Pond."

The trader's comment put a smile on my face. As promised, the trapper was spreading word about—and exaggerating—our great deeds. I didn't know how much his stories would help, but they were entertaining, anyway.

Agnes Meriwether opened her eyes wide. "Is that so? Well, there will be a party tonight, so you've arrived in time for some good eating."

"Thanks kindly. We're all hungry enough to eat a raw bear."

A nascent strategy solidified in my mind as I listened to their polite talk; the wagons were heavy with goods that Winterville desperately needed. With luck, the citizens could find things of value to offer in return, despite the circumstances. The townsfolk hurried off to gather scattered items to offer in exchange for fresh supplies. Longshot had told me that men traveled the trade runs during spring and fall, so we could expect to see more caravans, more targets for the Freaks too.

I sought Fade out to ask his opinion. He was sprawled beneath a flowering tree, its white blossoms sweet in the cool air. Even dirty and tired, he was the most beautiful man I'd ever seen.

"You look like there's something on your mind."

I nodded, dropping down beside him. "I was thinking that we should guard the trade routes. The fastest way to endear ourselves to the people in the remaining towns is to keep their economies thriving."

"You reckon that'll make them feel indebted, more likely to send men to bolster our numbers?"

"I hope so. It's the only idea I have left." Beyond securing more ground for Soldier's Pond, I couldn't imagine how our squad could make a difference against the horde.

"It's solid," he agreed.

"We have to add to Company D . . . or the minute the Freaks abandon Appleton, they'll roll right over the next town."

By proximity, Lorraine had the most to worry about, as the settlement was only four days away. A big group might take longer to arrive, but not long enough for the citizens to evacuate, and besides, where would they go? Urgency clutched at me with hot, sharp fingers, but there was nothing I could do at the moment. That didn't sit well at all.

Fade braced and reached for me then. It seemed to me that it got easier each time he did it, more natural. I hoped the day would come when he could do it without needing that mental pause, where touching me was the easiest and best thing in the world. "Try not to worry. For the moment, we're safe and we're together. Let that be enough."

That was more than enough; it was everything.

Defense

Stalker returned late that night, well after they set out the food. He caught my eye and nodded, letting me know he'd dealt with his grief. I was glad to have him back. After that silent exchange, he fixed a plate and joined the rest of his scouts. The town square was a cheerful place, lit by the electric lights that Wilson had explained in such tedious detail, plus the merry crackle of multiple fires.

By that time, everyone else had eaten. There were jugs of strong-smelling drink that made the townsfolk laugh and fall down a lot; I quietly instructed my men to stay away from it. Around that time, a Lorraine trader produced a fiddle, and I wondered if the Winterville citizens found the music improper for a night that was supposed to be about showing respect for the dead, but nobody protested. The notes sang out like silver light, until people's feet were tapping. Soon, dancing began, a whirl of feet and legs. The impromptu performance seemed to enliven Stalker further and he coaxed a local girl into dancing with him. Later, he stole a kiss from Tully, which made Spence try to plant a boot in his arse. Laughing, Stalker went back to his Winterville conquest. It was good to see him in high spirits, after the knock he'd taken earlier.

As the liquor flowed, stories tumbled out one after another. Many of them had the magical quality of the one Morrow had told about the boy who lived in the cupboard. I had a hard time listening to all of them, but the storyteller was in his element. Now and then I caught him scribbling frantically to be sure he didn't miss any of the details.

Tegan sat with Dr. Wilson, pestering him with questions, but rather than being annoyed, he seemed pleased by her interest. The scientist had endless patience for her curiosity, even if I didn't understand half the things he was telling her. She glowed by firelight, looking at Wilson as if he were the greatest present she ever got, even without the fancy wrapping. I laughed quietly, and Fade tightened his arm around my shoulders. Moments like these were few and far between.

"Do you ever wonder what happened down below after we left?" he asked, surprising me.

"All the time. I wish there was some way for us to find out." But we had come so far, not just in actual distance. I might even be frightened to go back down into darkness, fearing it would choose to keep me this time and not let me go back into the light.

"Me too. I know you had friends you left behind."

"Not very good ones, as it turns out. They believed the worst of me awfully fast." That was an old wound, one I'd hardly acknowledged.

"I'm sure they had their reasons," Fade said.

I gave a bitter laugh. "They trusted the elders, like I did before you got inside my head."

"Are you sorry about that?"

"How can you even ask? My life is so much better because you're in it—and not just because we went Topside."

He gave me a crooked smile, and his gaze lingered on my lips. "It's nice to hear."

I winced, taking that as a criticism. Deep down I knew I

wasn't the best at talking about my feelings, and Fade probably needed to hear how important he was to me, as much as I could express it. "I'll try to be a better partner."

"You're spot on with the killing," he told me, smiling.

That was a quiet nod at our time together down below when I was completely oblivious to the fact that he wanted to be more than my hunting mate. My cheeks heated. "I'll work on the talking."

The fact that my private thoughts mattered to him meant more than he knew. As I struggled to find the words to express them, the lights went out overhead. The fiddler paused his tune as the night darkened, leaving only the fires crackling. People quieted also, as if they remembered all too well how dangerous nights filled with monsters could be.

"I'm sure it's just a malfunction in the wires," Dr. Wilson said. "Or possibly the windmill that powers this part of town has broken down."

A dozen slurred voices added their opinions, but I recognized the prickle crawling over my bare arms. I signaled my men, and Company D was on its feet, ready for battle in less than thirty seconds. I spun until I located Stalker, but he was already coming toward me. He recognized this as his area of expertise.

"Will you see what's going on?" I asked, low. "But don't engage. We need intel."

This time, he took none of his scouts, heading off at a silent run. He moved with all the grace of a creature born in the wild, and within seconds, he vanished into the shadows. The party mood was gone, and the Winterville folk started packing up the food, hurrying toward the houses where they had hidden for days already. Most still had barricades for the windows and doors; I hoped they wouldn't need them tonight.

Mrs. Meriwether darted toward Dr. Wilson. In the confusion,

she thought nobody was paying attention, but I craned my ears to catch every word. "I thought we were safe. You made enough of that spray to treat the whole town."

His tired reply was unmistakable. "It doesn't last forever, Agnes, and Timothy is gone. I can't make more without him since the extract came from his reproductive glands."

"So we're defenseless?" Her horror was palpable. "I killed all those people for nothing."

I bit out a curse. The chances were good that we had Freaks in the windmills, destroying them. They might not understand what purpose they served, but they hated all human technology. They'd wreck these machines for the same reason they'd dug up our crops—because they thought it would weaken us in some fashion. And in most cases, they were right.

I didn't wonder long. Stalker came at a run, winded, which meant he'd pushed himself. He gasped out, "Freaks. At least a hundred, coming in from the east." As he caught his breath, he added, "I suspect they trailed the Lorraine traders. Not sure why the pheromones aren't discouraging them."

"It washes away," I said. "It's not forever. And Dr. Wilson can't make more."

"They won't fight." Fade was watching the townsfolk move in full retreat, preparing to cower inside their homes.

But barred windows and doors wouldn't deter a hundred intelligent Freaks. They'd use fire or some other strategy to take this town, and it wouldn't even require the rest of the horde, unless we did something about it.

"This will be a tough fight," I said softly.

Stalker nodded. "At night, against superior numbers? It'll cost us."

"I know. But the alternative is to leave Winterville to its fate." Under no circumstances could I give those orders. If the rest of Company D abandoned the town, I couldn't go. It might be the practical decision—one a Huntress would make—but I couldn't save these people from the feral humans, only to let them die.

"Men!" I called.

They surrounded me at full attention, row by row, and I recalled that was the style in Soldier's Pond. I didn't usually require it, but the occasion merited formality, I supposed.

I had no fancy words, but I gave them what I knew. "It'll be a rough night, our first big battle of the season ahead. Who wants to kill some Muties?"

"Company D," they called back.

Not a single voice remained silent; they all shouted their intentions to the skies. If they died tonight, they'd go out as Hunters, one and all.

I squared my shoulders. "Then we need a plan."

Fade turned in a slow circle, assessing the houses and the open terrain of the town square. "I think we can win. But we need to draw them here."

"Count on my scouts for that," Stalker said.

I thought I understood Fade's plan. "Spence and Tully, I need you on those rooftops. I want constant fire from you until you run out of ammunition."

"You're them," one of the Lorraine traders said in wonder. "Company D."

I hadn't noticed their approach, but it made sense they'd be here since they didn't have houses to hide in, and the wagons offered limited cover. The lead driver wore a rifle on his back as Longshot had, and I wondered if he was any good with it. He seemed to read my thought—or maybe my look—because he drew it and held it like a man who knew which way to point it.

"We are," I acknowledged. "But I don't have time for introductions at the moment."

I expected some disparaging remarks about my gender or

my age, but to my surprise, the rifleman said, "Put us on a roof-top. We'll fight with you."

A boy crept out of the shadows then, hardly more than a brat. He was dirty and thin, eyes too big for his face. He reminded me so much of the white-eyed brat from down below that my stomach cramped. A weapon too big for him to lift came behind him, leaving trails in the dirt.

"I can shoot," he said.

I saw the words forming on a trader's lips, *You can't even lift that thing, son,* so I cut him off. "How?"

"I can brace it. My dad taught me . . . before he died." There was a wealth of sorrow and anger in those words.

"Where's your mum?" Fade asked.

The brat lifted his chin. "Gone. You poured dirt on them both earlier today."

Guilt flickered through me; I hadn't even noticed him among the other mourners. Above the boy's head, Fade caught my eyes, and I nodded. We'd take this chance to do the right thing.

"Go with the traders. I want you posted over there." I indicated the tower where Fade had rung the bell. "Spence and Tully on the other side." That structure wasn't quite as tall, but it had a nice perch on the roof. "Barricade the door if you can, so they can't get at you. The rest, stay with me. Remember our drills." I planted the banner Momma had made in the ground, then told my men grimly, "Guard the flag with your lives. Don't let them inside our line."

"You heard the woman," the lead driver snapped. "Move."

Woman. That word felt as precious as my naming day; and maybe it was the first time Topside that anyone had looked at me and seen more than a silly girl. That man couldn't see my scars and he didn't know my story. He only knew what my actions told him, and apparently they said I was grown. But I had no time to savor the sensation.

Stalker's scouts came at a run with what seemed like a thousand Freaks charging behind them. I shuddered, remembering my mad flight with Fade through the horde. It had to be worse for him, but he was steady as a rock at my side. All around us, Company D readied their weapons. I drew my knives five seconds before the Freaks hit us like a hammer—and we stood our ground, shoulder to shoulder, as lead slammed into the monsters from above.

Bodies jerked and fell all around me. I stabbed and slashed, my usual style forestalled by the need to protect Fade on my left and Sands, who had staggered in on my right. Tegan fought between Stalker and Morrow, her staff knocking them down for other soldiers to finish. She didn't like to kill, but the girl had gotten deadly about defending herself. I held formation and turned my attention back to the next Freak charging toward me.

It snapped yellow fangs in visible threat. "Our land. Not yours."

"You'll have to take it," I growled, just before I plunged my dagger into its chest.

Fade knocked one away from me and cut its throat. He too was all efficiency, keeping them off me as well as the soldier on his other side. We fought as a unit, not as separate Hunters, and it felt good when the enemy fell in droves around us. The night air chilled my skin but sweat warmed it up again. I sliced like the threshing blade we'd used in the fields. The Freaks were ferocious, but they couldn't fathom the way we wouldn't yield, not even a single step. They couldn't surround us, couldn't use their usual tactics. These creatures fought like pack animals, three or four on one victim, who usually went down to the overwhelming blood loss, not due to any particular skill. They were less organized than the ones who offered us the truce near Soldier's Pond . . . and that made me think these were associated with the horde, possibly a vanguard. I risked a kick, though it pulled me forward a few steps, then someone from the church tower shot the thing, and Fade pulled me back.

"Careful," he scolded.

"Sorry."

A cry of pain from one of my men drew my eye. In the dark, I couldn't tell who it was, but the man dropped, and we tightened the formation. Freaks tested our defenses from all sides, but we didn't let them pass. They received bolts in the back, bullets in the side, and our knives everywhere else. Morrow was a lean shadow, dancing death with his slender blade. Now and then I caught Tegan watching him, and that made me smile, even as I blocked another lunge. The town square was a seething, snarling mess with bodies everywhere.

"Back up," I called.

The fight blurred into a mass of claws and fangs, cries of pain. I fought until my arms ached, until one more swing of the dagger might make my arms fall off. The rifles popped until they ran out of ammunition on the rooftops, and then we had Spence and Tully, and the traders on the ground with us. Around that time, the Freaks realized they were losing, so they ran. We gave chase, but a handful of them escaped in the darkness, dodging around the buildings. I hoped they would carry word that this town was well defended, but I feared they were going after greater numbers for the next onslaught. I panted, hunched over with my hands on my knees. Then I took stock. *Eight men down.* Mouthing their names, I closed their eyes myself.

"We did it," Tegan said.

Considering what we'd achieved, Silk would call this a win. I disagreed. Though we'd driven the beasts off, it didn't feel like a complete victory. The traders had taken some damage too. One hurt, another dead, and the leader looked stone tired.

"That was quite a fight. John Kelley might've exaggerated when he called you an army, but he didn't make up anything about your skill." He turned along with everyone else as the brat came down from the tower, dragging his father's gun. "You did good too, son. Saw three of them Muties go down under your fire."

"What's your name?" I asked the boy.

"Gavin," he said.

From what he'd said, he had nobody left. If he did, they likely wouldn't allow him to be here, fighting for a town that wouldn't defend itself. "How would you like to join Company D?"

Bright as the moon overhead, the kid's smile almost made up for all the men I'd lost.

Loss

By dawn, we had dug eight graves. My fingers were raw and blistered from the last twenty-four hours; there had been too much death and our numbers were decimated. In total, ten men from Company D died defending Winterville, and the townsfolk had hidden in their homes. The only real man among them was a brat named Gavin, who labored alongside me with as much grit as I'd ever seen.

Heart heavy, I signaled for the men to bring the bodies. We put them in the ground ourselves while I worried about the Freaks returning. We buried our dead together, and anger warred with grief inside me. I didn't call the minister to offer more soft words. Instead I asked the survivors to speak on behalf of the fallen. That lasted until mid-morning with quiet reminiscences and comments on the everyday things that had made these men happy. Afterward, I asked those who'd known them best whether they left family behind. And six of them had.

That cut even deeper.

"It's not your fault," Fade said softly.

I couldn't accept his comfort until I cleared my conscience. The look of those fresh graves lingered fresh in my mind as I strode through the silent town. When I arrived at the Meriwether house, I hammered on the door with both fists. To her credit, the mayor looked as if she hadn't slept all night when she answered.

There was no greeting for an occasion like this, and I didn't bother being polite. "The way I see it, you have two choices. You can form a militia or you can seek refuge in a town willing to take you in. I can't guarantee we'll get here next time. This is twice, and it's time Winterville started saving itself." I got up in her face. "No more awful potions, no more miracle solutions cooked up in Dr. Wilson's lab. You don't ask him for help again. Understand?"

"Not even in normal ways?" she asked, horrified.

I wasn't trying to tell them how to run their town. "Anything to do with defense." She offered a sorrowful nod, but all her sad looks wouldn't bring my men back. So I went on, "We're moving out, so whatever you intend to do, you'd best get to it. Hiding in your houses won't do the job forever."

"I understand. Thank you for everything you've done for us. We won't forget. I don't know yet if we'll have to abandon the town, but we'll have a meeting to decide today."

"As you like."

Whirling, I ran toward the rest of the company. Fade snagged my shoulder and spun me to face him. "Not this way."

"What?" I snapped.

"You can't let them see you like this, Deuce. Later, you can fall apart and I'll pick up the pieces, but right now, you have to be strong."

Taking a deep breath, I realized he was right. So I held still until I could fix my face in a more suitable expression. The men would rightly read my pain as weakness; I had no business leading troops into battle if I couldn't handle what came next. It was another hard lesson, but by the time we got back to the others, I had mastered it.

"Let's head out," I called.

Company D formed up, following me to where the Lorraine traders had bunked down beneath their wagons. "Did you get any business done?"

The lead driver nodded. "We took care of it last night, before the attack."

"Then the wagons are loaded and ready to go?"

He nodded. "Did you need something?"

"No, but if I guess right, you'll have a dangerous trip back to Lorraine. My men and I will make sure you get there safely."

"Why?" one of the traders asked.

"If the trade routes shut down due to Mutie attacks, all towns will suffer. I've seen what happens when a settlement becomes too isolated."

Salvation had been a good place, full of warmhearted people, but they didn't trust outsiders much, and they hadn't encouraged traders like these to come into town. From what my family had told me and I'd observed, Longshot handled all of that outside the town gates, allegedly preventing bad morals from getting in. But in the end, that seclusion didn't save them.

"Then we'd appreciate the escort. We can spare some provisions once we arrive, and I'll help you find a place in town to rest up for a night or two."

"Thank you," I said.

"I don't know if you caught my name last night amid all the revelry. I'm Vince Howe."

"Deuce Oaks." That was the first time I'd offered two names, and Fade shot me a surprised look, but he smiled. I needed to tell him that Momma Oaks had given her blessing for him to use their name too.

"Pleasure, ma'am. I guess you know, but you run a right remarkable group. I'm sorry for your losses, but I don't know when I saw more impressive battle." I acknowledged that with an inclination of my head, and he continued, "We'll be ready to go in less than an hour."

I took that opportunity to use the sanitary facilities one last time, so I jogged over to the lab and banged until the scientist appeared. Dr. Wilson was happy to let me in, and for a minute, I thought he might follow me all the way to the wash closet. He stopped in the hall, fortunately, and said, "Come see me before you depart, all right?"

With a distracted gesture, I agreed and then washed up. It felt wrong to start a new journey with grave dirt still smeared on my skin, embedded beneath my nails. When I came out, damp and clean, I felt renewed. For a few moments, I considered ducking out because I was in no mood to chat with the scientist. But in the end, I kept my promise and headed to the lab to speak with the old man.

"What's on your mind?" I asked.

He had two cups of tea steaming on the table, along with some buttered toast, so I joined him. On the road, I missed bread, and while this wasn't fresh, the melted butter made up for the rest. The drink was pale but strong with a medicinal scent. It tasted better than it smelled, however, with a gentle tang of mint. I drank mine because it was wet and hot, pleasant in a dry throat, and then I devoured the food.

The scientist watched me in silence, but once I finished, he said, "Your friend, Tegan, is quite extraordinary."

"Tell her, not me."

"I'm appealing to you as her commander. A mind like hers shouldn't be wasted on the life of a common soldier. Let her stay with me. I could use an assistant . . . and I've been looking for someone like her my whole life."

I laughed. "You don't know Tegan if you think I have any say over whether she stays or goes. But I'll fetch her and you can put the invitation to her yourself."

Leaving the dregs in my mug, I left the lab and went looking for Tegan. She was sitting alone in a patch of spring sunlight. The men gave her a wide berth, probably because of the tear streaks down her dusty cheeks. Dr. Wilson was right; she wasn't cut out for this life, but she was lucky in that there was no reason she couldn't cry when she felt sad.

"The good doctor would like a word," I said, offering my hand.

She seemed glad of the distraction, and we walked back to the lab together. Once inside, the scientist stated his case with more eloquence than he'd offered me, outlining all the opportunities for study and the wondrous things he could teach her. He concluded with "It's long been my dream to pass on my knowledge, but until now, I'd encountered no suitable candidates. But you, my dear, you're perfect."

Tegan considered, her lips parted in astonishment. "It's a kind offer, Dr. Wilson, but I'll see this through. Company D relies on me for healing, and the men will suffer without my care."

"I see you were right about not being her captain," Dr. Wilson said to me.

She frowned. "Deuce is my friend . . . she didn't order me to follow her. In fact she tried to talk me out of it. Should I survive, then I'll gladly come back to study with you."

"I'll endeavor to wait until that day," Wilson said dryly.

A hot flush colored Tegan's cheeks, and I smothered a smile. "I'm sorry. That sounded presumptuous, didn't it?"

"I *did* ask you to stay. It's not wrong to assume I'd like you to come back some day."

"Then I thank you for the opportunity, Dr. Wilson. I hope we meet again."

That seemed like the cue for us to leave, so we said our farewells and met the men in the town square. The wagons were loaded, and I was ready to see the last of Winterville. Despite their cowardice the night before, the townsfolk saw us off, and a few asked if I'd let them enlist. I was tempted to refuse, as I had with Rex, due to their inexperience, but I could tell by their guilt-racked expressions that they wanted to make up for their inaction. And in truth, we needed the bodies.

I looked the three men up and down. "Any of you know how to shoot?"

They shook their heads. But one of them said, "Please. I'm a smith. I can keep your weapons in good repair. Surely that's worth something."

He was a burly sort with broad shoulders and scarred hands. So I beckoned them all on. Since we had wagons to protect, this journey would take much longer than it did when the men ran at a Hunter's pace. More time on the road meant more chances for trouble, and we were all weary, but if we delivered the supplies safely to Lorraine, other volunteers might join our cause. John Kelley was spreading our story, and I suspected Vince Howe would add to it as well.

These things took time.

We were on the road for over a week, and Stalker's scouts did most of the heavy lifting. Sometimes we fought preemptive battles against the Freaks, so they had no chance to lay an ambush for the wagons. As I'd predicted, it was slow going, and there was little time to spend with Fade, apart from the way I treated the rest of the men. From his occasional looks, he was missing the way it felt when we were together, but the job came first, as it ever had. This was familiar from our time in the summer patrols, but I minded more than I had then. For the first time, I could imagine a quiet life with Fade, a little cottage like Momma Oaks had shared with Edmund in Salvation. I was tired of smoky campfires and nights spent alone in a bedroll on the ground. I'd learn to grow things, and he could find work that didn't require killing. On a starry night like this, those were dreams too distant for building.

On the eighth night, I woke to pure chaos. The mules were

screaming, Freaks were all around us. My men recovered as fast as they could, and the traders aimed their rifles, shooting into the dark. Between the crack of gunfire and cries of pain, I had no idea where anyone was. Gavin, the brat from Winterville, had climbed on top of the crates and was lying on his stomach, firing with complete calm. I spotted Fade fighting some distance away, but I didn't see Tegan or Stalker. There was no time to search further, because three Freaks were on me.

I whipped out my knives and whirled into the fight. As my vision sharpened, I spied Tegan on the other side of the wagon. Morrow fought madly toward her side, his blade a silver arc in the dark. By his worried expression, he didn't like how they were surrounding her. I didn't care for it either, but Stalker was closer. Another Freak charged her back; she was already blocking with everything she had.

Though she was good with her staff, she wasn't infallible. In a few more seconds, she'd go down. Stalker stopped defending and took four slashes across his back. He sprinted. I registered the precise moment when he realized he could save Tegan or land the killing blow, but not both. Not in time. A second later, he threw himself between her and the Freak that would've torn out her spine. He took both talons in the chest before Morrow and I reached them.

The Freak who went after Tegan from behind had a vicious scar across its face, received in some prior battle with human soldiers. It looked like a knife wound—and when it saw us—it loped off, more evidence that they were growing more cunning. This one preferred to live to fight another day. The rest of the monsters spun on us, but Fade and Morrow were there, fighting like wild things to keep them away. They died in piles beneath their furious blades.

Kneeling beside Stalker, I sealed my palms against the wounds. Blood bubbled up from between my fingers. The dawn showed signs of brightening into a sunny day, and he shouldn't be dying. Tegan sobbed, calling for her medicine bag, but by his crooked smile, he knew it was no use. Stalker pulled my fingers away and clutched them tight, until our skin was slick and red. His breath grew wet and harsh, his eyes winter pale in his stark face. I drew him up into my arms, as if I could force him to live if I held him tight enough.

"You said I could never make it right . . . but this helps, doesn't it? The world's getting the better deal, her for me."

Unable to speak for the tears thickening my throat, I stared down, memorizing his features. Though I couldn't care for him like he wanted, he'd been my friend since we made peace in the ruins. He'd fought brave and true by my side. His ideas, his genius, had helped me build Company D, and I didn't know how to win without him.

Stalker squeezed my fingers, his voice harsh and labored. "Promise, promise you'll finish this for me."

"By everyone I love, I swear it," I choked out.

"I'd . . . ask you to . . . kiss me good-bye," he whispered, "but—"

Before he could finish the wheezing words, I leaned down and pressed my lips to his cheek. He smiled, and it felt as if he were already gone, his body lighter in my arms. My heart broke over and over with each of his wet, rasping breaths.

His lashes fluttered like butterfly wings. "I could've made you happy, dove."

"You did," I whispered.

Not in the way he'd wanted, of course. But I had loved sparring with him, loved his pragmatic outlook, and his loyalty when he granted his trust. But he didn't hear. The spark that made him Stalker had gone, leaving a limp body in my arms. All around the campsite, Company D protected me from the straggling Freaks, but the battle felt far away. I was gone too, weeping in silence. It wasn't the way a leader behaved, but I was only a girl, mourning a fallen friend. So the battle raged on, but I had no fight left in me. My daggers lay useless at my sides.

"Let him go," Tegan said softly.

When she hugged me, I went into her arms, my eyes smeared with blood and tears. We wept together, and I felt Tegan shaking. She'd hated him so much, then she forgave him, and now this. Though I'd believed him when he said he regretted so many things—and that he'd changed—I never would've expected such a sacrifice from him. Until the moment when he decided her life was more precious than his own, I'd have said he was foremost a survivor.

Like me.

But in the end, Stalker chose to be better still.

And I had promises to keep.

Pledge

Company D rallied and carried the day, and there were no more casualties. Remembering Fade's words about being a strong leader, I pulled myself together and dried my tears. Yet the men had no trouble meeting my gaze, so I guessed they didn't judge me lacking because I'd grieved for a friend. It seemed unlikely anybody could sleep—too much blood and death, too much danger lurking just beyond the wagons.

"We're hours from Lorraine," Vince Howe said. "Let me load your fallen man, and we'll see him buried when we're safe."

I acceded.

That was a miserable march with sorrow gnawing through my backbone. Tegan wore a dead, awful look, one I recognized from when Rex lost his wife. She didn't mourn Stalker like that, but shock had a hold of her, as if something this awful couldn't possibly be true. I moved without thinking about where I put my feet, and six hours later, despite wagon speed, Lorraine rose ahead of us. In the morning light, it looked different from the first time we visited. Lorraine was a pretty town, a combination of Salvation and Soldier's Pond. The houses were made of wood, but the ramparts surrounding it were made of stone, like a picture I saw in a book once; Edmund had called it a castle. They had a standing militia, but they didn't patrol much. It was a common theme in the territory—people didn't go out looking for trouble if they had a choice. They'd let the Freaks push them back, until they feared the wilderness like drinking poison.

Better we stay safe, they said. *Better that those trained to do so go out to do battle with the monsters.*

If not for the men willing to brave the trade routes, these towns would be dead already. But for sheer appearance, Lorraine got high marks. It was more polished than Otterburn, less divided than Winterville. The buildings were old but well kept, of timber and stone. The roads leading up to town were made of dirt, but once the guard waved us past the gates, they had been swept, neat lines in the dust contributing to an orderly feel. People wore functional clothing here, both men and women. There wasn't a lot of variation in the dyes, but working with Momma Oaks had given me some idea about fabrics, and they had skilled weavers.

Arranging a proper funeral took most of the day. Vince Howe paid the fees and found Stalker a spot in the town cemetery. The undertaker took his body from us, and the next time we saw him, he was encased in a wooden box. There were men hired specifically to bury it, and people came from town because Howe asked them to. But I had the hardest job, for it fell to me to speak the right words in saying good-bye.

My throat tightened. "Stalker wasn't always a good person, but he was a fierce warrior, and he died well. Good hunting, my friend."

The men echoed it with one final battle cry, and then the gravediggers shoveled dirt on his casket. Howe set his hand on my shoulder. "I owe you. I doubt we'd have made it back in one piece without your men. So let me show you to your lodgings."

The last time we were here, they left us to fend for ourselves, but today, we received a heroes' welcome. The townsfolk offered us the town hall for our barracks and ladies of all ages promised to deliver warm crocks of food before the sun set. Before that, however, the local pubs sent us jugs of watered wine. I didn't want drunks on my squad, as they tended to be loud and unco-ordinated, but if any occasion called for some indulgence, it was this one.

It had been a devil of a week.

Once we were settled in the great room, I gave the orders in a monotone. "Get comfortable, men. Try not to think about the ones we lost. They died as they chose. Not every man gets to say that."

"True enough," Thornton answered. "I hope I go out half as well."

"I'll drink to that," Spence said.

They all raised their mugs, and I went over to Tegan, who still wore that odd, frozen look. "Anything I can do?"

She covered her face with her hands. "I shouldn't have come. That invitation from Dr. Wilson was a sign, and I ignored it. If I'd stayed in Winterville, Stalker would still be alive."

"You can't know that," I said firmly.

Fade joined us, folding down into a cross-legged position. "Deuce's right."

Tegan clenched a fist and banged it on her knee. "There was a time when this was all I thought about. I wanted him to hurt. I wanted him to understand how much I suffered at their hands. Sometimes I fantasized about his death. But . . . I never imag-ined it would be for me."

I couldn't decide what to say, but before I made it worse, she went on, "I'd appreciate it if you gave me a little time to make sense of things. I'll be all right."

Since that was obviously a dismissal, Fade stood and pulled me to my feet. I went over to Thornton and said softly, "I need some air. You're in charge until I get back."

The older man nodded. "I doubt these boys are going any-where. They're tired and hungry, waiting on the food we were promised."

"I'm sure it'll be here soon. Vince Howe seemed serious about looking out for us."

"We did him a good turn and he knows it. If honor means anything here in Lorraine, he won't go back on his word."

I was counting on that. Hurt expanded in my chest, until I felt like I'd choke if I didn't get away for a while, away from promises and expectations, away from death. Fade followed me out of the town hall, his steps echoing after mine. I ran through the twi-light, attracting strange looks from the people going about their business, until I arrived at the graveyard where we'd left Stalker. The men were gone, and the hole was filled in. They had planted a rectangular stone, which they promised would bear his name soon enough. A man with a chisel would cut the rock away until he shaped it just right.

Dropping down beside his grave, I cried as I hadn't even when I held my friend's body in my arms. The sobs tore out of me, loud against the quiet night. Fade knelt and wrapped his arms around me, so I sealed my face against his shoulder, hop-ing to muffle some of the noise. He didn't try to quiet me, offer-ing only silence and warmth. When I calmed, I noticed his hands stroking down my back.

"Better?" he asked at length.

"Not really. But I can handle it now."

"I didn't like him," he said quietly, "but I'm sorry you lost a friend."

"He won't be the last, I fear. And I couldn't stand it if you—"

Fade silenced me with his mouth; this wasn't a hungry, tak-ing kiss, but one that gave back comfort and tenderness, soothing my inner ache. This wasn't the place for such things, however, so I struggled to my feet and dusted off my knees. The ache might never go away, but I was strong enough to swallow it down and remember how a Huntress should respond. Lately, I was more girl than Huntress, and it was making my job more complicated. Down below, I would've reacted less emotionally, factoring our chances of success or failure without much regard for loss of human life.

Together, we left the graveyard and headed toward the town hall. At night, people stayed indoors, so the dirt lanes were deserted and the windows shone with golden light. Guards manned the stone walls with rifles and crossbows like the one Tully carried. If any human settlements stood a chance of survival, Gaspard and Lorraine did. Appleton was lost, and I didn't think Winterville had much longer, unless they made some drastic changes.

When Fade and I returned, the men were eating. I had no appetite but Fade persuaded me to drink some soup. Morrow sat beside Tegan, whispering in her ear. She wasn't smiling at his nonsense but from the light in her eyes, she was no longer feeling quite so heavyhearted. Once the food and drink were gone, we all rolled into our blankets and went to sleep.

In the morning, as promised, Vince Howe came to take me before the council. I hadn't even managed a meeting last time before they laughed me out of town, and that failure burned as I accompanied him to the restaurant. They didn't have those in Salvation or Soldier's Pond, but apparently, it was a place where you could buy prepared food. Inside, there were tables covered in pretty cloths and chairs with cushions. I attracted a few looks because despite my efforts in Winterville, my appearance was ragged. My plaits were disheveled and my plain brown road gear showed signs of hard use.

But I lifted my chin and strode past the onlookers like I had a right to be there. Five people sat waiting, three men and two women, all in late middle age, I guessed, according to Topside life spans. The men stood when I approached and gestured me to a seat. I glanced over my shoulder at Vince Howe, who sat beside me. He spoke all their names, but I didn't bother learning them. If any of them proved a worthy ally, then I would.

"This is the leader of Company D."

Remembering my manners, I extended a hand to each of them and gave my best "I mean business" shake. Then Howe went on, "Last night, I mentioned how much her men helped us and what they sacrificed to see our goods safely here."

"What would you like in recompense?" a fair-haired woman asked me.

She expected me to request money to trade in town, possibly provisions or the right to our current lodgings for as long as we liked. But I surprised them.

"Volunteers," I said bluntly.

Two of the council members exchanged a look. "For what?"

You promised Stalker you'd see this through.

"The army. We lost good men defending Winterville and more on the way here. The only way we can defeat the horde is to build a force capable of meeting them on the field. Lorraine's a strong town with good walls and sound defenses. You can spare some men for the fight."

"I understand the urgency," the councilman said. "We've had reports about Appleton, and I've been expecting to see Muties on the march for days now. But what if men don't step up?"

"Then we draft them," Howe snapped.

A young woman took requests for food; I let Vince Howe choose mine. Soon after, she delivered our plates, along with fresh bread. The speed and luxury of it amazed me.

I ate while they debated the morality of such a course. It was something like the lottery in Otterburn, only the men chosen would end up joining Company D instead of being sent out as sacrifices. To my mind, this was better, as they had a chance of coming home. The discussion raged all through breakfast, and I didn't hurry them along because I was enjoying the food so much. Fluffy scrambled eggs and hot buttered muffins, warm tea and a dish of fruit; it reminded me of the feasts Momma Oaks used to make. If I succeeded out here, maybe one day she'd have her own kitchen again. Between my desire to give my family a new home and my promise to Stalker, there was no way I could quit this task. I'd see the Freaks defeated or die in the attempt.

By the time I ate my fill, the council had made up its collective mind. "We'll call all able-bodied men—"

"No," I cut in. "Not just men. Everyone over the age of thirteen, male and female. If they're willing to learn to fight, we'll teach them. They only need to be brave enough to come with us. Company D will handle the rest."

That sparked another round of argument, but Vince Howe gave me an approving nod. I guessed he didn't see a problem. While they bickered, I had seconds on eggs and muffins, and wondered if the townsfolk had fed my men this well. Eventually they decided I was right, and that the call to action might even go better if they permitted my request.

So an hour later, we gathered outside the town hall with men running through town ringing their bells and shouting, "The council requires all citizens to gather at once."

It didn't take as long as one might imagine, so I figured they weren't used to this kind of commotion in Lorraine. I let Vince Howe speak for Company D since he was known, and his account of our deeds and sacrifices had the crowd rumbling in awe. When he tilted his head at me, that was my cue.

"You've heard what we've accomplished and what we intend to do. If you want to give your families more someday, more than just four walls, then join us."

At first nobody moved. But then Fade stepped forward with the banner Momma Oaks had made. The rest of the men began their drills, showing what our joint training had taught them. A surprised murmur stirred the townsfolk, and then the impossible happened—what I had been working toward from the beginning. Men and women, boys and girls, all of those old enough and bold enough to meet our needs, rushed forward, eager to take their place in our ranks, more willing bodies here than I'd dared dream.

This is for you, Stalker, this moment . . . and every battle henceforth.

Somehow, I hid my startled exultation. "Then line up," I said, "and give us your names. There's a war on."

three

terminus

"For then," he said, "the king himself can't part us."

—George MacDonald, *The Day Boy and the Night Girl*

War

That day in Lorraine, we more than doubled our number. Company D remained in town for two more weeks while we offered rudimentary training. It wasn't enough for the dangers we'd face in the wilderness, but scouts reported activity in Appleton; part of the horde was on the move. So we had to march, though our war band was still too small to face them.

By nightfall, we were camped alongside the river. I wished Stalker were here to offer tactical advice, but I'd left him planted in the ground, and I owed him a decisive victory. While the rest of the men tended to mundane tasks, I called a meeting: Fade, Thornton, Tully, Spence, and Morrow. They were my most experienced warriors, so it made sense to ask their advice.

"Of all the recruits, you've seen the most combat. What's the best move?"

"You're in charge," Thornton muttered. "I'm just here to kill Muties."

"But you acted like you knew what you were doing, the night we covered the retreat to Soldier's Pond." And it was true. He wouldn't get out of strategic planning by claiming ignorance. I'd seen too much of his skill over the past months.

"We can't fight them head-on," Tully put in.

Spence nodded his agreement. "Sands told me that three

hundred strong set out from Appleton. My guess is, they're heading for Lorraine. It's the next nearest town for plundering."

"But the rest of the horde is settling in?" Morrow asked.

I'd wondered the same thing. "We've assumed that they were all soldiers, but what if the horde's numbers are swollen by noncombatants? The warriors might've been searching for a safe place to leave them while they sack our towns."

"Like the village in the woods near Salvation." Fade's voice was soft, but etched in bitterness, as if the memory ate at him.

"How does that impact our strategy?" I glanced between them, willing them to volunteer some insight. Stalker had known the most about planning assaults, yet I had to push forward.

Thornton wore a tired look. "If you're right, then the ruthless thing to do would be to circle around to Appleton and hit their weak point."

"The females and the brats," I breathed.

Silence fell, as we all contemplated the value of such a strike. Greater numbers wouldn't matter so much then, as we'd be facing weaker opponents. Nursing Freak females and offspring weren't exactly defenseless, but they couldn't compete with trained soldiers like us. The brutal nature of the attack might break the enemy's fighting spirit, but it might also fuel their hatred, making them determined to exterminate humanity at any cost.

Ultimately I shook my head. "I can't wage that kind of war."

"Even if it's the only way to win?" Tully asked.

The decision hurt, but I stuck to it. "No, we'll find another way."

Fade added, "We don't know that much about Mutie culture. All of them might be trained to fight, so we could hit Appleton, only to find the females and brats are every bit as ferocious as the ones pillaging our towns."

Spence nodded. "Plus, I've seen some momma bears defending their cubs, and believe me, you do *not* want to mess with them."

"In some ways," I said, "Muties are more like animals. So it stands to reason they wouldn't react like humans if we attacked territory they've claimed."

"A hit-and-run campaign would serve best. Like in a book I read." Morrow wore a thoughtful look, as if he were trying to remember more details. "We have to keep our units lean and mobile. We'll move faster since our squad's still pretty lean. So we rely on Stalker's scouts to provide us with good intel, then we strike, kill some, and disappear. We use the land around us, the darkness, every advantage we can muster. Because this will be a long fight."

I gave a quick nod. "Excellent. You're in charge of tactics."

Morrow stared at me. "I'm just a storyteller."

"You're not. One of these days I'm going to ask where you found all of these books you've read, but right now, we need to plan."

Everyone agreed with that, and Morrow shared everything he could remember about that tale. Unlike *The Day Boy and the Night Girl*, we didn't have a copy of the war strategy book, so I had no way of knowing whether the smaller army achieved victory in the end. But it was the best idea we had.

In the morning, we broke camp. To my annoyance, it took longer than it should, and I vowed to work on that. The men needed to pack their gear in less than five minutes. I couldn't have them wandering around complaining about a night on the ground. So I set Thornton on them, as his thunderous scold was far more impressive than anything I could produce; and I had no experience yelling at people anyway.

I sought Morrow before we moved out. "Would you take over the scouts? They need a leader and I think you'd serve. But only if you're willing."

"You put a lot of faith in me, Deuce."

"Are you saying I shouldn't?" I had noticed his silent

movements, his careful grace. While he might not be as adept at slinking in and out of the shadows as Stalker had been, Morrow would be a fair replacement.

With a wry smile, he shook his head. "It's an honor. I'll do my best to keep them safe."

"I know. Now go get me some intel. We can't move far until we know for sure which way the Muties are heading."

It was a tense wait by the riverbanks. Company D occupied the time in drills. I put Fade, Tully, and Spence to supervising the sparring sessions. It was odd seeing normal townsfolk learning to fight, but they were all willing. Gavin worked particularly hard, hanging on every word Spence uttered. The brat had incredible heart to make up for his lack of size; each time his partner knocked him down, he came up swinging, and occasionally, he surprised somebody with his ferocity. I could tell he had a grudge to work off against the Freaks, and his anger troubled me, not because he was upset over the loss of his parents, but I feared it might get the best of him at the wrong time. Rage would get him killed.

I pulled him out of his current match and sat him down. He glared at me with green grass eyes, furious in his dirty face. "What? I was holding my own. And he's bigger."

This boy couldn't be more than fourteen years old, and his small size made me wonder if he was younger. "How old are you?"

"I'm over the recruiting age. You set that at thirteen."

"I know. Just tell me."

"I'll be fifteen in a few months," he muttered.

He seemed so young, maybe because the Topside world tried to protect its young more than they had done down below. It felt like much more than a year and a few months separated us. I guessed his world had been very different before the Freaks changed so much, Winterville panicked, and Dr. Wilson spread his poison.

I made my tone hard because I knew he wouldn't respect me if I was tender with him. He didn't want that, and couldn't handle it. This boy was after blood, not kindness. "If you get yourself killed fighting like a cow with two left hooves, you won't live to see the Muties in the ground. Is that what you want?"

"No, ma'am."

"Sir," I corrected. "In this army, it doesn't matter what people have in their pants. Now get back in there and use your head, not just your fists."

"Yes, sir."

Tegan came over to me as practice tailed off. "He reminds me of someone."

She had been less obvious about her anger, kept it locked up inside her, but I'd seen her fury when I first found her in Gotham. She'd let it out with each blow of the club; Tegan hadn't fought smart back then, either. The staff suited her better.

"You stay back," I cautioned.

"I know. I'm second line of defense and full-time medic. I won't be in the vanguard." She stared into the fields, watching the wind blow across the leaves. "It's unnerving to be out here, isn't it? Not knowing exactly where our enemies are."

I knew what she meant. The wilderness was quiet apart from the chirps of birds and the chitter of insects, the burbling rush of the river behind us. Springtime had greened the grass as far as the eye could see, but just over the next rise, could lurk violence and death. Despite myself, I shivered, hoping the scouts returned soon.

By noon I had my wish. They had done their work well and Morrow made the report. "They're moving northeast of here. From what we can tell, they're heading for Lorraine."

"Then we need to follow them, wait until they camp, and strike when they're asleep."

"Let's fight fire with fire," Fade said.

"Did we bring along any liquor?" Tully asked.

Since drinking left soldiers sloppy and careless, the answer should be no, but when we searched the packs, we found six jugs. I left Thornton verbally reaming the men who had violated the code of conduct while the others carted off the contraband. Tully popped the cork on one and sniffed it.

"It's strong," she said. "This will do nicely."

"For what?" I asked.

"We can make fire bombs. And with some rags, I can set my bolts on fire. These will scatter the Muties, induce panic, especially if we strike while they're asleep."

The remainder of that day we marched according to the scouts' directions. At Morrow's orders, they were constantly running back and forth, carrying messages about this portion of the horde. It wasn't the whole army I'd seen camped in the fields outside Salvation, but they didn't need all of their forces to take smaller towns. It made sense for them to protect the territory they'd already claimed—and at the moment, I didn't have sufficient numbers to take back Appleton, but I could keep them from overrunning Lorraine. Come nightfall, we were three miles from our intended target.

"Tonight, it's critical that you follow orders. Kill on the perimeter and fall back. Make them chase you. Anything that increases confusion and decreases visibility, do it. And run if you need to." I raked away the grass until I had a patch of dry dirt to serve as a map, then I etched some directions. "This is where we'll regroup. They may follow, trying to force a fair fight. We won't give it to them. This is where our forest starts, and if necessary, we'll fight in retreat. Ideally, though, we're going to hit them, kill as many as we can, then vanish. That's the plan."

"Any questions?" Thornton asked.

There were a number and he fielded them as I strode away. I hoped I sounded confident and prepared when my heart was pounding like a drum. So much depended on my instincts being right; I had no doubts that this needed to be done, but maybe I had no business attempting it. *Who am I to lead these men?*

"I'm with you," Fade said softly.

I wanted so badly to turn into his arms, but I was afraid he'd recoil—and it wouldn't be a good way to behave in front of the men, either. No doubt Tully and Spence were deeply in love, despite the fact that she was a good ten years older, but they never touched, never kissed where anybody could see. I just saw it in the way he gazed at her, like he'd fall over and stop breathing if she ever quit looking back.

"It's normal to be scared," he went on, "and I'm glad you are. It makes me feel better about the butterflies in my stomach. This will be the biggest battle we've ever fought."

"Thanks."

Though his arms remained at his sides, Fade whispered, "This is me holding you. And this is me, kissing you for luck."

That put a smile on my face. Maybe a battlefield was no place for such attachments, but I couldn't put away those feelings. He was part of me like my shadow.

"This is me, kissing you back."

"Deuce!" Morrow shouted. "I need you."

My eyes met Fade's and clung, and that look said so many things, and then I strode away to handle last-minute inquiries about troop deployments. The camp the Freaks had chosen offered us higher ground on a ridge above, so that was where I meant to plant our riflemen. Tully planned to start the fires, and six soldiers would carry the firebombs, which could be lobbed as far as somebody could throw them.

Just after moonrise, Company D moved out. A silver sliver in the sky, the moon cast barely enough light to keep the rest of the men from stumbling over their feet. For me, it was fine, and I could've navigated with my eyes closed. Which meant I was on point with the scouts to make sure the ambush went off smoothly.

I crept up over the rise, my stomach in knots. I hadn't seen so many Freaks gathered in one place since I ran from the horde, saving Fade. Fear boiled up in the form of bile, acid in my throat, but I swallowed it down. *You've taken enough,* I told the monsters silently. *This is all you get. This is where the end begins.*

After spotting the best vantage points, I set the riflemen in place. Once the fires started burning down below, it should help with targeting. After all, it didn't matter where they shot the Freaks; bullets never felt good going in. Once Tully was in position with the gunmen, I crept down to join the others.

"Thornton," I whispered. "You have command of the infantry. Don't let the inexperienced ones get swept too far into the mob."

"Will do my best," he said with Longshot's familiar salute.

Thornton wasn't the only man I'd seen use that gesture; it was common in the territories, a way of showing respect without acknowledging any superior rank. Yet it was inexpressibly poignant to see that just before the fight of a lifetime, a sign that Longshot was here watching over me. Maybe that was nonsense, but I'd take the hope of it because then I could imagine being united someday with the people I'd lost. If nothing else, it bolstered my courage, so I was able to give orders in a tone firm enough to make them believe we would triumph.

"The enemy's sleeping, men. Bring the pain."

Escort

From the first fiery bolt, the battle went according to plan. We got a bonus when the field caught, creating an inferno of snarling panic. The Freaks fled from the blaze and ran straight into our blades. Between the dark night and the bright fire, they hardly saw us as they died. The firebombs exploded in the center of the camp, immolating a number of the monsters. On the ridge, riflemen picked them off as they scattered. In the chaos, we killed them with impunity, until they realized how few we were and then they charged. I couldn't let them surround us. My men didn't have the experience to win at such steep odds.

"Sound the retreat," I shouted.

Morrow piped out the notes warning the squad to fall back to the agreed location on the forest's edge. The men responded, aware our tactics didn't allow for a stand-up fight; we meant to kill as many as possible before luring them to more advantageous terrain, where we'd fare better against superior numbers. Fade was nearby, so we fought together as we gave ground. I stabbed and slashed, careful not to turn my back on monsters that might impale me from behind. Thornton shot one over my shoulder and I turned. Fade ran with me, full out, until we put the war zone behind us. I counted as the soldiers stumbled in. In the end, we lost ten men. Well enough, I hadn't expected to defeat them in one ambush.

"How many did you get?" I asked the men, after they reached our rendezvous point.

The tally was close to a hundred—and I smothered their urge to cheer. It was a solid achievement, one third of the enemy's number. We fell back into the forest thereafter and these Freaks apparently weren't bound by the deal we'd made with the others, which confirmed they were part of the horde. They hunted us through the trees, but in such terrain, they couldn't fight as a mob, so we picked them off. Company D fought in constant motion, never letting them rest. On the sixth night, the Freaks fell back to set up camp in the grasslands beyond. There were only a hundred of them left by then, but I had no plans to offer them a fair fight.

Two weeks into the conflict, other problems plagued us. Between the Freaks in the area and our own men, it was difficult to find game. Fishing helped a little, but time spent on provender, as Thornton called it, left less time for evading their attacks and for planning our own. The situation had to be addressed before it got worse.

Before I could resolve that crisis, Morrow brought grim news. "There's a trade caravan heading from Gaspard to Soldier's Pond. My scouts think the Muties we've been harassing intend to hit it for supplies before circling back to Lorraine."

"We can't let that happen," I said. "Let's move."

That began a hard march east with little food and less sleep. Company D was thin and exhausted when we met the traders on the road. I expected them to greet us with rifles, but word of our exploits had spread, and they actually recognized the banner Momma Oaks had made. Most days, Gavin carried it proudly, the pennant flying in the wind.

"Oi, Company D!" the lead driver called.

"You intend to hang us too?" I joked.

Laughing, the man shook his head. "The guards are still talking about that, you know. I wouldn't expect a warm welcome in town anytime soon, but stories are different on the road. Vince Howe and John Kelley have only the best things to say."

"We'll get you to Soldier's Pond," I offered, "but you'll have to help feed us."

I hoped they could spare us something in Soldier's Pond since a good number of our men came from there. If not, we could surely share the traders' rations while we protected them.

The trader nodded without hesitation. "I can make the meal stretch to porridge if you can augment with fresh meat." There was some grumbling from his men because they'd expected skillet cakes, not gruel, but he leveled a stern look on them. "Do you want to live? This area's crawling with Muties."

He was right; only the skill of our scouts had let us reach the caravan before the enemy, and to get to Soldier's Pond, we had to circle the forest because of the wagons. There would be ample opportunity for them to hit us before then. A knot formed in my stomach because the last time we'd guarded supplies like this, Stalker *died*. I couldn't handle losing anybody else. But I put my fears aside and informed the men that we had a new goal—and at the end, there would be some rest in Soldier's Pond. That roused a weary cheer from warriors who had been subsisting on plants and berries. I didn't know about them, but I was starving and *so* weary of wild-leek-and-mushroom soup. It had been days since I'd eaten more than a scrap of meat, choosing to give my share to the soldiers instead.

"You're too thin," Fade had said, when he caught me doing so. "You can't keep up your strength if you don't eat."

"I am," I'd muttered.

There just wasn't much to be had. Between constant fighting and laying ambushes, then moving fast enough to stay out of reach, we didn't have time to hunt properly or bring down big game, assuming the Freaks had left any. There should be moose and deer, but it had been a week since the scouts saw any tracks. There was only smaller game like rabbits and squirrels, less worth the trouble of catching because it took so many to feed the soldiers. Sometimes we skinned them and put the meat in the pot for flavor along with the leeks, potatoes, and mushrooms, but it wasn't enough nutrition to keep us strong.

"I can't wait to see my family," a man said.

"Me either."

I left them to the talk of happy reunions, as long as they fell into formation when Thornton barked the order. And they did. My soldiers were young and old, male and female, but they all had courage to spare. We marched alongside the wagons with the Company D banner flying high; and it was dusk when the monsters came.

This was their first chance to strike at us in the open, a risk I'd known we were taking when I decided to protect the caravan. But if they got hold of these supplies, people in Soldier's Pond and Gaspard might starve, plus it'd strengthen the enemy. I couldn't let that happen. I recalled what Dr. Wilson said about how hunger made them digest their own brains. If we kept them from finding new food sources, they'd get dumber and easier to kill. They came at us in the loping run now so familiar to me, but there was no smell at all, except the sweat of unwashed soldiers and the general reek of the mules.

"Formation C," I shouted.

Thankfully, our drills had prepared the men for a number of contingencies, and they arrayed themselves with foot soldiers in front and riflemen in back. Tully vaulted on top of a wagon, then pulled Gavin up beside her. From on top of the crates they opened fire, gunning down two to start the bloodshed off right. The animals screamed in terror but the drivers sawed at the reins and didn't let them bolt in panic. I waited at the front, braced to receive their charge.

I had Tegan on one side and Fade on the other. She knocked one down for me, just like she used to do for Stalker, and I stabbed it through the neck. Tegan smashed one in the face as Morrow ran it through, and on my other side, Fade fought with economical grace, his moves a dodge and weave that never left my flank vulnerable. I stayed tight too, my blades spinning in the purple light. I lost count of how many I killed, but I heard Tully shout she was out of quarrels. A few riflemen said the same, and they pushed forward to fight with their knives.

Blood gushed, like spilled wine across the pub floor in Otterburn. The monsters knew they had to win this fight, so they never broke and ran, not even when Fade slew the last one with a blade straight through the heart.

The victory cost us twenty men, however. Before we moved, Company D dug another mass grave to keep scavengers away. Tully spoke the words on our behalf because I was too tired and I had nothing to say. As we shoveled dirt on their bloody faces, I noticed how young some of them were, a few barely meeting my age limit.

You did this. You took these boys and girls away from their mothers.

"But I didn't kill them," I whispered.

The words didn't assuage my guilt. When we moved on, we were a bleak, unhappy group, and the thin gruel we ate for supper didn't cheer anybody up. The scouts found us a clear path to Soldier's Pond thereafter, and while they saw smaller groups of Freaks prowling the hills nearby, none of them dared to attack. I was exhausted beyond description when we saw Soldier's Pond on the horizon. A weary huzzah came from the men, but they didn't look good. Many had developed sores; their shoes and boots were in rags, so their feet bled as we marched.

My dream hung in tatters, and though we were doing some

good, I was failing at keeping my men safe and healthy. I didn't have the experience for this, but the problem was, nobody did. Humans had cowered in their settlements for so long that they had forgotten how to fight without terrible potions and mysterious poisons. The only information we had came from Morrow's stories—and I still needed to ask him about those.

There should be time in Soldier's Pond.

The guards came out to meet the wagons, offering safe escort, and that was just as well, as I didn't think my men had any fight in them. The townsfolk might complain about us appearing to gobble up their provisions, but they wouldn't have these trade goods from Gaspard without us. And Soldier's Pond was far from self-sufficient.

"Thank you," the trader said as the caravan passed the town's defenses. "We'd have died on the road if not for your men."

His name was Marlon Bean, and I expected him to add his story to the ones circulating from Vince Howe and John Kelley. In the long run, their goodwill might save Company D, but for the moment, I merely nodded and led the soldiers to a much-desired homecoming. The guards had all kinds of questions, but I hushed them with an impatient gesture. It wasn't until I saw Tegan's brows go up that I realized how used to command I had become.

I frowned at her as I called, "I'm giving all of you forty-eight-hours' leave. The mess is over there . . . stick with a local if you don't know the way. Once you've eaten, find the bathhouse. Then locate a bunk and get some rest. Some of you need your wounds wrapped or bandages changed. I don't think anybody's likely to die overnight, so see Tegan and me in the morning. We'll fix you up. That's all. And enjoy the break."

The men surged off, grateful to be out of the wilderness. I knew how they felt.

Fade beckoned with a stern look. "That order to rest goes for you too."

Since I was dizzy by this point, I let him tow me toward the mess. If we were off schedule, I'd make the cook open the kitchen myself. Fortunately, however, Colonel Park was on top of things. She met us in the hall and she had two extra workers in tow so they could make more food quickly. As usual, it was tasteless, but we were all so hungry I would've happily eaten a bucket of the mushroom porridge they gave us down below.

As we ate, I realized belatedly that we'd sat in a cluster of officers. Nothing so formal had ever been declared, of course, but I always turned to Fade, Tegan, Thornton, Tully, Morrow, or Spence when I needed something. And here we sat, nobody else at our table. I wouldn't have sent anyone else away, but I guessed the others figured this was our inner circle, and we had clever plans to make. Or maybe they just wanted a break from the lot of us. I listened to the conversation with half an ear; it was an important issue, but I lacked the drive to tackle the problem straightaway when I had forty-seven hours of freedom.

"We have to ask all towns in the territory for a tithe," Thornton was arguing.

Morrow protested, "But we can't *make* them give us supplies."

Spence scowled, gesturing with his spoon so that he was in danger of losing the stewed poultry and dough he'd scooped up. "We can refuse to protect them if they choose not to."

It sounded hard, but maybe he was right. If they weren't willing to tighten their belts and donate to the soldiers keeping the horde at bay, then they could deal with the consequences. In so many ways, I'd bitten off more than I could chew; some days, only pure stubbornness kept me pushing forward when I felt so stupid, the least suitable person to be leading Company D.

Morrow shook his head, however. "Fear and intimidation

won't serve long-term. They'll only come to see us as tyrants, the reasons their families are going hungry."

"There's also the matter of hauling provisions," Fade said. "If we have wagons full of supplies, rather than just what we each carry, then it slows our movements. And we lack the numbers to face the horde head-on."

He was right about that. Before we joined up with the Gaspard traders, we'd sent scouts to Appleton, trying to get a handle on the actual number and there were still too many to count. It was impossible to send someone all through town, but from what Sands told us, the Freaks were living in the town, not ransacking it. They hadn't damaged the buildings; they were moving in and out of the houses like people, and *that* alarmed me as much as anything I'd heard.

"We won't solve this over dinner," Tully said at last. "Why don't we talk to the colonel tomorrow and see what she suggests? Her family has always been in the military and she's got a lot of old books full of historical campaigns."

I leveled a look at Morrow. The last time we were here, I'd noticed how he kissed the colonel on her cheeks, though he wasn't her husband. With a single raised brow, I invited him to elaborate, but he held his silence, and I made up my mind that I'd unearth his secrets before we moved out again.

Counsel

After a bath came a joyous reunion with my family. Each time I returned, they seemed a little surprised, as if they had secretly resigned themselves to my loss. Momma Oaks was thrilled with how the company had taken to her banner, but she wept when she heard about Stalker. I hugged her tight, fighting tears, and Edmund patted my shoulder, awkward as he always was with strong emotion.

"Where's Rex?" I asked, stepping back.

"Still at the shop," Edmund answered.

Momma Oaks bit her lip. "He's a tad angry with you."

There was nothing for it but to get the confrontation out of the way. So I headed down to the workshop, where I found Rex pulling a needle through some leather, trimming it. He glanced at me with a face like a thundercloud.

No greeting. "I saw how many new men you've taken on. Are *they* all trained warriors?"

Since that had been my objection to him joining up, I winced. "No. But they're not my brothers, either."

"Do you have any idea how it feels to be refused by your *mother*?"

"No. Because I never had one until I got yours."

"Ours," he corrected, losing a little of his righteous

indignation. But he soldiered on, "You should've told me in person, Deuce. Instead you slipped off without facing me."

He was right about that. I'd told myself I was in a hurry, but I just hadn't wanted to look into his eyes and say, *No, you can't fight. Stay home and make your momma happy.* Which was ridiculous, considering he had been married and living away from home for years.

"I don't want anything to happen to you," I said honestly. "It would break her heart. And I can't guarantee your safety out there."

"You can't in here, either."

That was true, especially after what happened in Salvation. "Do you still want to fight?"

"I do. The orders have slacked off . . . and I can tell Pa's just inventing work for me, trying to keep me busy."

"You're not looking to die to be with Ruth or something stupid like that?"

Rex shook his head. "I want to avenge my wife. It's a sin and goes against our ways, I know. But as many of those monsters as I can kill, well, I'd consider that a good day's work."

I understood this motivation. It shouldn't involve reckless heroics, either. Because he couldn't slay a bunch of Freaks if he got himself killed.

"Go see Thornton about weapons . . . and ask Momma for some fighting gear. Edmund will need to fix your boots too. We could use a lot more of them, come to think of it."

I contemplated my men with their bloody feet and thin faces. If Company D was to thrive and grow, I had to get better at providing for them. So I went back to the bunkhouse and caught the Oakses in a rare private moment. Edmund was holding Momma Oaks while she wept silently into his shoulder. Sucking in a soft breath, I crept away, not wanting to interrupt. Confused, I sat on the damp ground until I guessed it had been long enough for them to finish whatever that was. I had no idea if she was happily weeping because I'd come back or if she missed Salvation.

Half an hour later, I returned and a glance inside told me that Edmund must've gone to the workshop. I caught up with him there and made my request.

He nodded. "I'm happy to make whatever you need, provided I have the supplies. I've outfitted all the men here, and now I'm making surplus in common sizes. You're welcome to them, though if you have men with extra large feet or small ones, they'll need a custom fit."

"Thanks, Edmund."

"I'm glad to do my part for the war effort," he said quietly.

His sincerity moved me. My father believed I was doing something important, and he took me seriously. I had to hug him, even if that wasn't usually my first impulse. He looked surprised as I came around the counter, but he wrapped his arms around me like it was the easiest thing in the world. For him and me, though, it never was. For a few seconds, I enjoyed the warmth of his hold. Then I stepped back and told him about Rex.

He flinched far inside his eyes, but he nodded. "I saw that coming. I'll break the news to your mother."

I didn't correct him, even in my head. They weren't my foster anything. These folks had become my family, along with Fade, Tegan, and maybe, to a lesser degree, Company D.

In the morning, I went to see the colonel before breakfast. I found her in the HQ, listening to reports on Freak movements on the other side of the forest. Though they didn't go out looking for trouble, Soldier's Pond always had good intel, but the colonel erred on the side of caution. Deep down I suspected she felt unprepared for her position, just as I did, so she was reluctant to send men out to die. But while humans cowered, the horde grew.

"Colonel Park," the scout was saying. "There's no activity in the forest, but there are hunting parties circling around. It's only a matter of time until they reach us."

"If you want us to help defend the town, we'll need more men," I murmured.

"Good morning to you too," the colonel said. "You don't believe in small talk, do you?"

"Not so much. We also need provisions, whatever you can spare."

"I'd ask how many times you intend to make me turn you down before you give up, but I suspect the answer is infinite. Because you don't give up."

I smothered a smile. "I'm not known for it."

"I'll talk to the quartermaster and see what we can spare without running the risk of privation this winter."

"Thanks."

"Have you given any thought to your command structure?" she asked.

When I shook my head, I received a lecture on the necessity of running a tight ship, whatever that meant. She laid out how a proper army should be run, stressing the importance of a clear hierarchy. Colonel Park scanned the room as if checking for unfriendly ears, then she added, low, "I wish I could do more to help you. But my advisors are frightened, cautious men. They think if we maintain a neutral attitude, the Muties won't engage."

"I've seen that proven false, time and again. Salvation did nothing to provoke the monsters, just went about their business. Same with Appleton, so far as I know."

"I believe you. I just hope it doesn't take a tragedy here to motivate them."

"Why don't you overrule them?"

"Because when my father died, he left me only provisional power."

"What does that have to do with anything?"

"'Colonel' used to be an earned title, but I inherited the role from my father. Since I was younger than anyone expected, due to the bleeding fever, when I took over from him, there were conditions set on my administration of the armed forces." Likely she could tell I didn't understand, so she clarified, "My authority is subject to checks and balances from my advisors."

"So they can gainsay you. That's too bad."

With a few more polite words, I let her get back to meeting with the scouts. In that moment, I felt a bit sorry for her. It would be awful to be in charge, but not really, with people second-guessing every move. She had information and resources at her fingertips but she didn't have the freedom to use any of it as she deemed fit, at least, not without arguments and endless voting. Sometimes disasters required quick, decisive action.

We stayed in Soldier's Pond more than two days. It took longer for Edmund to outfit all the men, and Momma Oaks convinced the quartermaster to let her have multiple bolts of unused cloth; so while Edmund made boots, she was madly stitching uniforms. In that time, the colonel procured cornmeal, dry beans, and Morrow dug up a recipe for hardtack, which consisted of flour and water, baked multiple times until the ingredients were like small bricks.

"What're we supposed to do with this?" I asked, when the storyteller brought me to the mess to show me what the cooks had created.

At this hour, the room was empty apart from the harried workers, who had been experimenting with the recipe for hours, and us. Morrow frowned, likely at my lack of imagination. "If you crumble them, they thicken a stew. Crushed and mixed with milk or egg, they become pancakes. Or we can eat them like this if there's nothing else. They last forever."

With each soldier carrying his allotment of beans, cornmeal, dried meat, and hardtack, we should do well for the rest of the campaign, at least until the cold set in. Soon there would be tubers and fruit on the trees, more berries and wild greens. My concern was the scarcity of game with the horde hunting in our territory, but we couldn't stop fighting for fear of hunger.

"You think we'll run across cows and chickens in the field?" I teased. "That seems likely. I bet we'll have pancakes in the skillet every morning."

"You're cruel to a man who spent hours paging through dusty old books for you."

I raised a brow. "For me? Or Tegan?"

It was no secret, the way he looked at her when she was helping the men. I'd also observed how he sought her out during quiet moments and that he seemed to enjoy their training sessions a whole lot, maybe because he got to be close to her. I didn't think Tegan had noticed how he felt, but I had gotten better at paying attention to such details, after the misunderstanding with Stalker. My heart hurt when I remembered him, but the alternative was forgetting, and that was the final kind of death—when nobody told your story anymore.

"I'd like her to eat more," he admitted. "She's too skinny. So are you."

"That accounts for *everyone* in Company D."

With a small, sly smile, Morrow offered, "Well, I'm more concerned about the eating habits of some than others."

"Me too. Thanks for your effort on this." I turned to the cooks. "The colonel wants you to bake five hundred more of these."

They grumbled, but it was a measure of my status that they just went back to work. Morrow seemed impressed as we left the mess together, but I didn't let him run off. I wasn't done with this conversation yet.

"You've had access to all kinds of books," I said. "More than we've seen in any town or village we've visited. Gotham was the only place I ever saw that had so many. A lot of them were ruined, but plenty more could still be read. Have you been there?"

I knew Morrow was a wanderer—that he wasn't from Soldier's Pond—but he had been oddly reticent about his past. He sighed as he shook his head and started walking. I had no idea where he was going, but I didn't mean for him to leave me behind, so I quickened my pace. We ended up in the cowshed we'd used for training. There was nobody there, just the animals, so at least it was private.

"No. I'm from the west . . . a village called Rosemere."

I'd seen it on Longshot's maps, but I couldn't place it. Though it was listed, it wasn't on the trade routes he'd drawn. "Where's that, exactly?"

"On the Evergreen Isle."

That was why he hadn't traveled there. Longshot only covered land routes, and you had to cross the water to get to Rosemere. "You don't talk about it much. Was it bad there?"

"No," Morrow said softly. "It was heaven."

"Then why did you leave?"

"The usual story. I loved a girl who didn't feel the same, so I vowed to see the world and make her sorry I left."

"Did it work?" I asked.

He shrugged. "I don't know. I haven't been back."

"Tell me about it?"

The storyteller was in his element, painting a picture for me in words. He spoke of a jewel of a village with white stone cottages and charming gardens in bloom, of the market where all manner of lovely things were sold, of a sturdy dock where men went out in small boats to cast their nets and women in head scarves hung out their washing while calling cheerfully to one another. Of the Evergreen Isle, he said even more.

"You have to see it to believe. Forests all around, green as far as the eye can see. It's lush and unspoiled, no other ruins, and there have never been any mutants."

That seemed odd. "Why not?"

"They can't swim. I'm not sure why, but I've seen them try a few times from the ruins on the other side of the river, and they always sink like stones."

I bet Dr. Wilson would have a theory, but there was no time to detour to Winterville to ask him; with the delay for provisions, we had lost our momentum and needed to get back to the fight. But I filed that information away as a weakness I could exploit, provided I figured out the way to do it. Since the Freaks got smarter and more knowledgeable with each generation, they doubtless would be wary when it came to water.

"That doesn't explain all the books . . . or your fancy knife work," I pointed out.

Morrow seemed annoyed that I hadn't been distracted by his eloquent descriptions. "You're pushy, you know that?"

"I usually accomplish what I mean to."

"The first adventure I ever went on didn't lead me far from home," he said. "But it *was* dangerous. See, on the other side of the river, we have ruins, similar to what I imagine Gotham is like. So I swam across to explore, and in my wandering, I ran across a building full of books, you can't even imagine—"

"I can, actually. We found a place like that in Gotham. It's called a library."

"I know that," Morrow said. "I suspected you didn't."

"I so enjoy it when people assume I'm stupid."

He shook his head. "Not that, just very focused on killing."

"Go on," I prompted.

"I barely made it out . . . the ruins were crawling with Muties." That sounded like a story I'd like to hear, and maybe it was even akin to Fade's and mine. But I needed answers so that all the pieces added up, so I didn't ask him to elaborate. Morrow went on, "I was in bad shape when I stumbled out of the river, and my father was livid. As soon as I recovered, he dragged me to a man in the village who was teaching his sons to fence, a family tradition. And my father insisted I learn. He said I had to be able to defend myself if I meant to take foolhardy risks."

"You took to it," I observed.

"Yes, well. I had the proper build and I like the elegance of it, though I enjoy the bloodshed less."

"I've noticed. And the stories . . . ?"

Morrow nodded, slightly annoyed with my impatience. "I couldn't forget all those books . . . so I went to my father and I demanded the use of one of the boats. It took me weeks, but I recovered as many as I could and brought them to Rosemere. Now, we have the only library in the territories."

"Books people can borrow anytime they want?" I asked, impressed by the notion.

"Yes. I've read more than anyone I know." It wasn't a boast, just a statement, and that explained much about him: why he was so in love with stories and so set on writing his own.

"Thanks for telling me. I think I'd like to visit Rosemere someday."

"No offense, Deuce, but I hope you come as a traveler, not a Huntress."

I smiled at that. "None taken. I don't wish war or hardship on the only peaceful place in the territories. I just . . . I'd like to see something like that. That's all."

"I was wondering . . ." For the first time since I'd met him, Morrow seemed bashful. "You teased me but I'm recording all of our adventures. And someday, I'd like to hear your story in detail—everything you can remember from down below, what life was like, how you came to Salvation and then Soldier's Pond."

"Really?"

"Truly. I need your permission, though. It doesn't seem right otherwise."

"You have it," I said.

Campaign

I n addition to provisions, boots, and uniforms, we picked up forty more men, including Rex, before we left Soldier's Pond. I heard her advisors haranguing Colonel Park as we marched past HQ, but there was nothing they could do, short of rummaging through each man's pack.

This time, I was better equipped to provide for so many men and with warmer weather and better forage, the soldiers should stay healthy longer.

It hit me hard that I didn't have Stalker as my scout leader anymore. He had handpicked the scouts according to some private criteria, and I missed his expertise. Morrow did his best, but he lacked my friend's instincts. Their information was critical, however, so we all had to press on. I remembered what Colonel Park had said to me about structure, now that we were substantially larger than twelve men.

"Hold up. Tegan, Fade, Tully, Spence, Morrow, Thornton!" I called their names as soon as we left town, and they came over to see what I needed.

"I've looked to all of you repeatedly. It's time to make it official. I talked to the colonel about rankings and she said a company as large as ours needs command infrastructure, so the men know who to talk to and who's in charge."

Thornton nodded. "I wondered when you would get around to it."

"You didn't see the need to clue me in?"

"Nope."

I laughed. Though he was bigger and blunter than Longshot had been, sometimes Thornton reminded me of him. "You're staff sergeant, and I'm putting you in charge of provisions. If we need something, let me know. If you see a soldier going without or who's not taking care of his gear, tell me that too."

"Does this mean I get to scream when I see infractions?"

"Yep," I said, mimicking his delivery.

He actually cracked a smile. "Then thank you for that."

"Tegan, I'm officially making you company medic. Keep an eye on the soldiers because they may not come forward if they're feeling off. I know it's a lot to ask because there's so many of us now—"

"Do I get a fancy title?" she cut in pertly.

"Doc Tegan isn't enough?"

She smiled. "No, it'll do. And it's nice to have my talents recognized."

"I'm told I need a squad leader for every thirty men." At that point, I looked at Fade, Tully, and Spence. "I'm dividing the men up between the three of you. You have more like sixty men each at this point, but we'll have to make do."

"You're not taking a squad?" Tully asked.

I shook my head. "The colonel tells me that the captain—or whatever I am—has to be apart from keeping the peace like you three will. Should I have them count off?"

I studied the men standing in formation. At last, we looked like a proper army, no longer ragtag or mismatched, and with Gavin flying our banner proudly at the front of the column, a tremor of pride ran through me. Momma Oaks made this possible; she sewed until her fingers bled to get the uniforms done fast enough . . . because it was my dream. These men weren't bound to any town; they all shared a single cause—to defeat the Freaks or die trying.

I did this.

I didn't quit.

And I will not fail.

"That would be easiest," Tully said, responding to my question.

I shouted for the men to sound off in threes. Once they finished, I called, "Squad one, if you need anything, see Fade. He *is* the boss of you. Any problems he can't handle will be brought to me, and you *do not* want that." Not a single soldier snickered, probably because I was borrowing Momma Oaks's sternest voice. "Squad two, you're with Tully. Threes, look to Spence. If we separate for any reason, these are the leaders you follow. Understood?"

"Yes, sir!"

"If you forget your number, you'll dig latrines, even if we don't need them. Questions?"

"No, sir!"

"Then let's move out."

Thus commenced the summer of blood. We fought Freaks from the other side of the forest all the way to Gaspard and back again. The men were brave, even the inexperienced ones. The battles ran together, day after day, while we kept the trade routes clear. Company D got proficient at packing up their gear to move on to the next fight; the last time, it took less than two minutes and I was counting.

Now and then I caught Rex eyeing me but I couldn't read his expression. I treated him like everyone else, but I was happy to see him in one piece as time wore on. As for me, I had new scars and healing wounds, bruises on bruises from sleeping on the hard ground. I had seldom been so weary, but the Freaks never seemed to run out of bodies to throw at us. Each night, I dreamed of bloodshed and violence, of Freaks pillaging Soldier's Pond, as they had Salvation and Appleton. We kept the wagons moving, but accomplished little else because the horde wasn't stirring. Instead, they sent out hunting parties to test our abilities . . . and the survivors fled to report back with our scouts nipping at their heels.

The impasse made me nervous.

The days were hot and sticky; flies buzzed around the fields full of their dead. We burned the monsters when we could and left them to rot otherwise. I wished I could dream of Morrow's stories about Rosemere, but my mind was a dark and awful place. Sometimes it seemed that the killing would never end, and because they could breed faster, reach fighting age sooner, I didn't see a happy ending.

My naming day came and went unnoticed. This year, there were no sweets or presents, no party. Instead, I stood knee-deep in mud with a summer storm bearing down. The sky was all snaps of lightning, booming thunder, while my feet slid beneath me. It was hard to fight, tough to see with the rain sluicing through my plaits and into my eyes. But the weather didn't deter the Freaks, so we stood our ground. This was the biggest hunting party yet, close to our number, and it horrified me that the enemy could send so many while the bulk of the horde squatted in Appleton. It seemed like such a horrendous waste, but maybe the monsters had some plan my human brain couldn't fathom.

And that possibility scared the devil out of me.

I stabbed another, then another, its blood spilling away into the rain. My hands were cold, clumsy, and I lost my grip on the wet dagger. It sank into the mud; and I couldn't kick with the earth sucking at my boots. Fade slid in with a smooth strike, saving me, and I lifted my head in a weary, silent thank-you. He dug out my dagger and we pushed forward to help the rest of the men, all bogged down and stumbling.

We lost sixteen soldiers that day.

For the sake of my men, I hid my despair over those deaths . . . and the increasing intelligence of our enemy. Because we were winning our fights, mostly, Company D's spirits stayed fairly high as summer crept toward fall in a haze of multiple engagements. In the end, the scouts brought us dismal tidings as the days cooled again. The air was sweet with the scent of ripening apples; I had people in the trees, picking as many as they could carry. The last battle was two days behind us, and the men were ready to go again.

Sands delivered the worrisome news. "There's movement in Appleton at last. I think the horde's decided to engage."

So while we fought like mad to hold our ground, they'd rested, fattened up, and tested our strength. Now they knew our strategies and were ready to crush us. And I was . . . out of ideas. I'd done everything I could think of to recruit enough men to face the monsters, and at the current count, we had slightly less than two hundred with recent losses. Even when Company D won, soldiers lost their lives.

"Then we have to pick the battlefield," I said.

We set up camp by the river. We had come a fair ways west of Soldier's Pond, and I checked the maps, locating landmarks we'd passed. Appleton lay to the southeast; if we marched toward the horde, there was forest we could use for cover, but it would be impossible to hide two hundred men as we'd done on a smaller scale. Therefore, that tactic wouldn't work again. According to the routes, we were nearly to the Evergreen Isle. I tapped a finger against the paper, staring at it. There *had* to be a way to use the river against the horde.

Fade sat down beside me, looking as tired as I felt. Despite better provisions and good boots, life in the field took its toll, even in fair weather. He had to be tired of the lack of privacy and poor sanitary facilities, though men had it easier in a number of regards. Tully, Tegan, and I had complained more than once about how much more work it was for us while the male soldiers could urinate against a tree—and often did.

"Planning our next onslaught?" he asked with a half-smile.

There had been so little time to *be* with him . . . and I missed it. I ached from top to toes to be a girl as I had been in Salvation, all softness and smiles. For the first time in my life, I imagined hanging up my daggers in a place like Rosemere. I'd never seen it, but the way Morrow described it made me long to experience that peace for myself.

"I wish I could," I said tiredly. I repeated what the scout had told me.

Fade laced our fingers together, and I remembered when that gesture required a mental pause. "You've done so much with relatively little."

"It's not enough. If we can't break them, then it won't matter what we've achieved."

"Call the rest of the officers. Let's figure it out over dinner."

I bit back a sharp retort. There was no solution. The horde had too many for us to count, and even with our best fighters, they'd overwhelm us. I might be able to kill four or five, but the new men couldn't. Once our boys started dying, others might break and run. So far, the battles had been against equal numbers, a tactic I suspected had been employed so the Freaks could inform their elders how we reacted. *Or maybe their children.* It made sense that young ones might be in power, devising strategies, while the elders served as grunts. If that was the case, then we could expect smarter countermoves in the future. This insight sank my spirits further.

But I couldn't just ponder our inevitable defeat, so I invited the others to join us. They brought their stew, thickened with powdered hardtack, and gave us inquiring looks. In a few words, I shared all the details of the latest report. Part of me hoped they were smarter than me—Tegan definitely was . . . and probably Morrow; they might offer immediate suggestions.

Instead Morrow put down his plate and sighed. "Heroic stories aren't supposed to end this way. The monsters *never* win."

"No ideas?" Fade asked.

"I've been thinking about what you said." I tilted my head at Morrow. "About how the Muties can't swim. But I'm not sure how to use that."

"We can't fight in the river," Tully said. "The current would drag us down too and make it hard to maneuver."

"I wish there was a way to lure them into the water," I muttered.

Spence grinned. "That would be a fantastic trick. But I don't know if the river is big enough to drown that many monsters."

"It would need to be the ocean," Fade said.

"Somehow I doubt you'll get the Muties to go along," Tegan said.

Thornton had been quiet all this time. When he finally spoke, I hoped it meant he had something serious to contribute, as he wasn't known for wasting words. "You might be onto something with that idea."

"Drowning them?" I asked, doubtful.

"If we retreat to the big river to the west, we can fight with the water at our back. That means they can't circle around behind us and if need be, we can swim for the island when they hit us in force." He cut a look at Morrow, asking, "Would Rosemere welcome us? I know how your father feels about getting involved with outside affairs, but he's never been known for turning away travelers."

"Two hundred men is more than a few visitors," Morrow said quietly.

"Your father runs Rosemere?" I asked.

"He's the governor," the storyteller answered, looking uncomfortable.

"Of the town?" Tegan looked fascinated.

"The whole island, but Rosemere is the only settlement."

I pored over the map a second time, letting my dinner get cold and finally said, "I can't find better terrain to face them. Water at our back is the best we can do."

Tegan nodded. "I'll go ask the men if they know how to swim."

Tribulation

The horde found us before we reached the river.

Stalker's scouts carried the warning that saved us. Though Company D was full of brave men and women, we couldn't beat the enemy at ten to one odds. I called the retreat at the top of my lungs, Morrow echoed it on his pipes, then we ran for our lives. It wasn't brave; it wasn't glorious. But with two thousand monsters snarling, less than half a mile behind us, I did what was necessary to keep my soldiers alive.

Last night, we'd considered a last stand here, but when I saw their sheer number sweeping down toward us, I made a snap decision. There would be no battle against terrible odds; I wouldn't give my men's lives away. When we faced the horde, it would be on my terms. Rosemere represented safety, and while the horde was here, stymied by the river, they wouldn't be attacking any other settlements.

"Move!" I shouted. "Gavin, leave the banner if you must. Just get across!"

"I will *not*," the boy called back.

He was as stubborn as I had been, thinking that compromise was the same as losing. The Winterville brat waded into the water and hung on to the pole with one arm. Shaking my head, I watched him paddle. The current was swift, and I fought fear and despair that the water would drown half my forces. Still, they preferred that fate to being torn apart by monsters that intended to eat them, so Company D pushed on. My officers and I held the line on the shore, braced for the worst. I met Fade's eyes and he smiled, like the memory of my face was all he needed to steel him for the long walk.

Deliberately I crossed to him and whispered, "With my partner beside me, I fear nothing, not even death."

His answering look felt like a kiss. Behind us, men waded into the water, the monsters were nearly on us—and I felt the breeze from their snapping teeth and raking claws as I dove.

I'd never learned to swim.

Like the men struggling ahead of me, I preferred to choose my fate. I mimicked the motions of those who looked like they knew what they were doing, using my hands and feet to paddle, but the current sucked me under. The river hated me; it dashed me against the rocks and cast me back up again to torment me with a gasp of breath, only to pull me under again. My vision went dark, and I knew no more.

I didn't expect to see the world again, but I was on the opposite shore when I awoke with Fade pounding on my chest. A gasp, a splutter, and I vomited up half the river in a retching gush, then I fell back onto the damp dirt, curling my fingers in it. I hadn't expected to make it. Shakily, I pulled myself up and spotted Tegan circulating among the men. I couldn't tell yet how many had made the swim, but it seemed like a fair number.

Fade pulled me into his arms; he was sopping wet, shaking, but not with cold as the sun shone bright overhead. The island was close enough to the bank that I could see distant Freaks over his shoulder. They came a few steps into the water and then retreated with bared teeth. They wouldn't survive the crossing. If only they were stupid enough to drown themselves chasing us, that would solve our problems without the need for more dying on our part. But the monsters had become a clever, inexorable enemy, and their destruction wouldn't come so easily.

"How many did we lose?" I gasped.

"Twenty-two," Tegan said gently.

The officers arranged themselves around us, then Thornton said, "Some of them might wash up farther down."

I caught Morrow's eye and he shook his head. He was an island native, and he knew the currents. If he believed it unlikely, then I had to be realistic and count the men lost. Breathing hurt, probably from all the water I swallowed, but also from getting my soldiers killed.

"Find out their names," I told the storyteller. "Write them down. I want to be able to tell their families where they fell."

He got out his journal, wrapped in a treated cloth, and it was mostly dry when he opened it. "I'll get started right away."

"Before you go," I added, "how far are we from Rosemere?"

"It's a few miles to the east, all forest. I'd keep to the shore. As long as we do, you can't miss the village. It's built for fishing and sailing. If you catch a boatman on a good day, he'll carry you up the coast to settlements that aren't even on your maps."

Tegan brightened, her eyes sharp with what I'd come to think of as her hungry-for-knowledge expression. "Would you take me, sometime?"

"Someday," he agreed, moving off to fulfill my request.

I addressed Tully, Thornton, and Spence. "Tell the men to dry off and rest up. I want them all in solid shape before we look for the village."

"Understood."

Before moving off, Tully put her hand on my shoulder. "Glad we didn't lose you."

Against my ear, Fade made a sound of inexpressible pain. "Me too. You should've told me you can't swim!"

"When would I have learned?" I asked quietly.

He seemed to consider the question, sorting through what he knew of my past. Then he sighed and rubbed his cool cheek against mine. "I should've stayed close to you. When you went under, my life ended. I don't think I breathed until you did."

"You can live without me," I said.

"I don't want to."

I feared a love like this—that made us incomplete without each other. It was beautiful but treacherous, like snow that looked white and pure and lovely from the safety of your window, but when you stepped out to touch the softness, the cold first stole your breath, and then your will to move, until you could just lay down in it and let the numbness take you. Yet I didn't want to be without him either, so I didn't chide him for the statement. After all, I'd braved the horde to bring him back, even if Fade had believed he was broken beyond fixing.

He kissed me then in front of everyone, and I didn't mind at all. I lost myself in his arms and his lips, his heat and his presence. This man was everything I needed, my best and brightest dream. He tangled his hands in my hair, and I dug my fingers into his shoulders without thinking.

"Sorry. I forgot—"

Fade pressed two fingers to my mouth. "Stop. There is *nothing* I want more than your hands on me, anywhere you care to put them."

"Maybe you want to save that for later," Spence observed.

Heat suffused my cheeks, and I buried my face in Fade's chest as the men laughed. In an hour or so, the soldiers recovered enough to move and Morrow completed his census. He took down all the names of the fallen and showed them to me. After the war ended, if I survived, I would take this paper to all the towns across the territories and inform their families myself. It was the least I could do.

"Thank you," I said to the storyteller. "Can you lead the way to Rosemere?"

The storyteller nodded.

"What will your father say when he sees you?" Tegan asked.

"'James, what have you done now?'"

I smiled at Morrow's answer.

The trip took two hours, according to Fade's watch, which had survived the river and was still keeping time. *Morrow was right*, I thought. *It's beautiful here.* Of the Evergreen Isle, I could honestly say I had never seen a more tranquil place, though part of that came from knowing no Freak had ever set foot here. I wondered if all islands were the same, havens of safety that the monsters couldn't reach. Pale, raucous birds dove after fish and insects along the rocky coast, which gave way to dense and mysterious forest farther inland. We came around a curve to find Rosemere perched like a perfect secret.

The village stole my breath; my chest ached in a way that I experienced only when I looked at Fade. Just as Morrow had described, the place was pure beauty, neat cottages with flowers growing in boxes beneath the windows. The roofs were painted tiles in colorful contrast to the milky stone of the cottages. Though the buildings weren't tall, they had a sweetness I couldn't explain, as if they beckoned me to come explore the tidy cobbled streets and see the shops and markets. Everything the storyteller had said was true.

In the streets, people greeted us with friendly smiles. Many of them had coppery skin, more like Tegan's, though that could be a result of the sunshine. Their hair came in all shades from fair to dark, and the women favored head scarves and baggy trousers wrapped multiple times around their hips. Here, the men treated the women with respect, but I heard no deference on either side as they greeted one another. There were no fences or gates or bars; the river kept these people safe. At the far end of the village, I saw the dock Morrow had mentioned with boats tied and bobbing in the current. Farther on, there was a grist mill for turning grain into flour and a long rectangular shop that the storyteller had said was for building boats.

"It's incredible," Tegan breathed.

She spoke for all of us. The tired faces of the men around me reflected the same wonder. I had never seen a place before that was so bright and full of joy, so utterly without fear. In a small, scared corner of my mind, I wondered if we were all dead and in a better place, as Momma Oaks believed.

"Head for the market," Morrow said, pointing. "It's straight down that way. I need to find my father and arrange accommodations. We have an inn for travelers, but it's not big enough to house everyone."

"You heard the man."

I led the way and the villagers seemed interested to see so many armed soldiers marching through their square, but not alarmed by it, possibly because they recognized Morrow. If not, they were the last trusting souls left in the world, and I would die happily to protect them. Along the way, Company D took in the sights, and I felt overwhelmed. It was so hard to imagine that the end of everything was camped across the river.

Down the street, the market was busy and colorful with stalls selling all manner of things. The vendors brightened when they spotted us; they'd be disappointed when they discovered we had no local currency. But we all enjoyed examining what they had to sell: grilled fish folded in flat bread, wood and bone carvings, hooks that I imagined were best used for fishing, bolts of fabric dyed in bold, bright patterns, ready-made clothes and shoes. The thing I noticed first—there were no weapons, just knives I guessed were used for eating.

What's it like to be born in a place where the people don't need to be armed?

I understood more about Morrow's odd fighting style, why it seemed more ceremonial and graceful than the purposeful killing the rest of us had learned. He came from a village where they fought for sport and to show athletic prowess, not for their lives. It was a distinction I'd never conceived until this moment.

"Have you ever seen anything like this?" Tully's normally hard expression gave way to awe as she gazed around. I couldn't ever remember seeing her without her lips pulled into a taut line, expecting the worst. But she was smiling now.

"We could just stay," Spence whispered.

I wished the thought hadn't occurred to me too. We could all be happy here, and the island was big enough that the village could expand. Trees could be felled to make room and Morrow had told me there was a quarry on the far end of the island where they dug their stones for the cottages. We could all plant gardens and fish in the river, learn to build boats and carve things out of wood and paint the clay tiles on our houses.

But Tully was a stronger woman than I was. She shook her head. "I wouldn't be able to enjoy it, knowing I let everyone else die. I'm in this fight to the end."

With those words, she sealed my fate. I turned to find Fade watching me. He read the renewed commitment in my eyes, and for a few seconds, sorrow darkened his. Sometimes I suspected he wished I would turn away, choose a different path, but like Tully, it would haunt me if I just gave up. Momma Oaks and Edmund were in Soldier's Pond; they had given me a home in Salvation, and I wouldn't rest until I could offer them the same.

Aloud, Fade only said, "It's beautiful here."

I nodded.

And when Morrow returned with his father, a lean older man with gray-shot dark hair and silver temples, I said softly, "I will never understand why you left."

Reunion

The logistics took several hours to sort out.

First Morrow introduced us to his father, Geoffrey, the governor of the Evergreen Isle. Then there were a number of pertinent questions, like, "What the devil do you mean by arriving with a small army?"

At that point, I explained about the horde on the other side of the river and the governor paled. "You brought them *here*?"

"Not on purpose," Morrow said. "But they would have come eventually, Father. Somehow I don't think you want to be the last settlement standing."

"Not at all," his father said soberly.

The older man sprang into action then, organizing the hospitality for his unexpected guests. He sent runners all through the village, seeking volunteers to host a soldier or two. Soon the replies came back positive. So many people were willing to help, no questions asked, and it told me I was right about the spirit of this place. When the families came to show the men to their temporary homes, they glanced at me for permission.

"Go ahead. I'll send a message if I need you to assemble."

One of the men asked, "Should we treat this as leave time, captain?"

I nodded. "That's fine. Be respectful to the locals."

It was an unnecessary request; Company D was full of

honorable soldiers, who would remember their manners and be thankful for the kindness offered. Before I got my house assignment, however, Fade stepped closer, making it clear we wouldn't be separated. Tully and Spence had the same idea, and I think Morrow wished Tegan would look at him the same way, but she had wandered off to admire the bone carvings at a nearby stall. I went over to see what had caught her eye and Fade followed, a quiet shadow at my back.

"It's called scrimshaw," the vendor informed her. "My daddy taught me, his before, and so on. We've been working at this craft for a long time."

Tegan touched a gracefully carved spine. "What is this?"

"It's a dolphin, miss. You find them in the open sea. In good weather, the sailors head that way." The man leaned forward in a confiding manner. "I went on a whaling voyage once. Never was so scared in all my life."

"I'd love to see it all someday," she said dreamily.

That was where she differed from me. With this war behind us, I could see myself happy here and never wanting anything more. But Tegan had a big, hungry mind that soaked life in like a sponge. She was the smartest person I'd ever met . . . and one of the strongest. She was also pretty as a spring day with her dark hair and coppery skin, her big brown eyes and her sweet smile. The vendor was clearly charmed as he pressed the carved bone dolphin into her hands.

"It's a gift. Keep it."

"I couldn't." But her fingers were already curving around the pretty thing.

"She has great skill at doctoring," I told the man. "If you need any help while we're here, she'll be glad to tend you or your loved ones."

Tegan gave a grateful nod. I knew her well enough to understand that she'd love to keep the carving, but she didn't feel right about offering nothing in return. This let her salvage her pride and for the vendor to enjoy the generosity of his gesture. I stepped away from the stall to let them continue their conversation, and as I moved off, I heard her asking about whales.

A few minutes more wouldn't hurt anything, I decided. So I passed among the stalls, admiring the shiny items. One woman made adornments like the necklace I had borrowed from Momma Oaks—and all of them glimmered in the sun. I touched a short coil of silver wire, interspersed with brilliant stones.

"That's a beautiful bracelet," the vendor noted. "It would look lovely on you."

Fade murmured agreement, something about it being perfect for my wrist. That was his way of telling me what I was supposed to do with it; I didn't know whether he'd noticed my weakness for sparkly things. I smiled, aware I had no chits to buy it. But I wanted to. Quietly wishing I could, I turned away to find the governor, as I'd wandered off before he could tell Fade and me where we'd be sleeping. My clothes were sticky and uncomfortable, and I hoped our hosts would be kind enough to let me bathe. It was surprising how awful river water felt, drying inside your shirt. From across the market, someone shouted my name.

I knew that voice—*knew* it—but it wasn't possible. It wasn't. I broke away from Fade on a burst of impossible hope. I shoved through the crowd, running, because I heard it again.

"Deuce. Deuce!"

Then I saw him. Stone was tan, like the rest of Rosemere, and his shoulders seemed even broader. He carried a small boy on them, striding toward me with an eager expression. In the Rosemere sunlight, his blue eyes shone brighter, contrasting with his mop of brown hair. Carefully, he set the brat down and then he swept me into a tight hug, smashing all the breath out of me. He'd always been as exuberant as a puppy, unconscious of his own strength.

Telling the boy, "Don't move, Robin," he spun me around until the market was a blur around me, just movement and color and my stomach felt sick, but on top of everything, I knew only the fiercest and most incredible joy, as if a secret wish had come true.

"Is Thimble with you?" I asked, hardly daring to hope. She'd been one of my closest friends in the enclave, a Builder who was always inventing clever things.

Stone nodded. "She's at home. I came to offer our loft when I heard there were soldiers in need of shelter. I never dreamed I'd be lucky enough to find you."

He let me go long enough to pick up the boy gazing up at me with huge blue eyes. Close up, I noticed the resemblance to my brat-mate, who had been a Breeder down below. "Yours?"

Stone's look turned shy as he cradled the child closer. "Yes."

"How in the world did you end up here?" I wondered aloud.

"It's quite a story, an adventure you might even say." His handsome face turned serious. "Along the way I wasn't sure we'd survive, but Thimble always figured it out. I'll tell you everything over supper."

Beside me, Fade cleared his throat, glancing between Stone and me. He didn't say more, but I heard the unspoken question. *Am I invited to this party?* If he wasn't, then I wouldn't be going either.

"Do you remember Fade?"

"Of course. I don't know if we ever talked down below." Stone offered his hand, Topsider fashion, and they shook. "I'm Deuce's friend. Or I was. I'm not sure how she feels about me now. I've figured she must hate me and wish me dead, if she survived."

The pain and anger of his betrayal felt like a long time ago.

So I joked, "If I'd known you were this resourceful, I'd have let you take your own punishment."

He flinched. "I know. I've been wishing all this time that I could explain . . . and say I'm sorry. Come with me and give me that chance?"

"That sounds good," I said.

I felt oddly lighthearted as I followed my old friend through Rosemere. Along the way, he greeted the villagers, and a number of them had small gifts and smiles for the boy, who alternately giggled and tucked his face against Stone's shoulder. He acted more like I'd seen topside sires behave with their brats than anything we'd learned down below, which meant he was better at adapting to circumstances than I had believed. Clearly I hadn't given him enough credit when I martyred myself, thinking I was the only one strong enough to survive the exile.

More *hubris*, Mrs. James would say.

Stone and Thimble's cottage was perfect, snug and small, built of the stone they quarried on the island and framed in raw timbers. Their roof was painted mossy green in contrast to the copper of their neighbors, and the front door stood open with my dear friend in the doorway. When she saw me, she dropped the box of tools she was holding and ran. Either her foot was better or she had crafted something to make it appear so because I hardly noticed her limp. We hugged tight and long; and the sun itself seemed to shine brighter, glowing on the white petals of the flowers growing in her window box.

"How?" she demanded. Then she seemed to think better of the question as she let go of me. "Food, first, I think, then explanations."

Thimble looked more mature in her tidy brown skirt and white blouse. She wore an apron to protect it from whatever she had been working on. With busy hands, she beckoned us into the cool shade of the cottage. I came first, Fade next, and then

Stone with the brat. Inside, there were wooden chairs with brightly sewn cushions and a sturdy table, a box full of toys near the door. A ladder stretched to the loft they had promised while a doorway led to the back of the house. There was a fireplace for cooking, and windows cut on either side to let in the light. Shutters would protect them from the elements. For a few seconds, I just admired their home.

While she hurried around setting crocks on the table, Stone performed the introductions, in case Thimble and Fade didn't remember each other. Then I said, "Is there someplace we can clean up? The river isn't as refreshing as it looks."

"I should've offered," Stone answered, handing his brat to Thimble.

He led us to a washhouse out back, where Fade and I tidied up. Afterward, we enjoyed their hospitality, the best meal I'd eaten in weeks. Thimble fed us soft cheese and dark bread, fried fish and sliced apples, fresh greens and chopped nuts. Fade and I tried not to be greedy, but after field rations for weeks, we quietly accepted seconds and thirds. As we ate, I told our story and explained how we'd arrived in Rosemere. They were interested in everything Fade and I had to say and concerned about the horde. But with the river as a buffer, the immediate danger seemed remote.

"I suppose it's our turn," Thimble said, once I finished talking.

Stone covered my hand with his, tentative, as if he expected me to pull away. I didn't. "Me first. You gave up everything for me, and I let you leave thinking I blamed you. I'm so sorry, Deuce. You have no idea how much."

I set down my spoon. "It would help if I knew why."

"Robin," Stone said.

The brat glanced up from his place on the floor, where he was stacking wooden blocks. "Yes, Da?"

"He's why. I wasn't supposed to pay attention to him after I did my part, but I always knew he was mine. And I loved him. When they said I was guilty of hoarding, I could only think that I'd never see him grow up, never be there for his naming day, and I would've done anything to stay with him . . . even let a friend suffer in my place."

Thimble picked up the story, seeming to sense that Stone wanted her to. "And we were both frightened of what was happening in the enclave. We hoped we'd escape reprisal if we pretended to condemn you along with everyone else. It was . . . cowardly. I'm sorry too."

"Did it work?" Fade asked coldly.

I had never seen such sorrow in my friend's eyes as she shook her head. Then she told us of the massacre down below—how my exile, along with Banner's death—led to open insurrection. Silk put down the rebels, but by that time, it was too late, and the Freaks took advantage of the weakness and disorder to sack College as they had Nassau. She shared the rest of their tale then; after she laid the traps and Stone played bait, they escaped to an old-world shelter, accessible through the tunnels. For a time, they stayed there, letting Thimble's foot heal and Robin recover from the ordeal. He seemed like a happy brat, so it must've worked.

"That was when we named him," Stone concluded. "I didn't want to wait until he was older. That seems like you're asking the world to take your child away."

Pain blazed through me when I thought of Twist and Girl26. I'd left people behind, and until this moment, I'd tried not to remember them. Looking at Stone and Thimble, I couldn't help it. "What happened to Twist?"

Stone bent his head. "He fell in the initial fighting. Hunters cut him down."

That seemed worse than dying to Freaks. For a moment, I

remembered the small, weak Builder, who had saved our lives by providing forbidden supplies. We were supposed to leave with no food, no water, but unlike the others, Twist hadn't been so cruel. Without him, Fade and I wouldn't be here . . . and our benefactor was gone.

"Were there any other survivors?" Fade asked.

"I heard some as we were leaving, but we couldn't save them," Stone answered. "I was afraid a larger group would draw too much attention."

Thimble's expression hardened. "They didn't help when the Freaks were chasing you. They hid and cried. If not for my traps and your speed, we'd be nothing but bones by now."

"So others might have made it out," I said.

"Maybe." Stone shrugged as if he didn't care.

I shouldn't, but Girl26 had no say in how the elders had run the enclave. So I clung to the possibility that she was like Fade— that she'd hidden from the Freaks and crept away quietly. To what, I didn't know, as by then, the ruins were likely overrun, but a smart girl might find a way to survive, as Thimble had proven.

"So how did you get from the shelter to Rosemere?" Fade wondered.

I was curious too. Thimble was clever and Stone was strong, but neither had any experience defending themselves, so I couldn't believe they'd made such a long journey. Yet here they were in their own cottage, settled in the prettiest village I'd ever seen.

Stone took up the story. "Eventually the tinned food ran low and we felt strong enough to venture out. So we climbed up. Topside couldn't be worse than darkness and filth, we thought."

"It was so bright," Thimble said, remembering. "It hurt my eyes, and I was so scared."

With easy affection, Stone scooped her into his lap. "We both were. For a time, we wandered and hid. I killed birds and we ate them raw. There were packs of Freaks fighting humans, most of whom wore the same colors."

"The gangs," Fade guessed.

Stone continued without prompting. "Eventually we went into a building and Thimble found a useful paper. A map," he added, as the word came to him.

"I knew we needed fresh water, so I guided us toward the blue on the page. And that was when we saw the boatmen." Thimble smiled in recollection; and I grasped how relieved they must've been with food scarce, a brat depending on them, and the ruins alight with violence.

Fade touched my hand. We'd gone to the water too, but there were no boats bobbing on the waves. If we had come earlier—or later—our path might've been so different. But maybe our journey happened as it was supposed to, so I could meet my new family and learn to love Fade as he deserved.

Stone said, "I called out and the fisherman heard me. He told me he couldn't risk the shallows . . . and that I'd have to swim to him. So I put Robin on my back and got into the water."

A shiver rolled through me. "It's a miracle you survived."

"Only because of Thimble. She found a piece of driftwood and called me back. We used it to float out to the boat, and then we sailed with them up the coast and down the river to Rose-mere. They promised us it was safe—"

"And we've been here ever since," she finished.

"That's quite a story," Fade said.

"It's the best kind," Stone told us, smiling. "Because it has a happy ending."

And *I* brought the monsters here.

Unprecedented

After dinner, I stepped outside to clear my head. Fade was eating another slice of Thimble's honey cake, but I couldn't stop thinking about the evil on the other side of the river. Stone and Thimble's story was incredible, and I envied the happiness they'd found in Rosemere. I was tired of killing; I wanted to build too.

"Wait," Stone called from the doorway.

It was dark by then, moonlight shining down. "I won't go far. And I'll be back soon."

"No . . . before you go, please say you forgive me, Deuce."

Such a small thing. "Of course. You love Robin so much . . . and that's the way a sire should feel about his son. I've come to realize that the enclave was backward in so *many* ways."

He hugged me tight. "Thank you."

"Tell Fade and Thimble I'll be back soon."

"I will. It's safe here, so feel free to explore."

My head whirling, I walked through town, admiring the pretty cobbled streets and the lamps that lit them. Morrow had been right. This was the most peaceful place, and you could see it in the children's faces as they played. They didn't know how it felt to be hungry or frightened.

I want the world to look this way . . . or at least the whole of the territories.

My path led me down to the sturdy pier, where the boats were moored. Men fearlessly sailed up and down the river, casting their nets. During the day, the area was full of fresh fish and people arguing about its worth. By night, however, it was quiet, so I was unprepared for the touch on my shoulder. Reflex took over; as I whirled, I drew my knives and dodged back a step.

In the moonlight, I made out only a shadowy, hooded figure. It was impossible to glimpse his features, but when he spoke, shivers of dread ran over my skin. "You're the Huntress."

I had heard Freaks rasp out words before, but never with such fluency. Their voices always sounded broken and garbled, as though it hurt them to speak our tongue. *But this . . . how can he be here?* My thoughts scattered like frightened fish. At this point, terror should grip me fully, but numbness crept over me instead. My hands trembled and sweat beaded on my brow, but I couldn't let him have the upper hand.

So I feigned calm. "I am. Push back your cowl so I can see you."

He moved slowly, but as he did, his sleeves fell back to reveal gray skin and taloned hands. Starlight illuminated sharp, savage features. His eyes were inhuman, glowing amber-gold like a cat's. He might even see in the dark better than me, possibly part of their continued evolution. He appeared young, his body lean and strong.

"What are you doing here?" I demanded.

Outwardly I displayed anger, but I was quaking inside. If the monsters had worked out how to cross the water and were mounting an invasion, I couldn't bear it. Company D had scattered with my permission; I'd thought it best to give them a few days of peace while I decided what to do about the two thousand Freaks camped across the river. But now I had no way to summon them fast enough to defend Rosemere, should that become necessary.

"I came to talk," the Freak said.

My grip slipped on my knives. Given my history against these monsters, I'd expected this was an assassination attempt, but if it had been, he could have ripped out my spine from behind. Touching me to alert me to his presence ran completely counter to any hostile aim. Since coming topside, the skills I'd learned as a Huntress down below had served me well—and despite my misgivings, I sensed this Freak was different from the rest, mostly because he chose words over violence. His fluency with our language also marked him as special, and I'd regret it if I didn't find out what he wanted. Hands shaking, I sheathed my blades. Maybe this was madness, but I'd hear him out.

"I can be armed again in two seconds," I warned.

"Your speed is well-known to us, Deuce the Huntress."

"How did you find me?" I was proud of how steady my voice sounded, as if he weren't turning my world upside down with each moment we stood with the river flowing behind us in the moonlight.

"We followed your banner. It, too, is well-known."

Momma Oaks would be pleased to hear it. Gavin had kept the pennant safe through summer and fall, until the Freaks recognized it and charged in rage . . . or avoided us, depending on their goals and allegiances. I had so many questions, but they wouldn't coalesce in my brain. Conflicting emotions warred for dominance, leaving me dull.

"I thought your kind couldn't swim," I managed to say, as fear rushed in.

If these Freaks had found a way across the river, it couldn't be long before the horde followed. Rosemere would be decimated. Sickness roiled in my stomach, churning the rich food I'd eaten moments before at Stone and Thimble's table. I had to think of a way out of this mess, and there was nobody here to help, just my inadequate wits against endless weight.

"No," he replied. "But we can build."

That is not good news.

"Boats, you mean?"

He inclined his head. "They are not so fine as yours, but they suffice."

Now I pictured them lashing logs together—as we had for the primitive town we built in the forest—constructing rafts that would carry them across the river. *Please don't let the horde have seen them. They don't need any help to destroy us.* Taking a deep breath, I reined my dread.

"Say your piece quickly."

I can't believe I'm not attacking this strange creature.

"I am Szarok. In your tongue this roughly means He Who Dreams."

Astonishment stilled me for a few seconds. I'd never imagined that Freaks named their brats or that their language could translate with such elegance. Before this moment, I saw them only as monsters to be destroyed at all costs. Cold prickles crept up my spine as I considered how many of Szarok's brethren I had slain.

"You speak it well," I whispered.

He acknowledged the compliment with what I'd take for a smile in a human face. "I studied. I learned. This is the way of the young."

"Why? Killing us is your favorite pastime."

"No. This is all our forefathers know because they remember too much about the hate and pain of their creation. But the lastborn see farther. We have memories of kindness."

"Kindness?" I asked.

"Will you take my hand, Huntress?"

I couldn't credit how peculiar this seemed. If this was a trap, it was too bizarre for me to fathom. Maybe this creature knew it couldn't defeat me in a fight, and it had some new trick in mind, some new ability I'd never seen, like venomous skin. Yet I heard

Tegan whispering in my ear, as if she were standing here. She had become the new voice in my head, replacing Silk.

Trust has to begin somewhere. For peace to take hold, one person must first stop fighting.

I pushed out a shuddering breath. "Go ahead."

Szarok's hand was strong and warm. The claws prickled as he wrapped his fingers around my wrist. Impressions flickered through my mind; I had nothing to compare it to, but I saw a young Freak wounded and near death. A child in Otterburn tended it; she was too small to understand they were enemies. She saw only pain, not ugliness, and she healed the creature. And that beast fathered Szarok. I saw the connection in blood and bone, and I realized he could spin these memories in his mind, just as Dr. Wilson had predicted.

When he let me go, I reeled back, not in hurt but wonder. "What's it like to be able to trace your path back so far?"

"Beautiful. And ugly. The world is always both."

Those words resonated with me. "It is. Are the memories you carry from your forefathers always that sharp and clear? Can you call them at will?"

"Yes," he said. "It's blessing and curse, I think, as you can see in the old ones. They cannot forget or forgive. They cannot move past the pain."

I imagined the mad jumble of images the Freaks in the horde stored in their heads, marching all the way back to their human origins. No wonder they hated us. People never raged so hard as against the flaws they perceived in themselves. The feral Freaks weren't smart enough to understand their instinctive antipathy, but I did. And it saddened me.

"You said your name means He Who Dreams. So tell me yours, Szarok."

"I dream of peace . . . and a world where neither side judges the other by their skins."

It sounded like a worthy goal, if an improbable one. "What did you have in mind?"

"An alliance."

I gaped at him, as that was possibly the most startling statement in a night already fraught with more shocks than I could process. "You can't be serious."

"We've spent the last year keeping the horde in check, Huntress, arguing with them about the wisdom of their course." He leaned forward, seeming skilled at reading my reactions. "You didn't avoid them out of luck; my clan is why they stayed in Appleton so long, sending only a portion of their strength against you. But the old ones will listen no longer. Most have less than three years left, but before they die, they will wipe your kind from the territories. There's no time for peace to flourish as it will. We must make it so."

That explains so much. But Company D would never accept this. "I don't think—"

But Szarok made an impatient gesture, one familiar to me from other angry men. In that instant, I saw him as a person, not a monster. "Do you think this is easy? We must join our hated enemies to slay our mothers and fathers. But this is the only path. They cannot stop killing, so we must make them."

"Are you so sure I can be trusted?" I had murdered an awful lot of his people, after all.

"You kept to the terms of our agreement before."

Just when I thought I couldn't be more surprised, he produced another shock. "The emissary came from you? When we fought in the woods near Soldier's Pond?"

"It was my suggestion to see if you were open to peace," he admitted. "Many tribes met and discussed the best way to handle your war band. My clan has always been opposed to human extinction . . . and we didn't want to make livestock of you, either, unlike some. After the slaughter at Appleton, I proposed many solutions but the old ones would hear none. And so the young split from the horde. Tonight, I offer you five hundred warriors willing to die because *one* of your people was kind. Can you say the same?"

I started to say I'd never met a gentle Freak, but then I realized I was looking at one. The pain he must feel at betraying his own people to make the world a better place . . . I understood it, because I was facing the same dilemma. Company D would see this alliance as perfidious, and they might hate me for it.

I hesitated, seeing the unmistakable benefit, but unsure if I could make it work. "I have less than two hundred men. Even if we join forces, it seems like a lost cause."

"Other allies will come," he said mysteriously.

"Who?"

"I will tell you nothing further until you agree to my terms. My men are camped on the far end of the isle. Meet them . . . and decide if, together, we can make the world better. That's what the young Uroch want."

"Uroch?" I repeated. "Who . . . ?"

Szarok seemed to grasp what I was asking. "It means the 'People' and it applies to my clan, those willing to fight our kin to end this war." He paused, as if weighing whether he should say more. "That's why I'm willing to work with you. We can learn from one another."

How astonishing. I marveled at the complexity I had never imagined—that Szarok's tribe had a name. At that point, I suspected I must be dreaming—to hear him echo my own desires when I'd killed so many of his brethren. *For peace to begin, someone must lay his weapons down.* But that was a choice the Huntress could never make. My whole body trembled; the risks were so high and this could be the biggest—and last—mistake of my life.

"You could be leading me into a trap," I said.

Szarok tilted his head in challenge. "And you could call down the whole village upon me. Yet you have not."

When the enemy chooses to talk instead of fight, only a fool rejects the overture.

In my mind's eye, I touched two fingers to my brow in a farewell salute to the merciless warrior they'd trained me to be, down below. I wasn't a Huntress, not even close. I'd chart a new course from here, guided by the gentleness I'd learned from Tegan and Momma Oaks.

"I'll go with you."

"No!" To my astonishment, my brother, Rex, ran down the dock toward us, knife drawn. "I was waiting for you to gut this lying monster. Don't trust it!"

"What are you doing here?" I asked softly.

Szarok stilled but he didn't take hostile action. From what I could tell, he was leaving this complication in my hands. In the taut silence, broken only by the rush of the river behind us, I waited for Rex's reply.

He burst out, "I had some ideas about how to handle the horde, and I came looking for you. When you went walking after dark, I followed, thinking I'd get to play the protective big brother for a change. And it's a good thing too. I never dreamed you could be so gullible. When he delivers you to the horde, Company D will surrender. The war will be lost."

Rex lunged then, and I threw myself between Szarok and my brother. He glared at me, knife upraised. "Get out of my way, Deuce. I vowed to kill every last one of these bastards for what they did to Ruth."

I shook my head, desperate. "Don't. Ruth wouldn't want this. It's wrong to blame him for what someone else did. You wouldn't hold all men accountable for the crimes of one."

Rex snarled, "But *this* isn't a man. It's a monster."

Szarok said softly, "You hold a knife poised to strike your sister down, beloved of your mother and father. Who is the monster here?"

My brother stumbled back with a cry of horror, the blade falling from his fingers to clatter on the ground. I hugged him tight and he was shaking. Over and over, he whispered, "What, what have I become?"

For long moments I held him and Szarok was wise or kind enough to hold his peace. Eventually Rex stepped back, picked up his blade, and sheathed it. "I'm sorry. That was madness. But . . . I won't let you do this thing alone."

I glanced at Szarok in silent inquiry, and he responded, "If your brother can promise civilized behavior, I have no objection to two visitors in our camp."

It went unspoken why; he had five hundred warriors on the Evergreen Isle, and if we proved aggressive, it would be easy to dispose of us. And any misbehavior on our part might result in death sweeping down on an unsuspecting Rosemere. On its own, that was more than enough to keep me in line, but I believed Szarok's offer was sincere. He had not come lightly to the decision to fight his own people.

As we left, I whispered to my brother, "You seem to be taking his eloquence awfully well. I'd expect you to be more shocked."

Rex aimed a rueful look at me. "I was, at first. But remember, I was listening to you two for a while, before I stepped in."

It took most of the night to reach the western corner of the isle. As we approached, I spotted multiple campfires, small enough that they wouldn't draw attention. Out here I detected only the wet silt scent of the river and the crushed pine aroma from the bed of needles where the Uroch camped, along with smoky wood. Szarok led us through his soldiers with complete confidence, and though they stared, none of them moved toward us. Fear quaked through me; I'd never been so close to my enemies with no defensive measures in place. Memories of my flight through the horde threatened to drown me.

"You see," he said when we reached his fire, tended by a young Uroch. "They fear you, for you have killed so many of their mothers and fathers, but they will not harm you. We want the same thing."

"A better world," Rex said.

I was flummoxed by the idea that these powerful creatures feared me. Was *I* the terrible story that Uroch mothers told to their brats in order to persuade them to behave? I sank to my knees, unnerved by the way the world had spun tonight.

I don't want to be the monster that haunts a child's sleep. A small voice added, *And neither do they.*

Szarok nodded. "Do you wish to converse with them? A few speak your tongue as I do."

Freezing, I had an awful thought. "My man was taken a while back, treated like an animal, and he suffered greatly. Did you learn our language from human captives?"

"I'm sorry," he said. "A number of the old ones saw humanity as a useful food source. We argued, but when only a small minority supports your view, you cannot always stop awful things from happening."

That, I understood too well. With a pang of regret, I recalled the blind brat Fade and I had let the Hunters kill down below. "You didn't answer my question, though."

Sidestepped it, at best.

"They weren't captives when they taught us," Szarok said.

"You freed some human hostages?" Rex sounded surprised.

"One night on the plains, there was a disturbance," the Uroch explained. "We saved as many as we could when the old ones gave chase. But your people were weak. They required care before they could return to their homes. As we looked after them, they taught us your tongue."

My mouth hung open. "I . . . I'm pretty sure you're talking about the night I saved Fade."

I'd finally startled Szarok. From his wide-eyed reaction, he hadn't known I'd crept into the horde and opened the slave pens. "How extraordinary. It seems as if our paths have been converging for some time."

I agreed. And until dawn broke, I talked with the Uroch warriors. Szarok had shown them the Otterburn girl who saved his father's life, and unlike their parents, the young Uroch could choose another course. Hatred was not emblazoned in their bones.

"I want to learn to plant things," one young Uroch whispered to me. "To put seeds in the ground and make the greenings grow."

"So do I," I admitted.

That was the skill I coveted most. Last summer, I had envied the planters who knew what to do with the earth, how to treat the plants, and make them strong. I wanted to grow food people could eat and flowers they would admire. It was one secret I'd never admitted aloud because it was so silly for a Huntress, yet I told this Uroch with eyes clever as a cat's.

Rex moved amid the camp too, his hostility fading. I recognized the moment when he accepted that these weren't monsters, but another people. With the proper support, he and I could pave the way to peace. My spirit lightened when I imagined an end to the war that might not result in complete annihilation on our side.

"Do you accept the alliance?" Szarok asked as dawn broke.

Though I trusted my instincts, I couldn't be sure this wasn't a trick . . . and I still had to persuade my men to work with their former enemies. Exhaustion flared in a headache, tightening my temples. *I don't want to make such a big decision.* But there was nobody else.

"It will take some convincing," I said, "but I'll bring the men around. Your warriors will need to wear armbands or something, so there's no confusion when we attack."

And if you betray me, I'll die trying to make you sorry. Yet I was willing to gamble everything on the promise of a lasting peace. If I was wrong about Szarok, that'd be a sad thing for someone to carve on my grave marker.

Here lies Deuce Oaks. She was gullible, but she tried.

"I'll find a way to distinguish us from the old ones." He offered his hand and I shook it.

This time, no images or memories came with the contact, so he must control that ability; the Uroch were fascinating when they weren't trying to kill you. He released me with a tip of his head, and I had seen enough of the way they interacted with one another to take that as a sign of respect. Since I came up from down below, I had gotten skilled at recognizing other people's customs, mostly because I learned them anew, everywhere I went.

"You mentioned other allies," I said.

Between his five hundred and my two, it was hard to fathom the battle ending well against two thousand feral Freaks. And they squatted on the banks of the big river, poised to destroy the last bastion of peace in the territories. Rosemere.

They come no farther. It ends here.

Szarok nodded. "I've made contact with the small folk. They live in the caves and tunnels and they, too, have suffered from the endless fighting."

"The small folk?" Rex asked.

I thought of Jengu and his kind, then I described them to the Uroch leader, who said, "Then you know of them. They call themselves the Gulgur."

"How many are there?" I asked.

"Willing to fight? A hundred or so. They're few but cunning, masters of remaining unseen. They'll slip in while the old ones sleep and poison their meat."

"Can you be ready two days from now?" That would give me time to make arrangements and persuade the men.

Szarok nodded. "I'll coordinate with the Gulgur and ensure they carry out their role."

"My men will attack from the east. You strike from the west. And let's hope it's enough."

If the horde was weak and sick from the tainted meat, eight hundred of us might be able to defeat them, though we would take heavy casualties. I shared a glance with Rex, who said, "It's time to tell the others. We can win."

Resistance

he village was in an uproar when Rex and I returned. I was reeling with fatigue after so long without sleep, so my head was fuzzy as to why. For obvious reasons, we left Szarok in the Uroch camp, and as we strode into the village, I saw that Company D was already assembled and listening to orders shouted alternately by Tully, Spence, and Fade. Thornton had our smith checking all the weapons; it was like they'd decided to go to war overnight.

"What's going on?" I called.

At hearing my voice, Fade spun and covered the ground between us in three strides. He crushed me against him, shaking. For a few seconds, I couldn't breathe . . . and I was confused about his reaction. Then I knew. Before he spoke, I knew.

"I thought they took you, somehow."

Like they did you.

With everything that had happened, I hadn't considered how worried he must be. *I go out for a walk and I don't come back? Stupid. You should've sent Rex with word.* Shock from the night's events had driven all other considerations out of my head . . . but I couldn't get enough breath to speak, let alone apologize.

"I realize you're glad to see her," Rex said, "but you're crushing my sister's ribs."

I didn't fight to make Fade let go, though; instead I hugged him back as tight as I could. The rest of Company D, currently watching, could wait. It took a while for him to calm down enough to release me, and when he stepped back, his dark gaze glittered with fury. I could expect a proper quarrel later. Since I wasn't injured, his eyes said, and clearly I hadn't been taken, there was *no excuse* for putting him through that much grief.

And he didn't have Stalker to help him figure out the way I went, either. He must've felt so helpless.

Personal matters had to wait, however. "There's been a most unexpected development," I said, loud enough for everyone to hear. "If you'll come with me, I'll explain everything."

Since we were standing in the middle of the market, I thought it best *not* to talk about the Uroch camped on the western part right then. The villagers might panic, and that was the last thing we needed, two days before engaging the horde. Company D was well trained, luckily, so they fell in and followed me past the docks, along the coastline to the east. I marched until it was safe to talk. The only fishermen I saw were out on the river, not working from shore.

"I'd sure like to know why I gave up a night's sleep searching for you," Thornton said. "When you're clearly fine."

Taking a deep breath, I answered, "I'm glad you asked. You may not like what you hear, but don't say a word before I'm done. There will be a chance to talk afterward. Not during." I scanned all the men's faces and added, "That's an order."

Rex put a hand on my shoulder in moral support. Then I explained where I'd been all night—and with whom. Shock and rage governed most faces, although Tegan and Morrow looked intrigued rather than angry. That was about what I expected. When I wrapped up the story, Company D exploded with outrage, protests, and disbelief. I didn't address their collective fury until it started to die down. Once they realized I wasn't arguing with them, the men paused and glanced among themselves, as if wondering at my tactics.

Since it was our only chance against the horde, I didn't much care what they thought of the idea. "I don't expect you to like them . . . or even trust them. But your goal hasn't changed. You're still tasked with defeating the horde. The only thing I ask is that you don't harm the Uroch. They'll be fighting alongside us . . . and if you reckon they can't think, feel, and hurt . . . well, you'd be wrong. They're people. Not like us, true, but they're not monsters. The fact that they're willing to fight their own to save us proves it."

"We don't get a say?" one soldier shouted from the back.

"You can walk," I said. "But then you have to live with knowing you were too much of a coward to complete your mission. It's your choice. I won't make anyone fight, but I'll be awfully proud of those who do."

My brother stepped forward. "Last night, I almost stabbed my sister rather than listen to reason. I hope you won't make the same mistake. I was there with her. I talked with them too. They may not look like us, but they're not violent, unthinking beasts."

"My men will stand," Tully said, fixing a hard look on the crowd.

A rumble of assent greeted her words. Fade was ominously silent, but I thought that was because he was angry with me for scaring him. He might also have a deep objection to cooperating with the Uroch; I just hoped I could make him understand that the young ones weren't the same as their parents, just as he and I weren't like the elders in the enclave. It was crazy that I had become an advocate for the monsters.

"Tully doesn't go to war without me," Spence said. "And I'll make sure my boys are ready to bring the pain."

Morrow added, "I wouldn't miss this for the world."

Thornton spoke up then. "Company D may not like your orders, but we follow them. When does the assault commence?"

Relief surged through me. At least I hadn't lost my officers. "I need everyone assembled here, three hours before dawn, two days from now. Before then, I'll speak with the boatmen about ferrying us across. We can't strike if we're all exhausted and waterlogged from the swim."

"Good call," Tegan said.

"The Uroch will be wearing something—I'm not sure what—to help us tell them from the elders. It may be hard to track in battle, but a good rule of thumb is, if they're fighting other Muties, they're on our side, so leave 'em alone."

That sparked nervous, uncertain laughter from the men. I imagined it was hard for them to accept this idea. Fortunately, they would have almost two days to digest the new reality. If some of them left the unit or refused to fight, so be it.

I went on, "One last thing. Not a word to the villagers. There's no need for them to worry. All the fighting will happen across the river, and they might panic. Understood?"

"Yes, sir," the men answered as one.

"Dismissed. I'll see you day after tomorrow, three hours before dawn."

As the men went about their business, some discussing the incredible idea of the Uroch helping us, others saying they'd rather kill Muties than fight alongside them, Morrow pushed through the men, looking troubled. I thought I understood what was bothering him, but I let him start the conversation.

He paced as most of Company D headed back toward town. "This is my home. I don't know if I can let this go without telling my father. He's the governor, responsible for people's safety. He needs to know about the army on the other side of the island."

"Can he handle the information?" I asked. "If the Uroch

meant to hurt Rosemere, they'd have attacked last night. Szarok wouldn't have crept into town quietly, looking for me, so we could build an accord."

"That's probably true, but silence feels like betrayal."

I nodded. "Follow your conscience, then. But if the situation blows up, your father informs the town council, they panic and a mob of villagers descends on the Uroch, it'll be a bloodbath. You know that."

Tegan stepped up and put a comforting hand on his arm. "Maybe we could meet them? I must confess I'm curious—and it might set James's mind at ease to verify that these Muties—I mean Uroch—are everything you claim."

Morrow gazed at her as though she were the answer to every dream he'd ever known. "That way, I can be sure they're not moving against Rosemere. Would Szarok agree to that?"

"I'm sure he would." Glancing around, I found Rex nearby. "Would you mind guiding Tegan and Morrow to the camp?"

My brother smiled. "Not at all. I'm glad to finally feel useful. I'm the worst in the company with *any* weapon, apart from a skinning knife."

Tully and Spence had been listening to the conversation and at that point, she said, "We'd like to go with them. I have some questions for our new allies. Not that I don't trust you, Deuce, but if I'm ordering my men to fight alongside them, I want to satisfy myself on some issues."

"Just do me the kindness of being polite?" I requested.

They all nodded, like that was a given. A small party, made up of Tegan, Morrow, Tully, Spence, and Rex, shouldn't alarm the Uroch. So I gave the expedition my blessing with one condition. "I'd prefer that you return by midnight before the attack. My officers can't be wandering the shoreline when they're supposed to be here."

"Done," Tully agreed.

They moved off, leaving me alone with Fade, who had been seething at my side for the last fifteen minutes. His silence was like a sunburn. The rest of the men were halfway back to Rosemere, but I thought it best to let him yell at me in private . . . if he ever spoke to me again.

I swallowed hard to get my apology past the lump in my throat. "I'm so sorry. I didn't mean to scare you."

His reply, when it came, was a low snarl. "Do you have any idea what last night was like for me? What I imagined they were doing to you? We thought the horde had you. Company D was ready to go to war, even though we had *no chance* of winning. They were all ready to die for you, and if you had been half an hour later, we'd have been across the river."

My heart dropped all the way to my toes. In disbelief, I said, "Even if I had been taken, none of you should react that way. I'm one person. I'm not irreplaceable."

Fade grabbed my shoulders, as if he couldn't help himself. His fingers bit down, not quite enough to hurt, but I felt the ferocity coursing through him, his pulse hammering in his wrists. "You are. How can you not know that?"

I started to answer, but his mouth took mine, and his kiss was hard and hungry, angry and voracious, until my mouth felt swollen and tender, but I held on to him, sparked by the need he had always hidden. Fade tried to be gentle with me but that wasn't the whole of him. He was furious and starved, desperate, and I felt it too, until we were both trembling. His breath mingled with mine when he eased his head back.

Against my lips, he whispered, "Sometimes I could almost hate you because you don't understand how much you mean to me, how dark and empty I was before. *Solnyshko moyo.*"

I didn't think I'd ever heard those words, but I was wobbly from exhaustion as well as his anger. "What does that mean?"

"It's in my father's tongue. I can't remember more, but he

used to say that to my mother. *Solnyshko moyo.* It means 'my sun.'" Fade leaned his brow against mine, closing his eyes. "Each time Stalker called you 'dove,' I wanted to hit him. Because you're not a little gray bird . . . you're all the light in the world."

"So are you," I said, flattening my hands on his chest. He jerked at the contact, but not in a bad way. His breath hissed through his teeth, and he opened his eyes to gaze at me with desire blazing like a signal fire. "And I *do* understand. You're all that's kept me going when it seemed like this was hopeless. It's also why I did whatever was necessary to bring you back. You're my beating heart, and without you, I cannot live."

"*Now?* You say that to me now?" Fade seemed peculiarly indignant as he gestured at the empty, rocky coastline. "Here? When we've both been up all night, Stone and Thimble are waiting for us at the cottage, and there's not a bed in sight."

Ah. Heat washed my cheeks when I understood what he meant. "There's a mossy bank."

He sighed at me and pulled me closer, gentle this time. "Let's get some rest and tomorrow, we'll talk to the boatmen."

"I was afraid you wouldn't—"

"If you swear they're different from the rest, I believe you. I can't pretend I'm happy about it, but if the alternative is having our settlements destroyed, then . . . I can handle it."

Fade ought to rant at me some more because I deserve it. I hadn't meant to frighten him—and the consequences could've been so grave. I shuddered as I envisioned my soldiers dead on the wrong side of the river, all because I hadn't thought to send word that I was safe.

"I'm sorry," I said again, as we strolled toward the village, too tired for a faster pace.

"I'm still angry, but I'll think of a way for you to make it up to me."

I angled a teasing grin at him. "I'll let you beat me the next time we spar."

"Not what I had in mind," Fade muttered.

Back in town, I made up a ridiculous story about walking along the coast and getting lost. By their dubious expressions, Stone and Thimble suspected I was lying—and I didn't know whether to be pleased that they thought better of my abilities—or dismayed that my deception disappointed them. Still, they put aside their qualms and invited us back to their home, where they fed Fade and me. Talk was scant and stilted while my former brat-mates held whole conversations with their eyes.

Finally, Thimble said, "You're exhausted. Don't mind us. Get some rest."

With her blessing, we crawled up into the loft without delay. Downstairs, Stone set to household chores and played with Robin while Thimble went to her workshop. Fade pulled me close and settled me against his chest. For a few seconds, I listened to his heart.

"When did you know?" I wondered sleepily.

"What?"

"How you felt about me."

"I always admired your skill," he said, sounding thoughtful. "You were so intense about your training that I wondered if you'd focus so fiercely on somebody you loved."

"And do I?"

Fade kissed the top of my head. "More than I could've imagined. That's part of why I asked Silk to partner us."

That astonished me. "Truly?"

"She didn't want to waste you on me, you know. I spent weeks convincing her I deserved a second chance."

I shivered, imagining how different my life might be if he'd failed to persuade her. "I'm glad she agreed. But that's not what I asked."

"I'm prolonging the suspense."

Smiling, I set a hand on his chest, which made him draw a sharp breath. "Tell me."

"For me, it started when you let me put my arm around you on the way back from Nassau. So many girls in the enclave treated me like I was a filthy savage, one step away from killing all of you in your sleep."

"You must've wanted to, sometimes."

"Not after I met you. I felt . . ." He paused, as if struggling to find the words. "Like you needed me a little, as if you might let me in. But as for the moment when I *really* fell . . . we'd just opened a can of cherries and you licked them from my fingers. Then you looked at me like I was every wonderful thing in the world. And I thought, I'd give anything for her to feel that way forever. It just about killed me when I imagined that you preferred Stalker."

I shook my head quickly. "I'm sorry. I didn't understand, whereas you remembered your parents . . . and how they were together. I wish I hadn't hurt you while I was figuring things out."

"I hurt you too." Fade was referring to his harsh words on my naming day, when he'd told me everything was over between us.

To convince him that was all in the past, I scooted up and brushed my lips against his raspy jaw. I had a fuzzy idea that we might manage some quiet kissing, but oblivion took me before I did more than nuzzle his cheek. We were so weary that neither of us stirred all day. Some point after dark, I woke and Fade nudged me down the ladder, where my brat-mates fed me. Blearily I acknowledged him helping me to the facilities out back, then upstairs again. He stayed close, a warm comfort in my sleep. All told, I was out for almost eighteen hours. Given that I'd been living rough for weeks, had nearly drowned, then hiked to the west side of the island and back, staying up all night, it was no wonder I was too tired to function.

When I roused next, it was time to prepare for battle.

Meld

I spent the day dealing with last-minute details, making sure we were ready for the fight. That included various errands, begging a few items from the vendors, and dealing with the boatmen. Morrow asked his father to smooth our way—and the governor was willing to help, even without knowing why. I liked him more for that; it meant he trusted his son's judgment. But it was a good thing I'd slept most of the prior day because I wouldn't rest again before the appointed hour. The villagers didn't know what was going on, only that the soldiers they housed were saying thanks and farewell.

That night, after I wrapped up my work, I met the officers of Company D at the Cup and Bowl, Rosemere's only pub. It was nicer than the one in Otterburn; the furniture was finished, and the people were friendly, not frightened. But that came from their safety due to the river more than any natural tendency. As a girl approached our table, I wondered if all islands had fared so well. It comforted me to imagine pockets of joy and security around the world, untouched by chemicals, Freaks, or violence.

"Nothing for me," I started to say, as I didn't have any local chits.

Morrow spoke over me. "I'll pay for the group."

I shrugged. If the storyteller wanted to buy our drinks, that was fine. In response to his request, she brought us a pitcher of ale, which I privately thought was disgusting. The smell should persuade a person not to drink it, but the others seemed pleased as Tegan poured. They'd just returned from the Uroch camp, their expressions stunned and hopeful. While they drank, Morrow and Tegan talked nonstop about Szarok, their voices pitched so nobody but our table could hear.

"I trust him," Tegan murmured. "He seems sincere about the alliance. And I was surprised by how many physiological differences I noted between these and the older ones." She elaborated on that, but I wasn't interested in the properties of their blood or other distinctions.

When she paused for breath, Morrow added, "I find their culture fascinating. Did you know they share memories with a touch?"

"Szarok showed me . . . a girl in Otterburn changed everything."

"What do you mean?" Spence asked.

In answer, I told the story about how one little girl, saving an injured Freak, led us here.

Once I finished, Tegan was teary. At first I didn't understand why until she said, "If we survive, it's because of her, and she'll never know."

"She might still be alive," I suggested, hoping to cheer her. "Since I plan to ride around notifying the families of our fallen men, afterward, I'll look for her too."

She nodded. "That would mean a lot to me."

Tully seemed less moved by the story. Her mind was clearly on the battle ahead, not what came after, and that was wise. "I don't know how this arrangement will work long term, but we need their numbers."

Spence downed his ale in a gulp. "No question. I still don't like the odds, but it's the best chance we're likely to get, provided those Gulgur do their part."

"Did you see any when you visited the camp?" I asked.

Morrow broke into a smile. "A group was arriving as we left. I spoke with them for a few moments. Funny little fellows, aren't they?"

Nodding, I contemplated the coming battle. There were so many variables; the fight might turn into a massacre, but without help, Company D was doomed. I'd carried them as far as I could on our own. There was no way to produce soldiers from thin air, so we had to accept aid from strange sources. Briefly I wished I could say good-bye to Edmund and Momma Oaks in case things went wrong at the river, but at least Rex was here; and I'd do my best to protect him.

Tegan pulled something out of her bag and offered it to me. When I unwrapped it, I held an odd artifact; it had a long, slender red tail, a small cylinder at the top, wrapped in paper, then a string hung down. "What is this?"

"Szarok said they're useful for sending signals. When we're ready to attack, plant the stick in the ground, light the wick, and step back."

I studied the strange item for a few seconds more, then shrugged and stowed it in my pack. "If he says it'll work, then we'll try it."

"He said to wait to a count of two hundred once we light it and then begin the attack. They will do the same from the west."

"They're smarter than I expected," Spence said.

"And better spoken," Morrow added.

Fade was quiet; the idea of working with the Uroch must be bothering him, after what their brethren had done to him. I touched his leg and he nudged it closer to mine, so our thighs nestled while the others talked. It hit me hard that this could be the last time . . . for all of this. Any of us could fall tomorrow;

there were no guarantees—and my heart hurt with the finality of it.

I raised my glass. "I just want to say, it's been an honor to know you all."

"I'll drink to that," Tully said.

"Does anyone have questions?" I asked.

There were a few, and I answered them. Once we finished the ale, we agreed it was time to get some rest, as we'd soon be meeting the boatmen at the dock. Since there were so many soldiers, they'd make multiple trips. Once we crossed, there was no turning back.

But I'd passed that point when Tully said she couldn't live with knowing we'd let everyone die so we could live, if we gave up and stayed in Rosemere.

Morrow stopped me as we left the Cup and Bowl. "You were right about the Uroch. And about the villagers too, I think."

Alarm sputtered to life. "What happened?"

"Nothing. But when I saw them encamped, I *knew* how people here would react. It would've been terrible . . . and so completely avoidable."

"Did you tell your father anything?"

Morrow shook his head. "He wouldn't thank me for keeping this secret, but the council would've insisted on some imprudent, hastily concocted defense strategy, and instead of new allies, we'd be fighting on two fronts. We can't afford that."

"True."

He smiled, glancing down the lane. "I should get on. Tegan's waiting for me."

"You took her home to meet your parents, did you?"

The storyteller ducked his head. "Not like that. But, yes."

"And she doesn't realize?" I guessed. "Give her time."

"I'm made of it." He flourished a mocking bow and strode off to where she stood beneath a lamp. When she took his arm, I glimpsed the future, and it beckoned like the wind blowing through a field of wildflowers.

The moon glowed overhead, though its curve was waning. I liked it best when it was a slice of silver in the night sky, not so full that it overwhelmed the stars. Here, they shone like chips of ice, so bright that the darkness seemed almost blue by contrast. The sky over Rosemere might be the loveliest I'd ever seen. Fade walked back to where I stood, staring up.

Then I realized I hadn't told him what might make this pact easier to swallow. Quickly, I repeated Szarok's explanation for how they'd learned our language. I concluded, "So . . . what you went through? It mattered. If I hadn't come for you, the Uroch would never have slipped away with the other captives. They wouldn't have been able to communicate, even if they'd wanted to." I took Fade's hand. "You're the reason we have any hope of winning."

He stood very still, as if listening to the stars. "That's not true. You've carried us this far, my sun. But yes . . . it helps, knowing I didn't suffer for nothing."

"I'm glad. It's hard to believe we're finally here," I said softly.

"On the eve before the reckoning?" At my nod, Fade trailed his fingertips over my wrist, his eyes glimmering. "It's a night for taking risks, I think."

I gazed up at him. "And for not leaving things undone."

The memory of his last kiss swept over me. I had been too tired then . . . but between all the sleep I'd stored up and the looming battle, there was no way I'd close my eyes tonight. In that moment, I wanted only Fade.

"I bet Stone and Thimble are asleep by now," he whispered.

"Likely." They kept early hours, driven by Robin. "We'll need to be quiet."

"I hope that's possible." Fade's grin held a wicked edge.

And I shivered, because he was so obviously talking about more than creeping up the ladder. My fingers tightened on his, and we were running. Fortunately, there were few people about to see our urgency and question it. When we reached the cottage, the door was unlatched. I slipped in with Fade close behind me.

The fire was banked low in the hearth, all the supper things put away. There were two rooms at the back of the cottage, one where Stone and Thimble slept, the other for Robin. Just inside, I bent and removed my boots, then carried them with me to the loft. Fade followed soon after; above lay a cozy space with a feather mattress, just big enough for me to sit up at the tallest point. Fade and I had nestled here together, but I remembered only bit and pieces of it.

Tonight, I'd memorize every moment.

Fade knelt at the edge of the pallet, the hearth downstairs lighting his features enough for me to see his uncertainty. "Do you want this too? I can wait if—"

"No." I swallowed hard, aching, nervous, and excited all at the same time. "I don't want either of us to regret that we never did."

That was as close as I could come to admitting how scared I was that he wouldn't be around when the fighting ended. The prospect of my own death didn't bother me as much, except for how it would hurt Fade. I'd come up with the expectation that I might die protecting others, and my nature hadn't changed entirely, though I was now able to perceive the beauty of living without a knife strapped to your thigh.

"No regrets," he whispered.

I opened my arms, and Fade came to me on his knees, but only because that was what the low ceiling required. There was no begging between us. He kissed me in soft, delicate glides of lips and tongue, as if I'd become fragile. I sank my fingers into

-- 363 --

his hair and fell into him; that was enough for a while, until he got brave and his hands roved down to my hips. Since I wasn't a Breeder, nobody had ever told me how this worked, though I'd figured out the gist from noises down below and being close to Fade. I wished I wasn't nervous, but it was tough, especially considering how little I knew.

He pulled off his shirt, probably guessing that would spook me less. I didn't know if I was ready to be naked with him, but I didn't want to wait, either. "Can I touch you?"

When my fingertips found his chest, he shivered. "Anywhere."

It helped that he let me lose myself in his lean body, learning his lines until he was shaking. He pressed his mouth into my shoulder, breathing fast, especially when I raked my nails down the nape of his neck. To test his reaction, I did it again, and this time, he groaned.

"You like that."

"I'd like anything you did to me."

While I doubted that was true, it made me bolder. I pulled him down on top of me, and we kissed some more with my hands roaming up and down his back. Soon, he was moving on me as if he couldn't help it, and it felt good, even the parts that were new and strange.

"Fade . . ."

His voice deepened, his words ragged and choppy with longing. "You feel so good. Need to . . . just let me . . ."

Feeling brave, I wriggled out of my shirt and that drew another pained sound from him when he lay down on me again. He explored with lips and hands. Then I lost track in the squirming and touching, so I didn't notice when the rest of our clothes went away. The night was all heat, firelight, and Fade, breathing hard into my skin. He pressed my hand to him, but it didn't take long until he was gasping. There was madness born of need in his eyes but I wasn't afraid, never of him. He had restrained himself more than once, and I knew if I asked, he would stop. Instead I urged him on.

It hurt a bit, but I'd had worse. As he held me, kissed me so deep I tasted nothing but him, the rest turned beautiful. I figured out my part pretty fast, and when we finished, we were both sweaty and smiling. He cuddled me close, and I decided I didn't mind being naked with him. With the wrong person, this would be awful, but I loved Fade with all my heart.

"So that's how brats are born," I said.

He propped up on an elbow. "We might have made one."

"Is it possible the first time?" Maybe there was a learning curve.

"I think so. I'm not clear on the details." Fade kissed my temple. "Was it all right?"

Teasing him, I pretended to consider. "I'd do it again. It's probably like fighting, and we'll get better with training."

"I don't know if I should be sad it wasn't perfect or excited about the practice."

"The last thing," I advised.

Fade reached down, pulled up the covers, and settled me against his chest. We had lain like this together before, but never without clothes or blankets between us. To my mind, this part ran a close second to the touching and kissing.

"Are you scared?" he whispered.

I closed my eyes against the inexorable tick of time. "Very."

"We have a few hours yet," he pointed out.

As it happened, there was a lot to discover in that time. The second effort was better, and I understood why Momma Oaks spent so much time cautioning me. It was probably a good thing most Hunters were kept ignorant, or there would've been more brats than we could feed.

In silent accord, we gathered our clothes, dressed quickly, and crept out to the bathhouse to clean up before we met the rest of Company D. I'd never felt closer to another person in my life, as if breeding had destroyed the barriers between us. He waited while I took my turn, then I did the same. When Fade stepped out, I couldn't resist kissing him; it seemed unthinkable that a night like this must end in death.

Not his, I begged silently. *Not Fade. Please don't take him from me.*

Onslaught

Three hours before dawn, we assembled on the shore as agreed. The boatmen met us and ferried us over in shifts. I ordered the men to sit quiet and wait; I wasn't sure how good the enemy's hearing was, and this attack didn't start until I gave the signal. It took about an hour to get everyone safely across. On arrival, I counted and realized we were short a few men. Apparently they couldn't live with their orders . . . and I understood.

"Is everyone ready?" I asked.

"Yes, sir."

Fade drew me aside. The men turned away—and I appreciated their discretion. We weren't the only ones who had just-in-case good-byes to say, however. Around us, other people paired off: Morrow with Tegan, Tully and Spence, and a couple of men too. My heart hammered in my chest, so hard it hurt, and those moments of sweetness and safety up in the loft felt so far away. I went into his arms without asking if he wanted me there because I knew he did. His breath stirred my hair, and for a moment, I just listened to his heart beating.

"The odds still aren't good," I said softly.

I fought tears, as I had to be strong and brave at this moment, everything I didn't feel. Fade loosened his arms enough so he could tip my face up to his, and I could've drowned in his eyes. "For us, they never were. Look where we found each other."

He had a point; it was pretty awful down below. "I'll never be sorry that we went Topside together. I'll never be sorry about anything."

Including what we did tonight. I left that part unsaid, but Fade knew. He always did. Back when Silk partnered us, he seemed to understand me better than I did myself, sensing what I wanted and things that would make me happy. I remembered how he'd comforted me with an arm around my shoulders, and that was the first step toward a world where he meant everything to me, and his touch was as much my home as any cottage could ever be.

"If this is the last time, let me say it so you never forget. I will always love you, Deuce. No matter where souls go, mine will be looking for you, *solnyshko moyo.*"

Those words tore me in two. "No. I want a promise instead. Promise you'll fight like you never have, so when the dying stops, you'll be on your feet looking for me here."

"I swear," he said.

But there were no guarantees. I knew that, even as I extracted the pledge. So I kissed him because if the end came for me in the form of fangs and claws, I wanted to die with the taste of him on my lips.

There should be a speech for a moment like this one, but it was chilly, and we were all ready to have the fight done. So I held out my hand to Fade, who put his sire's lighter in it. I jammed the artifact in the ground, as Tegan had said, lit the wick, and then we all backed up. Sparks flew, then the thing shot straight up in the air in an orange arc, making a popping, whistling noise, then it exploded in a cascade of colors. For a few seconds, we all stared up in awe because none of us had ever seen anything like it.

"I'm counting," Morrow said.

As he hit two hundred, an answering light rose on the other side, just high enough that we could see it. I took a deep breath, scared as I never had been. I didn't believe that I was a Huntress anymore—and therefore, destined for a great and glorious death. If I died in battle, it would hurt as much as it did for anyone else, and there were so many things I'd never do. But courage wasn't an absence of fear; it was fighting despite the knot in your stomach.

"That's our cue. Good hunting, Company D."

The men echoed it back to me; and in the faint, predawn light, I saw all of their fear, all the uncertainty. I had no remedy for it. Morrow took his scouts while Tully, Fade, and Spence rallied their soldiers. Thornton stuck close to Tegan, hanging back, and I was glad he meant to protect her. I wanted to grab Fade and beg him not to be too brave or too reckless. Instead, I led as I'd always done, by rushing the enemy with my knives drawn.

The camp was mostly asleep, though some of the Freaks were retching. I'd never seen them vomit before. It was disgusting, the way bile funneled to either side of their fangs. They hardly had a chance to raise the alarm before we were on them. Company D ran straight into the heart, and then stabbed it for good measure. Tactics that served us before worked again. The men were armed with all the liquor the pub owner was willing to spare without knowing why we needed it, and we lobbed ten firebombs into the horde. Rifles barked and I heard the smooth *shing* of Tully's crossbow. In the confusion and snarling bodies, I lost sight of my lieutenants at once. The beasts were all around, so many that I couldn't breathe, but they were sluggish and clumsy, as promised, which meant the Gulgur had kept their part of the bargain.

The air thickened with smoke, until it was hard to see who we were fighting. I stabbed one Freak, then another as it stumbled toward me. Another burst out of the miasma, but he wore a white strip of cloth around his arm, so I raised my blade in salute and we attacked the next enemy together. I hurt for him; it might be his sire or dam suffering beneath his claws but he didn't falter.

My ears echoed with the screams and curses, snarls and cries of pain. There were corpses everywhere, gunshots cracking out, the coppery tang of blood heavy in the wind. I had no sense for how my side was doing, only the certainty that if I stopped fighting, I would die. The horde was huge, their numbers formidable, even with poisoned meat churning in their guts. Ten of them surrounded me, and beyond them, there were ten more and ten again, far past what the night and the smoldering reeds permitted me to see. Bodies splashed in the river nearby, fighting or fleeing, I couldn't tell which.

The Uroch near me slashed a Freak that tried to lunge past him to get at me, and I finished his kill. These monsters were puzzled, unable to grasp why they were fighting their kin. I parried and sliced until my arms ached and the dead piled up around me. Still they came on as the dawn broke. It should've been an inspiring sight, sunlight on the water, but instead it only illuminated how long our odds were. The combined might of Company D, the Urochs, and the Gulgur didn't seem to be enough. We'd killed so many, but as many of our soldiers lay injured and dying on the bloody battlefield, and they had a thousand more to throw at us.

Across the way, I heard Tully screaming at her men to regroup while rifle fire came slower and slower. The men were running low on ammo, I guessed, as I swiped sweat and blood from my brow, and fought on, focusing on my immediate danger. A Freak impaled the Uroch beside me, and I was too slow to save him. Blood bubbled from the young one's mouth, then he fell, never having said a word, and I was alone in the middle of the horde.

I need Fade.

But my throat was parched and tired from the hours of fighting. Calling out was a waste of breath. Freaks surged as far as the eye could see, and they were exultant despite their weakness because they sensed how this fight ended. With a burst of renewed energy, I struggled on, powered by the memory of all the people I would never see again if I gave up. My shoulders burned, my arms twin columns of fire.

Another wave of the monsters rushed me, and I was engulfed, unable to see, just the snarling mass of claws and fangs lashing at me. With sheer determination, I brought up my knives, but willpower wasn't enough. My body had limits, and I'd reached them. More of their strikes got through; it was just a matter of time until one of them got lucky and struck the killing blow. *Heart, throat, thigh. One of those places, and I'm gone.*

A Freak sank its teeth into my forearm, another scored my shoulder. With a move Stalker had taught me, I cut the first one's throat, and spun low, slicing at their legs. *If they can't stand, they can't fight as well.* It also made me a smaller target. I sliced the veins in their legs and nearly puked at the rush of blood that caught me in the face.

How many more? Too many.

Three of them died at my feet, and I stared, unable to grasp what I was seeing. But Tegan had broken one of their skulls, Thornton accounted for the other, and the third, well, Gavin of Winterville stood with our banner in his hands, the flag flapping in the wind; he'd impaled the Freak with the pointy end. Before I could thank them, Thornton's head snapped to the side and his neck gushed red. The veteran fell before I could react, and then there were eight more monsters on Tegan, the brat, and me. He jerked the banner from his victim and used it like a polearm, but the kid didn't have the strength to do that for long. Tegan and I covered him as best we could, but I was so tired, and from her movements, her leg was paining her. A doctor shouldn't fight on the battlefield, but there was no time for her to treat the wounded. One of our men screamed for mercy, and anguish flickered across her face because she couldn't break from the battle and do her job.

I'm sorry, I tried to say, but I had no breath. The stitch in my side came from a complex blend of exertion and pain, both emotional and physical. I'd never fought in a conflict that had no end, but this felt as if there were nowhere to go and no conclusion except the grave. Tegan stumbled and I grabbed her; somehow we held on as Freaks shoved toward us. Gavin was so gallant, flapping the pennant as if its power alone could drive the monsters away.

Tegan knocked down a Freak and I stabbed it while Gavin impaled another. He was actually pretty good with that blasted banner. But there were too many.

"I'm not dying!" Gavin shouted. "I promised my mum!"

His defiance gave me the strength to kill one, then another. Tegan appeared to take heart as well, and we pushed past the pain, until we had a pile of bodies so tall before us that I could stand on them. And I did. I climbed the corpses and stumbled down the other side, through the smoky air. There was more fighting farther along the river.

I spotted knots of Uroch battling their brethren and the Gulgur slinging stones with leather straps from the fringes of the battle. When a Freak turned to give chase, the small folk darted away and were gone, and in that time, the monsters took more damage from behind. Exhausted, I paused to catch my breath while my two comrades did the same.

"Are we winning?" Tegan asked.

I shook my head. "Don't know."

Then hope appeared, incredibly, unbelievably. From the south and east, men came marching. I recognized Morgan at the head of one column, so I identified them as Soldier's Pond men. I saw people I had met in Gaspard, Otterburn, and Lorraine; they had tired faces but they all wore identical expressions of determination. Most were poorly outfitted and equipped. They had no uniforms and some were armed with hoes and shovels, whatever they could grab quickly. Marlon Bean lifted a hand in greeting, as did Vince Howe.

John Kelley rode at the front of the lines and when he saw me, he called, "You started without us, Huntress. Do you mind if we take some of these Muties off your hands?"

"Don't attack the Uroch or the Gulgur," I yelled back. "They're with us."

Quickly Tegan called out the description of our allies, and Kelley looked astonished, but he acknowledged with a nod, relaying the instructions to their men. Nobody argued. There was too much movement for me to get any idea how many had come to join the fight or how many Freaks were left, but hope flickered deep within me.

Catching my second wind, I ran at the remaining Freaks with renewed fury. As I fought, I searched for Fade. Sometimes I thought I heard his voice calling out orders, but I couldn't break off to search for him. I did see Spence, out of bullets and using his shooting iron to club the monsters in the head to stun them before he stabbed. He smiled at me, teeth white in his filthy face, and it heartened me to see that he'd made it this far. His men surrounded him, the twenty that were left . . . out of the fifty he had before, and their deaths hurt, but I couldn't stop.

Not when we were so close.

In the melee I lost track of Tegan and Gavin. Then I saw the boy raise his banner high and jam it into a Freak Tegan had flattened for him. *"That's* for Stalker."

I didn't know how he could be so sure, but I sliced my way toward them. When I looked at the dead thing on the ground,

I recognized the scar cutting through its left eye. Maybe it shouldn't matter, as it didn't bring my friend back, but I nodded at the brat.

"Good work."

Within minutes, the tenor of the battle changed. These weren't soldiers, but they were brave men, and the rest of us fought as hard. It could have been an hour or five, but eventually the horde broke. The Freaks tried to run, but riflemen from Soldier's Pond had been practicing for years for this day, and they cut them down.

On the enemy's side, there were no survivors.

Death

Ravens and crows swept down on the dead, even as I tried to tend the living. Tegan was distraught; we had no plan in place for victory, no facilities for the wounded. She shouted at people to help her carry litters away from the killing field and men responded to her call. Tegan found a capable-looking woman to serve as her nurse, and they discussed the best way to save as many lives as possible.

As for me, I was looking for Fade. I walked among the corpses, staring down into their bloody faces. Each time I saw a lean young man or a shock of black hair, I lost my breath and my courage. It took all my willpower to keep searching. I found Zach Bigwater cut down . . . and I hoped he'd found peace, redemption from his conviction that he was a coward. To me, it looked like he'd fought hard and I whispered, "Thank you."

A few minutes later, I rolled Harry Carter over. The older man was smiling, as if he'd seen something lovely before he died. Fear took deep root in my belly. *Fade promised. He's fine. You just have to find him.*

I stumbled across Spence by accident. He was half hidden by a rise above the river, bodies all around him. The beady-eyed black birds crept closer on forked feet and his scream sent them scattering in a flutter of wings. Too late, I saw Tully cradled in his arms. The container that held her bolts hung empty, and her knives were nowhere to be found. Her blood had clotted, going brown in the sun, but he didn't let go of her. He just held her and rocked. His eyes opened when he saw me; and he seemed too young for such grief with his ginger hair and freckled face.

"I couldn't find her." His voice was a song born of pain. "I was too late."

Dropping to my knees, I put my hand on his shoulder. "I'm sorry. I'm so sorry."

"She always said I'd get tired of her. She never—never—"

Tears sprang to my eyes. "Maybe she didn't say it out loud, but she knew you loved her. I could see it between the two of you."

"I can't do this." Without warning, he dropped her body and went for his gun.

Terrified, I grabbed his arm and wrestled him for it, using all my strength to pull the barrel away from Spence's body. He actually hit me, hard enough to make my vision sparkle, but I dug my fingers into his arm and didn't let go. We rolled in the mud, end over end, and I came up on top, barely hanging on. I couldn't let this man die.

Fortunately, his burst of fury didn't last long, and when he yielded, I hurled the weapon into the water.

"I can get another," he said dully.

"Do you think she'd want this for you?"

His blue eyes went hard as ice. "No. But she's dead, and she doesn't get a say."

"Pull yourself together. People among the living still need your help, and I haven't given you permission to quit."

Spence offered a terse suggestion as to what I could do with my orders; and if I wasn't so worried about Fade, I might've cracked a smile. Instead I shoved to my feet and pointed. "Pick her up. Move Tully to where the medical team can look after her. Once we take stock of who's left, we'll see to our dead."

He argued a little, but in the end, he swung his beloved into his arms and he was weeping unashamedly when he delivered her to Tegan. She registered at once who he carried and what she'd meant to Spence. Tegan waved frantically at Morgan, who had some carts. His men must've gone across the river to ask Rosemere for help.

Tegan said, "I need you to take care of her for me."

"I will." Morgan had proven he was steady as a rock, so his word was good.

"How the devil did you get here just in time?" I asked.

"Thank your traders. They've been haranguing all towns in the territories to send men for weeks. On their last trip, which they made without your protection, they swore there would be no more supplies unless we all manned up and did our share."

"We owe them our lives." I pitched my voice low, casting a glance at Spence, who stood like a ghost beside Tegan. "He's not all right. Keep an eye on him while I search the battlefield? I'm missing some men."

Fade, Morrow, and Rex. I couldn't speak of the ones I'd lost.

Morgan agreed with a ready nod. "You know, Colonel Park wants to speak with you, as soon as you get the chance."

It was funny to me how formally he referred to his own wife, but her position made their relationship a quiet, private matter, glimpsed primarily in a subtle look.

"I have a lot to take care of first, but I'm heading to Soldier's Pond when I'm done."

With no more conversation, I returned to my mission. I found Rex soon after, and my stomach lurched when I saw him lying there. Momma Oaks would never forgive me for taking another son from her. But when I put my fingers to his throat, I felt a pulse. I searched him from top to bottom and uncovered a flesh wound on his chest and a bruise on his jaw. He was bloody enough, however, that the poison-fogged Freaks had thought he was dead.

Shaking him gently, I set a jug to his mouth and poured. At first the water just trickled down his neck, but apparently that was enough irritation to bring him around. He slapped my hands away and struggled upright, his eyes fuzzy at first. I knew the second he focused on me and realized he was still alive.

"That's a bit of a surprise," he said.

"A good one. On your feet. I need you to help me find Morrow and Fade." Actually I was more interested in seeing if he *could* get up, which should help me gauge how badly he was hurt.

With my help, Rex clambered up and he looked around, his face going green. "This is . . ."

"Yes," I said softly. "It is."

Though Rex was unsteady on his feet, he seemed sound enough, so he stayed with me as I sorted the living from the dead. Three times, we found men who looked as if they were done, but I found a heartbeat and called Tegan's workers to treat them. It was terrifying and exhausting, there among the wounded. Somewhere past midday, Szarok found me. His sharp features were familiar in a way I found strange, considering we'd only spent one night talking. Rex stepped closer in reflex until he remembered that the monsters were dead.

"Your soldiers fought well," he said.

"As did yours. One of them saved my life."

"I wish there was a way to take the memories from the dead," he said somberly, "so they're not lost." Before I could reply, another Uroch approached, and they hissed and growled a conversation. Then the other hurried away. "I've been reminded to state my terms for our alliance. We keep Appleton. While it's regrettable the way we acquired it, I doubt any of your people care to settle there now."

"I don't have the power to—"

"The devil you don't," Rex cut in. "You led this army. You united every able-bodied person willing to fight in the territories.

You beat the horde. So if you offer Appleton to our allies, nobody will argue with you."

Could that be true? I supposed it was. "All right. Appleton's yours. This isn't the time to talk about such things, but there will need to be . . ." I didn't even know the words.

"Treaties," Rex supplied. "Trade agreements. And the Uroch will probably want to wear those armbands, at least until the last of the old mutants are gone."

A flicker of pain registered in Szarok's golden eyes. Those were his people Rex was casually dismissing. We hadn't killed all of them; there would be stragglers in forest and field, but if we were careful, they'd die out in a few years and their legacy of violence with them.

But I couldn't help wondering, "Can the few remaining old ones breed . . . and start the cycle all over again?"

Szarok shook his head. "They're past the age of reproduction. The future of my people rests in our hands now."

"That's good to hear," Rex muttered.

The Uroch favored him with a sharp glance, before saying, "We're returning to Appleton now. These bodies are nothing to us since we can't collect their memories. So the crows are welcome to them."

That was a way in which we differed, but I didn't judge him for it. "Might be best. I don't know how the men will react, now that the fighting's stopped."

Rex nodded. "Peace takes time."

Szarok went on, "The Gulgur have returned to their burrows. They told me to ask you to bury their dead along with your own. I don't know if they're interested in treaties or trade agreements, but they're pleased it's safe to come into the light, if they so choose."

"I'll take care of it. Thank them for me," I said.

With a lift of his taloned hand, Szarok turned and signaled

his surviving warriors with another of those exploding things. They loped away, along the river and out of sight, leaving me to continue picking up the pieces. With each body I turned over and each face I searched, my hope grew fainter. The sun was past its zenith when I found Morrow.

"Tegan!" I shouted, knowing she'd drop everything to tend him.

He was covered in so many wounds that I didn't know how he was still breathing. Two men came with her, drawn by my sharpness, and we carried him to the tent set up away from the bodies. I figured it, too, had come from Rosemere, and I silently thanked them for their help. There were fires burning and water boiling in huge pots, and women from the village moving among the wounded soldiers with bandages that looked like they had been torn from sails.

"Someone should fetch his father," I said.

In case he doesn't make it.

I wished I'd let him inform the governor, as he'd wanted. Then they could've had a just-in-case farewell. But Tegan fixed a look of such ferocious denial on me that I stumbled back to the tent's entrance. "Nobody is going anywhere. Get me a damned pan of water, some clean cloth, and my medical bag."

I did as she demanded, then Rex and I washed up and assisted her as she cleaned his wounds and then prepared the tincture that had saved Harry Carter. With steady hands, she poured the noxious mixture into the bites and stitched Morrow's wounds. His men heard about his condition, and fifteen of them paced outside the tent. We'd suffered such losses before reinforcements arrived—I cut the thought as I daubed away the blood leaking from his side. I couldn't afford to let fear and impending grief distract me. A friend's life hung in the balance.

It seemed like it took forever before Tegan finished working on the storyteller. He was so pale that it didn't look like he had any blood left in his body. She dropped to her knees and pressed her cheek to his, and that seemed like my cue to back out of the tent. Along the way, I stumbled, but there was nothing to trip me, only the smooth roll of grassy ground.

Rex steadied me with one arm and said, "You have to eat something."

"I can't. I have to find Fade."

"Eat," he demanded gently. "Or I'll tell Momma that you don't listen to your brother."

Shakily, I assented, but only because I'd never locate Fade if I collapsed. If he was wounded and unable to call out for help, buried in a pile of corpses—I shook all over, just thinking about it. This battle would never end for me if he didn't keep his promise.

Rex led me to a fire where village women were warming soup. I took a wooden bowl of it and drank in a few furious gulps—anger because pain would drown me without the protective shell. Then I downed some water and glared at Rex.

"Happy now? Can I go back out there?" Even as the words spewed out in *that* tone, I knew my brother deserved better than this.

To his credit, he only nodded. "Let's keep looking."

More bodies rolled beneath my hands, more dead faces to haunt my dreams. Beside me, Rex was grim and silent, but I was glad to have him. With Tegan tirelessly treating patients and the men looking for their own friends and loved ones, I'd be alone otherwise. And without his calm determination, I might be screaming and tearing out my hair. We'd been searching for some time and it was starting to get dark when Gavin rushed at us.

The brat was so breathless he could barely talk, so the words juddered out in fits and starts. "Deuce, this way . . . please. Hurry."

His urgency was contagious. I pushed to my feet and stumbled after him, the riverbank a mass of bodies, so much death. There were small forms, the Gulgur, and larger ones: Uroch wearing armbands, townsfolk with hoes beside them, and the fallen men of Company D. The stench was becoming dreadful. If we didn't do something about the corpses, they'd poison the river, ruining the tranquil beauty I'd so admired. Rex ran behind me, steadier on his feet.

I hoped with all my heart for good news.

Ahead of us, Gavin led the way with the bloody banner still flying in the wind. The brat ran lopsided, but if he was capable of moving on his own, then he was low on the list of people Tegan needed to see. There were so many who wouldn't last the night, maybe including Morrow. My own injuries cracked and stung as I churned the earth, trying to keep up.

When the boy stopped, he stood beside a lean figure sprawled upon the ground. And there was so much blood, so much, all over his face, that I was afraid to look closer. As I braced to scream, Fade opened his eyes.

Relief drowned me, and I lost my breath. "You promised you'd be on your feet."

Memorial

It took thirty-two stitches to put Fade back together. While Tegan sewed, I hovered and paced, shadowed by Rex, who seemed to think I might do something drastic. Mercifully, Fade passed out before she finished. Her eyes were bleak as she raised her head.

"This wound could be tricky."

"Give me everything that Doc used on you. I'll take care of him and fight the infection."

Without another word of protest, as she had other patients to tend, Tegan handed me a collection of dried herbs and bottled remedies. I listened to her instructions, memorized them, and then turned to Rex. "I need your help getting him to Rosemere. We can't stay here."

In reply, my brother swung the man I loved up into his arms, and we left the medical tent, leaving Tegan to hover over Morrow and wait for the next soldier to be carried in. Gavin went with us, and I was eager to escape the smell of death. Flies were thick in the air, buzzing in the reeds and laying eggs in something I didn't want to see. Rex shouted to a boatman; they were in constant motion, ferrying supplies and wounded back and forth across the water. I was desperate for the sanctuary Rosemere represented. Though there might not be any danger on the mainland, I needed to get away from the battlefield.

The fisherman came in response to Rex's call. He couldn't come all the way to shore, lest his boat founder, so we waded out, and I helped my brother lift Fade into the boat. Gavin clambered in on his own, the banner still in his hand. It looked more like a rag, smeared with mud and blood, but my symbol was still discernable in the center. Wearily I climbed aboard myself, and the man sailed us silently back to the Evergreen Isle. On the docks, the fishermen chattered about the battle and more volunteers had assembled to help with the wounded.

Our boatman went back out, along with two more, in case they were needed. Villagers peppered me with questions and I answered in a monotone, thinking only of getting Fade to safety. Just when I was about to lose my temper, Stone shouldered through the crowd, his handsome face lighting with relief when he saw me.

"I can take him," Stone said, but my brother shook his head.

It must have been a matter of pride since Rex had to be as exhausted as I was. With Stone leading the way, I trudged to his cottage, where Thimble stood with Robin balanced on her hip. She stepped back and made room, her face creased with worry.

"How bad is it?" she asked. There was no answering that yet, so I kept quiet, and she turned her attention to Gavin and Rex, who seemed pleased by her care. "If you'd like to wash up out back, I'll feed you, then you can rest in the loft."

Stone carried Fade into Robin's room; it was small, little more than a nook, but large enough for a narrow bed with a feather mattress. He laid him down and said, "Robin will be fine with us for a few nights. Do you need anything?"

"Some soap and water. Clean bandages."

As he left, I stripped Fade out of his torn and ragged clothes. He had a number of less serious slashes on his shoulders and chest, none as serious as the wound on his side. My stomach clenched when I thought of Tegan pinching his muscle together and sewing tight, before stitching another layer in his skin. Stone returned with the supplies I'd requested and I washed Fade from head to toe. Mercifully, he was still unconscious.

It never occurred to me that he could die, even when his fever spiked later that night. He sweated and thrashed while I bathed him and plied him with the treatments Tegan had provided. There were special teas and poultices to draw out infection before it deepened. While I tended Fade, others buried the dead, burned the Freak corpses, and cleared the battlefield. I didn't sleep much; a blanket on the floor beside his bed didn't offer much comfort, but I had to be close enough to hold his hand. I was convinced as long as I didn't let go of him, his fever would break and his body would heal. I might've been delusional by that point from lack of sleep and food, but there was no budging me. Thimble tried, but I snarled at her, and she backed out of the room.

On the third day, Thimble came to the doorway again. "How is he?"

"Better, I think. Have you heard anything about Morrow?"

"Tegan's with him at the governor's place. He nearly died in the night, but she opened one of his wounds and brought him back."

"Multiple infections?" That explained why she hadn't checked on us.

She nodded soberly. "Why didn't you tell us about the battle, Deuce?"

"Because I knew you'd fight. So would Stone. You both feel like you need to make amends with me, and you have Robin to think about, which is more important than guilt."

"Topside's been good for you," she said, smiling. "You're smarter than you used to be."

"I understand more how people think now. It doesn't always make me happy." I thought of Stalker when I said it, and melancholy twisted my heart.

Fade moaned then and I spooned some water down his throat. Thimble tiptoed out. Fade's lips were dry and pale, his cheeks flagged with color. Knowing it would hurt him, I changed the dressing on his wound. It was seeping a little as Tegan had warned, but the poultices kept it from swelling up and turning red. I made more of the black goop and smeared it down the stitches; it didn't look clean or healthy, but she'd promised that was what Doc Tuttle said had saved her life. And after it dried, it smelled horrible, like it was really drawing out the impurities. I washed it off and started all over again with the bandages.

My monthly started the next day, which Momma Oaks had told me meant I wasn't breeding. That was a relief; and I made a mental note to ask her how to prevent brats when I saw her next. It wasn't that I was against the idea, but I wanted us to be ready when we had our own. With him so hurt, it sure wasn't the time.

Five days passed in more or less the same fashion, but that night, his fever broke. And when his eyes opened, they were clear as the night sky; and he knew me. I wasn't even surprised, just overcome with love and satisfaction, as if my stubbornness had any impact on his health. His beautiful mouth curved into a smile.

"You look awful," he whispered.

"Then we're a matched set."

"My side feels like somebody's branded me with hot irons."

"I'm not surprised. A Freak talon opened you up."

He pushed out a breath, then reached for me. The movement prompted a cry of pain, so I scrambled onto the edge of the bed. "Stop, I'm here. I haven't left you for a single minute."

"I remember the battle . . . and seeing the Gulgur dodging around, slinging stones. They're not fierce, but they're annoying. I killed a lot of Freaks who were dumb enough to chase them."

I nodded, smiling. "They pulled their weight. I wonder if Jengu's still out there."

"I hope so." He winced, probing the stitches with his finger-tips, and I stilled them by covering his hand with mine. "After our reinforcements arrived, I got careless. I tried to reach you, but I must've blacked out."

"Gavin found you. I had been looking all day."

"I owe him, then." Fade shifted to favor his injured flank and drew me close. I must have smelled awful, but compared with the stuff slathered on his wound, maybe he didn't notice.

"So do I."

For the first time in days, I curled up and went to sleep. He improved steadily after that, enough to stay awake for hours at a time, eat on his own, and drink endless cups of herbal tea that Thimble claimed would hasten his recovery and Fade said tasted like weeds. I relaxed enough to take a bath and brush my hair.

"How's Morrow?" I asked, the first time Tegan came by.

"Healing, slower than Fade."

The deep shadows under her eyes said she was nursing him with the same care I'd granted Fade, but she probably didn't re-alize what that meant yet. I wondered how long it would take for her to figure out that she loved him. She had help from his family, however, whereas I was like a mother bear with a single cub; I'd snarled and threatened to take the hand off anyone who came near my man.

"How many are left of Company D?"

"I've been going through Morrow's journal while I tend him. Less than seventy."

I bowed my head for a few seconds. "I need all their names."

"I'll put Sands on it." Soon after, Tegan left.

Only one of Stalker's original scouts had survived the battle. Since he'd been with us from the beginning, Sands would likely know the names of the dead and where they'd come from. *Time for me to keep my promise.* A little food and sleep had worked wonders, especially since I knew I could cross the river, and there was nothing much to fear anymore.

The next day, Fade protested when I kissed his forehead and said, "I'll see you soon."

He tried to follow me, but he wasn't strong enough. A blue streak of cursing ensued, quickly staunched when Thimble stuck her head in the room wearing a ferocious scowl. "If my son picks up that language from you, Fade, there *will* be a reckoning."

"Let me come with you." Fade's desperate voice followed me, and I turned.

"You need to heal . . . and I need to get this done before the first snow. Don't worry. This is the last time we'll be apart. That's *my* promise to you."

He didn't like it, but he settled against his pillows. I ran back and kissed him properly, just to give him some motivation, then I hurried out of the cottage, knowing I couldn't linger or my resolve would falter. I didn't look forward to this task, but my conscience would plague me if I didn't give these families the news about their loved ones. They deserved to know what happened, why their sons and daughters were never coming home.

After a little searching, I found Rex in the pub with Spence. Morgan had taken my request seriously, and before he'd left, he assigned my brother to look after Spence because he wasn't even half sane after Tully's death, and he still sought ways to do himself harm. I hoped his grief would ease in time.

"When Fade's better," I said to them both, "I need you to take him to Soldier's Pond. Wagon is fine. I'll come as soon as I finish one last thing."

"Carrying word." Spence's blue eyes were flat and sad.

I agreed that was so. "Will you?"

"We'll take care of him," Rex promised.

Thimble met me at the cottage door with my pack; she was every bit as resourceful as I remembered from our days down below. She must've figured I'd be heading out as soon as possible, better to get the grim journey out of the way. I hugged her tight, but I didn't say good-bye. Now that I knew they were here, I'd be back. I just had some traveling to do first.

To my surprise, Gavin met me at the docks. He still had the Company D banner, but he'd taken it off the pole, and he wore it around his shoulders like a cape. I didn't have the heart to tell him he looked ridiculous; he seemed so proud of the dirty, disreputable thing. Maybe Momma Oaks could sew him a proper cloak when we got to Soldier's Pond, possibly with our emblem, if it would make him happy.

"I'm going with you," he told me.

I didn't try to talk him out of it. "You know it'll be a long, sad trip."

He shrugged. "I don't have anywhere else to go."

The survivors of the company had split up while I tended Fade, leaving Rosemere in twos and threes, to return to their homes. Part of me wished I could've given them something worthy of their courage, but there were only words, and I had never been skilled with those. So it was best they went before I could ruin whatever good thoughts of me they might carry away.

A boatman took us across with an oddly deferential air, and when I stood to clamber out of the boat, he kissed the back of my hand. I pulled away, eyeing him in abject confusion.

"Why?" I asked.

"Because you're the Huntress," he said. "And you won the War of the River. You made the territories safe again."

I hadn't done so without a lot of blood and pain, many sacrifices from people smarter, braver, and better than me. But I was so flummoxed by his words that I let Gavin drag me out over the side, into the water, and all the way to shore. I cast a look back, but the man was already trimming his sail and turning the little boat back toward the Evergreen Isle.

When Gavin and I returned to the battlefield, it had become a graveyard. Row after row of wooden markers stood neatly commemorating where brave men and women died. I stood for a few seconds, my throat too tight to breathe. The brat's fingers stole into mine, and I squeezed them. It seemed so wrong that we were here when Stalker wasn't, when Tully and Thornton were probably buried beneath these fresh black mounds.

"Do you ever wonder why them and not you?" Gavin asked.

"All the time."

The trade routes were oddly clear. Breaking the horde had driven any straggling elders into hiding, where they would doubtless hunt small game until they died. If they grew bold again, the Uroch would send word. Now and then we saw our allies on the road, going about their business. They wore white armbands and lifted their clawed hands in greeting. I wondered if I would ever get used to that.

So blasted strange.

Gavin and I traveled without trouble; and in the fall, it was easy to find forage—berries and nuts, ripe fruit on wild trees and fat hares lazy from eating all summer long. In that fashion we traveled from town to town carrying our tidings. Gavin stayed with me as I found the families and told them, one by one. In Gaspard, there weren't many, but the weeping was fierce in Lorraine. We stayed there for two days, telling stories so that grieving relatives could comfort themselves with the knowledge that their loved ones had been heroes. And they were, of course, every last one of them. It didn't require daring deeds, only the courage to stand when everyone else was running.

In Lorraine, I also visited Stalker's grave. As promised, the stone marker had been carved with his name, Stalker the Wolf, and I touched the letters with reverent fingertips. Gavin watched me in silence for a few moments.

"Do you miss him?" he asked.

"Every day."

We won, my friend. I wish you were here to see it.

We went to Otterburn next, and it surprised me a little because I hadn't expected them to send anyone, ever. The counterman had been so definite about the tithe and their determination not to get involved in the war. But there were fifteen names on my list, men and women who decided they'd rather fight than cower.

"This is an ugly town," Gavin said, as we approached.

Though I agreed, it wasn't polite to say so where the residents could hear. I shushed him. People were already gathering; at first I didn't understand why, but then John Kelley called, "I wondered when you'd get here."

As he had before, the trader must've carried word about my mission. So the people were already braced and waiting. Without further delay, I read out the names, and two women fell to their knees crying. Others comforted them. I was tired of walking, tired of bearing bad tidings, but I still had Winterville before I could return to my family in Soldier's Pond. Rex, Fade, and Spence should be there by now.

I hoped so, anyway.

"Thank you," I said, striding through the dispersing crowd to meet the trader. "The only reason we won at the river is because you blackmailed the towns into sending help."

The trader grinned. "Not just me. Vince Howe and Marlon Bean got in on the action too. We all did some shooting that day. Haven't felt so alive in years."

"It was a day to remember all right," I admitted.

Not just in good ways. But I wouldn't spoil the moment with my dark memories.

"Where are you headed next?"

"Tomorrow, we're off to Winterville," I said. "Then Soldier's Pond."

"I'll buy you a round at the pub, if you like."

I shook my head. "There's somebody I need to find, here."

"Who? I might know him. Otterburn's a pretty small place."

I tried to picture the girl Szarok had put in my head, then I did my best to describe her. "I'm not sure of her name . . . and she'd be older now, maybe by as many as ten years."

"There aren't too many black-haired, blue-eyed girls living here. Let me ask around." Before I could say this was my responsibility, John Kelley took off.

And, honestly, I was weary enough that I didn't mind. I opened my pack and ate some nuts and berries we'd picked on the way to town. Sitting nearby, Gavin devoured his share; I'd noticed how he always stayed close enough to touch me, nothing obvious, just a bump of his foot or an awkward jab of elbow. At some point over the last few weeks, we'd become family.

A bit later, John Kelley came back with news. "There are two girls that could be who you're looking for. Should I send for them?"

"If you don't mind."

Confluence

One look, and I recognized the child from Szarok's memory, so I dismissed the other. She seemed nervous when I did so. She was a year younger than I was, with long black hair and eyes like the heart of a flower. Before I could stop her, she dropped to one knee, like I was a princess from one of Morrow's stories. Wide-eyed, I glanced at Gavin, who shrugged. He had spent too much time smelling me on the road to think I was special.

A number of Otterburn folk lingered to hear what I wanted from her, and I ignored them. When I pulled her to her feet, the girl was shaking. She kept her gaze turned down.

"What's your name?" I asked gently.

"Millie, ma'am."

I debated inwardly whether I should tell her in private, but then I decided such recognition would probably raise her status in town—and she deserved it. "Do you recall tending an injured creature in the woods when you were small?"

Her head jerked up. "Yes, ma'am."

"She's always dragging home some wounded thing and doctoring it," a man volunteered.

"But this wasn't a rabbit or a squirrel, was it, Millie?"

She paled. "No. Am I in trouble? I never brought it near the village."

"The exact opposite," I assured her. "I've actually come to thank you. Because what you did when you were a little girl saved our lives."

By the look on her face, she had no idea what I was talking about . . . and she suspected I was crazy. So I explained what Szarok had told me—omitting the part where he shared the memory directly—and by the time I finished, everyone in Otterburn was staring at her as if she were the biggest hero they'd ever seen.

"So he remembered me?" she asked in a tiny voice.

"He did. And he told his son how kind you were. It's what made the Uroch decide to ally with us instead of fighting alongside their kin. You first gave them hope that we could be persuaded to make peace."

"*I* did that?"

I smiled at her. "Never underestimate your importance, Millie. You're a hero, same as anybody who fought at the river . . . and maybe more. Because it takes more courage to heal the world's hurts than to inflict them."

They threw a party in Otterburn that night in Millie's honor— and in celebration of the permanent end to the tithes. Gavin and I crept away while she basked in the attention, and we got half a day down the road before I was too tired to continue, and we made camp by moonlight. In the morning, we walked on, and a few days later, we made Winterville, where I repeated the tidings with the same results that I'd received in all the towns.

Dr. Wilson hadn't lost anyone but he came out to see me before we left. "Is Tegan well?"

I laughed. "She is. Tending the wounded in Rosemere, last I heard."

The scientist nodded. "Good. You remind her she promised she'd study with me if she made it through your mad war."

"I will."

"Are we done here?" Gavin demanded.

He had been patient, but the days were cooling off, and I was weary of wandering. We caught a ride with a trader I didn't know on his way to Soldier's Pond—and though the mules were slow, I didn't complain. That night, I dreamed of Longshot; it was the shortest dream I ever had, but one I would cherish until the day I died. We stood in a field of gold, the sun shining down. He was hale and whole as he walked with me.

For a little while he said nothing, then: "I'm proud of you, girl."

Then he turned, melting into the light, until I could see only his face. He offered me one final two-fingered salute, and I woke smiling. Gavin was staring at me because I didn't usually awaken in such a cheerful mood. The mules were flatulent too, so there was precious little to be happy about, crammed in the back of a wagon amid crates of trade goods. Yet I was.

"We're almost there," he said.

I hadn't asked if he wanted to stay in Winterville. No doubt he didn't, as he'd lost both his parents, and he'd seemed truly eager to get away. At this point I didn't know what to do with him, but I'd figure it out. A few hours later, Soldier's Pond appeared in the distance. It took forever for the wagons to reach the fences. *They don't need them anymore,* I thought. The security measures were unhinged for the first time in my memory, and the guards rushed to greet us. I thought they were eager to check out the supplies, but instead, they pulled me out of the wagon and tossed me up on their shoulders. Other towns had welcomed me, but never like this.

As the soldiers carried me, the crowd beyond the gates chanted, "Huntress! Huntress!" until I couldn't hear anything but that. The wild nature of the greeting was unsettling, as if in their eagerness they might pull me apart, like dogs too hungry for the same bone. I tolerated the attention until we got some distance into town, then I shouted, "Put me down!"

"Give the heroine some room," the colonel ordered.

Colonel Park pushed through the mob toward me, gesturing so that everyone backed off. I appreciated that, even as I said, "I don't want a party. Tell me something of substance."

"I've received word from Appleton . . . your Szarok wants to draft permanent peace treaties . . . and trade agreements. As part of the accord, they're offering to share some new technology with us. They've apparently found some fascinating things in the ruins and they're working out how to use them."

I remembered the exploding sticks Szarok and I had used in signaling each other, and I nodded. "It would be a mistake to underestimate them . . . or to treat the Uroch with anything less than absolute courtesy."

They had done a brave and awful thing by killing their brethren. If my elders all went mad, I didn't know whether I could ally with the enemy to end the threat, no matter how much they deserved it. Just thinking about it turned my stomach.

"It's a new world, Deuce." The colonel smiled.

I leveled a hard look on her. "I can trust you with this, right?"

Colonel Park didn't take offense at the implication. "I'll offer fair terms and respect their customs. Nobody wants the hostilities to resume."

Satisfied, I figured it was time to leave the details to other people. Councilmen and mayors in towns all over the territories could sign documents and make promises. To my mind, I had done enough.

"I thought your hands were tied," I said then. "Your power limited."

She shrugged. "I ignored them. They blustered for a while, but the men demanded to march, especially when Vince Howe started yelling about how we'd never see a single wagon load of anything if we were such yellow cowards that we'd let you die."

"Sounds like quite a speech. Where's my family?" I rose on

tiptoe and peered through the milling crowd. These men had known me for a while, but they all seemed unduly impressed, like I was about to be amazing while starving, cranky, and covered in road dust. My back was sore, too, from the wagon.

"Here," Momma Oaks called.

I swear she pushed two men down in her haste to reach me. Her face bore heavier lines, but her eyes were warm and calm. When her arms wrapped around me, I breathed her in so deep. I clung and clung to her, promising myself that I'd never worry her so again.

"Did Rex get back safe?" I asked, stepping back.

"He sure did. Fade, too, and that poor boy, Spence." By her soft tone, I could tell she'd claimed him, too, so the mothering would never end. It might even be enough to save him.

Gavin peeped around my shoulder, catching my mother's attention. I grinned. "Then I have a surprise for you. I marched one son off to war, but I brought back two."

Both her brows shot up. "It's not nice to tease, Deuce."

"I'm not," I told her. "Gavin lost his mum and dad, and he needs a place to stay. Do you think Edmund could use another assistant in the shop?"

With sharp eyes, she catalogued how badly he needed a bath, all the rips in his clothing, then she put an arm about him. "I'm sure he could. And we have plenty of bunks."

Though I was eager to see them, I was glad the others hadn't come to the gate. I didn't want to greet Fade with so many witnesses and Edmund might cry, but he'd pretend he had dirt in his eyes. Momma Oaks shouldered people out of her way, and if they complained, she fixed them with her sternest look. It worked incredibly well, so that she cleared a path in no time.

First thing, I saw Fade waiting outside, well enough to stand. Forgetting my exhaustion, I ran to him and he caught me with an arm around my waist. In front of my family, he kissed the life out of me, as if it had been longer than a month. When we broke apart, Edmund was tapping his foot.

"Is there something you want to say to me, son?"

My cheeks went hot, and I started to protest. Luckily Momma Oaks intervened by introducing Gavin, then she pointed out how poor the boy's shoes were. Nothing ever motivated my father like the sight of a child in torn footwear, and he was off to his workshop like a shot. For a moment, I frowned because I hadn't gotten a hug from him or a pat on the shoulder, even.

Momma Oaks winked at me. "You have to expect that sort of thing. You're not an only child anymore."

I laughed and put away my mild annoyance because it was so good to be back with them. Rex gave me the tight squeeze I had been looking for and he spun me, planting a noisy kiss on top of my head. "It's so good to see you. I was starting to worry."

"It's not dangerous anymore," I said. "Well. Just the normal road hazards."

After that, I broke away from Fade, reluctantly, for a bath. Then Momma Oaks did my hair. For the first time in longer than I could recall, I put on a dress, not because someone was making me, but because I wanted to look pretty, as much as I could, anyway. Life in the field had pared me down, so I didn't look womanly or even strong but Fade lit up when he saw me.

I hope he never stops looking at me that way.

Whether I wanted one or not, they threw me a party. It was a wild night with piping, drums, and dancing. I sat out because Fade wasn't up to such acrobatics. The worst thing about this town was the lack of privacy. Late that evening, we crept away and couldn't find a quiet corner to save our souls. The empty houses had been filled with men who had come from other towns and traveled to Soldier's Pond with the survivors from Company D. All told, it was probably a good thing, as I hadn't spoken with Momma Oaks yet about certain private matters. So we came back to the party and nestled close, content just being together.

The days soon fell into a routine with Fade recovering, Gavin and Rex working with Edmund at the workshop, and Momma Oaks keeping busy as best she could. But she wasn't happy in Soldier's Pond; and it was time for me to offer a gift in return for those she'd given me.

So two weeks after I arrived, I sat down with her for breakfast. It was late morning—she'd let me sleep in—so there were few people around. The movements outside were so familiar, men running in formation and soldiers sparring. For some people, this probably felt like home, but to me, it was only a place that sheltered us for a while.

First, however . . .

"I was wondering if you'd tell me the best way to keep from making any brats?"

She startled me by providing the information in detail. By the time she finished, *I* was bright red, but considerably enlightened. Her eyes twinkled at my expression. This woman never stopped delighting me, so I kissed her cheek and thanked her.

"I don't want to stay here," I added quietly.

Her chin lifted in surprise, and I suspected she was braced for me to name some other crazy job that needed doing, which would end with me tired and hurt and her with more gray hair from sitting at home, worried. "Where are you going?"

There were never any complaints from her, no arguments or attempts to change my mind. I teased her a little, though. "A town called Rosemere."

"Tell me about it?"

So I did. With eloquence I seldom owned, I described the village in detail. Her face softened as she listened and a smile formed. Momma Oaks covered me in questions about the people, the customs, the boats, and the market. She seemed half in love with the place before I concluded my account, and she didn't even know what I had in mind.

"But I'm not the only one moving," I said at last. "You and Edmund should pack your things. Soldier's Pond is a worthy place, but it's not for us."

"Will they let us in? Is there enough space?"

She was still thinking like a refugee, like someone who had lived her whole life bound by Salvation's restrictions. I put my hand over hers. "Momma, there are no walls. Evergreen Isle is huge, and the village has lots of room for new houses. You'll love it. Trust me."

"I do," she said with teary eyes. "I'm sure it's everything you say."

"I don't plan to winter here. If we hurry, we can get there before the first snow. And we might be able to build before the ground freezes."

With those words it was like I lit a fire under her. "You'd be surprised how fast I can pack when I'm driven."

"Nothing good about you would surprise me at all," I whispered, but she was already out the door, ready to uproot their lives on my word.

I don't deserve to be this lucky.

Fade met me outside the bunkhouse. "I hear we're moving to Rosemere."

"Is that all right?"

"It's a little late to be asking my thoughts, isn't it?" In the morning light, I couldn't read his expression. Sometimes I worried that things were different between us, but I hoped it was because we slept in a room with my parents, not because he was mad that I'd left him to heal up alone while I did my duty to the families of the fallen.

"We were so happy there," I whispered.

Then he smiled, assuaging my anxiety. "I can't conceive of anything I'd like more. I loved everything about it."

"Tegan's still there with Morrow. Maybe she'll stay." That would please me mightily, as I'd have all my friends and loved ones close by.

"I hope so," Fade said.

It occurred to me then that he might be wondering, but feeling too shy to ask. So I whispered, "I'm not breeding, by the way."

Fade hunched his shoulders. "I think Edmund knows. He keeps staring at me."

"That only works if you have a guilty conscience, son." My father's comment made both of us jump. He stood on the path with his arms folded, tapping one foot. "I thought you said your intentions were honorable."

I might die of this, not in battle.

"They are," Fade said quietly.

"Then it's time to make good on those promises, if you mean to build a life together."

"What are you talking about?" I demanded.

But Edmund was already calling for Momma Oaks. "You need two witnesses."

I stared at Fade, wondering what was going on. My mother came out with a bolt of fabric in her hands, looking annoyed at the interruption. "What's all the bother?"

Edmund studied me with sweetness in his eyes. So whatever he was about, he didn't have bad intentions. "Fade, do you promise to be hers, always?"

"I do," he answered.

"And, Deuce, do you swear to be his, forever?"

"Yes," I said, annoyed. "He's already mine, and I'm already his."

Edmund muttered, "Thought so. That's why you needed to make it official."

"You have *no* sense," Momma Oaks chided him.

Fade and I traded bewildered looks and I asked, "What just happened?"

"You didn't tell them they were plighting their troth?" my mother demanded.

"They knew." Edmund showed no remorse.

"A wedding should have more ceremony. She should be wearing her best dress, and there should be food and guests, music, a cake—"

"Did you want any of that?" my father asked.

I shook my head. I'd only ever wanted Fade, and from what I could tell, this didn't change anything. I'd already promised him forever, just not in front of witnesses, which seemed to be the crucial part. So if Edmund wanted me to tell everyone in Soldier's Pond, I would.

Fade was mine, and I was never letting him go. As I'd told him once, and as I'd proven time and again, I'd fight for him.

And I'd never stop.

Adieu

Two days later, Soldier's Pond didn't want us to leave.

In the end, I talked Colonel Park into it by promising to send letters with the traders when they came to Rosemere. She clutched my hands, more personal than she'd ever been with me. "You'll advise me if I need it? You've dealt more with the Uroch than anyone. I'm worried about offending them."

"Treat them like people," I said. "You can't go wrong like that. But, yes, I'll help if you need me to."

I hoped there would be no pleas, no emergencies. The world should sort out its own business, so far as I was concerned. I saluted her and left HQ for the last time to join my family at the gate. The guards had loaded a wagon for us, full of fabrics Momma Oaks had begged or borrowed, Edmund's supplies, and the few personal effects the rest of us had accrued. Rex snapped the lines and the mules trotted forward. Spence was a reluctant companion on this journey, but we agreed he couldn't be left on his own. Fade sat in the back with Momma Oaks while Edmund perched up front beside his son. Gavin and I walked alongside because I had rested long enough, and I'd traveled by wagon often enough to be sure I didn't want to do it more than necessary.

As we drove away, the sentries shouted, "Huntress," like I wasn't tired of hearing it.

Rex cast a look over his shoulder. "Doesn't that get wearisome?"

"You have no idea," I muttered.

We took the journey in easy stages, and it was nice to journey with my family. Now and then we passed other travelers—and not just traders making supply runs as it had been in the days before the victory at the river. Some were human, some Uroch, and occasionally we spotted small groups of Gulgur, though they seemed shy and didn't speak.

The days were chilly but not freezing, but the nights dropped down cold, and we huddled together under the wagon for warmth and comfort. Gavin acted a bit nervous at first, like he suspected this was all a trick, and when he got comfortable with the idea of being part of a family, we'd take it all away. But by the time we arrived at the big river, he was cuddling up to Momma Oaks. I knew exactly how he felt because I had walked in his shoes, wary and distrustful, unable to believe anybody could care about me without asking for something in return.

By then, the trees flamed with color on the Evergreen Isle. The name was deceptive, as only a portion of them had perpetually green needles while the rest turned crimson and gold, framing the village barely visible from this side. Rex paused on a rise, the mules shifting nervously in their traces. Edmund's hand rested on his shoulder and Momma Oaks pushed to her feet to get a better look. She focused on row after row of grave markers in the field nearby. It hadn't been long enough for grass to grow and it was too late in the year besides, so the graves contrasted sharply with the brown grass.

"So many dead," she whispered. "It could've been any of you, all of you."

Edmund shifted in his seat and dug for a smile. This was why I loved him; his steadiness kept her from sorrow. "But it wasn't."

As they spoke, Gavin nudged me, offering the tattered banner. "This is yours."

But I had noticed how much he loved it. So I got out my knife and cut away the fabric Momma Oaks had used to sew my token in place. I reclaimed the card. "No, *this* is mine. The pennant's yours. You guarded it well."

Gavin ducked his head and curled up beside Momma Oaks. I could tell I'd pleased him.

"Let's go," Edmund said. "I'd like to see the place I'll be calling home."

The wagon trundled on, all the way to the water, where sailors worked the river. Rex whistled and I shouted until one of them saw us. He turned his craft, willing to help us cross. I cursed when he recognized me because his manner went from friendly to reverent.

"I can't take everyone," he apologized, looking stricken. "But I'll send more boats to carry the rest, plus all your belongings."

"You and Edmund go with him." I hugged Momma Oaks, and she looked so excited as my father helped her into the boat.

She held on tight as the man adjusted the sail so the wind would send him back to the isle. Relatively speaking, it didn't take long for more boatmen to arrive. It was lucky we had relatively little—and none of it heavy—but Edmund and Momma Oaks were skilled crafters, so we'd be comfortable soon enough.

Rosemere hasn't changed, I thought, as Rex helped me ashore. My parents stood nearby, marveling at the beauty of the place. As soon as he got word, the governor came down to welcome us, shaking my hand firmly and expressing pleasure that I'd brought my parents. They seemed awed by the attention, and though I was past the point of savoring it, their enjoyment was reason enough for me not to run off with Fade or go looking for Stone and Thimble.

"How's Morrow?" I asked when he paused in his polite remarks.

"He's well, though it was a near thing. I have Doctor Tegan to thank for his life."

"She's amazing," I agreed. "I'm sorry he got hurt. You probably blame me for getting him into trouble, and I'm sorry about that too."

To my surprise, the elder Morrow laughed. "Not at all. Nobody has ever been able to prevent James from doing exactly as he pleases, not even me. The only thing I can do is be here when he comes home."

Momma Oaks aimed a pointed look in my direction. "It seems we have something in common, sir."

The governor smiled. "So I notice. You've an impressive number of bags and boxes for a visit. Have you come to stay?"

"If you'll have us," Edmund said.

Before I could respond, he was telling Mr. Morrow about his skill as a cobbler and how fine a seamstress Momma Oaks was. I could've hugged the governor when he said, "We can definitely use people of such skill."

If there was one way to make my parents feel at home, it was by implying they were needed. I listened to them idly, leaning against Fade for warmth, until the governor decided nothing would do but for us to stay as his guests. I declined, preferring to occupy Stone and Thimble's loft, but Momma Oaks, Edmund, Rex, and Gavin accompanied Mr. Morrow. His family lived in the largest house on the island, so there would be plenty of space.

Fade and I went along to our friends' cottage. I rapped on the door, hoping they'd be glad to see me. Thimble's face lit with pleasure when she answered and she swept me into a tight hug; I wasn't the only one who had put aside lessons learned down below in favor of better and brighter ones.

"Dare I hope you've come to stay?" she asked.

"We have. Not with you," I added. "At least not forever. But I'd appreciate it if we could board here while we figure out something more permanent."

Thimble smiled as she stepped back to let us in. "Of course you're welcome."

Stone echoed her warm acceptance, and he seemed genuinely glad to see us. We'd all changed so much, but not to the point that we were strangers to one another. That night over dinner, we talked until our throats were hoarse, filling in all the gaps and smoothing the rough spots. Robin was adorable, and while Thimble cleaned up from supper, I held him, and Fade caught me smelling the brat's hair. I ducked my head, conscious of how absurd I likely looked, but his eyes were hot when they lingered.

Later, in the loft, Fade whispered, "I've been dying for some time alone with you."

He'd spoken those words before, more than once, but this time, I knew what he meant. I rolled over and kissed him, then we practiced some more, quietly, and this time, we got it exactly right. Afterward, I traced the scar on his side. Fade shivered at my touch, pressing closer.

"I came so close to losing you," I murmured.

"You never will."

I kissed him once and again, counting back all the times he'd kissed me, until I lost track of the numbers. That got him worked up again, so it was a while before we settled. But a quiet doubt trickled into my mind.

"What was that?" Fade had always been good at reading me.

"Is it all right? When I touch you."

"It's the best thing in the world." But that wasn't what I was asking—and he knew it. So he added, "I don't know if I'll ever be completely fine. And sometimes I have bad dreams. But when you're near, everything feels better."

"Then I'll stay close," I promised.

Unexpectedly he stirred, digging around in his pack. "I have something for you."

I sat up, intrigued. "What is it?"

In reply, he produced a shiny silver wire, festooned with sparkling stones, and I lost my breath. "What . . . when?"

Somehow he interpreted my incoherence correctly. "I bought it after you left. I remembered how much you admired it. I probably should've given it to you when Edmund married us in Soldier's Pond. But I was waiting for the right moment."

As he fastened it around my wrist, I whispered, "It's perfect." And silently vowed never to take the bracelet off.

In the morning, we began our life together.

After breakfast, we strolled through the village hand in hand; I had no particular destination in mind, but when Fade led me past the docks, I realized he did. He didn't go far, past the last cottages, up a gentle knoll, where the view was incredible. From this vantage, I saw the market, the boats on the river, and the governor's house on the other side of Rosemere.

"This is where I want to build," he said. "If you're willing."

Since I'd decided where we would live without asking him, it seemed fitting for him to choose the site where we'd raise our home and—if life was kind—grow old together, not as people did down below, but like Edmund and Momma Oaks. My heart swelled with the possibility; we could have years and years here in this beautiful place. It was so much more than I ever could've dreamed.

"It's beautiful. Do we need permission?"

"I already asked."

I canted my head in surprise. "When?"

"Before you got up this morning. For some reason, you were extra tired." Fade wore a wicked grin, such pure temptation that I considered pushing him down into the bracken to show him what tired felt like.

But we had work to do first.

As I saw it, there was one benefit to being the Huntress. The way people watched me when we walked back through the village annoyed me, but also meant that volunteers came out in droves to help build our cottage, once we assembled the materials. With half of Rosemere pitching in, the walls went up fast, then the builders filled in the stones and laid the floors. Stone and Thimble helped, as they'd crafted their cottage, and Thimble had worked out all manner of cunning tricks to make a home snug and cozy.

The only dark cloud came from Tegan. One day, while I was working alongside Fade, she made her way out to the site; she stood watching us with a thoughtful expression. I set down my stone and hurried over to her. In my haste to get our house finished, I hadn't seen her as much as I'd have liked. I had reckoned there would be plenty of time to visit this winter. But the melancholy in her expression told me that probably wasn't so.

"You can't go," I said quietly. "I can't say good-bye to you, Tegan. Don't ask that of me."

My heart broke a little when I recalled Stalker whispering those words to me, just before I ran into the horde. I thought of him often, amid my happiness, and his death was one of my fiercest regrets. I saw that shadow in Tegan's face too.

"Deuce," she whispered. "It's time for me to keep my promise."

I knew the one she meant—to Dr. Wilson—and I was supposed to remind her of it, but selfishly I'd hoped she would forget. She didn't belong in Winterville . . . or maybe she did, and I just wished she didn't because I needed her nearby.

"He knows so much, and I want to learn it all. I feel like I have to."

I understood that impetus, too, but I wished I could convince her that she didn't have to be anything in particular to be worth saving. Choking up, I reached for her, and she hugged me too tight for long moments. Somehow I managed not to weep into her shoulder. We whispered to each other that it wasn't forever—we would visit and send letters with the traders as they came and went—but we both knew we had come to the parting of the ways. From this point on, there would be no more adventures, no more wayfaring. She would go to Winterville and become a learned soul while I stayed here on the isle.

"Let me go," she commanded.

And I did.

I turned around so I didn't have to watch her leave, then I sank to the ground and cried. Sometimes it felt as if all happiness came at a price. You could never, ever, have perfection. Life gave you beauty so you could bear the pain. At length, I dried my tears because Fade wore his fierce and brooding look, and I never knew how he would react. Tegan wouldn't thank me if my man charged after her and brought her back because her path was making me sad.

Then I paused my work on the cottage to go to the governor's manor. One person in Rosemere would share my sorrow in equal measure.

Morrow opened the door when I knocked as if he had been expecting me. His face was thin and pale, newly marked with a red scar. The rest of him seemed sound enough, though he still hadn't regained his full strength. I gave him my arm as he escorted me to a large room with a crackling fire. When I was working I didn't notice the nip in the air as much as when I stopped.

"She's gone," I said softly.

He lowered his head, the hair falling into his clever face. "I know."

"How long before you go after her?"

"I'll give her the winter, long enough to miss me."

"And if that doesn't work?" I guessed he hadn't told her how he felt about her; I could've explained why she was so leery of men. But as promised, I had kept Tegan's secret, and nobody knew what she'd suffered in the ruins. With Stalker dead, the truth would die with me.

"Then I'll come and go until she asks me to stay." His smile was a sweet and somber thing. "I'm working on your story, you know. It's keeping me busy during my convalescence. I hope to have a draft ready for you to read by spring."

I smiled at that. "Fade can read it to me. It's not my strong suit."

For a few seconds, I imagined curling up with my man before a fire, listening to Morrow's words. I couldn't imagine anything better. We talked a little longer, enough for me to be sure he'd be all right in Tegan's absence, but the storyteller was stronger than he looked and he had one precious gift that rendered him invincible—eternal hope. Either that, or he was mad, which might explain why he'd followed me.

"I plan to call it the Razorland saga," he told me.

"Why?"

"Because of something you said when you were telling me about your journey north . . . about how the world's all razors that cut you no matter what you do."

"It isn't anymore," I said softly.

"Thanks to us." Morrow flashed his charming smile, but I saw the bittersweet tinge to his gaze. He would miss Tegan too.

"One thing I've always wondered . . . why do you greet the colonel by kissing her on both cheeks? It seems like that would annoy Morgan."

"I'm Rosemere's diplomatic envoy," he replied. "My father knew he had to find work to satisfy my need to wander. That's the customary kiss of peace."

"Ah." I should have known he was more important than he

let on, just a storyteller indeed. "Then why didn't you identify yourself when you were traveling with me?"

His look turned sheepish. "Because I didn't have approval for the mission. My father wouldn't have gotten involved. So I couldn't claim to represent Rosemere when we were building Company D. That, I did as James Morrow."

I stood, kissed his cheek, and said, "I'll always be grateful."

Then I went back to work, along with half the village. The construction seemed to focus Spence, giving him something else to think about, and Rex kept him company. Spence liked him best because they shared a common loss. They didn't talk much, but a certain bond was forming between them. They were also working on a house for Edmund and Momma Oaks, a fact that delighted me. I'd kept the promise to myself at last—and given them a new home. Gavin cavorted more than he worked, proud as a young peacock in his new cloak, which bore the insignia from Company D.

With constant labor, it took under a month to complete the cottage, just before the first snowfall. Awed and delighted, I stood inside with Fade, unable to believe we had a place of our own. People soon arrived with housewarming gifts, a tradition on the isle. Stone delivered furniture that Thimble had built while Momma Oaks brought cushions and curtains for the windows. She fussed and helped me hang them while other village women offered dishes and pots for cooking, linens, blankets, and boxes I didn't open straightaway.

It was late in the day when they all departed—and along with the small touches, we had a table, chairs, and a bed with a newly stuffed mattress. The cottage was designed much like Stone and Thimble's; for a moment, I let my mind wander, imagining how the years would pass. While I pondered, Fade built a fire in the hearth, the first in our own home. Wonder stole my breath and called tears to my eyes. I refused to let them fall.

I opened our first gift. Someone had given us a picture frame and I knew what to put in it. "Do you still have your token from down below?"

"Of course," he said. "It's stupid, but I can't make myself discard the thing."

"I'm glad." I placed his paper and my card inside the frame, and then I went in search of hammer and nail.

Our talismans adorned our new home, and that seemed fitting, part of the old life to carry into the new one. Next I rummaged in my pack and laid out my two greatest treasures: Longshot's maps and the book Fade and I had found in the ruins. He came to see what I had, then he touched the leather with reverent hands, as if the story meant as much to him.

"I can't believe you still have it. And it's still intact, too."

"I kept it wrapped in oilcloth. Would you read me the end?"

Fade pitched his voice low—and the story had more resonance now.

They were married that very day. And the next day they went together to the king and told him the whole story. But whom should they find at the court but the father and mother of Photogen, both in high favor with the king and queen. Aurora nearly died with joy, and told them all how Watho had lied and made her believe her child was dead.

No one knew anything of the father or mother of Nycteris; but when Aurora saw in the lovely girl her own azure eyes shining through night and its clouds, it made her think strange things, and wonder how even the wicked themselves may be a link to join together the good. Through Watho, the mothers, who had never seen each other, had changed eyes in their children.

The king gave them the castle and lands of Watho,

and there they lived and taught each other for many years that were not long. But hardly had one of them passed, before Nycteris had come to love the day best, because it was the clothing and crown of Photogen, and she saw that the day was greater than the night, and the sun more lordly than the moon; and Photogen had come to love the night best, because it was the mother and home of Nycteris.

"But who knows," Nycteris would say to Photogen, "that when we go out, we shall not go into a day as much greater than your day as your day is greater than my night?"

When he finished, I kissed him and whispered, "I love you, Fade," because that was what I'd failed to say when I lay feverish in the wagon. Wearing a smile so broad it threatened to crack his cheeks, he scooped me up and carried me to a chair, a capacious seat with broad arms and fat cushions, cozy enough for two. Idly I wondered if Thimble had designed it for sparking. Today, my muscles ached from work more pleasant than constant fighting.

Silk was wrong, I thought. *I have a Builder's heart.*

"I'm glad the story ends that way. So that even the king couldn't part them. Like us."

"What are kings to us?" Fade asked with a cocky grin. "We changed the world."

Incredibly, it was true. I rose to set the book on the mantelshelf above the hearth. Then I added Longshot's folio. "There. That's perfect."

"What will you do with those maps?" Fade asked, following me with his gaze.

"Give them to our brats," I answered.

It was the best legacy I could envision, like giving them the world.

"I don't want to wait to name them."

By Fade's expression, he felt strongly about that.

"Me either. We'll follow topside tradition like Stone and Thimble."

"Did you see how much food they put in our cupboards?" he asked lazily, changing the subject.

I was glad; it was a little soon to be talking about expanding our family. Cheeks hot, I shook my head. I'd been busy with Momma Oaks, making the place cozy. "A lot?"

Fade watched me with silent admiration. In a moment or two, it would ripen into desire, and we had every right to wander into the back room. Nobody would interrupt or summon us to other business. That was . . . astonishing.

"Enough for the whole winter, I expect."

"We've earned a few months of leisure," I told him.

"What will you do, come spring?" He reached for me then.

I sank onto his lap. Fade nuzzled my neck, and I put my hand to his jaw. "Be with you."

And I kept my promise. Always.

Epilogue

On Evergreen Isle lies the town of Rosemere, and within the bounds of that village, there's a white stone cottage where an elderly couple lives. Pink roses twine around a whitewashed lattice out front, and ivy climbs the garden walls in back. It's a peaceful place, all sunlight and dappled green. There's a cherry tree in the yard, and when he's asked, "Why cherries?" the man who planted it years ago smiles and says, "Because she loves them."

Inside the cottage, a frame on the wall holds an old scrap of paper and a playing card, the deuce of spades. Above the hearth, there's a shelf, where two books sit between wooden statues. One is very old, produced by the world before, and its spine is imprinted with the title *The Day Boy and the Night Girl*. The other is written on parchment in a fine hand, illustrated in colorful inks, and hand bound in leather. The first page reads, *The Razorland Saga* by James Morrow. Though they have a library full of books to choose from, village children often ask for this story, for they're enchanted by Tegan of the Staff, Stalker the Wolf, Deuce the Huntress, and He Whose Colors Will Not Fade. They're comforted by these familiar legends and the account of how the world came to hold its current shape.

When he's not reading to children who have stolen away from their chores, the man spends his days making armor for young people determined to seek their fortunes and see the world. Until recently, his wife taught those adventurers how to fight, preparing them for the journey. But now that his hair has gone white and hers silver, she prefers to tend her garden. They have children, this pair—long since grown and gone away, exploring through a legacy of maps. Sometimes they, too, visit with stories; they ask the boatman to bring them home, and their parents are always pleased, welcoming them with the same gladness they learned long ago from people who loved them too much to make them stay when the world was calling.

Tales abound regarding the role these two played in the War of the River, before the Gulgur rose from down below, before the Uroch signed the peace treaties, but as time wears on, their neighbors can hardly credit that this sweet couple is as dangerous as the legends claim. Therefore, folks suspect their friend, Morrow the Storyteller, must have exaggerated the accounts. Sometimes, a cloaked figure is spotted slipping in and out of the house, but nobody can say who it might be. This aged pair enjoys their small intrigues even yet.

Most locals would dismiss the folklore entirely, except that once a year—on the Day of Peace—the pilgrimages commence. People travel from as far away as Gaspard, from Winterville, Otterburn, Lorraine, and Soldier's Pond, all over the free territories—and they bring gifts. For three days and nights, they camp outside the cottage in Rosemere, hoping to meet the Huntress and He Whose Colors Will Not Fade. Once a year, these two tell the tale in their own words, not Morrow's, to those who care to listen.

Because these two believed their actions mattered, because the Huntress chose peace, forgave her enemy, and laid down her knives, the territories changed forever. That is the lesson of ultimate courage, taught by Tegan of the Staff, who devotes her life to learning in honor of a sacrifice made so very long ago. This is the story written in the bones, and that homage will continue as long as the world turns, until it loses its ragged edge, and new heroes arise.

But those are other stories.

Author's Note

This book required extensive research on what a ground war would be like, set in conditions similar to the American Civil War. I read endless articles on provender, weapons, field medicine, survival rates, and privations unrelated to actual combat. For Tegan's role, I learned about herbs, primitive remedies, and a vast number of ailments. I now know what a chilblain is and that it's literally possible to walk your boots to leather tatters. Some of the data didn't make it into the story because it didn't fit Deuce's point of view, but it was fascinating.

For more information, try these sites: www.civilwarhome .com/strategyandtactics.htm and www.historynet.com/civil-war -soldier. The following books are excellent too: *Battle Cry of Freedom: The Civil War Era* by James McPherson, *American Heritage Picture History of the Civil War* by Bruce Catton, and for military buffs, I recommend *The Twentieth Maine: A Classic Story of Joshua Chamberlain and His Volunteer Regiment* by John J. Pullen. War isn't glorious, however, and I tried to convey that in *Horde*. There's a reason Deuce is ready for peace.

Town names in the territories are taken from actual settlements in present-day Maine and Canada, but their locations have been shifted to suit certain catastrophic events. I chose these familiar names to lend the land a certain verisimilitude, which roots readers in reality as I created a new world for them to explore. For those who are curious, the action takes place between present-day Maine, New Brunswick, and Quebec, though the topography has definitely changed over the centuries. If you use Google Maps, type in "Cabano, Témiscouata-sur-le-Lac, QC, Canada" to get an idea where they started out in Salvation. All the towns are arrayed from there. Marching west as they did, you'd reach Soldier's Pond, whereas Gaspard lies to the east.

I promised you'd have all the answers about the Freaks by the end of the saga, and I think I covered everything, but if you still have questions, feel free to e-mail me.

This is how the world ends . . . and begins again. Thanks for sticking with me, and I hope you enjoyed the ride.

Acknowledgments

Here's where I mention all the people who have helped along the way, starting with Laura Bradford, who believed I could pull this off. She's never once told me I'm crazy (though I clearly am), and for that, I'm sincerely appreciative. Thanks for everything.

Next, there are the wonderful folks at Feiwel & Friends: Liz Szabla, Jean Feiwel, Anna Roberto, Ksenia Winnicki, Rich Deas, Kate Lied, sales, marketing, PR, and the rest of the stupendous staff. Finishing the trilogy has been pure joy. It's rare that I can say I look forward to copyedits, but I adore working with Anne Heausler, whose efforts are peerless. All told, this team creates the most beautiful books and I'm so proud to partner with them.

Now I send a thank you to my early readers: Karen Alderman, Sarah Fine, Majda Čolak, Robin LaFevers, Rae Carson, and Veronica Rossi. That's a seriously star-studded beta group, and if there's anything wrong with *Horde*, blame me, not them. Their advice was awesome.

Thanks to the Loop That Shall Not Be Named, though I may not look directly at you, lest I go blind from your glory. You're my dearest friends, and I love you more than pancakes and racing frogs. Thanks for your support while I went quietly insane and tried not to gibber on the Internet.

Much gratitude to my phenomenal proofreader, Fedora Chen. She always makes my work shinier.

Thanks to my fabulous family, who put up with all kinds of crap. It can't be easy to live with a workaholic who forgets what day it is, but you fill my real world with sparkly unicorns, rainbows, and puppies. Mostly puppies.

Finally, thanks to my readers; you've taken my books to your hearts and for that, I will always keep you in mine. Don't forget to write.

HORDE

BONUS MATERIALS...

GO FISH

QUESTIONS FOR THE AUTHOR

ANN AGUIRRE

© Lifetouch

What did you want to be when you grew up?
A writer.

When did you realize you wanted to be a writer?
I've wanted to be a writer since I was eight years old, and I won a chance to hear Shel Silverstein read from *Where the Sidewalk Ends* by virtue of my self-illustrated seminal work, *The Mystery of the Golden Doubloon*. It was an epic tale of two best friends who went to Florida on vacation together and uncovered a ring of illegal treasure hunters. They also met two cute boys. I suspect the value of this work is now immeasurable.

What's your most embarrassing childhood memory?
There are, honestly, too many to list. I was awkward and bookish, a bona fide geek, which led to many such moments.

What's your favorite childhood memory?
Going to Old Chicago, which was an indoor amusement park, with my cousin, Danny.

As a young person, who did you look up to most?
My cousin, Danny.

What was your favorite thing about school?
All the books.

What was your least favorite thing about school?
Math.

What were your hobbies as a kid? What are your hobbies now?
Then? Reading, writing stories. Now? Music, movies, video games, yoga, taking walks with my family.

What was your first job, and what was your "worst" job?
My first job was at a movie theater. I worked the concession stand and came home smelling well-buttered. My worst job? I used to be a clown. I'm sorry. If it helps any, I have moderate coulrophobia myself, which means I was traumatized every time I looked in the mirror. If you can suggest anything less cool than a college student driving a bright orange Plymouth Horizon to a gas station grand opening in full clown regalia, including red nose and frizzy yellow wig, I'd love to hear it. Worst college job ever, and I say that having worked in a nursing home, changing bedpans. That was better than being a clown. Seriously.

What book is on your nightstand now?
None. If I'm reading a book at night, I carry it around with me during the day until I finish it.

How did you celebrate publishing your first book?

When I got my first author copies, I cried hysterically. On the actual publication date, I went out with my family for a nice dinner, had some wine, and kept pinching myself surreptitiously.

Where do you write your books?

On my MacBook. Seriously, though, it depends on the scene. Some scenes must be written at night; those I work on in bed. Other scenes need noise and furor, so those I write on the love seat downstairs in the middle of the household action. I never write at a desk; I pretty much only use my desk for printing these days.

What sparked your imagination for the Razorland Trilogy?

Generally, there isn't one single event that germinates an idea. My inspirations come from a multiplicity of sources; they're stew, not pot roast. I had wanted to write a YA novel, so I gradually built the world in my head until it was wholly accessible and then I got the story down on paper.

What challenges do you face in the writing process, and how do you overcome them?

It can be hard, sticking to a schedule day after day. Some days, you wake up feeling lazy and uninspired. On those occasions, it's crucial for me to press on because if I get in the habit of not working, my books won't get written.

Which of your characters is most like you?

None of them are really like me. They have adventures. Scary, terrible things happen to them. In general, I stay home to avoid that sort of thing.

What makes you laugh out loud?

Red Dwarf and Monty Python spring immediately to mind, but I also love music by Jonathan Coulton for quick laughs (especially "re: Your Brains" and "Skullcrusher Mountain"). I'm also a sucker for goofy Internet memes, like the llama song and badger, badger, mushroom, mushroom, OMG It's a snake! I may well break down and buy some honey badger swag.

What do you do on a rainy day?

I *love* the rain. There's nothing more soothing. I curl up with a book and a cup of hot tea.

What's your idea of fun?

A free day where I can do whatever I want, whether that's make cookies, read a book, or play video games.

What's your favorite song?

This is a tough call. Music is a huge influence on my work and most books have sound tracks, but I don't have a favorite. It goes according to my mood.

Who is your favorite fictional character?

Too many to list.

What was your favorite book when you were a kid? Do you have a favorite book now?

As a kid, I was totally in love with Madeleine L'Engle's work. *A Wrinkle in Time* was the first one I read, and it's still beloved to this day. These days, I'm an eclectic reader. Like music, I read according to my mood. Sometimes, I want shameless emotional gratification. Other times, I want explosions.

What's your favorite TV show or movie?
Right now, my favorite TV show is *How I Met Your Mother*. The writing, acting, and characterization are consistently top-notch. I haven't felt this involved with a group of people since *Friends*.

If you were stranded on a desert island, who would you want for company?
My family.

If you could travel anywhere in the world, where would you go and what would you do?
I'd love to spend a month traveling around Australia and New Zealand. I'd see major cultural attractions, do a helicopter tour, some hiking (but nothing too grueling).

If you could travel in time, where would you go and what would you do?
I'd head to the future to see how it looks in a thousand years. This is probably due to a long obsession with Matt Groening and *Futurama*.

What's the best advice you have ever received about writing?
"If you can quit, do. There are easier ways to make a living. But if you can't, if the stories have to be told and the characters in your head won't shut up, then never give up."

What advice do you wish someone had given you when you were younger?
Nobody owes you anything. Make your own dreams come true.

Do you ever get writer's block? What do you do to get back on track?
Generally, no. Some days, the words are harder than others and I don't feel like they're good enough, but I press on.

What do you want readers to remember about your books?
They're meant to be entertaining.

What would you do if you ever stopped writing?
Die.

What should people know about you?
I'm a proud geek.

What do you like best about yourself?
That I never give up.

Do you have any strange or funny habits? Did you when you were a kid?
Oh, I could fill pages on them. I'm biased against odd numbers. I don't like talking about book ideas before I write them. Crowds freak me out. Clowns make me uneasy. I hate being poked (I don't actually know anyone who enjoys that), and I could go on. . . .

What do you consider to be your greatest accomplishment?
Raising my children to be responsible, self-sufficient young adults.

SQUARE FISH

What do you wish you could do better?
Math. Mostly because my kids sometimes ask for help and I refer them to their dad. Fortunately, he's good at it.

What would your readers be most surprised to learn about you?
That I really believe frogs are lucky. Which is why everyone should own a pair of underpants with frogs on them.

RESTORATION

by

Ann Aguirre

My vision was veiled in gray, and I had been dying inside for hours.

Grimly, I stared at the ceiling and listened to the silent house surrounding me. The wind nudged at the eaves, whistled in the cracks, until I could pretend I wasn't alone. I lit no lamps and I didn't kindle a fire in the hearth. Darkness suited me better.

Forget me. Stop staring at me with those begging eyes. I can't be what you need, now. I had said that to Deuce on her naming day. There was only silence between us, and then . . . she brought me a gift.

Earlier, I had been working in Edmund's shop when I heard her come in. She murmured to her father; I didn't hear what she said.

But his voice carried. "Fade's in the back, cutting patterns."

"Do you mind . . . ?"

"Go on. He's welcome to take a break. Hard worker, that one . . . doesn't talk much, though."

That's because my words are gone. I lost them in the pens.

I closed my eyes for a few seconds, bracing to see her. From the darkness in Deuce's eyes when she regarded me, she thought it was easy for me to walk away, but it was like a dance across a field strewn with razors, and I bled with every step I took. Never in my life had I been so far from deserving what I most desperately wanted. She strode into the back room, a tight space littered with tools and scraps of leather, with a fierce, determined look.

Joy, there was *always* joy for an instant whenever I saw her, but awareness chased it away. *She deserves someone better, stronger.* My face froze. I set down the awl I had been using to punch holes in the leather and tilted my head.

"What are you doing here?" I asked.

I didn't expect it would take her long to give up—and to figure out what I already knew—that she could do better. *I'm not whole. I'm livestock.* And even if I lived to be an old man, I could never, ever forget how it felt to watch the Freaks turn Frank into haunches of meat, tied up for roasting. Parts of him, they devoured raw, blood smearing their monstrous fangs, and then they dragged me on. Taking a breath, another, I kept from shaking so she could see, clenching my hands on the underside of the workbench until my knuckles whitened.

"I see that you're unhappy . . . you feel trapped. But I can help."

"What do you mean?"

She explained. "Longshot left me his house. I wouldn't like living alone, and I don't mind Edmund or Momma Oaks. So you can stay and take care of the place. It'll give you more peace . . . more privacy. Nobody will bother you there."

There were no words sufficient to express my gratitude, but I tried. "I . . . really appreciate this."

"Do you know where it is?"

I nodded. "Longshot had me over once."

She put the key on the counter, and I picked it up. The metal was cool and heavy in my palm. *That's her legacy, not yours. But you'll take it, so you have a place to hide. Coward.*

You should've heard them. You should've fought harder.

"That's all, then," she said.

Deuce hesitated, and I could tell she wanted me to ask her to stay. If I could wind my watch backward and be the person I was before, I'd do it, but I couldn't, and it seemed kinder to let this end. In some bleak corner of my heart, I remembered my father and how he had been after my mother died.

That's what happens when the sun goes dark.

Before, he was full of stories and laughter. We moved around a lot, running, hiding, but there was always brightness. My father had a slim bag of books that he carried no matter where we sheltered, and each night, he read to me from one of them. During the sunny season, he taught me to swim in the river with my mother looking on. There were dangers, but we were cautious, and my father had friends around the city. I liked visiting Pearl and I loved listening to tales wherein people didn't scavenge to survive, learning about better ways to live.

We'll go when you're older, he'd say. *You must be strong enough to keep up.*

Only we never left. Instead, my mother got sick, and she went so fast. I watched her get pale and thin; she couldn't keep her food down. After that, my father was a shadow. He tried, but his smile was a dead and frozen thing. It didn't even surprise me one frosty morning when I crawled out of my blankets to find him cold and still. That same despair rolled through me, echoes of how I felt sobbing and pounding my father's chest.

Her eyes were dark as thunderclouds as she stared at me. I held her look for as long as I could bear and then I dropped my eyes to the leather on the table before me. I wanted to reach for her, but my hands were filled with lead.

"Deuce . . . thank you."

"Welcome," she muttered.

And then she left.

I worked a little longer, but Edmund heard stirrings in town that made him shoo me out of the shop and hurry home. Unmoored, I strolled through Salvation, head down. Close to the green, I heard Caroline Bigwater ranting, but that was so common that I didn't stop to listen. Nobody spoke to me as I let myself into Longshot's cottage, the sanctuary Deuce had given me. There was nothing in the house to eat, just dust and cobwebs, but that suited me fine.

The shadows were lengthening when I settled in the chair before the dead fireplace, and I was still sitting there when the knock sounded, though I had shifted my gaze from the ceiling to the empty chair across from me. With a faint sigh, I got up to answer it, ready to wish my unwelcome guest to the devil. The caustic words died in my throat when I found Edmund standing there with a basket covered by one of Momma Oaks's embroidered napkins.

"Can I come in?" It was still light enough for me to read his expression, and he appeared to have something weighty on his mind.

"Of course, sir." I stepped back and let Edmund in.

Things had been cool and uncomfortable at the shop since Deuce's naming day. He loved his daughter, and he blamed me, rightfully, for hurting her. But sometimes there was no cure but a clean break; in my case, I'd only bring her down with me. I considered what she'd risked to pull me out of the horde, and I couldn't take the chance she'd repeat the foolishness.

"My wife sent dinner."

"Please thank her for me," I said, unfolding the cloth.

Inside the basket, I found a dish of hearty stew, a round of bread, butter, and a wedge of apple spice cake. It didn't seem right to eat while Edmund sat watching, so I wrapped the meal back up and said, "Care to sit?"

"For a spell," he answered.

Joining him before the ashen hearth, I waited for him to speak. He didn't fidget, only fixed me with a steady look that made my stomach churn. Shame made me drop my eyes, and I braced for him to tell me I wasn't welcome in his shop—that he had no desire to teach me about leatherworking any longer. I was ready for that.

So what he actually said landed like a kick in the teeth. "Deuce is leaving tonight. Elder Bigwater made it sound like a rescue mission, one she has a chance of succeeding at, but I'm afraid he's sending my girl out to die."

The basket slipped from my hands, hit the floor with a thunk, and desperation cracked my voice. "You can't let her go."

He wore a wry, weary smile. "Did you ever try to stop that girl when she's running? I'd have more luck roping the wind."

"I can't talk her out of it," I said quietly. "We're not on the best terms, as I guess you figured out."

"I've come to ask you, man to man, to go with her. Whatever maggot you've got in your head, I know you care about her. I can't fight, so I'm begging you, Fade. Don't let her go out there alone."

My eyes stung, but I'd rather die than expose myself as weak and broken before Deuce's father. Somehow, I swallowed it all down and managed to say, "I can't. I'm not man enough."

"You think a man doesn't fall down, son? A real man falls down nine times and gets up ten. You think real men don't get scared? We do, all the time, especially when the people we love can be taken away from us. The key to manhood is *being there* every morning when she wakes up, every night before she goes to bed. That's what a man does. It has nothing to do with how good you are with some shiny knives. And if you let her do this thing alone, then by God—"

"I'll go," I said, staggered by the intensity in his voice, in the way he was leaning forward in his chair, like he might very well choke me if I didn't agree.

"Glad you saw reason," he said, pushing to his feet.

Edmund didn't offer his hand to shake, which told me he'd noticed the way I shied away in the shop. Not a reflex I wanted or controlled—to my own eyes, I was like a whipped dog that shivered any time people got too close. But the older man did dip his head in silent thanks as he headed out. At the door, he paused. "Eat some of that supper. You'll need the strength for the road."

I took him at his word and devoured the contents of the basket as quick as I could, then I set it on the shelf in Longshot's kitchen. It was easy to picture him here, so happy with his wife. Some loves could never be replaced, and men spent their lives chasing that light into the shadows, until the long walk opened up, one last journey before the final homecoming.

Deuce is that love for me.

This time, when someone rapped on the door, I was expecting it, but I took my time about answering, tremors shaking over me. Each time, seeing her ripped my heart out like the pain was brand-new, like I'd just bleed out on the floor. But the darkness leveled me out, kept from showing her how wrecked I was.

The pale oval of her face gleamed in the moonlight. She stepped back half a pace when she saw me, and my fingers curled. *It's starting already. Things can never be the same. You'll always be the one she found trussed up like an animal.*

In reaction, sharp words snapped out before I could stop them, poison I feared would eat through any warmth she had left for me. "Did you forget something?"

I'll never let you fight alone. I promised your father, and I'll watch after you, best I can. If I can't be with you, I can die for you. In time, you'll remember me the way I was, before. And that'd probably be best.

"Just this." Stretching up on tiptoe, she pressed her lips to my cheek. The heat sparked through me, making me yearn for so many beautiful, impossible things that I actually recoiled from the weight of that want. "Good-bye, Fade."

If she had whipped out her blades and stabbed me in the side, it couldn't have hurt more. For a few seconds, I couldn't get my breath, drowning in the icy water of that rejection. "I deserve that."

"What?" She was already turning. Elder Bigwater had given her a mission, and it didn't matter if she left me behind.

I shouldn't mind. That's what I wanted. I told her to forget me. But getting what I'd asked for had never felt worse. In that moment, I doubted my impulses hard, as Edmund's words echoed in my head. *The key to manhood is being there.* So dying for her might not be the answer. Maybe . . . maybe I didn't have to be perfect. Maybe it was enough to . . . try.

I choked out, "That you don't trust me enough to ask for my help. Or maybe you think I'm not strong enough to be of any use."

"I don't think that." Her shoulders were set, spine straight, and her loose plait wrapped around her shoulder. The nape of her neck was beautiful, a sliver of cream against the contrast of her hair. Any other time, I'd come up behind her, wrap my arms around her, and kiss her right there while whispering an apology for my idiocy, but I didn't deserve her forgiveness. Yet.

Someday, though, I'll fight my way back—fall down nine times, get up ten.

"We're still partners, aren't we?" I feared her answer. Maybe I'd used up all my chances, and by being stupid and stubborn, I could never, ever win her back.

Deuce turned then, and her gray eyes gave me hope. They were all softness, tilted to mine in a look as sweet and tender as a kiss. My heart gave a ferocious thump when she whispered, "I never left. I didn't request your help because I was trying to do what was right for you. Obviously, having you there is *always* best for me."

That seemed too magnificent to be true, yet I believed her. My girl never, ever lied. For some reason, she still lit up when she gazed at me. The first time I saw that expression, she was licking sweet cherries from my fingers and the memory stole my breath, along with the power of speech.

Don't ever stop looking at me. I'm the shadow behind your light, and I might just disappear without you. I don't deserve you, but I can't give you up, either.

My voice came out hoarse. "I don't want to stay here. I don't even want to be in my own skin. Can I come with you?"

I can't let her say no. Besides the promise to Edmund, I'd go crazy if she walked away from me. Right then, she was my sole reason for living, even if I was doing my best to drive her away. The logic had seemed sound on her naming day—I couldn't reveal the full extent of my shortcomings when I knew how she felt about being a Huntress. How Silk would laugh at the weakling I'd become.

No Hunter would let himself be taken. You should've died. You're not a man. You're food. Then I almost threw up; it took all my will to choke it down.

Deuce reached for me, then drew back, as if remembering that touch wasn't what I wanted anymore. I *did*, but close contact had so many echoes, like a child weeping at the bottom of a well. My foster father, the Muties, years alone in the dark . . . there had been so much pain, so much loss, but being taken? Changed me. I couldn't silence the scream in my head that said I should've been strong enough, smart enough, to stop it. No matter how I tried, that accusation never ceased.

"Fade, you said you can't be what I need, but you're everything I want. Even if you give up on yourself, *I* never will. I'll fight for you."

"You shouldn't say that," I muttered. "I'm not worth it."

"That's not true." She lifted her face so I could read the sincerity there. That smile was a promise, and I clung to it like I had my father's hand, long ago, in the river, while my mother sunned herself on the rocky shore.

As she studied me, my chest ached until I couldn't stand it. For inexplicable reasons, she blew me a kiss, and I raised my hand to catch it. Though it was an ephemeral thing, intangible, I daydreamed her warmth against my palm, and for the first time since I came back, hope fluttered its fragile wings. My heart throbbed her name, all the way to my fingertips, as I watched her walk away.

Once she was gone from sight, I ran into the house to pack my bag. Though she hadn't said so, I knew from Edmund that this assignment came from Elder Bigwater, so it made sense to search for her there. As I passed the blacksmith shop, and with a cheerful tune preceding him, Stalker came out, a pack slung over one shoulder.

My jaw clenched.

"Did she take pity on you, ask you to tag along?" he asked, sharp as a knife. "I wonder if she kissed you. She's like a secret berry patch, all thorns on the surface and sweetness beneath." He licked his lips pointedly.

Killing him would've been perfect. My fingers trembled on my blades, but I kept them sheathed out of respect for Deuce. She seemed to find something in him worth saving. I disagreed. In my eyes, this animal would never be anything but a weapon, fodder to keep the Muties from eating someone else. What he'd permitted to happen to Tegan assured me he was filth, and if that wasn't enough, he'd hunted Deuce and me for sport. Finally, if not for him, Pearl would still be alive.

Deuce might be able to forgive you. Not me. I'd rather stab you in your black heart, wolf boy.

"She will never see you," I said quietly. "You're a sparring partner, convenient to her, useful even. You may trick her now and then, because she's not bent like you. But she'll never, ever offer what you want of her own free will."

He sneered, the ugly expression pulling at his scars, but I saw from the desolation in his eyes that I'd drawn blood. "And what do you think I'm after?"

"Her heart," I said. "Which is too bad. You see . . . that's mine, and it always will be. Odd as it might seem, she'd rather have me broken than you whole."

When Stalker shoved past me, he wasn't whistling anymore. I watched him go, knowing I should feel a little guilty, but for the first time in days, a smile broke over me, and it felt like a sunrise. This was a deep, clean breath, bracing me for the trouble that lay ahead. The danger hardly seemed to matter, as long as I was with her.

Be patient, solnyshko moyo. I'm still here. And I'm coming back to you.

Edie wants revenge on the beautiful people at Blackbriar
Academy. Their cruelty drove her to the brink of despair.
She soon finds herself alone in a world teeming with secrets.
In this murky morass of devil's bargains, she isn't sure
who—or what—she can trust. Not even her own mind.

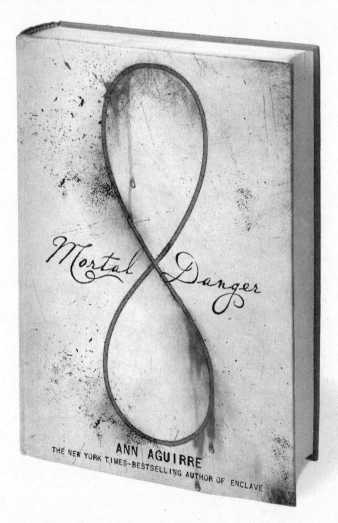

Mortal Danger

ANN AGUIRRE
THE NEW YORK TIMES–BESTSELLING AUTHOR OF ENCLAVE

Keep reading for a sneak peek of Ann Aguirre's

Mortal Danger

DEATH
WATCH

was supposed to die at 5:57 a.m.

At least, I had been planning it for months. First I read up on the best ways to do it, then I learned the warning signs and made sure not to reveal any of them. People who wanted to be saved gave away their possessions and said their good-byes. I'd passed so far beyond that point; I just wanted it all to stop.

There was no light at the end of this tunnel.

So two days after the school year ended, I left my house for what I intended to be the last time. I wrote no note of explanation. In my opinion, it never offered closure and it only made the survivors feel guilty. Better to let my parents think I suffered from some undiagnosed mental illness than to have them carry the knowledge that maybe they could've saved me; that burden could drive my parents to the ledge behind me, and I didn't want that. I only wanted an ending.

Earlier I had walked toward the BU T station I used for other errands, like shopping and school. There was plenty of time for me to change my mind, but I'd done all the research, and it was meticulous. I'd considered all sorts of methods, but in the end, I preferred water because it would be tidy and quick. I hated the idea of leaving a mess at home for my parents to clean up. This early—or late, depending on your perspective—the city was relatively quiet. *Just as well.* I'd gotten off at North Station and trudged the last mile or so.

Jumpers loved this place, but if you picked the wrong time, somebody would notice, call the authorities, and then you'd have cars honking, lanes shutting down, police cars . . . pretty much the whole media circus. I was smart enough to choose my opportunity carefully; in fact, I'd studied the success stories and compared the times when the most deaths occurred. Constrained by public transport hours, I arrived a bit later than the majority of those who died here, but my leap would still be feasible.

At this hour, there wasn't as much traffic. The bridge was a monster, but I didn't have to go all the way to the other side. Predawn murk threw shadows over the metal pylons as I faced my fate. I felt nothing in particular. No joy, but no sadness either.

The last three years had been the worst. I'd seen the well-meant *It Gets Better* videos, but I wasn't tough enough to make it through another year, when there was no assurance college would be better. The constant jokes, endless harrassment—if this was all I could look forward to, then I was ready to check out. I didn't know why people at school hated me so much. To my knowledge, I'd never done anything except exist, but that was enough. At Blackbriar Academy—an expensive, private school that my parents thought guaranteed a bright future—it wasn't okay to be ugly, weird, or different. I was all of the above. And not in the movie way, either, where the geek girl took down her hair and swapped her horn rims for contacts, then suddenly, she was a hottie.

When I was little, it didn't bother me. But the older I got, the meaner the kids became, particularly the beautiful ones. To get in with their crowd, you needed a certain look, and money didn't hurt. Teachers fell in with whatever the Teflon crew told them, and most adults had enough secret cruelty to believe somebody like me had it coming—that if I tried harder, I could stop stuttering, get a nose job, dye my hair, and join a gym. So clearly it was my fault that I'd rather read than try to bring myself up to the standards of people I hated.

Over the years, the pranks got worse and worse. They stole my clothes from my gym locker, so I had to go to class all stinky in my PE uniform. Not a day went by that they didn't do something, even as simple as a kick or a shove or a word that dug deep as a knife. I used to tell myself I could survive it—I quoted Nietzsche in my head and I pretended I was a fearless heroine. But I was as strong as my tormentors could make me, and it wasn't enough. Four months ago, the last day before winter break, they broke me.

I pushed the memory down like the bile I swallowed on a daily basis. The shame was the worst, as if I'd done something to deserve this. Being smart and ugly wasn't reason enough for what they did to me. Nothing was. At that point, I implemented plan B. I had no friends. Nobody would miss me. At best, my parents—oblivious academic types—would see me as ruined potential. Sometimes I thought they had me as a sociology experiment. Afterward, they'd retrieve my body and mark my file with a big red FAIL stamp.

The sky was gray and pearly, mist hanging over the river. Drawing in a deep breath, I gathered my courage. To my amusement, I'd passed a sign that read, DEPRESSED? CALL US. Then it listed a number. I'd ignored that, along with a massive heap of pigeon shit, and continued across until I was far enough out that the water would drown me fast, provided the fall didn't kill me on impact. Now I only had to climb over quietly and let go.

The end.

A jagged shard tore loose in my chest; tears burned in my eyes. *Why didn't anyone notice? Why didn't anyone do anything?* So, maybe I was like the other lost souls, after all. I wanted a hand on my shoulder, somebody to stop me. Shaking, I put my foot on the guardrail and swung my leg over. On the other side, metal at my back, the dark river spread before me as if it led to the underworld. For me, it did. My muscles coiled, but I didn't need to jump. All I had to do was lean into space. There would be a few seconds of freefall, and then I'd hit the water. If the impact didn't kill me, the stones in my pockets would.

I'd planned for all contingencies.

I stepped forward.

A hand on my shoulder stopped me. The touch radiated heat, shocking me nearly to death. I couldn't remember the last time anyone had touched me, except to hurt. My parents weren't huggers. So long as I got straight As, they had little to do with me. They said they were rearing me to be self-sufficient. It felt more like they were raising me to self-destruct.

Mission accomplished.

I turned, expecting a corporate drone jonesing to start his cubicle time early, and on target to screw up my careful plans. In that case, I'd have to talk fast to avoid police involvement and incarceration in a mental facility. They'd put me on death watch and stare at me for three days in case I relapsed with the urge to kill myself. The lie hovered on the tip of my tongue—how I was researching suicide to make a sociology essay more compelling—but the guy who'd interrupted my exit also stole my ability to form a coherent thought. His hand remained on my shoulder, steadying me, but he didn't speak.

I didn't either.

I couldn't.

He had the kind of face you saw in magazines, sculpted and airbrushed to perfection. Sharp cheekbones eased into a strong jaw and a kissable mouth. His chin was just firm enough. He had a long, aquiline nose and jade eyes with a feline slant. His face was . . . haunting, unsettling, even. His layered mop of dark hair gained coppery streaks in the halo of passing headlights that limned us both. In a minute or two, somebody would see us. Though traffic was light, it wasn't nonexistent, and eventually some concerned motorist would pull over or make a call. I saw my window of opportunity narrowing.

"What?" I managed to get the word out without stammering.

"You don't have to do this. There are other options."

I didn't try to bullshit. His direct, gold-sparked gaze made me feel that would be a waste of time. Part of me thought I might have already jumped, and he was my afterlife. Or maybe I was on a ventilator after they fished me out of the river, which made this a coma dream. I'd read studies where doctors posited that people experienced incredibly vivid dreamscapes during catatonia.

"Yeah? Like what?"

I figured he'd mention therapy. Group sessions. Medication. Anything to get my butt off this bridge. Right then, only the strength of his biceps kept me from flinging myself backward. Well, that . . . and curiosity.

"You can let me help you."

"I don't see how that's possible." My tone sounded bleak, and it gave away more than I wanted.

I didn't mean to tell a random stranger my problems, no matter how pretty he was. In fact, that appeal made me trust him less. Beautiful people treated me well only when they were setting me up for something worse. In hindsight, I should've been wary that day, but I was just so tired, and I wanted so bad to believe they intended to stop tormenting me. I was ready to accept the apology and move on. *Everybody grows up, right?*

"Here's the deal. We'll get something to drink, and I'll make my proposal. If you don't like what you hear, I'll escort you back here and this time, I won't stop you. I'll even stand guard so nobody else does."

"Why should I? You could be a murdering weirdo."

"You intended to kill yourself anyway."

"I was going to be quick. You might not be. Being suicidal doesn't mean I'm stupid."

He laughed. "See, this is why I didn't bring my car. I *knew* you wouldn't get in."

Weird. That sounded like we were old friends, but I'd remember someone like him. "You got that right."

"You can walk five feet behind me if it makes you feel better."

I wasn't sure it did, but with his help, I climbed back over the guardrail. His argument made sense, and I was curious. What did I have to lose? He might try to recruit me into a cult. Nervous and wary, I trudged behind him, my eyes on his back at all times. I was ready to end things on my terms, not wind up living in a hole in somebody's basement. That would definitely be worse. I shivered, wondering if this was the best idea. Yet curiosity refused to let me back out.

He led the way off the bridge, quite a long walk the second time around; the rocks in my pockets gained weight with each step. Eventually, we reached the street, passing a number of closed restaurants, Italian places mostly. He stopped at a twenty-four-hour diner called Cuppa Joe. The place had a giant mug out front, outlined in red neon. Inside, the vinyl booths were cracked and sealed over with silver duct tape. On the wall, a neon blue-and-pink clock buzzed, a low drone just inside my range of hearing. According to the position of the hands, it was 6:05 a.m., and I'd missed my deadline.

A couple of waitresses wore the ultimate in polyester chic, while old women sat nursing coffee with lipstick imprints on chipped cups, makeup caked into their wrinkles. There were elderly couples as well; men in plaid trousers and white belts, ladies in shirtwaists. Everyone in the diner had an odd look, like they were players on a set, and some otherworldly director was saying, *Now* this *is what a diner looked like in 1955.* I also counted too many customers for this hour. Finally, there was an expectant air, as if they had all been awaiting our arrival. I dismissed the thought as symptomatic of how surreal the day had become.

The hot samaritan sat down next to the window, so that the red light from the giant coffee cup on the roof fell across the table in waves. I took a seat opposite him and folded my hands like I was at a college admissions interview. He smiled at me. Under fluorescent lights, he was even better looking than he'd appeared on the bridge.

It didn't make me happy.

"So is this where you call the cops? You lured me in quietly. Good job." To my astonishment, I got the words out without a hitch. In his company, I wasn't nervous at all, mostly because I half suspected he was a figment of my imagination.

"No, this is where I introduce myself. I'm Kian."

Okay, not what I expected. "Edie."

Short for Edith, who had been my maternal great-aunt. No one used my nickname, except me—in my head. At school, they called me Eat-it.

"I know who you are."

My breath caught. "What?"

"I didn't find you by accident." Before I could answer, Kian signaled the waitress and ordered coffee.

She glanced at me with an inquiring expression. *What the hell.* If I was dying after this conversation anyway—

"I'll have a strawberry milk shake."

"Hey, Hal," the waitress called. "Shake one in the hay."

An assenting noise came from the back and then the woman went behind the counter to pour Kian's coffee. She served it with a flourish, along with a sugar bowl and a pitcher of cream. "That's how you take it, right?"

He smiled up at her. "Good memory, Shirl."

"That's why I get the big bucks." She winked and sauntered to her next table.

I picked up the thread as he stirred cream and sugar into his drink. "Explain how you know who I am and where to find me. It sounds stalker-y, and I'm inclined to bail as soon as I finish my shake."

"Then I have time to make my case," he said softly. "Misery leaves a mark on the world, Edie. All strong emotions do. Rage, terror, love, longing . . . they're powerful forces."

"Right. What does that have to do with me?"

"Your pain came to my attention months ago. I'm sorry it took me so long to act, but I'm constrained by certain rules. I had to wait until you reached the breaking point before I could offer you a deal."

"If this is where you offer a fiddle of gold against my soul, I'm out."

His smile flashed. A little shiver of warmth went through me because he seemed to appreciate my wit. "Nothing so permanent."

"I'm all ears," I said as the waitress delivered my shake, hand-dipped with whorls of fresh whipped cream and a bright red cherry on top—almost too pretty to drink. Deliberately, I stirred it with my straw, ruining the beauty, and sucked up a huge mouthful.

Delicious.

"When humans of exceptional potential reach the breaking point—what we call extremis—we can step in."

I choked on my drink. "Humans. Which makes you *what*, exactly?"

Now I felt sure this was the lead-in to the most spectacular punk ever. I craned my neck, looking for Cameron, Brittany, Jen, Allison, or the cheer mascot, Davina. She had too much melanin for Blackbriar squad standards, so they kept her in a lion costume half the school year, and when she got out of it, she ran errands for the Teflon crew, who treated her more like a minion than a friend. I didn't see anyone from school, but that didn't mean they weren't in somebody's bedroom, laughing their asses off through this guy's button cam. This would probably end up on YouTube.

Like the first video.

Kian shook his head. "I can't answer that unless we come to an agreement."

"Let's cut to the chase," I said tiredly. "I don't know what they're paying you, if you're a struggling actor, or what, but I'm not interested. This isn't even the meanest prank they've pulled. Are they watching right now?"

"Edie—"

"Wait," I cut in. "I bet you don't get paid unless I play along. Fine. Tell me more about this awesome deal. Can I get it for four low payments of nine ninety-five?"

He didn't answer. Instead, he leaned across the table and took my hand. *Now that's commitment to the bit,* I thought.

Then the world vanished, a static skip in an old VCR tape. I remembered those from elementary school, the low-rent one I attended before my parents published, filed their first patent, and could afford a pricey prep school. That fast, the diner was just *gone.*

Brutal wind whipped my hair against my face. My glasses frosted over and my skin tightened with goose bumps in the icy air. A mountain stared back at me, rocky and wild. If I took four steps forward, I'd pitch off the edge. Vertigo spun my head, and I clung to Kian's hand, unable to say a word. This looked like Tibet—or the pictures I'd seen anyway. Deep down, I'd always wanted to go . . . to kneel in a holy place with the silent monks. Could he *know* this about me? I glimpsed no civilization, just trees, rocks, and stars. The cold gnawed through me; I was dressed for late spring in Boston, not in Sherpa gear. Shock paralyzed me for a few seconds.

God, I had to be out of my damn mind. *Hey, coma dream, how you doing? Let's see where this takes you.* But on the off chance it was real, I whispered, "Stop. Make it stop."

Another shift, and we were back at Cuppa Joe. My hands felt like chips of ice. His, still wrapped around mine, radiated the same heat I'd noticed when he touched my shoulder. I glanced around wildly, wondering if anyone reacted to our disappearance. The other patrons showed no signs that anything was wrong, but people didn't *do* that. Vanish and materialize, like somebody was beaming us in a transporter.

But maybe that was key. *People* didn't. Kian had called me an exceptional human, implying he wasn't. I'd been full of breezy skepticism before; it died on that mountaintop. I drew my hand away, took a couple of deep breaths, trying to calm my pounding heart.

"How come nobody even blinked? That was some straight-up *Star Trek* stuff."

"This is our place," he said. "Company owned. I can't tell you more right now."

"Well, that jaunt registers pretty high on the she'll-take-me-seriously meter."

"I don't usually have to resort to it this early in the conversation," he admitted.

My milk shake was still sitting on the table, melting into baby-pink goop. "Sorry I cut you off. You said something about extremis?"

He nodded. "That's when a human is about to die."

Oddly, that cheered me. "So I was going to succeed."

Kian didn't seem so pleased. "Yes. In a sense, you're already gone, Edie. If your fate wasn't currently in limbo, I wouldn't be permitted to talk to you. There's a pivotal moment just before death, when bargains can be made. I'm authorized to offer you three favors now in return for three favors later."

"I don't understand. What kind of . . . favors?"

"Anything you want," he said.

"*Anything?*" By my tone, it had to be obvious I meant things bigger and more impossible than tickets to Tahiti.

"My ability to change your life is limited only by your imagination."

"But then you can ask me for anything," I pointed out. "Three times. What if it's not something I can deliver?"

"The favors requested in return will always be within your power to grant. That's the way it works."

"But there are no parameters of what you might ask . . . or when. It might be terrible. Or illegal." Too well, I remembered "The Monkey's Paw," the burden of being a reader. Somebody who spent less time lost in books might've already signed on the dotted line.

"You were ready to throw your life away," Kian said. "But are you brave enough to change it?"

"You never answered me. What *are* you?"

"How would that help you decide? If I'm a demon, I'm unlikely to admit it, so I could say anything. How would you know if I'm telling the truth?"

He had me there. I scowled and sipped my shake, the possible dangers and consequences banging around my head. Since I'd accepted I didn't have a future, it seemed less scary to consider everything that could go wrong down the line. If my life imploded twenty years later when the bill came due, wouldn't it be worth it to be happy first? It had been so long since I laughed that I couldn't remember what it felt like to walk around without this awful weight in my chest.

"In a theoretical sense, say I agree to your deal. Is there a time limit on when I have to use my favors?"

Appreciation sparked in his gaze. Kian inclined his head. "The first must be used within a year. The rest within five."

"To prevent people from getting what they want with the first, then sitting on the others until they die, thus blocking you from asking anything in return."

"Exactly. The return favors may be collected anytime after completion of our side of the bargain."

"So repayment could be due anytime. Talk about living under the hammer."

"Some people feel that way. Others live in the moment and don't worry about what might come."

I jammed the straw deep into my glass, chewing my bottom lip. "This sounds pretty diabolical. I hope you know that."

"I'm aware." Sorrow threaded his tone, making me wonder what could make someone like *him* sad.

"Can you tell me anything about the people you work for?"

"At the moment, no."

I'd like to glean some more information before making a decision, but his response implied he could only answer questions after I agreed to the terms. That seemed shady; it couldn't be good if my benefactors preferred to hide in the shadows. One thing could be said of this situation; curiosity had supplanted despair as my dominant emotion.

"You said you come to exceptional humans. Why me?" I was brainy, but not the kind of smart that cured cancer.

"If I told you *why* we want to save you, it could screw up your timeline."

"You mean if I learn that I solve cold fusion, then I might not. I might decide to breed rabbits instead."

"You hate rabbits," Kian said gently.

"Yeah." I did—since one bit me in the fourth grade—but how weird that he knew.

"The deal is on the table. Choose, Edie."

From here, I sensed it was up to me. "Can I have some time to think about it?"

"No. I'm sorry."

"It comes down to a leap then, either way. You can put me back on the bridge . . . only this time you don't stop me. Will it be like we never came here or went to the mountain?"

"Yes."

I smiled. For someone like me, there could be only one reply.